1

The Amber Road

The Amber Road

A Warrior of Rome Novel

DR HARRY SIDEBOTTOM

MICHAEL JOSEPH
an imprint of
PENGUIN BOOKS

MICHAEL JOSEPH

Published by the Penguin Group

Penguin Books Ltd, 80 Strand, London WC2R 0RL, England

Penguin Group (USA) Inc., 375 Hudson Street, New York, New York 10014, USA

Penguin Group (Canada), 90 Eglinton Avenue East, Suite 700, Toronto, Ontario, Canada M4P 2Y3
(a division of Pearson Penguin Canada Inc.)

Penguin Ireland, 25 St Stephen's Green, Dublin 2, Ireland (a division of Penguin Books Ltd)

Penguin Group (Australia), 707 Collins Street, Melbourne, Victoria 3008, Australia
(a division of Pearson Australia Group Pty Ltd)

Penguin Books India Pvt Ltd, 11 Community Centre,
Panchsheel Park, New Delhi – 110 017, India

Penguin Group (NZ), 67 Apollo Drive, Rosedale, Auckland 0632, New Zealand
(a division of Pearson New Zealand Ltd)

Penguin Books (South Africa) (Pty) Ltd, Block D, Rosebank Office Park, 181 Jan Smuts Avenue,
Parktown North, Gauteng 2193, South Africa

Penguin Books Ltd, Registered Offices: 80 Strand, London WC2R 0RL, England

www.penguin.com

First published 2013
001

Typeset in Dante MT Std 11/13pt by Palimpsest Book Production Ltd, Falkirk, Stirlingshire
Printed in Great Britain by Clays Ltd, St Ives plc

A CIP catalogue record for this book is available from the British Library

HARDBACK ISBN: 978–0–718–15595–7
PAPERBACK ISBN: 978–0–718–15596–4

www.greenpenguin.co.uk

ALWAYS LEARNING   **PEARSON**

To Peter Cosgrove and Jeremy Tinton

Contents

The Himling Dynasty

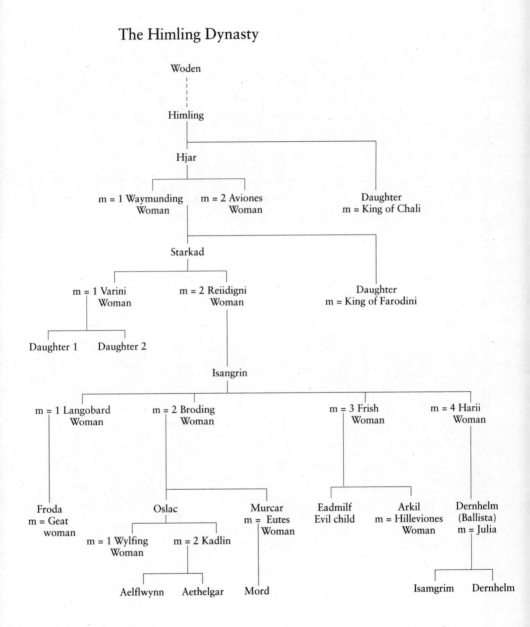

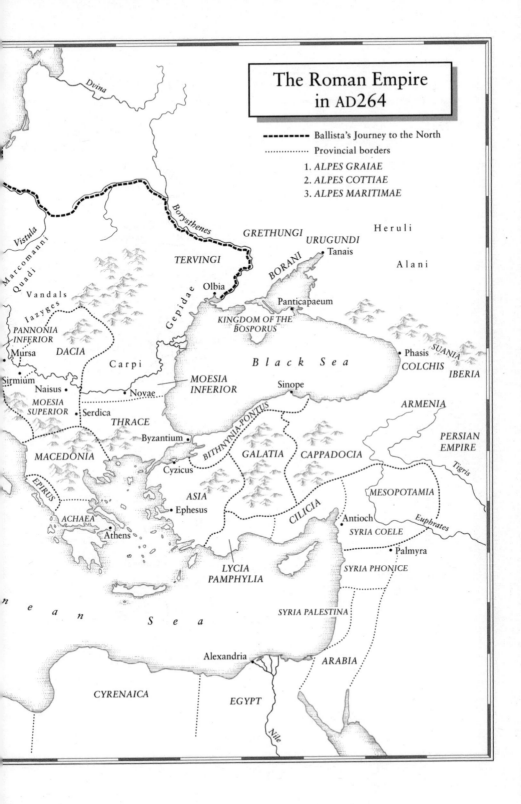

The Roman Empire
in AD264

- - - - - - - Ballista's Journey to the North
.... Provincial borders
1. *ALPES GRAIAE*
2. *ALPES COTTIAE*
3. *ALPES MARITIMAE*

Dvina

Vistula

Borysthenes

GRETHUNGI

URUGUNDI
· Tanais

Heruli

TERVINGI

BORANI

Alani

Marcomanni
Quadi

Vandals

Gepidae

· Olbia

Panticapaeum

Iazyges

PANNONIA
INFERIOR

· Mursa

DACIA

Carpi

KINGDOM OF THE
BOSPORUS

· Phasis

SUANIA

COLCHIS

IBERIA

Sirmium

Naisus ·

· Novae

MOESIA
INFERIOR

Black Sea

Sinope ·

ARMENIA

MOESIA
SUPERIOR

· Serdica

THRACE

· Byzantium

BITHYNIA-PONTUS

GALATIA

CAPPADOCIA

PERSIAN
EMPIRE

MACEDONIA

· Cyzicus

Tigris

EPIRUS

ASIA

· Ephesus

MESOPOTAMIA

ACHAEA

CILICIA

· Athens

· Antioch

Euphrates

SYRIA COELE

· Palmyra

LYCIA
PAMPHYLIA

SYRIA PHONICE

n

ean

Sea

SYRIA PALESTINA

Alexandria ·

· ARABIA

CYRENAICA

EGYPT

Nile

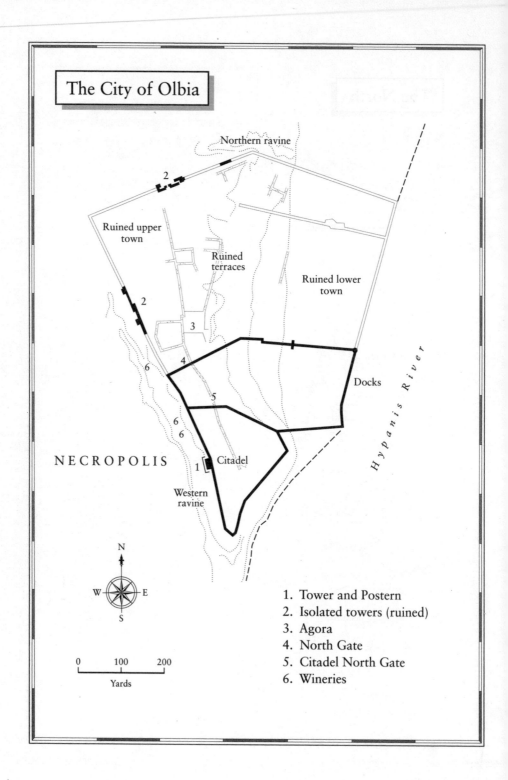

The City of Olbia

Northern ravine

Ruined upper
town

Ruined
terraces

Ruined lower
town

2

2

3

Docks

6

4

5

Hypanis River

6

6

NECROPOLIS

1 Citadel

Western
ravine

N
W — E
S

0   100   200
Yards

1. Tower and Postern
2. Isolated towers (ruined)
3. Agora
4. North Gate
5. Citadel North Gate
6. Wineries

The North

1. Gudme
2. Gudmestrand
3. Hlymdale
4. Norvasund
5. Island of Abalos
6. Island of Hindafell
7. Island of Solfell
8. Island of Varinsey
9. Island of Hedinsey

N
W — E
S

- - - - - - Ballista's Journey to the North

FAUONAE

FINNI

SCRITHIPHINI

Mons Saevo

SUIONES

FIRAISI

Tastris

CHAEDINI

DANI

GEATS
7

CIMBRI

EUTES

LEUONES

AVIONES

FUNUSII

Sinus Codanus

DAUCIONES

6

WYLFINGS

CHALI

HILLEVIONES

VARINI

4

8

1 2

9

3

BRONDINGS

5

AESTII

MYRGINGS

HEATHOBARDS

RUGII

FARODINI

REUDIGNI

LANGOBARDI

Vistula

FRISII

HERULI

SAXONES

FRANKS

HARII

Prologue I
Gallia Belgica, AD262

Afterwards, towns always wear the same scars.

It had been too easy, Starkad thought. In the long, long voyage, only one ship had gone missing. There had been no Roman patrol boats in the Gallic Channel, no watchers on the bluffs flanking the estuary. The fishermen's huts where they beached the longboats had been deserted. Not a soul had disturbed them as they laid up the remaining hours of the day. Only their bulky shadows and a vixen about her own murderous business had made witness to their march inland in the treacherous starlight. The small market town of Augusta Ambianorum was unwalled. No geese had cackled, no dogs betrayed the approach. Neither call of nature nor providential deity had pulled a citizen from his slumber to raise the alarm. The sea wolves had ringed the town, a party on each road. When the *atheling* Arkil was satisfied, he had made the signal. The Angles had set about their rapine with practised enthusiasm and the zeal of men long at sea. After the incomprehensible suddenness of the onset of catastrophe, it had proved a long night for many of the wretched women of the town, all too short and final for some of their men.

In the dead, grey half-light before dawn Starkad stood near the ornamental gate and looked back down the main street to the forum. Unlike many of the warriors, he had neither raided into the *imperium* nor served in the Roman forces before. The buildings were unusual to him: bigger, squarer, made of stone with tiled roofs. Yet otherwise it could have been a settlement on Scadinavia or around the shores of the Suebian Sea. There were all the usual signs of a sacked town: the kicked-in doors, the casually smashed heirlooms, the weeping women, small children wailing, and here and there the splayed, humped dead. The smell of spilt alcohol, of vomit, excrement and blood; the rankness of unwashed men. Starkad thought only a man of no imagination could regard what he and his companions had wrought and not consider the implicit threat to his own family, to his own home.

Clumsy and bleary with fatigue and drink, the Angles were shuffling into a column of some one thousand along the wide street. The *eorls* who commanded the ships chaffed the *duguth*, and each of the latter did likewise to the ten warriors under them. All were well laden with plunder. They were not taking too many captives with them. These were divided into two groups, one of young women, the other of men of all ages. That night the former had experienced a foretaste of their fate. If the male captives knew what their future held, the cowards among them might envy the lot of the women.

The crewmen of Starkad's longship were all present and in some form of order, drawn up roughly five abreast and ten deep. He told his friend Eomer, the *duguo* of one of the tent-groups of ten, to take over, keep them from more drinking, and he walked off to the head of the column.

Arkil was talking to two of the *eorls*. Like all the Himling dynasty, Arkil was tall, very broad-shouldered, with long, blond hair. Like all the Himlings, his arms were bright with gold. The *atheling* smiled at Starkad. One of the *eorls* spoke.

'Your crew are still slower than mine,' Wiglaf said.

Starkad shrugged.

'He is still a puppy.' Arkil's tone was light.

'Twenty-five winters, you could hope for more,' Wiglaf replied. 'I said he was too young to be one of the *duguth*, let alone an *eorl*.'

Starkad smiled in a way he hoped conveyed the gathering senility of his elders. A big man himself, he had some confidence in his own skill at arms and his ability to exact obedience. He did not bother to point out his men had been tasked with the rounding up of prisoners.

The chiefs of the other fifteen ships began to come up in ones or twos. Arkil had a few words with each *eorl*. It was not just stature Arkil had inherited. All the Himlings of Hedinsey had the gift of commanding men in war. It came naturally to them. They were Woden-born. Even Starkad's stepfather, Oslac, quiet, studious man that he was, had led several successful expeditions in his youth. Starkad's thoughts ran from Oslac to his mother, Kadlin, and from her to his father. He did not want to think about his father.

Starkad looked at the arch spanning the road. It was a gateway that could not be shut and that connected to no walls, a thing of elaborate impracticality. In the torchlight its relief carvings shifted: men heavily armed Roman-style or stark naked killed trousered warriors whose faces were grotesquely bearded, almost bestial. Why had the townsfolk commissioned such a monument? Presumably they identified with the Roman fighters and had forgotten that once they had been free men, before the legionaries had massacred their trouser-wearing forefathers, taken their weapons and made them pay taxes. Starkad had little but contempt for men who paid others to defend them.

'It has all been too easy,' Starkad said.

'And you would know,' Wiglaf said. Some of the older *eorls* laughed.

'The boy might not be wrong.' Arkil was known as a thoughtful

3

man. 'No one can tell what the *Norns* have spun. Great misfortune often follows hard on the heels of success. But Morcar and I spied out this place last year on our way back from the west. We were thorough. Morcar questioned the locals we caught. He did not spare himself.'

Everyone smiled; some wincing at the thought of the ingenious cruelty Arkil's half-brother delighted in using. Not all the Himlings were gentle.

'It is fifty miles to Rotomagus, the same to Samarobriva. There are no Roman troops nearer than Gesoriacum, and that is further by road and its harbour has few warships. There was no burning in last night's work. No beacons have been seen. There is no time for a message to reach Gesoriacum and the soldiers to return before we are gone.'

The chiefs nodded at the sagacity of the *atheling*.

'There is nothing at which the gods can complain. We have promised much to Ran that she will spare us her drowning net, and Woden will have the rest and much booty on our return.'

A low *hooming* of approval at the old, stern ways of blood ran through the leading men.

'We have done what we can by gods and man,' Arkil said. 'Put out the torches. It is time to get back to the ships.'

Starkad walked back past the first three crews to his own men. Although sitting casually, some even prone, they were in rough marching formation. None was drinking more than might be expected. The roped captives were huddled in the street between them and the warriors of the next longboat. At Starkad's command, his followers began to clamber to their feet. They extinguished the torches, hefted their weapons and plunder and shouted at the prisoners until they got up as well.

At home the old men said that until the reign of the *cyning* Hjar, just three generations before, the Angles had gone to war in no great order. They said the Angles had brought discipline back from fighting for the Romans on the distant banks of the Ister in their great wars against the Marcomanni. Starkad found it hard to imagine his people going into battle in a chaotic mass no better than the primitive and savage Scrithiphini or the Finni of the far north. But he had no reason to think either the old men or the travelling *scops* who came to the halls of the Himlings and sang the deeds of Hjar should lie.

A war horn sounded, and the column, somewhat unsteadily, bunching and surging, started forward.

The light was strengthening as Starkad emerged from the gate into the necropolis. Like all young well-born men at the court of Isangrim, a little Latin had been drummed into him. The *cyning* himself could speak the language fluently, and his son Oslac, Starkad's stepfather, was noted for his unusual interest in the poetry of the *imperium*. Starkad knew what the Romans called their burial grounds, but the previous night the stars had been too dim and his apprehension too tight to take his first view of one. As its name implied, the necropolis was a veritable city of the dead. As well as many sculpted and inscribed gravestones and sarcophagi, some columns and a couple of miniature pyramids, there were lots of small houses for the deceased. They began as soon as the homes of the living ended, and flanked the road as far as could be seen in the gloom.

It was all strange to Starkad. The Angles interred their dead in fitting barrows at a suitable distance from their settlements. There was something odd about this Roman necropolis nestling up to the town, something faintly disturbing about building houses for corpses as if they might still be alive. He had heard the southerners believed they would have no afterlife except flitting disembodied through the dark like bats or shadows. He wondered how their young men could bring themselves to endure the arrow storm or stand close to the steel with no hope of their courage and deeds bringing them to Valhalla.

As they cleared the necropolis, the horses of the Sun hauled her over the horizon. The dark fled away from her, as she herself ran from the wolf Skoll. The land spread out around; a cultivated, pleasant place of fields and meadows, rustic tracks and stands of trees. Buildings were dotted here and there; comfortable villas commanding fine views, more humble farms in sheltered spots. It was a fertile land, well worked, and Starkad admired their husbandry.

The road stretched on, and the sun shifted up. The morning was going to be hot. It was only five or six miles to the boats, but after the first the raiders were already suffering, their nocturnal excesses catching in their chests, making their feet shamble.

Starkad shifted the shield and pack slung over his back. It brought no ease. He did not care. He was happy. His discomfort was a measure of his success, and this road was the start of his journey home. It would be good to be back. There were no problems between him and his stepfather, and he loved his mother. As was the custom of the north, he had spent several years of his youth in the hall of his maternal uncle. Heoroweard Paunch-Shaker lived up to his name: a huge, jovial bear of a man, a legendary drinker, and, despite his girth, a warrior to be feared. In most ways he was the father Starkad had never known. It would be good to return to him – and to his mother – in triumph. And then there was Heoroweard's son, Hathkin. Starkad and Hathkin were of an age, had grown up together and could not be closer. Certainly Hathkin meant more to Starkad than the younger half-brother and half-sister his mother had given Oslac.

The road breasted a rise. On the reverse slope a broad sward ran down to a line of mature trees. It was in a clearing in this wood the previous night that the vixen had watched their passing. They were getting on for halfway back.

'Shieldwall! Form on the *atheling*!'

Starkad was repeating the call down the column before he realized its meaning.

'Shieldwall! Form on the *atheling*!'

The threat must be ahead. Starkad calmed himself, thought quickly. His was the fourth crew in the column. He must go to the right. He remembered the prisoners. The fucking prisoners. They were his responsibility. He made rapid calculations.

'Eomer, your men stay with the prisoners. When the line is formed, bring them up behind us.'

The command was acknowledged with a wave.

The crew in front was already moving off to the left. Starkad gestured to the rest of his men to follow him and set off at an encumbered jog, angling off the road. The grass underfoot was long. It caught at his legs. He hoped he had done the right thing. There were eighty captives. Eomer had ten men. But the prisoners were roped; half of them were women. Starkad put it out of his mind, concentrated on bringing his men to the correct place.

There was Wiglaf's red *draco*, flying bravely. Starkad panted up beside the right hand of Wiglaf's warriors. Blowing hard, like a close-run animal, he motioned his forty men into position. They jostled into a line ten wide and four deep, then dropped their packs and sacks of loot, planted their spears in the ground and took their shields in their left hands. A violent retching, and a man stepped forward and threw up. A moment later another followed. Some laughed.

Starkad's standard-bearer was beside him. He looked up at the white snake his mother and her women had sewn for him. The *draco* writhed; its tail lashed. Starkad had not noticed the westerly breeze get up. The next crew were shuffling together on his right. So far nothing had gone wrong. Finally he had time to assess the cause of the alarm.

The enemy were drawn up in front of the wood. A long line of oval white shields marked with a red design. Steel helmets glittered in the sun, and above them a mass of spearheads. Over all, various standards – again, all white and red – flew. A knot of horsemen stood out before the centre; a large *draco* floated over them. There were about two hundred paces of open grassland between the forces.

Starkad shaded his tired eyes and peered across the gap. He caught the shimmer of mail between the shields. The enemy were arrayed several ranks deep. He estimated the width of the enemy formation, then stepped forward and looked along the almost-formed Angle shieldwall. Roughly the same width, so the numbers should be about equal. He moved back into his place.

'The Horned Men,' one of the older warriors said to Starkad. 'Your first Romans, and they turn out to be our cousins. Most auxiliary units of *cornuti* are recruited in Germania. They may well be Batavians.'

Starkad grunted. Apart from their shields being oval, not round, and all bearing the same design, they did not look much different to the Angles.

'A double-strength cohort, should be about a thousand men,' added the older man.

What sort of child did old Guthlaf take him for? It was not as if he had not stood in the shieldwall and faced the ranks of the *fiend* before. He could estimate numbers, and an enemy was an enemy. Starkad turned away and pretended to watch Eomer bringing the captives up.

'Someone is coming over.'

A lone rider was walking his mount slowly across to where Arkil's big standard – the white horse of Hedinsey – flew at the centre of the line. He held his spear reversed in one hand and some sort of staff in the other.

'The thing he is carrying is their symbol of a herald. He wants to be sure we will not kill him out of hand.'

Starkad was fast running out of patience with Guthlaf.

'How did they get here?' a voice in the ranks asked.

Starkad had no idea. 'Silence in the wall. Let us hear what he has to say.'

The rider took his time but eventually reined in a short javelin cast from Arkil. The man wore no helmet. He had short, dark hair, and a short, dark beard. To give him his due, he looked composed enough.

'In the name of *Imperator* Caesar Marcus Cassianus Latinius Postumus Augustus, Pius Felix, Invictus, Pontifex Maximus, Germanicus Maximus, you Angles are commanded to surrender.' He spoke in Latin. His voice carried well.

There was a pause. The herald's horse ruckled down its nose.

Just when the rider was about to speak again, Arkil took a pace forward.

'Stand aside, and we will be on our way.' Arkil's Latin was heavily accented, but serviceable.

'That cannot happen.'

'Then you had best go back, and the steel will decide.'

'This does not have to end tragically, Arkil of the Angles. My commander, Marcus Aurelius Dialis, Governor of Germania Inferior, offers you terms.'

The herald stopped, and again no one spoke.

'Tell us the terms.' Arkil's voice had a sharp edge. This was dragging on too long.

'Lay down your weapons, leave half your plunder, and you can go on your way.'

'You had best go back.'

The herald did not move. 'If you swear a truce and remain where you stand, it may be Governor Dialis will offer more lenient terms.'

Arkil strode further out from his men. 'Go back now.'

'If you just . . .'

Arkil unsheathed his blade. The Himlings possessed several swords of ancient renown. This was Gaois, the growling one, half as old as Woden and responsible for nearly as many deaths.

'Go back now,' Arkil said again.

Undiplomatic, but Starkad thought the *atheling* was right. Time was not on their side. Any moment could see other units of Roman troops appear from any direction.

The herald reined his horse around, walked it back towards his line. And no one among the Angles could say he had acted without courage.

'The prisoners!' Arkil roared. 'One in ten!'

A lane parted in Starkad's men, and he walked through to the rear. To be an *eorl* demanded hard choices, and this was one of them. Starkad stood by Eomer in front of the captives. 'Him,' he pointed, 'and him. That one . . .' He continued until eight men, none young, had been dragged out. 'Cut the others free.'

Their bonds gone, the women and younger men stood, irresolute and fearful.

'Go,' Starkad said.

They did not move, but gazed at him with round, uncomprehending eyes. He realized he had used his native tongue.

'Go,' he repeated in Latin. 'Your gods hold their hands over you.'

Still they did not move. Perhaps they suspected some cruel trick.

'Go.' He pointed in the direction of the town. One individual, then another, tentatively shuffled in the direction they had come. When nothing untoward happened, they moved faster. Others joined in, until they were all running as fast as they could back towards their shattered lives.

Starkad jerked his thumb at the eight remaining. 'Front of the line.'

They were distributed along the shieldwall. One was Starkad's duty. He did not relish it, but it was a necessity. An *eorl* had to do what was right by his men and the gods.

Arkil began the dedication. Starkad and the others joined in. 'Ran, goodwife of Aegir . . .'

Starkad looked down. The man was on his knees, bound. He had grey hair, grey eyes, a gentle, delicate face. Probably he had a wife, most likely a child, certainly he had been someone's son.

'Ran, turn your pale, cold eyes from us . . .'

Starkad drew his sword.

'Spare us your drowning net, take these instead.'

Without hesitation, Starkad swung the blade. The man threw himself sideways. Not quite quick enough. The steel bit into the side of his neck. Blood sprayed bright in the sunshine. The man squealed, high like a pig. He was on the ground, not moving, but not dead. He was moaning. Starkad stepped up, and finished him with two hard, chopping blows to the back of the head.

A baying of outrage rolled across from the Roman lines.

Starkad cleaned his weapon on the dead man's tunic, and slid it back into its scabbard.

'Swineheads!' Arkil's voice carried along the Angle warhedge of shields.

Guthlaf walked a few paces in front and planted himself four-square. Two other experienced warriors went and stood on either side and just behind him. Starkad took his place at Guthlaf's back. His chest felt all tight and hollow at once. His breath was coming fast and shallow. Without thought, he loosened his sword and dagger in their sheaths, touched the piece of amber tied to his scabbard as a healing stone. Taking up his spear, his palm was slick.

As each crew shifted into a wedge formation, a song rang out:

> The sword growls
> Leaving the sheath,
> The hand remembers
> The work of battle.

The Swinehead was formed. Starkad had Eomer on one shoulder, his standard-bearer on the other. Buoyed up by the singing and the proximity of his companions, he felt his anxieties slipping away. He would be a man; let down neither his friends nor himself.

'Advance!' Arkil's bellow was followed by the bray of a horn. Normally, those warriors touched by Woden or another god would jump out beyond the formation and dance. Leaping and turning, casting aside their armour, they would draw down into themselves the ferocity of wolf, bear or other fanged, clawed beast. As they worked themselves into a murderous, slathering fury, the hearts of the rest would be lifted. Today there was no time. If one Roman unit could appear, against all expectation, so could more. The Angles had to break the *fiend* in front of them, and win through to their ships.

A low sigh, like a breeze through a field of ripe barley. Soft and deceptively gentle, the Angles began the *barritus*. As they moved off, the war chant swelled. They raised their shields in front of their mouths; the sound reflected, growing fuller and heavier.

Stepping in time, the *barritus* rose to a rough, fitful roar. It faded, and they could just hear the answering war chant of their enemy. The Angles lifted their voices and, like a great storm, drowned out everything else. The *barritus* foretold the outcome, and their *barritus* sounded good; a measure of manhood.

Between the nodding helmets of Guthlaf and the front rank, Starkad could see the enemy. They were stationary, close packed, awaiting the onslaught. Their leaders had chosen cohesion over momentum. Downhill, they had made a bad choice. Starkad was glad to be moving.

The Angles were picking up speed. Jogging, the thunder of their boots, the rattle of their war gear added to the din of the *barritus*. Starkad saw Guthlaf lower his spear. Carefully he brought his own down underarm; its point jutted out between Guthlaf and the shield of the man to the old warrior's right.

They were close, no more than forty paces. Every detail of the shield-burg of the enemy was clear. The front rank were kneeling, spear butts planted, white shields half overlapping. The second rank had brought their shields down over the first, bases locked on to the bosses of those below. A dazzling wall of white wood and red-painted horned beasts. Everywhere wicked, glinting spearheads projected, waiting to tear the life from those the *Norns* decreed must fall.

The Angles broke into a full charge, legs pounding. Thirty paces, twenty. The fearful and the foolishly brave swept along together. The *barritus* echoed back like a huge wave crashing against a cliff. Something flashed to the right between Starkad and Eomer. Above, the air was full, as the rear ranks of both sides hurled their spears. Screams cut through the clamour. Chin down into chest. No time to think.

The noise – like nothing else in Middle Earth – wood and steel smashing together, buckling, breaking. It hit Starkad before the savage impact jarred up his right arm, into his shoulder, bringing wrenching pain. The haft of his splintered spear was torn from his grip. Full tilt, he ran shield to shield into a *cornutus*. One of his own men thumped into his back. Wind knocked out of him. No room to move. The enemy face behind the shield; snarling, brutish. Hot breath in his nostrils. Crushing pain. The enemy falling back and down – eyes wide with horror. Guthlaf above him, climbing, scrambling over the locked enemy shields, using their bosses as footholds. *Cornuti* stabbing up. Guthlaf hacking down, like some demented woodsman. The edifice swaying back, collapsing. The pressure on Starkad easing a fraction. Gasping for air, he dragged his sword free.

A shove from behind. Starkad stumbled over the enemy writhing on the grass. Lose your footing here, and you were dead. Friend and foe would trample you to nothing. Shield well up, Starkad thrust down with his sword. The point of the blade met the resistance of a mailcoat. He put his weight on the hilt. The steel broke through the rings and slid into soft flesh.

A blade arced down from Starkad's right. Coming over his shield. He hauled his sword up, a clumsy parry with the guard. Something hit the left side of his helmet, hit very hard. Stunned – the clangour ringing in his head – he staggered, his vision swimming.

From all directions the deafening, terrible din of battle. Trapped in a surging crush of bodies. Feet scrabbling, Starkad fought to stay upright in its eddies.

A vicious edge of steel bit into the top of his shield, through the leather binding, down into the linden boards. A splinter gashed his forehead. His legs were shaking, so tired. He hunkered down behind his shield. Another blow landed, took out a chunk. He bent his knees, tried to dig in his heels, get a firm stance. He had to fight back, lead by example. He was an *eorl*.

A flash of light to Starkad's right. A ghastly scream. The sword embedded in Eomer's stomach. His friend's face white with shock. The *cornutus* withdrawing the blade. Eomer crumpling. Starkad twisted, lunged, his body behind the blow. Another scream. Starkad's blade slicing deep across the soldier's thighs, scraping on bone. Starkad and the *cornutus* tangled together. Starkad shoved him away. He fell. Two neat steps and Starkad brought up his sword.

'Please . . .' A bloodied hand raised in supplication.

Starkad smashed the heavy sword down; one, two, three times.

The press was clearing, the movement now all in the direction of the enemy.

'Out! Out! Out!' The triumphant, traditional cry of the Angles rumbled down the hillside, pursued the *cornuti* as they fled into the wood.

Starkad took in the stricken field. Everywhere were discarded and broken spears and swords, shields and helmets, even mailcoats. Everywhere the dead and the dying lay in their own blood and filth, and the living stood bent over with the enormity of it all. A grassy sward reduced to a shambles. But it was over. Now to count the cost.

Eomer was sitting, supported by another warrior. His hands were pressed to the jagged hole in his war shirt. The blood was flowing slowly but already had pooled in his lap, clotting the rings of his mail, staining the thighs of his trousers black.

'I will get . . .'

'No,' Eomer gasped. 'Gut wound. No point.'

Starkad dropped his sword, got to his knees. He tried to remove his helmet, but the blow had dented it out of shape. Someone levered it off for him. Blood from his forehead ran into Starkad's eyes.

'Enough to enter Woden's hall.' Eomer tried to smile. 'I hope.'

Starkad shuffled forward. The other warrior moved, and Starkad cradled his friend.

'Tell my mother, and Aeva.' Eomer winced. 'Tell them I died well.'

Starkad buried his head in his friend's neck, crying.

'Time to go.' Guthlaf was standing above them, bloodied but unhurt. 'The *atheling* has ordered we move.'

Five times at the point of the Swinehead and Guthlaf was still alive, this time seemingly unscathed. It should have been him, not Eomer. Starkad could not reply.

'Time to go,' Guthlaf repeated.

Starkad sobbed.

'You are an *eorl*,' Guthlaf said. 'Show yourself one.'

Starkad glared, about to curse the old man, curse him to Niflheim and Hel.

'He is right.' Eomer gripped Starkad's arm with a bloody hand. 'You are my *eorl*. Do the last thing for me.'

Starkad shook his head.

'The Choosers of the Slain will take me.' Eomer gripped him harder. 'Do it, as I love you, do it.'

Starkad knew they were right. He kissed Eomer, held him close, told him he loved him, whispered Woden's last words to Balder in his ear. Then Starkad drew his knife, and cut his friend's throat.

After, Guthlaf helped him to his feet. 'Leading men is not all feasting and giving gold. You did well. You are *eorl* to all in the crew.'

Men were busy all over the meadow. Starkad took his place under his *draco*. Four of his crew had died in the clash, two had been helped out afterwards. There were six with serious wounds but who could still march. Starkad sent men back to collect such of the plunder as was light and would not hold back their progress. As they did so, he got the remainder in order.

Arkil's horn sounded, and the reduced column resumed its limping march to the sea.

The trees – mature oak and beech – made a dappled world of shadow. Under their spreading branches the undergrowth was sparse, but enough to conceal an ambush. Starkad put it out of his thoughts. He had seen Arkil send out scouts. The *atheling* was a true leader, a true Himling.

'We must have been seen,' said a voice in the ranks.

'No,' Starkad said, 'they knew Arkil's name.'

They trudged on, pondering the bad implications of that.

'Arkil was here last year, with Morcar,' Guthlaf said.

Starkad smiled, but with no humour. 'Morcar would have left none alive to say their names.'

'They must have taken Ashhere's missing boat,' someone said.

'None with Ashhere would betray us.' Starkad was certain.

'Yet they knew Arkil was coming,' Guthlaf said.

There was no answer to that.

Through gaps in the foliage a high sky of mackerel-patterned clouds could be seen. Lower, light clouds pushed to the east. A fair wind, if they could make the ships. Not more than three miles to go.

Ahead, the column was marching out into the sunlight. Before Starkad reached the edge of the wood, he knew it was not good. A low groan of disappointment from the men at the front. Then he heard Arkil's horn, and the order came back down the track.

'Shieldwall! Form on the *atheling*. Last crew as reserve. Wounded form as their rear ranks.'

Again Starkad brought his men into the warhedge on the right of Wiglaf's crew. They were about twenty paces out of the wood, the reserve at the tree line.

This time it was an army they faced. The Romans were drawn up on a gentle hill, a stream at its foot, open country in front, smudges of smoke in the sky behind. Red-crested legionaries in the centre, auxiliaries on either side, all backed by archers. A formidable phalanx, with cavalry further out on both wings. Starkad counted their standards, their frontage, gauged their depth, tried to estimate their numbers. Three thousand or more, perhaps quite a few more, a third of them mounted. In a good position, standing in good order.

'Well, that would seem to be that,' Guthlaf said.

'Heart and courage. Some of us may win through.' Starkad did not believe it, but he felt it was the sort of thing an *eorl* should say.

'Heart and courage,' some of the men muttered uncertainly.

'It is no more than a mile to the ships.' Starkad added the lie gamely, and none of the *duguth* or the warriors chose to correct him.

The wind sighed through the big trees behind them, hissed sibilant in the jaws of the *dracones* above. A horse neighed in the enemy array.

'Another herald.'

The Roman rode down the slope, forded the stream in a cloud of spray, cantered towards the Angles. Mounted on a magnificent black horse, this was an officer of high rank, his muscled armour gilded and chased. He reined back to a walk, and brought his charger to a standstill about as far as a boy could toss a stone from the shieldwall. Bareheaded, hair and full beard artfully curled, he looked like a portrait on a coin of an emperor from a previous age.

'Arkil, son of Isangrim.' The Roman spoke the language of Germania with an accent from somewhere near the Rhine. 'You lead brave men. Too brave to waste their lives in a hopeless cause.'

Arkil stood forth. 'No man can predict the course of events.' He raised his voice. '*Wyrd* will often spare an undoomed man, if his courage is good.'

The horseman nodded, as if at the wisdom of the lines, then pointed over his shoulder. 'Your longboats are burned.'

Beyond the Roman army Starkad could see the smoke had grown into a thick column. It rose vertical, then billowed out to the east.

'The Augustus Postumus would have men like you in his *comitatus*, if you would give him your oath.'

Arkil took off his helmet, so his face could be seen. 'My father, the *Cyning* Isangrim, long ago pledged his friendship to your enemy the Augustus Gallienus. Isangrim is leader of our people. It is not for us to go back on the word of our *theoden*.'

The black horse tossed its head, and the Roman quieted it with a practised hand. 'The tyrant in Rome does not merit the friendship of men such as the Himlings of Hedinsey or the brave Angle warriors they lead. Gallienus has treated your half-brother Ballista shamefully. He has shown him no honour for his years of service, no honour for the risks he has run or the wounds he has taken. Instead, it is said, he has sent him into exile in the distant Caucasus mountains, sent him to his death among strangers.'

At the mention of the hostage, there was a low *hooming* from the older warriors in the warhedge. Starkad felt his own emotions rise.

'Gallienus wastes his time in idleness in the baths and bars of

Rome. Dressed in jewels and silk as a woman, he leads a *comitatus* of pimps and catamites. There can be no shame in renouncing the friendship of such a man.'

'What of our booty?' Arkil asked.

'What you left behind on the field of battle beyond the wood will be divided among my soldiers. What you have with you will remain yours.'

'Where would the Augustus Postumus send us?' Arkil asked.

'If you give him your oath, the Augustus Postumus will lead you first against your hereditary foes, the Franks. He will reward you with an open hand. It is in my mind you will not find Postumus lacking in courage.'

Arkil laughed. 'That I can see already.'

Postumus acknowledged this with a civil gesture.

'The decision is not mine alone,' Arkil said. 'I must consult the *eorls*.'

'It is a pleasant day. I will wait.' The emperor, all alone, sat easy on his horse.

Starkad and the other *eorls* clustered around their *atheling*.

'We could kill him,' one of the *eorls* hissed. 'They would not fight then.'

Arkil rounded on the man. 'That is the thought of a *nithing*. Only a man of no account would think to harm a man who came as a herald, trusting our word.'

'I have no desire to stay here,' Wiglaf announced. 'We should fight.'

'Fight this army, then the army on the Rhine, and on the far banks the Franks? We are far from home,' Arkil replied.

'After we have defeated the *fiend* in front of us, we should seize a port, take their ships.'

'My old friend' – Arkil spoke gently – 'the battle madness is on you. If we fight today, we will all dine in Valhalla this evening.'

A murmur of agreement ran through the ring of *eorls*.

19

'Then it is agreed.' Arkil turned back to the emperor, raising his voice. 'We will serve in your *comitatus* for two years.'

'Five,' Postumus replied equitably.

'Three, with the same pay as Praetorians.'

Postumus laughed. 'The *stipendium* shall be as you say, and you will receive such donatives as are fitting, but you will serve for five years.'

'Five it is then.'

'Will you swear the military oath on behalf of your men?'

Arkil nodded.

'Then take the *sacramentum* here in the sight of men and gods.'

Arkil drew his sword, placed his left hand on its edge, and spoke in Latin. 'By Jupiter Optimus Maximus and all the gods, I swear to carry out the emperor's commands, never desert the standards or shirk death, to value the safety of the emperor above everything.'

Five years, if he lived. Watching from the line, Starkad had to reconcile himself to five years before he could hope to return home.

Prologue II
The Island of Abalos in the Suebian Sea, AD263

The Roman was very far from home, beyond even the great forests of Germania. He was alone and afraid. This island, which had looked so small when first sighted in the restless grey expanse of the Suebian Sea, now seemed endless.

He could run no further. The wood here was mature timber, aspen and birch. There was little underbrush, no obvious place to hide. He looked about. Off to his left a big tree had fallen, its roots fanned up in a rough arch, a damp hollow where they had grown. He hobbled over and huddled there.

He listened, but could hear nothing over his own laboured breathing. The thick folds of the toga which had so hampered his flight were hot and heavy. He tugged and pulled until the voluminous thing fell away. Clad in just a sweat-stained under-tunic and sandals, he crouched, fingering the hilt of his knife. It was more suited for peeling an apple than a desperate fight.

His breathing quieter, he strained to catch any sounds of pursuit. Nothing except birdsong and the sounds of the wind moving through the trees. He leant back against the roots, exhausted.

Marcus Aurelius Julianus, a Knight of Rome, *Vir Egregius*, reduced to this. Only the gold ring of an equestrian distinguished him from a fugitive slave. When he was young, his father – may the earth lay light on him – had taken him to Nemi to see the priest-king. They had crossed the fence into the sacred space. It was festooned with strips of material, offerings to Diana of the Lake. They had found the runaway slave. He had emerged from a thicket, suspicious, blade in hand. When he had decided they were not of his own kind come to kill and replace him, he had moved off on the endless, fearful patrol of his haunted, diminutive kingdom.

Julianus knew this was all his own fault. He remembered his delight at the invitation. A formal banquet on the Palatine with the emperor himself in attendance was an honour beyond the hopes of most in the equestrian *ordo*. Many of the great had been there: Nummius Ceionius Albinus, Prefect of the City and *Consul Ordinarius* for the second time; Censorinus the Praetorian Prefect; Plotinus the philosopher; Cominius Priscianus, the new *a Studiis*; and several eminent military men, including the Danubians Tacitus and Aurelian and the Egyptian Camsisoleus. Julianus had been on a table higher than some of the *principes*, no distance from the imperial presence. Gallienus had been wearing a magnificent amber amulet to aid his recovery from tonsillitis. Julianus had admired the piece. The emperor had been graciousness itself, asked if he was interested in amber. A collector himself, and warmed by the Falernian and other noble wines, Julianus had not been able to stop himself expounding on the errors of the Greeks concerning its origins. Liguria, Iberia, Ethiopia, all nonsense, as were Egypt, Numidia and the Pyrenees. The only true amber was washed up on the shores of the Suebian Sea. Julianus had gone on to talk of its colours and properties. And the very next day Censorinus had come to his house. It was not a social call. The Praetorian Prefect carried an imperial command. A discreet diplomatic mission was leaving for the north. Julianus's deep knowledge of amber would act as a Trojan horse. He must have longed to travel to the Suebian Sea, to the fabled Cimbric peninsula and the islands where the precious resin was washed ashore. Now he could fulfil that desire, provide good service to his emperor, and purchase all the amber he might dream about. An imperial command was not to be disobeyed.

Too much wine, too much talking – hubris, even – had combined to lead Julianus to this dismal forest beyond the north wind.

Still no untoward sounds, but he could not stay here. Bundling up the toga, he did his best to conceal it under the roots of the tree. The sun was visible through the branches. It was directly overhead, no help in determining his course. There had been a fishing village on the southern coast, seen before they had rounded the headland and run up to the port. With money in his belt, the knife in his hand, he might get a boat. Casting around anxiously, he set off in what he hoped might be the right direction.

The wind stirred the branches and the sun dappled down. Julianus slipped from one sylvan glade to another. He had always loathed the countryside. Like most of his acquaintance, he preferred it tamed, the hand of man having transformed it into something like the garden of a villa. It was all very well in bucolic poetry or a Greek novel – clean-limbed young goatherds playing their pipes and innocently falling in love. But the reality, even at home in Campania, was threatening, full of outlaws and shepherds, and they amounted to the same thing. He remembered being frightened when his father had taken him to Nemi. But that had been nothing compared with the journey north from the last outpost of the *imperium* in Pannonia. Eight hundred miles or more through *barbaricum*. He had been terrified, even in the company of Tatius the ex-centurion and their several slaves.

When they had reached the shores of the Suebian Sea nothing had been as literature had led him to expect. There had been no hint of the Hyperborean good fortune of which Aeschylus had spoken. Contrary to the *Odes* of Pindar there had been sickness, baneful old age, and toils. Certainly there had been no avoiding Nemesis. The northern chief they had travelled to see dwelt to the west. Far from conveying them to him, these barbarians had insisted they accompany them to this island. Were they guests or prisoners? Julianus understood little of politics.

A bough creaked in the wind. Julianus was alone. What had happened to the others? It had been pure chance he had not been taken as well. He had always suffered from a weak bladder. Waiting to be summoned for their second audience with the sinister chief of this island, Julianus had stepped out of the hovel that formed their lodging. He had been relieving himself – not easy in a toga, hard not to splash yourself – at a polite distance, when he heard the uproar. At first he had thought it some rough barbarian custom or sport; their ways were unaccountable. Until he had seen Tatius dragged out and knocked to the ground. And then . . . and then the slave tried to protect his master, and the barbarians killed him.

Had they killed Tatius as well? Julianus had not stayed to discover. He had gathered up the skirts of his toga and fled into the forest. What had they done with the boy? If he were a hero, he would go back and rescue Giton. The gods knew he loved the boy. But Julianus knew it was not in him. He had done his military service half a lifetime ago. A year as a tribune with Legio II Adiutrix on the Ister had convinced him his courage was a finite commodity. He was not a hero. He was a 43-year-old landowner who enjoyed poetry and had a taste for pretty boys and fine amber artefacts.

Out of breath, Julianus rested against a tree. The sun had shifted. He was heading the right way. Surely not far now to the shore. He was about to set off again when he heard it. A horn, its note deep, full of menace. Hard to tell its direction. Behind, he thought. He plunged forward.

Running blindly, feet sinking in the thick leaf mould. A branch whipped his face. He stumbled, lost a sandal. No time to get it. He ran on.

Diana of the Lake, save me. A heifer, horns gilded, for you, hold your hands over me. Hercules, saviour of men, my finest piece – the red amber with the fly – for my safety.

A shout – harsh, guttural – all too near. They had sighted him. Like a hard-pressed beast, Julianus forced himself faster. Splashing through a rivulet, on hands and knees up the far bank. The muscles in his thighs screamed with pain. His breath came in agonized gasps. He detested hunting. Its exertions bored him, and he never failed to feel a pang of sympathy for the cornered quarry. He could not go much further. Soon he would have to turn like a stag at bay, waiting for the sharp teeth of the hounds.

A glance over his shoulder. Movement between the tree trunks. They were gaining. A root tripped him. Face first, sprawling in the dirt, then rolling down a slope. Winded, his knife knocked out of his hand. The reek of the forest floor and his own fear.

They were all around him, at the top of the incline. Horrible, pale faces, steel in their hands.

'Why? Why me? I have never harmed you. It was not my choice to come here. Politics is nothing to me. Tatius, he is the one you want. Take him.' The Latin pleas meant nothing to them.

They pulled him to his feet, bound his hands behind his back, a rope around his neck. Like a haltered animal, they led him off down a forest track.

They offered him no cruelty, just kept him moving. Occasionally they spoke to each other in grunts he could not comprehend. After a time the woodland changed. Birch and aspen gave way to oak. Julianus could smell open water. The works of man appeared. Not the shaded walks and marble statuary of *humanitas*. Here and there, in no discernible order, stark poles. On each a skull, dog, horse or human.

At the heart of the sacred grove was a clearing, yellow flowers in the grass. The sun glinted on water through a tangle of alder scrub on the far side. Men were waiting there, clustered around a massive idol. The deity was seated, hands in lap. A carved bird perched behind each shoulder. The god was scarred, blind in one eye.

The one who called himself Unferth the Amber Lord stood in front of the god. His constant shadow, the Young Lord, as ever with him. The hunters pushed Julianus to his knees before them. The one-eyed divinity looked down implacably over them all.

A whimper drew Julianus's attention. Giton, his boy, his beloved, was there. Muddied, huddled off to one side, but alive, seemingly unhurt. The boy was not looking at Julianus, but above his head. Julianus followed his gaze across the open ground. Tatius was alive – naked and bloodied, hung in the high branches of an oak.

'Punishments should fit the offence.' The voice of the Amber Lord boomed strangely from behind the metal face mask of his helmet. 'Those who offend against the people should be made a public example. Deeds of shame should be buried out of the sight of men, stamped down, trodden deep.'

That he had no idea of the meaning did nothing to lessen Julianus's terror. He thought his bladder would give way, shame him.

'Take them.'

Julianus was hauled to his feet. Too frightened to make a sound, he heard Giton pleading. Julianus was manhandled, half dragged down a path through the alders. He lost his other sandal. The rope was cutting into his neck. Reeds then open water ahead. The sky very big above. Bare feet scraping, he was pulled along a wooden walkway out into the marsh at the edge of the lake. He heard a scream, cut off by the sound of something heavy hitting the water. Urine ran hot on his thighs.

No, no, I never wanted any part of it.

The men seized him. Thrown forwards, he landed face down

in the mud. He twisted, came up spluttering. Hands still tied behind his back. The wattled hurdle loomed over him. He screamed. The hurdle pressed down. The mud and water rose. Julianus held his breath. The water was in his eyes, his ears. Everything went dark. At last, he had to breathe. The water rushed into his throat. He started to die.

PART ONE

Oikoumene,

(Spring AD264)

I

THE TOWN OF OLBIA TO THE
NORTH OF THE BLACK SEA

Some damaged walls and any number of ruins. Ballista's first impression of Olbia was not favourable. The pilot who had come aboard at the Castle of Alector as they left the Euxine had negotiated the long, marshy confluence of the Borysthenes and Hypanis, skilfully avoiding both the shallows and the many rafts of logs being poled downstream, and then taken them up by the far channel of the latter river. Now he was threading their way across through the numerous islets and mudflats. There were duck and geese on the water. Its margins were teeming with waders. Progress was slow, and the passengers on the *trireme* had plenty of time to view the remote outpost of Hellenism and empire.

'Another shitehole,' said Maximus.

'Yes,' Ballista agreed with his bodyguard.

A citadel on a cliff dominated the south of the town. The narrow pediment of a temple and a jumble of other roofs jutted above its curtain wall and rectangular towers. At the northern foot of its slope, quays, slipways and sheds huddled against more walls. Several fishing boats and some local river boats were pulled up out of the water. Near the indigenous craft four small trading vessels from the south and one small warship were moored. Behind the docks the incline was steep. It was terraced, close packed with houses, tiled roofs overlapping, seemingly built on top of each other. A line of mean one-storey dwellings backed on to another low wall, which snaked up towards the gate of the acropolis and marked off the inhabited quarter. Beyond it, away to the north, was desolation. Smoke hung over parts of it. Isolated towers, once part of a much greater defensive circuit, showed here and there through the haze, and a couple of huge conical barrows for the dead had been erected in what once must have been the heart of a thriving Greek *polis*.

Ballista had no more wish to be here than in any of the places he had been since the dreadful events of the previous autumn. It had been months of unhappiness and frustration. From the even more far-flung *polis* of Tanais they had crossed Lake Maeotis to the faded splendour and vicious political infighting of Panticapaeum, capital of the Roman client kingdom of the Bosporus. From there, just before the close of the sailing season, they had taken ship across the Euxine to Byzantium. At the Hellespont an imperial official had waited, the bearer of new, most unwanted orders. The pleasures of Byzantium – the famed seafood and wine, the games and chariot racing, the public displays of wisdom by philosophers and sophists – had meant nothing as they were constrained to winter there. Now they were heading north again, misery unabated, vengeance unfulfilled.

As the warship edged in to Olbia, a lifetime of training took over and moved Ballista's thoughts from his troubles. A closer study of the acropolis revealed vegetation growing in fissures in both curtain wall and towers. In places some of the dressed stones had fallen, tumbled down the gradient and been replaced with make-shift rubble. Despite this the cliff made the river side of the citadel almost impregnable, if defended with any application. There was nowhere to site artillery against it, no way to bring up rams let alone siege towers, no chance at all of undermining. A storm with ladders would bring incalculable casualties, almost certainly fail. The only access there would be surprise or treachery.

'Clear fore and aft,' the *trierarch* called. 'Bring her about. Ropes for mooring.'

The long galley slowly swung around. Her triple banks of oars took the way off her, and then gently backed her up against a ramshackle jetty. Deck crew jumped ashore and secured the vessel. Others ran out the boarding ladder from one side of her stern ornament.

Toga-clad and purposeful, Aulus Voconius Zeno, sometime *a Studiis* to the emperor Gallienus himself, before that governor of Cilicia, processed down the ramp, his usual display of *dignitas* only slightly marred by a less than dignified stumble as his feet stepped on the unmoving ground.

With even more self-regard, and far more exotic in a floor-length, gold-fringed red cloak over snow-white tunic, the portly eunuch secretary Amantius went next. He, too, was unsteady as his silk slippers trod the dock.

Ballista followed with Castricius, who would be his deputy when he assumed command of Zeno's escort. The rest of the party, Maximus and Tarchon, the two fighting men from Ballista's *familia*, and the five slaves, trooped down in the rear.

Zeno looked up and down the quayside. He was as clearly unimpressed by what he saw as might be expected in a man who had once advised the emperor on things of culture, and much else more political.

'We must make our arrival known to the authorities,' he announced.

'You do that,' said Ballista.

Zeno bridled. 'Gallienus Augustus has despatched us on an official mission.'

'Tell the local magistrates about the amber,' said Ballista.

Zeno glowered. As the real mission could not be mentioned, he was unsure what to reply.

'Take Amantius with you,' Ballista continued. 'The slaves can unload our baggage, look after it until we have been assigned lodgings. The rest of us are going for a drink.'

'Our escort, the crew of that warship from Moesia . . .'

'Will find us.' Ballista spoke over him. 'Now, I need a drink.'

'Where?'

Outside a shed, unimpressive even on that waterfront, two elderly men sat drinking. 'Over there.'

Zeno and the eunuch swept off, waving away a customs official who tried to speak to them. The *telones* next approached the men with Ballista.

'Fuck off,' said Maximus.

The *telones* regarded Maximus and the other three armed men, and withdrew.

The inside of the bar was bigger than the exterior suggested, although possibly even less appealing. A rough wooden counter ran down the left-hand side. Storage jars sat in holes cut into its surface. Amphorae were stacked behind, and there was an oven next to a closed door at the far end. The only light was from the front door, but nothing looked very clean. Ballista had no intention of eating here.

'A pitcher of wine, please, one quarter water,' he said.

'The best you have,' added Castricius.

As they took places at benches around a plank table, the only other customers, six men and two whores sitting together, hard-eyed them. Maximus and Tarchon stared back. Ballista and Castricius pretended not to notice.

34

'The best,' said the barman. 'A local speciality.'

He poured it and they drank. It was not too bad, although it tasted oddly of elderberry. They drank some more.

'Another,' said Maximus.

As the barman returned, Ballista checked over the other table. The men wore military-style belts with daggers. They were evidently drunk. It was mid-afternoon. He motioned Maximus to look less challenging. There had been several unpleasant incidents in Byzantium over the winter. Not surprising, given the amount everyone in the *familia* had been drinking and what had happened before out on the steppes.

From where he sat Ballista could see a section of the dockside through the open door. An old fisherman was sitting cross-legged in the spring sunshine, mending his nets.

Outwardly at ease, Ballista listened carefully to everything in the bar. The knife men had turned to a loud, drunken conversation among themselves: women, money, drink – the usual subjects. They laughed, moronic in their cups. The whores simpered. The violence had retreated from the room. For now, at least.

Outside, the fisherman was using pot shards as weights. He must have bored a hole in some, as he was stringing them on to the net. Others, he was tying. Perhaps he had scratched a groove in those, so the sharp edges would not cut the cords. An amphora was easy to break, but when broken its fragments were nearly indestructible. Almost a paradox, Ballista thought. A philosopher could make something of that.

Ballista drank more. He felt the wine buzz in his head. The false wellbeing and confidence of alcohol were creeping over him. The melancholy would come later.

Castricius was talking. The short, pointy-faced Roman officer was teasing the other two members of the *familia*. 'You pretty barbarian boys had better watch out. Men from Miletus founded Olbia. Brought the love of boys with them. The locals here are addicted to it, like sparrows in their lechery. Their lust will be inflamed at the sight of you two – a pretty Hibernian and a tender little Suanian.' Maximus and Tarchon gazed back at him with no expression. Each of their lined, battered faces showed its owner's forty-odd years. The Hibernian Maximus was missing the end of his nose.

'I was in Miletus once,' Maximus said flatly. 'Another shitehole.'

There was no obvious catalyst to violence here – unless the knife men were locals who might take offence at being dubbed pederasts. The drink in him, Ballista did not care if they did. He would back himself and his three companions against the six opposite.

A smallish sailing boat had tied up to the wharves. Stevedores were bringing off its cargo. Bales of hides were being piled next to boxes of wax, which suggested the coarse grey amphorae contained honey. Guessing the produce of the neighbouring land could not keep Ballista's mind from why he was here. He was going home. Twenty-six winters since he had been taken as a hostage into the Roman *imperium*. Well over half his time on Middle Earth, and finally he was going back to the lands of his people, to the Angles of the Suebian Sea in the far north. Twenty-six winters waiting to go home. And now he did not want it.

Ballista drank more. No, he did want it. Part of him did. He wanted to see his father, his mother. Of course, Eadwulf, the half-brother he had been closest to, would not be there. But – he smiled – he would see Kadlin, the first girl he had loved. And he could drink again, as he had in his youth, with her brother, Heoroweard.

But the north was not where he should be going now. Calgacus his companion and friend was dead – murdered last autumn on the Steppe – and his killer escaped. In Tanais, Panticapaeum and Byzantium, Ballista had asked everywhere for news. No one knew anything of a Greek called Hippothous. That was what Ballista should be doing – scouring the *imperium* for the Greek bastard. They had taken Hippothous into the *familia*, and he had killed Calgacus. He had killed many others, but it was Calgacus who counted.

Ballista took a long pull from his cup. The flavour of elderberry was getting cloying. Most things did, if you drank enough on an empty stomach. If not hunting Hippothous, he should be at home in Sicily, at home with his wife and sons, keeping them safe. Certainly things had not been right between him and Julia for a long time – he was unsure why, it might be his fault. But with his boys it was different. Two winters since he had seen them. Isangrim would be twelve now, his birthday the *kalends* of this month. Dernhelm turned five last November. The younger would have changed more, maybe out of all recognition.

Poor old Calgacus had loved them. The Caledonian had been a miserable, ugly old bastard. But he had always been there, since Ballista himself was a child. Calgacus had travelled into the *imperium* with him, served on every distant frontier. Maximus was a good friend. They had been together years. They were close. Castricius less so – he was strange. But, on and off, the little Roman had been with him for years, too. Tarchon the Suanian was loyal, even if often incomprehensible. But none of them was Calgacus. The one man Ballista had talked to in the worst of times, in the most uncertain and unguarded moments.

Ballista knew he was already drunk, his thoughts sliding around, maudlin, full of self-pity. Perhaps he should eat. He concentrated, trying to focus on the dock outside.

A big trading vessel up from the south had now been pulled in to the side. Dozens of amphorae were being lugged ashore, men everywhere. Incongruous in scarlet cloak and silk slippers, Amantius was weaving his way through the bustle, half imperious, half diffident.

The eunuch walked into the bar. Instantly the knife men fell silent, their eyes on the outlandish newcomer.

'Ho, precious,' one called out in rough Greek, 'we have whores already.'

They laughed. One made the sign to avert evil. Everyone knew eunuchs were like monkeys or cripples, things of ill omen.

Amantius stopped, irresolute.

'Fuck off, we do not want your kind in here.' One of the toughs got up from their table.

'Apologize.' Ballista found himself on his feet, face close to the standing knife man.

'And who the fuck are you?' It takes most men a few moments to work themselves up to violence, at times an unfortunate weakness.

'Apologize to the eunuch.'

'You can fuck —'

Ballista smashed his cup hard into the man's face. His head snapped around, blood spraying as the shattered earthenware lacerated his skin. He crumpled to the floor, hands to his face.

From the right a whore swung a heavy wine jug at Ballista. He swayed back. When it had passed, he punched her in the face. The bones in her nose broke under his fist. She went down.

'Blade!' Maximus yelled.

Ballista dropped, turned, tugged his dagger free. As he did so pain lanced through his left arm. He rammed the tip of his weapon up where his assailant's stomach should be. Nothing. The man had checked his momentum, stepped away, dropped into a fighting crouch. Ballista did the same, no room for swordwork. Blood ran down his arm. A bad cut high up. There was a sickness deep in his guts. Noise battered his senses. *Watch the blade. Watch the blade.*

The man's dagger weaved like a sightless steel predator scenting warm blood. Ballista felt a wave of nausea rise. Ignoring the pain, he gripped his sword scabbard in his left hand, held it clear of his legs. The man shifted his blade to his left hand, made a pass.

Ballista stepped clear, jabbed. The man evaded, passed his weapon back into his right. He had done this before. *Watch the blade.*

At the edge of his vision, Ballista saw the man on the floor move. He took a step towards him. The one on his feet blocked him. Ballista sidestepped away. The din buffeted back from the walls, Ballista and his opponent a pocket of silence in the chaos.

The injured man was trying to haul himself up. Ballista had to act. He tossed his dagger in the air, caught its blade on the first rotation, spun it at the standing knife man's face. Surprised, his opponent jerked sideways, off balance, his guard disturbed. Ballista drew his sword, flicked it straight out, lunged. Two quick steps. The heavy *spatha* battered the dagger aside. Its steel tip ripped in below the chest, two foot of steel following. The man grunted, dropped his weapon, clutched at the blade. Not looking into his face, Ballista twisted his sword, pushed him away, retrieved his *spatha*, turned to deal with the other on the floor. The man was scuttling off under the table.

A crash of splintering wood; light flooded in from another angle. Someone had kicked open the back door. Figures flitted out. The man from the floor last, staggering but fast.

Ballista checked the room. His three friends all on their feet, seeming unhurt. The eunuch cowering under a table. The stabbed man at his feet, gasping out his life in a spreading pool of dark blood. Another very motionless in front of Maximus. A whore unconscious on her back, her face a bloodied ruin.

II

CAMPANIA IN ITALY

The emperor Gallienus stifled a yawn. It had been a long day already, enjoyable but tiring. Having dressed by lamplight, they had mounted up well before dawn. They had ridden through the rich fields of Campania, then up into the foothills of the Apennines, where well-surfaced Roman roads had given way to narrow, rustic paths flanked by stands of oaks. A gentle spring zephyr had played through the foliage and, above, swallows darted high in a perfect blue sky. It had been a good morning for riding. All the imperial party had been on horseback, except for the philosopher Plotinus. Thinking of his years and various ailments, Gallienus had given dispensation for the Platonist to travel in a light, two-wheel carriage. Such consideration was the mark of a *civilis princeps*. Of course, no emperor but the most civilized of rulers would have embarked on such a day in the first place.

His first view of their destination had moved Gallienus to recite Homer:

For I know this thing well in my heart, and my mind knows it:
There will come a day when sacred Ilion shall perish,
And Priam, and the people of Priam of the strong ash spear.

The same words of Hector recited by Scipio as he gazed on the ruin of Carthage some four hundred years before. Unsurprisingly, the imperial entourage – the philosophers included – had shaken back their cloaks and quietly lauded the appositeness of the quotation. Only Freki the Alamann and the Germanic bodyguards he commanded had not joined in the applause. *Paideia* meant nothing to them – it was doubtful any of them understood Greek – but even on a day devoted to culture an emperor could not be without armed guards.

The town was a ruin. Its outer wall could just be traced as a low grassy bank from which poked occasional blocks of weathered stone. Inside, the streets were choked with weed-covered rubble. Mature trees grew in what had once been the *agora* and gymnasium. The walls of few houses remained above a couple of feet. Lonely columns, some at dangerous angles, marked the site of temples long abandoned by gods and men.

The citadel had fared a little better. In places, its wall still stood, if insecurely. At its height, their condition defying the ages, loomed one huge tower and a temple to the Egyptian gods. Dark and primordial, it was as if they still waited, for guards, for priests and worshippers.

And over everything soared the heights of the Apennines, gorgeous, bright and remote in the spring sunshine.

Alighting from his carriage, Plotinus had conducted Gallienus around the site. Supported on one side by his philosopher's staff and on the other by Amelius, his fussy, aging chief disciple, Plotinus was indefatigable. In practical demonstration of his belief that the body was no better than a prison, he had made no concessions to the ulcers on his feet. Pushing through undergrowth, clambering around fallen masonry, disturbing small lizards where they basked, throughout the heat of the day he had set out his vision. Courtiers and German bodyguards flagged – the latter were never good in hot weather – but Plotinus had not let up. Gallienus thought the philosopher's old eyes had become less bleared; certainly his voice had gathered strength.

Once, this desolation had been a city of the Pythagoreans. Their worn inscriptions and strange symbols were discernible through ivy and moss. In their way they had been seekers after wisdom and the divine. But they had chosen the wrong path. They had erred into dark magic and political tyranny. For these, rightly, they had been condemned. Now, with the favour of the emperor, this place could rise again, rise in justice and truth under the tenets of Plato.

It would cost the imperial fiscus little, probably no more than a million sesterces, for contributions had been promised by many affluent followers of Plato. The senators Firmus, Marcellus Orontius and Sabinillus already had pledged large sums. Five thousand settlers were needed. Military veterans would be best, as used to discipline, but landless peasants, members of the urban plebs, even barbarian refugees or prisoners would be acceptable – true philosophy can enlighten the most ignorant, tame the most savage. A select group of eminent philosophers would form the Nocturnal Council. These guardians of virtue would govern the town. Platonopolis would be the wonder of this and future ages – a city run by the *Laws* of Plato, a utopia made real by the *paideia* of Gallienus Augustus, by the wisdom and learning of the emperor.

At last it had been time for the midday meal, and it was Gallienus's turn to amaze. In a shaded olive grove on a slope overlooking the projected city, the emperor had had his servants prepare rustic couches and cedarwood tables spread with out-of-season delicacies. Boys dressed as Pans played pipes, and pretty young shepherdesses tended their artfully groomed flocks.

For postprandial rest there were *cubicula* of roses. No expense had been spared creating this transient ideal of bucolic simplicity.

Garlanded and replete, Gallienus lay back, cup in hand, a handsome Greek boy at his feet. Other comely servants glided through the grove, their smooth youth a delicious contrast to the gnarled silver trunks of the trees. Gallienus noted that most of Plotinus's followers exhibited a detachment suitable to their calling. One Diophanes, however, despite his rough cloak and untrimmed beard, appeared far from indifferent to their charms.

On the couch next to Gallienus, the elderly senator Tacitus was utterly unmoved by either the pulchritude on display or the food and drink. Solemnly he nibbled at a piece of dry bread, which from time to time he dipped in a little olive oil. The only other items on his plate were a morsel of cold pheasant and some leaves of lettuce. He had drunk just enough watered wine to be polite. He had unbent no more than loosening his sword belt.

Gallienus knew all about Tacitus's austere domestic regime. The Danubian subscribed to the belief that lettuce cooled the desires of the flesh – he was very opposed to the desires of the flesh. Likewise, Gallienus knew why Tacitus had journeyed from his estate at Interamna and requested permission to be one of the imperial *comites* today. Naturally a figure of such seniority and influence – a powerful military man from the Danube risen to the rank of consul – was watched by the *frumentarii*. The imperial spy in Tacitus's household had given ample forewarning of the request and its reason.

Platonopolis had aroused vehement antagonism. Stoics, Cynics, Epicureans, Peripatetics and, of course, latter-day Neo-Pythagoreans had united with Megareans and Cyreneans and followers of doctrines of yet greater obscurity to denounce the whole concept. No sect wanted to see another singled out in imperial favour. They had all been most unphilosophic in their complaints.

More telling opposition had come from within the military. Some years before, struck by the sworn-bands of the northern barbarians who would not leave the field alive if their chief fell, and thinking a little of the companions around Alexander the Great and his successors, Gallienus had instituted the *protectores*. Part bodyguard, part senior officer, a *protector* took a personal oath on a naked blade to fight to the death for the emperor. Their oath brought the right to bear arms in the imperial presence.

The *protectores* had appeared united in their hostility to Platonopolis. Their loyalty gave them a certain latitude. Aureolus, the Prefect of Cavalry, had used smooth words for one raised as a shepherd among the semi-barbarian Getae. Domitianus had argued in the sonorous tones of a man who claimed descent from an emperor. However, others had gone further. The Praetorian Prefect Volusianus had spoken as the blunt ex-trooper he was. Camsisoleus had waved his hands about, as excited as might be expected of an Egyptian. Aurelian – the one they called *Hand-to-Steel* – had even raised his voice in the imperial *consilium*; to the horror of the *silentarii*. Tacitus was one of their number, and he was the last throw of the *protectores*.

Gallienus had decided to grant the petition of Plotinus. An emperor's reign demanded monuments. The architects had produced nothing but problems, delays and additional expense with the new colossus of Gallienus on the Esquiline. No more than its gigantic feet existed. And future generations might mistake its size for something hubristic. A city dedicated to *paideia*, to Plato, could never incur that charge.

Yet Gallienus would give Tacitus a hearing. A *civilis princeps* did not act on a whim, on personal inclination, like an oriental despot. A good emperor consulted his friends, let his *amici* speak their minds. Free speech should be allowed in formal council, and also away from the *consilium* at a rustic meal in the foothills of the Apennines.

'*Dominus.*' Tacitus obviously thought the moment auspicious.

Graciously, Gallienus said his friend should speak what was on his mind. Tacitus's lined face, never a canvas of levity, took on a cast of deep profundity, and he launched into his considered discourse.

No one, Gallienus thought, with the exception of an intellectual at the Alexandrian Museum or an habitué of the schools of philosophers or sophists, could have the experience of an emperor in appearing to listen intently to speeches while thinking of something completely different. Gallienus knew what Tacitus would say. This foreknowledge was nothing to do with the *frumentarii*. The arguments against Platonopolis had been rehearsed on many occasions in many forms.

Advancing one school of philosophy would alienate all the others. While the tenets of none necessarily led to opposition to monarchy, often they had provided moral underpinning to men contemplating assassination of a ruler. Brutus had been a Stoic, Cassius an Epicurean, and Caesar had died. Less drastic, but possibly more damaging in the long run – the gods would foil any insane attempt on the life of the *princeps* – intellectuals shaped public opinion. The speeches and writings of philosophers might deform the image of the glorious reign of Gallienus. Street-corner Cynics were ever ready to howl against even the best of emperors.

'What of this place itself?'

The rhetorical question brought Gallienus back to his surroundings.

'The Pythagoreans came here seeking enlightenment, but ended mired in foul superstition and lust for temporal power. It puts one in mind of Cicero's speech against the proposal of Rullus to settle men at Capua. The land there is luxurious, it made men who dwelt there the same, and that made them enemies of Rome.'

Gallienus smiled in recognition of the novelty of this cultured argument. Those among the traditional elite who sneered at the military men from the Danube were fools. The family of Tacitus had owned wide estates time out of mind; many of his compatriots were rougher – Aurelian *Hand-to-Steel*, for one. But the thing that united these hard men from the north was their reverence for the traditions of Rome. In many ways they were closer to the *mos maiorum* than the pampered and plucked rich who were born in marble palaces on the seven hills or opulent villas on the Bay of Naples.

Tacitus had moved on to finances. Gallienus was well aware what this would entail. Plotinus had vastly underestimated the true cost. If building were to be undertaken, better the emperor's own plan for a portico along the Via Flaminia. Unlike this out-of-the-way spot in the Apennines, it would provide work for the always restless plebs of Rome.

Tacitus was bound to end with the argument that, in these days of usurpation and barbarian assault, money was better spent on the army. The safety of the *imperium* must take precedence over everything in these days of iron and rust.

At the thought, Gallienus felt his skin tighten. There was a new clarity to the light; faint music among the trees. He knew Hercules, his divine companion, was with him. The deity reached into Gallienus's soul, drew it out of his body.

Wrapped safe in the skin of the Nemean lion, Gallienus was lifted through the air. Past the heights of the Apennines, he was carried north. Higher and yet higher, until his divine friend set him lightly on the utmost peak of the Alps. From there they gazed down on all the land and all the sea. Hercules laid his hands on them, as one might an instrument capable of playing all modes, and under his fingers they all sang together.

The whole *imperium* and everything in it was spread out, an animate map, with mountains for bones, rivers and roads for veins. In the east, Odenathus of Palmyra took the war to the Persians. Gallienus could see Ctesiphon in flames, the easterners fleeing in panic. To the north of the Euxine, out on the vast plains, nomad horsemen wheeled as the Alani fought the Heruli and Urugundi. None of them had the leisure to turn on the empire. Moving west, the King of the Bosporus once again performed adoration to the imperial standards. Of little use in a fight, he would at least sound the alarm should the piratical tribes of the region – Borani, Grethungi, Tervingi, Gepidae and Taifali – take to their boats and venture south. Along the Ister, all was quiet. Loyal men governed the armed provinces of Moesia and Pannonia. Aided by Attalus of the Marcomanni, they watched the bellicose hordes of the Carpi, Sarmatians, Quadi and Vandals.

The west was different. The vile pretender Postumus – oath-breaker, child-murderer – squatted in Gaul. Corrupt, self-seeking courtiers, traitors to a man, whispered foulness in his ears. The fickle legions along the Rhine swore their sacrilegious oaths to him. The provinces of Britain and Spain – stately matrons reduced to whores – grovelled and submitted to his will. Even the proud barbarians of the distant north had taken his tainted subsidies. The Frisii, the Saxons, even the Angles had ceased to raid the territories he tyrannized. This year the latter at least should change – Gallienus had sent *mandata* and men to put his plans for the far north in motion. This year also he would deal with Raetia, the rebellious province nestling at his feet north of the Alps. These things done, next year, Gallienus Invictus would march at the head of the field army, cross the Alps and unleash the full terror of his revenge.

Across the glittering sea, away to the south, the sun beat down on Africa. All was soporific. But in the haze of the heat strange rumours coiled up. The native rebel Faraxen was not dead. Somewhere, in a cave in the High Atlas, his disembodied head sang songs of revolution and apocalypse.

Gallienus dismissed the fragments of this fevered dream and turned his eyes back to the east. If Odenathus, the man he had appointed *Corrector Totius Orientis*, remained loyal, nothing could halt next year's descent into Gaul. If Odenathus remained loyal . . .

III

OLBIA

Achilles' hair was thick, lovelier than gold. His nose was not quite aqui-
line, but almost so; his brow the shape of a crescent. The bluish-grey
eyes of the hero held a certain eagerness. A soft breeze moved through
the tops of the poplars and elms around the sanctuary. Herons and
cranes glided low, the seawater falling like dew from their wings. Patroklos moved closer; head held straight, as if in a wrestling school, nostrils
flared like an impatient horse. His olive skin looked good to touch. Dark,
black eyes gazed at Achilles. The act of desire begins in the eyes.

The trampling of horses. High, shrill, female yelps. A myriad of gulls
took flight raucously. The Amazons streamed towards the sanctuary,
crying aloud and driving on their mares. Achilles bounded up, shouting
his great shout. The mares refused, the war cry inflicting on them terror
greater than any bit or switch. Rearing and plunging, they threw their
riders. The Amazons sprawled, bruised and dazed, on the ground. The
horses took on the habits of wild beasts, bristled their manes, pricked up
their ears like savage lions. They fell on their former riders; tearing at the
forearms of the supine women, stamping down with their sharp hooves.

After they had broken open their chests, they devoted themselves to the entrails, gulping them down. The sanctuary was a slaughterhouse, horrible beyond measure. The women were lying everywhere, still breathing and half eaten. Everywhere, severed limbs and pieces of flesh, slobbered with bestial saliva.

Amantius clutched the threads of the dream, the mingled lust and revulsion. He opened his eyes. The small attic room. His boy, Ion, asleep across the threshold. Space was at a premium in the inhabited quarter of Olbia, let alone here on the acropolis.

He woke Ion, sent him to buy fresh fruit and *oxygala*, and honey to sweeten the yoghurt. There was no need to live like a barbarian, even if surrounded by them. He told Ion to get himself bread, not slave bread. Amantius fancied himself a kind master.

When the boy had gone, Amantius propped himself up on his cushions, his considerable paunch rising and falling with his breathing. He thought he should write to Censorinus. Privacy was hard to come by to write secret letters. His chubby fingers reached for his writing block and stylus. They stopped in mid-air. What was he to report? In the past two years of travel in the *barbaricum* to the savage Caucasus and the end of the world on the Steppe, Amantius considered he had provided good information. As far as he knew, nothing had yet come of his coup in discovering the possibly treasonous correspondence between Gallienus's *Corrector Totius Orientis*, Odenathus, and Naulobates, king of the savage Heruli. But he flattered himself the return of the King of the Bosporus to friendship with Rome was in large part his doing. The Praetorian Prefect was not a man to be bothered with trivialities. What could he tell Censorinus about now – a drunken fight in a bar?

Amantius lay back, trying to put it out of his mind – hiding under a table, while two men died. He admired the jewels on his hands: garnets and sapphires set in gold. No one could steal rings, unless you were already dead. The thought made him shudder.

He so wanted to be at home. Gods forbid not in Abasgia, where he had been born. Few memories remained, and those bad – the pain of the knife, being told his family were dead. He had not wanted to be a beautiful child, to be castrated or unwittingly become the cause of the deaths of his parents and brothers. He lacked the courage to seek revenge. Abasgia held nothing for him. What he wanted – desired with all his soul – was to be back among his own kind in the palace at Rome. Companionship, imperial favour, civilization and safety; he had been happy there.

It was unfair. He had survived Albania, Suania, even the sea of grass. Miraculously, he had survived when many others had died. He had been on his way home. Amantius had never known such misery as the day in Byzantium when the new orders came to act as secretary to this mission to the far north.

And the mission was inauspicious, if not already doomed. To begin with, there had been nothing worse than the discomforts of travelling on a warship, the enforced proximity with rough men who held the prejudices of the entire against his sort. He had seen them, thumb between index and middle finger, making the sign to avert evil. He had ignored the mutterings – monkey, crow, neither dove nor raven, thing of ill omen.

It now seemed an age since the storm had hit when they were off the mouth of the Ister. The Argestes had got up in the north-west, cresting the waves, driving the *trireme* out into the wild Euxine. When, through spray and low, scudding clouds, the Island of Leuce had been sighted, their delight had brought them to tears. They had embraced each other at their deliverance. All except Amantius. No one hugged a eunuch, no more than they would a monkey.

The galley had rounded the northern cape and anchored in a small rocky bay which gave some shelter. The boarding ladders in the surf, over treacherous rocks, they had floundered ashore, soaked to the skin.

The storm still raged when behind the clouds the sun went down. Zeno had said they must return aboard. Amantius had supported him. Leuce was the Island of Achilles. No one spent the night except at the risk of his life. It brought down the wrath of the hero.

The *trierarch* had dismissed the idea. The ship was double anchored, but it was a bad holding ground. She could drag her anchors at any moment. If the wind shifted, it was a certainty. Only a fool would put himself in a present danger to avert something intangible in the future. They would propitiate Achilles in the morning.

In the dark and the rain, they had trudged through the woods up to the centre of the island. There was a portico adjacent to the temple. They bedded down there, sodden and uncomfortable. Amantius had hardly slept, huddled a little apart from the others, full of dread, like a hunted animal in a temporary lair. Divine prohibitions were not to be flouted.

When the sun came up, the storm had blown itself out. The last few clouds ran like ink away to the east. The leaves of the sacred grove glistened. Gulls and sea-crows spiralled about the cliffs. The island was small, but wild goats abounded. The crew soon caught one. Before it could be sacrificed, they had to discover if it was acceptable to Achilles. The formula was well known. Zeno put out an offering on the round altar in front of the temple. It was generous and fitting; a silver bowl, with scenes from the *Iliad* chased in gold. They waited for the sign that told the hero approved. His attendants stayed away. After a time, Zeno placed silver coins in the bowl. The sky over the altar remained empty. Finally, gold coins were added. There were innumerable birds, over the sea, around the cliffs, high over the treetops. Not one swooped low over the altar, to fan the offering with the beat of its wings, to anoint it with falling seawater.

Boldly, Zeno announced it was as he expected. In the night

Patroklos had appeared to him in a dream. The son of Menoetius had told him Achilles had gone to Thessaly, to roam the plains and hills of his childhood. Zeno had announced the goat must go free. The offerings would remain. They would please Achilles on his return. Before they sailed they would make libations.

The lie was so obvious. Sailors were among the most superstitious people in the world. Unhappily, they had trooped down to the bay, gone on board, made the *trireme* ready. Dark looks were cast at the eunuch, sure bringer of bad luck. Wine tipped into the sea with pious words lightened their mood not at all.

Yet the remainder of the voyage had passed well. The prevailing north-easterly wind had not reasserted itself. Argestes continued to blow, but gently now. The breeze on the beam or quarter, the *trireme* proceeded mainly under sail. Soon the rowers, lounging on their benches, sang and joked when not quieted by the officers. Like plebs or barbarians, sailors were quick to change, unthinking. The terrible anger of Achilles was out of their minds. Amantius had not forgotten the implacable anger of Achilles.

Lying in bed, waiting for Ion to return, Amantius brooded on the Island of Achilles. It was created by and for love. Achilles' mother, Thetis, had asked Poseidon to make an island where her son and Helen could live together after sloughing off their mortality. The god of the sea had granted her petition, minded that it might also serve as a refuge for seafarers. Poseidon and Amphitrite, and all the Nereids and water spirits had attended the wedding. And there through the ages Achilles and Helen had made love and sung together. But it was also an island of blood. Apart from the hideous fate of the Amazons, there was the story of the Trojan girl.

A merchant was in the habit of putting in to the island. Achilles not only deigned to appear, but had entertained him with food and drink. When all was convivial between them, Achilles asked the merchant a favour. The next time he visited Ilion, would he buy him a particular girl who was owned by a certain man? Astonished at the request, and emboldened by wine, the merchant wondered why the hero needed a Trojan slave. Because, my guest, Achilles said, she was born of the lineage from which Hector came, and she is what remains of the blood of the descendants of Priam and Dardanos. Thinking the hero was in love, the merchant carried out the task. The next time he came to the island, Achilles praised him, and asked him to guard the girl overnight on his ship. The island was inaccessible to women. That afternoon Achilles feasted the merchant royally and gave him many of the things such men are unable to resist. The next morning the merchant put the girl ashore, and cast off. He had not gone much more than a hundred yards when he heard the screams of the girl. There on the beach Achilles was pulling her apart, tearing her limb from limb.

Ballista sat in the pool in the hot room of the *thermae*. They were the only public baths functioning in the town of Olbia. The water was not as hot as it should have been. Despite that, the sweat was lashing off him. It was to be expected when a man stopped after drinking for two or three days.

Through the gloom of the *caldarium*, Ballista looked at the wall painting by the door. It was a dwarf with a hunchback. From under its ridiculously short tunic poked an erormous erection. The artist had lavished care on the bulbous head, tinting it purple. Causing Ballista a certain disquiet, it brought Calgacus to mind. The memories remained vague shapes below the surface. Ballista's head hurt and his chest was tight.

Ballista had seen many similar grotesques across the *imperium*: dozens of the deformed in mosaics and paintings, often negroes, with huge penises and testicles. Their very abnormality was intended to provoke laughter, and it was common knowledge that laughter scared away *daemons*. So the misshapen often performed their apotropaic function in doorways and in bathhouses. It was not just against *daemons* the Romans thought they needed protection. There was the danger of *invidia*, or *phthonos* as the Greeks called it, the very human malign envy that directs its ill will at others. Those who possessed the Evil Eye were said somehow to be able to penetrate their victims with invisible particles of grudging malice, causing illness, madness, even death.

It was hard to imagine there was much to envy here, certainly nothing about either the looks or characters of Ballista's three companions. They were all naked in the pool. The scar where the end of Maximus's nose should have been gleamed white through the steam. His small eyes were screwed shut against the pain of his hangover. If anything stirred behind them, most likely it involved some unfeasible combination of women, alcohol, cannabis and extreme violence. Castricius moved an arm now and then, but the lined, pointed features of his face remained in repose. The little Roman was not one to be afraid of supernatural threats. He never tired of recounting the power of the *daemon* that always accompanied him; the very *daemons* of death were terrified of the two of them. His looks were equally unprepossessing, but Tarchon the Suanian was a different case. *Thermae* were still strange to him. Perhaps it was some perception of threat – physical or mental, human or *daemonic* – or merely the unaccustomed proximity of naked men, but there was no relaxation in the tribesman from the Caucasus. He shifted this way and that, trying not to brush his legs against those of the others. Continually, he peered around into the shadows. Ballista felt a surge of affection for all three, even as the loss of Calgacus pierced him yet again.

Following Tarchon's gaze, Ballista doubted the *thermae* themselves could induce much envy. An old-style moralist who inveighed against the luxuries of contemporary bathing would find little for complaint. The hot room was small, dark and dingy.

There appeared to be mould on the ceiling. Apart from the *caldarium*, there was only a changing room. A cold plunge pool had been wedged in a corner of the *apodyterium*. The four of them were the only bathers, yet it was still cramped. It was as well they had not brought a single slave with them. The baths in Ballista's home in Sicily were bigger and better equipped.

In his tired and weakened state, the thought of home threatened to overwhelm him. He wanted nothing more than to be with his boys, with Julia. He loved the villa high on the cliffs of Tauromenium, loved sitting in the shaded garden looking down at sun shining on the Bay of Naxos. But was it really home? The villa had come with Julia as part of her dowry. It had been in her family for generations. Ballista had added his own touches to it; some trophies and weapons hanging on walls, an expanded library, the odd work of art. But it was not his in the way it was Julia's, in the way it was his sons'. They had always known it. For him it was a brief sunlit interlude. It had been years since he had been there. The place had assumed a mythical status, like Alfheim or the Islands of the Blessed.

The sweat was stinging his eyes. He rubbed it away, along with his maudlin thoughts. There was no point in dwelling on Tauromenium now. He was bound for the far north, Angeln, his original home, and there were no bathhouses there. A line of Tacitus came into his mind. The Britons rushing to embrace togas and baths; mistaking those signs of servitude for *humanitas*. In which case, his journey should be a flight from slavery into freedom. Somehow he doubted it.

A man moved quietly past the dwarf into the room. There was no sound of clogs protecting his feet from the heated floor. In his hand there was a gleam of metal. The water erupted as Tarchon surged up out of the pool. Ballista slipped and struggled to his feet. Maximus and Castricius were up, knives magicked out of their towels.

The newcomer screamed as Tarchon slammed him against the wall. A bucket rolled away and a strigil scraped across the tiles. Tarchon had his hands around the man's throat.

'No!' Ballista shouted. 'Leave him. It is just a bath attendant.'

The slave fled when Tarchon let him go.

Ballista smiled at the Suanian. 'You were quick, but more killings would not be good. We still have the two dead sailors from the waterside hanging over us.'

The drinking had to stop, the guilt reined in, discipline re-asserted. Ballista knew he and his *familia* were a danger to themselves as well as any who crossed their path. This had to stop.

IV

OLBIA

Aulus Voconius Zeno, *Vir Perfectissimus*, special envoy to the far
north of the Augustus Gallienus, Pius, Fortunate and Invincible,
sat in the seat of honour, such as it was, in the council house of
the city of Olbia. Light came from the open door and windows.
There was no glass in the windows. Obviously, the building, high
on the acropolis, had once been the *praetorium* of a Roman army
unit. The *Boule* must have moved into the officer's quarters when,
after the disaster at Abritus thirteen years before, the new
emperor Gallus had withdrawn the troops from the north of the
Euxine. By the look of it, the council had spent nothing on repairs
or decorations since.

The meeting had been in session for an hour or more. A lifelong career in imperial service had equipped Zeno with deep
reserves of patience. After lengthy prayers to the gods, a magistrate titled the *agoranomos* had taken the floor, and showed no
signs yet of relinquishing it. First he had set out, in bad Greek
and exhaustive detail, the grain shortage afflicting the town. The

public granaries were virtually empty, prices rising steeply; there were dark rumours of hoarding and profiteering. A citizen of Olbia now resident in Byzantium had donated a shipload of wheat. The *Boule* had decided to recommend the assembly vote this man a statue at public expense. Given the straitened circumstances of city finances, an old statue should be rededicated. Despite this godlike generosity, the *agoranomos* had continued, much more was needed. With no overt reluctance, two councillors had announced they would provide grain from their private stores. More fulsome praise had followed, and two more forgotten benefactors of an earlier age lost the dedications on their statues.

The *agoranomos* now was talking about temple treasures. Zeno's thoughts drifted towards the baths and dinner. At least one of the baths was still operative, diminutive and foul though it was, and he had instructed one of his boys to buy oysters and bream. Seafood was wonderfully cheap in this backwater compared with Byzantium, let alone Rome. Raised voices with uncouth accents brought him back. Apparently, the previous year the *Boule* had authorized the priests of Apollo to pawn some sacred vessels of gold. The foreigner who held them was threatening to take them abroad and melt them down. The somewhat acrimonious apportioning of blame continued for some time, growing steadily more heated, until the first *archon* Callistratus announced he would reclaim them with his own money. The loan would be for a year, interest free. The members of the *Boule* then had to endure Callistratus launching into an extempore oration on *homonoia*; did they not realize civic harmony was the greatest treasure a *polis* could possess?

There were only twenty members of the *Boule*. Zeno studied them. They were all dressed in native style: embroidered Sarmatian tunics and trousers, small black cloaks, long swords on their hips. Zeno thought of the story of Scyles in Herodotus. Scyles had been king of the nomadic Scythians in these parts, but his mother had been a Greek woman. She had taught him that language, and brought him up to love all things Hellenic. When Scyles had come to Olbia he had left his army outside the walls and entered the gates alone. Inside, Scyles had changed his Scythian clothes for Greek. He had a home in the city, in which he kept a woman he treated as his wife. Maybe they had children; Herodotus did not say. Each time, he had stayed for a month or more. This state of affairs had persisted for a number of years. In the end a citizen of Olbia had told the Scythians, who could say for what motive. Rejected by his people, hunted and finally betrayed, Scyles was decapitated.

Looking at the councillors of Olbia, Zeno thought the cultural influences now ran strongly the other way. They had done so for a long time. The citizens of Olbia had been wearing nomad garb over a hundred and fifty years before when the philosopher Dio of Prusa had come to the town. Yet Dio had judged them Hellenic, had found merit in them. They were brave, knew Homer by heart, some of them loved Plato, and – always an important factor with Dio – they had listened to his philosophizing and honoured him. Dio had been a slippery man, often saying more or less than was true about himself and others. Zeno knew one thing which Dio had suppressed about the Olbians. Many of them carried barbarian names, like this *agoranomos* Dadag, or Padag, whatever he was called.

At long, long last the Greek magistrate with the Sarmatian or Persian name ceased talking. The floor was taken by the *strategos* in charge of the defence of the city. The name of this one was entirely Roman. Marcus Galerius Montanus Proculus, like many in the *Boule*, was clean-shaven. Zeno smiled at the recollection of Dio claiming only one man in the whole town had shaved – in flattery of the Romans; and all his fellow citizens had reviled him for it. Maybe fashions had changed, or maybe again Dio had played with the truth. Many intellectuals were not to be trusted.

Montanus told another story of woe. A group of slaves had run. They had stolen a boat and made their way to somewhere called Hylaea. Evidently, this place was nearby, somewhere in the great marshy estuary where the rivers Hypanis and Borysthenes came together. There were altars and sacred groves there, which the slaves had violated. The heavily wooded terrain was blamed for the failure of the Olbian militia under Montanus to kill, capture or dislodge them. Lately, the runaways had turned to piracy.

Zeno was wondering if he needed to relieve himself, when he realized he was being directly addressed. So there was a reason beyond the killings in the waterfront bar why his presence had been requested. Montanus was claiming a providential deity had sent an imperial warship and its forty crew to aid the city in this trial.

In the hush, Zeno got slowly to his feet, walked the three paces to the centre of the shabby room. He looked at Montanus, then at the floor, furrowing his brow, nodding thoughtfully. He did not care much for modern sophists – much preferring a recitation of Homer – but he had attended enough of their display oratory to learn a trick or two. He let time pass before looking up sharply, as if his weighty deliberations had reached some inescapable conclusion.

'It is a grave situation, and my heart urges me to help.' Again Zeno paused, the very image of philanthropy wrestling with duty. 'Yet in all conscience, I cannot. I have the honour to be charged with a mission by the most noble Augustus himself. To delay would amount to disobeying imperial *mandata*.'

There were loud mutterings about the triviality of his task. Some, perfectly audible, questioned what type of emperor concerned himself with amber ornaments over the wellbeing of his subjects. One called out Gallienus's infamous line on being informed of the revolt of Postumus in Gaul: Can the *Res Publica* be safe without Atrebatic cloaks?

'It must be remembered, failure to carry out imperial orders is nothing less than *maiestas*.'

At the Latin word for treason, the *Boule* became very quiet.

'As I understand, the city of Olbia falls under the military competence of the governor of Moesia Inferior, and you should apply to him.' Zeno resumed his seat. Whenever possible, pass responsibility. All he had said was true, as far as it went, and this backwater meant nothing to him.

The councillors fell to wrangling about what measures, if any, they could take about the slaves.

Gods below, thought Zeno, it was hard to imagine Olbia was once a powerful city that had defied Alexander the Great, defeated an army of thirty thousand men and killed his governor of Thrace. Now what sort of *polis* hoped one river patrol boat and forty men would bring them salvation? Was Olbia a Hellenic *polis* at all?

To take his mind off his growing need to urinate, Zeno turned over the question in his head. What made a *polis*? An urban centre, buildings of course; Olbia had these, if in a much reduced state. Certain institutions were vital: magistrates, council, assembly. The latter had been mentioned. Zeno wondered what it was like, given the *Boule* seemed just to consist of four or five rich men who dominated the magistracies and some fifteen others who lacked the means or initiative to leave this beleaguered outpost. Then there was culture. Did the Olbians possess *paideia*? It was true they worshipped the traditional Greek gods, among them Zeus, Apollo and Demeter. Zeno had witnessed no barbaric religious practices. They spoke Greek, if with bad pronunciation and strange word order. Wearing Sarmatian clothes could be dismissed as a thing of no importance. But blood will out. Some philosophers might argue that a man of any race could become Greek if he adopted Hellenic *paideia*. Zeno did not agree. These Olbians were descended from waves of nomadic horsemen. Their names gave them away: Padag, Dadag, the names of dogs or slaves. They could never be truly Greek. Zeno himself was born in the heart of the Peloponnese, in Arcadia, under the sheer peak of Cyllene. He would remain a Hellene, even if he lived alone in a hut on the side of a remote mountain, cut off from men and gods, never speaking his native tongue.

Callistratus brought the debate about the slaves to an end by volunteering to equip and serve on an embassy to the governor of Moesia Inferior. The first *archon* moved on to raise matters he described of the utmost importance. This spring the king of the Gothic Tervingi had not appeared with his men on the borders to demand his customary gifts. The councillors called out like a disturbed flock of birds. Zeno, his bladder ever more urgent, could not see the cause of their alarm. Surely given the impecunious state of their civic treasury they should welcome the absence of the Goth?

There was more, Callistratus continued. Word had come downriver that the Castle of Achilles, the most northerly fortified settlement on the right bank of the Hypanis, was deserted; the half-Greek inhabitants had fled. Zeno nearly snorted with derision. Who were these Olbians to judge others half-Greek?

What was he doing in this barbarous place? How had it come to this? Four years before, he, Aulus Voconius Zeno, *Vir Perfectissimus*, had been governor of Cilicia. In the revolt of Macrianus and Quietus, he had remained loyal. Although unable to defend his province, his *fides* – and his devotion to *paideia* – had been rewarded by Gallienus with the post of *a Studiis* at the imperial court. Zeno had carried out his duties with diligence, searching out the texts Gallienus wished to read and the intellectuals he wanted to talk to, discussing them with him. He had spoken out in the *consilium* with the freedom of speech expected of a friend of the emperor, always arguing for the traditions of Rome. Despite it all, last year he had been dismissed, sent away to the Ister as deputy to the senator Sabinillus on a diplomatic mission to turn the tribes of the Carpi, Gepidae and Tervingi against each other. Of course the attempt had failed. Yet – and here he could barely stomach his bitterness – Sabinillus had been summoned back to court, while he had been ordered to undertake this most likely equally hopeless and certainly far more dangerous embassy.

Zeno had had enough of this; his bladder could take no more. On the point of leaving, he was addressed by Callistratus.

'*Vir Perfectissimus*, those under your command have committed public affray. Two men are dead. What –'

Zeno cut him off. 'All the men involved, the killers and the victims, are under military law. It is of no concern to the *polis*.' He stood. 'Now, if you will excuse me.'

Sat on the latrine, relief flooding through him, Zeno thought about the impression he had made on the *Boule* of Olbia. Pompous, abrupt, even rude; a typical, arrogant imperial functionary employed on a trivial errand. Perhaps they would change their minds, if he were able to reveal the real intention behind his journey to the north. Although the odds against its success were long, even to try to bring the tribes around the Suebian Sea ruled by the Angles back into allegiance to the rightful emperor Gallienus, to break their recent alliance with the pretender Postumus and once again to turn their ships against the coasts he tyrannized, was a noble undertaking.

As he dried his hands, Zeno wondered if, should they know it, the members of the *Boule* would also appreciate the irony that one of the killers he had just removed from their justice was the very man who had driven him from his province of Cilicia. Zeno despised all barbarians, but there was a special place in his animosity for Marcus Clodius Ballista.

V

GERMANIA INFERIOR

Marcus Cassianus Latinius Postumus Augustus, Pius Felix, Invictus, Pontifex Maximus, Germanicus Maximus sat perfectly still on the raised throne in the great apse of the Basilica of Colonia Agrippinensis. The five years he had worn the purple had inculcated in him one of the vital skills of an emperor, the ability to sit motionless, alert yet remote, godlike in his imperturbability, while men made speeches.

It was the same the *imperium* over. In a sense, Postumus thought, it was not men under arms, not money and materials, not even ties of *amicitia* that held the *Res Publica* together, but men delivering and listening to formal, public orations. By their mere presence they pledged allegiance to a specific regime, more generally to a way of doing things, to an ideal of *humanitas*, to Rome itself. Yet the Gauls who formed the core of his breakaway regime were particularly addicted to rhetoric. They were as fond of verbosity as the Greeks. His son, Postumus Iunior, was as bad as any. Educated by the finest, and most expensive, rhetors in

Augustodunum, Lugdunum and Massilia, left to his own devices the boy did nothing but scribble and declaim speeches for imaginary law suits. His *Controversiae* were said to show skill. Postumus was no judge of such things. He had sent the boy away south to act as Tribune of the Vocontii. It was a minor administrative post, but Censor, the governor of Narbonensis, would make sure he applied himself. It was necessary he acquire proficiency in governance: one day the youth would be Caesar.

'To proffer advice on an emperor's duties might be a noble enterprise, but it would be a heavy responsibility verging on insolence, whereas to praise an excellent ruler and thereby shine a beacon on the path posterity should follow would be equally effective without appearing presumptuous, as the excellent senator from Comum once said to the best of emperors Trajan.'

Postumus looked at the speaker, a smooth, rounded figure in a toga, standing beyond the low altar where the sacred fire burned. Simplicinius Genialis had done well by the regime. When, at the outset, Gallienus had invaded across the Alps, Simplicinius Genialis, as acting governor of Raetia, had declared for Postumus. The implicit threat of an invasion of Italy in his rear had sent Gallienus back over the mountains. Since then rebellions – the Macriani in the east, Mussius Aemilianus in Egypt, the prolonged defiance of Byzantium – and barbarian incursions – above all, the Goths in the Aegean – had held Gallienus back. But war was coming, if not this year, certainly the next, when Gallienus had completed his preparations. When it came, Simplicinius Genialis would be in the front rank. Gallienus was gathering a huge field army on the plains around Mediolanum. There were only two ways he could march; west into the Alpine provinces and then into Gaul, or north into Raetia. Whichever way he chose, a diversionary force would have to take the other route to prevent a descent into Italy when his *comitatus* had left.

The forces in Raetia were not numerous, but they were of

proven worth. The one legion in the province, III Italica Concors, unusually for the times, was near up to strength, with about four thousand men under the eagles. Their commander, the Spaniard Bonosus, was renowned as a drinker, but also as a fine fighting officer. The legionaries were matched in numbers by auxiliaries, divided into two *alae* of cavalry and eight *cohortes* of infantry, all much below their paper strength. When the Semnones and Iuthungi had crossed the Alps on their way back from plundering Italy, Simplicinius Genialis had had to beg *vexillationes* of troops from Germania Superior and levy the local peasants. Despite his ad hoc army and his urbane and well-upholstered appearance, he had won a great victory.

In recognition of the importance of Simplicinius Genialis to his regime, Postumus had appointed him one of the two consuls of the year. Now, as tradition demanded, Simplicinius Genialis had travelled from his province to give his thanks in this panegyric.

'For what gift of the gods could be greater and more glorious than a *princeps* whose purity and virtue make him their own equal?'

The introductory invocation of the gods was moving into the concept of divine election. Tactful, Postumus thought, given the reality of his accession. Doubtless it would be followed by the Gauls, oppressed by the tyranny of Gallienus, left undefended from the savagery of the Germans, spontaneously acclaiming a reluctant new emperor. The whole *actio gratiarum* would take quite a time. Postumus blamed the long-dead Pliny of Comum. Once, the speech of thanks by a consul was a brief thing. Then Pliny had reinvented the genre as this interminable parade of flattery.

Postumus had never wanted to be emperor. He did not now. From a modest beginning among the Batavians, he had risen through the army to be a general, to be governor of Germania

Inferior. He knew himself a good commander. It had been enough. Ironically, it was his own skill – that and the jealousy and greed of that bastard Silvanus – that had made him emperor.

At Deuso near the Rhine, Postumus, at the head of his mounted bodyguard, and one legion had intercepted a war band of Franks returning from Spain. He had defeated them. Almost all of them were killed or captured, their booty distributed among his soldiers. Silvanus, the governor of Germania Superior, was *Dux* of the whole frontier then and had charge of the Caesar Saloninus, the young son of Gallienus. In effect, Silvanus had been left in charge of the west when Gallienus had hurried back to Italy to fight a marauding horde of Alamanni. Postumus had received a peremptory command from Silvanus to hand all the booty over to him. In point of law Silvanus was right; all *manubiae* should go to the imperial *fiscus*. That had all been very well in the silver age of the Antonine emperors. In this age of iron and rust the troops had to be mollified. Postumus had been left between Scylla and Charybdis. If he had attempted to get the plunder back from the soldiers they would have killed him. If he did not, Silvanus would have accused him of *maiestas* and executed him for his treason. Postumus had consulted those with him in the field, Lollianus the *Praefectus Legionis* of XXX Ulpia Victrix, Victorinus the *Tribunus* of his Equites Singularis Consularis, and Marius, his *Praefectus Castrorum*. The commanders of the legion, horse guards and camp agreed – he had no choice but to bid for the throne.

A donative had been given to the troops. The images of Gallienus and his family had been torn from the standards; idealized portraits of Postumus had replaced them. A purple cloak had been taken from the sanctuary of Hercules Deusoniensis and draped around the shoulders of his devotee, the new Augustus.

Perhaps there had been a way back, even then. A message had come from Gallienus, ambiguous in its brevity: 'What are you doing? Behave! Do you seek battle?' Postumus had written back, playing for time: 'Do not come north across the Alps, do not put me in a position of fighting Roman citizens.' Gallienus's response had smacked of madness. 'Let it be settled by single combat.' By then events had gathered their own momentum. A judicious distribution of some more of Postumus's share of the Frankish loot had won over I Minerva, the other legion in his province, along with its commander, Dialis. The same cause lay behind Laelianus and Servilius Rufinus, the commanders of the two legions in Germania Superior, declaring for Postumus. The defection of the legions in his own province catching Silvanus by surprise, he had retired with Saloninus and a handful of loyal troops behind the walls of Colonia Agrippinensis. Postumus had laid siege to the town.

It might be a negotiated settlement had still had a chance. Postumus had written to Gallienus saying he had been elected by the Gauls and was content to rule over them. But no answer had come back. The siege had dragged on, and the attitude of those camped outside the walls had hardened. When the citizens ran short of food, they bought their own salvation by handing over Silvanus and the young imperial prince. And then – Lollianus and Marius had urged him to it; Postumus regretted it now – and then both Silvanus and Saloninus had been beheaded. With that, all hope of peace had gone. Postumus knew Gallienus would not rest until one of them was dead. He could not blame him. If someone killed his son, he would do the same.

Postumus had not wanted to be emperor, but once you had taken the wolf by the ears you could not let go. He would do everything in his capacity to keep his grip. He would do anything, absolutely anything, to ensure the survival of his family and himself, and, if it were possible, of course he would be of benefit to those he ruled.

'By his presence he will safeguard the soldiers in the camp, civil rights in the forum, law-suits at the tribunal, the *dignitas* of the senate house, and he will preserve for each one his personal possessions.' Simplicinius Genialis had moved his oration into an exegesis of qualities thought by the elite desirable in their ruler.

Postumus shifted his gaze to the high, shadowed beams of the ceiling. A *princeps* cannot scruple at deceit or betrayal. Love the treachery, hate the traitor – unless circumstances dictate you love him, too. The agents of Vocontius Secundus, his *Princeps Peregrinorum*, had brought him the names of those who served Gallienus whom they considered might be suborned. The *frumentarii* had been diligent, but the list was not over-long, nor, with a few exceptions, were its contents over-mighty. Four caught the eye. Placidianus, the *Prefectus Vigilum*, still owned lands in Gaul near his birthplace, Augustodunum. The *vigiles* comprised seven thousand paramilitary firemen in the heart of Rome. It could be useful. Then there was Proculus. He was the Prefect of a unit made up of *vexillationes* of soldiers drawn from the legions of Pannonia and was now stationed with the *comitatus* of Gallienus at Mediolanum. Proculus hailed from Albingauni in the Alpes Maritimae. Many of his family were still there, and his cousin was no less than Maecianus, Prefect of Postumus's Equites Singulares Augusti. For what it was worth, Proculus was an inveterate womaniser, always bragging of his conquests and prowess. The third man of interest was a young officer called Carus, recently appointed a *protector*. No one was closer to Gallienus than the *protectores*, and they were assigned the most important tasks. Carus was from Narbo, and retained property there. Finally, there was Saturninus. His long and distinguished career of civil and equestrian offices had been rewarded with the signal honour of being Gallienus's colleague as consul this year. The ancestral estates of Saturninus spread across Narbonensis into Aquitania.

Postumus's eyes followed the smoke of the sacred fire as it coiled through the dark patterns of the ceiling. One of the stranger aspects of this undeclared but truceless civil war was that – despite its potential efficacy and the disposable wealth it would yield – so far, neither he nor Gallienus had threatened to confiscate the properties in their territories owned by the families of men serving on the other side. Tempting as it was, Postumus would not take the first step. He had more to lose. The old law that every senator must have one third of his property in Italy was not always observed. Yet many of the key supporters of his regime had holdings in lands under Gallienus. His *amici* Ragonius Clarus and Trebellius Pollio were from Macedonia and Italy respectively. Lollianus came from Syria Phonice. Tetricius, his governor of Aquitania, might be a native of that province, but he possessed one of the finest houses in Rome, a beautiful building on the Caelian Hill, between two groves and facing the Temple of Isis. Postumus would remember to tell Vocontius Secundus to have the *frumentarii* keep an especially close watch on Tetricius and the others.

'Under the tyrant, humanity's former blessing of friendship had withered and died, and in its place sprung up flattery and adulation, and, worse even than hatred, the false semblance of love. It was you, Caesar, who brought friendship back from exile. You have friends because you know how to be one.' The consul's words rolled out, sonorous with sincerity, seemingly never-ending.

Enthroned in lonely eminence, Postumus's thoughts ran their own course on loyalty and betrayal. His gaze tracked down to his German bodyguards at the doors of the basilica. *Heart and courage.* Arkil and his Angles would keep to their oath. Yet it had been a timely act of treachery by one of their own that had put them in Postumus's power.

VI

OLBIA

'Back in line!'

Ballista watched the ten sailors shuffle back to rejoin their colleagues. They were hot and tired, dragging their feet. There was not one of them who did not look mutinous.

'Next,' roared the *optio* Diocles.

There were just eight in this *contubernium*. Under their brows they looked pure hatred at Ballista – as well they might after what had happened in the bar down by the docks. Ballista gave no indication that he noticed. He shifted the weight of the mailcoat on his shoulders and studied the impromptu training ground. The old *agora* in the largely abandoned north of the upper town of Olbia was the only area of open, flat ground near the walls. On three sides were ruins: a collapsed row of shops, a fallen portico backed by the remains of two temples and a less easily identified jumble of buildings. On the fourth side stood a granary. It had been built recently, on the site of what might have been a gymnasium. Its construction had cannibalized the surrounding buildings.

Thus passed the glory of the world. Nothing was permanent, not even the gods.

'Javelins ready,' Diocles ordered. Ten wooden posts, each six-foot high, had been hammered into the ground about thirty paces in front of the men.

'Run and throw.' The heavy, blunt training missiles arced away. Five found their mark; the other three fell not far off.

The troops were getting better. Ballista had had Diocles keep them at it all morning. There had been much room for improvement. The crew of the Ister patrol boat *Fides* were under military law. They were expected to be proficient in military drill. They were not. The fault lay with Regulus, their *trierarch*. Ballista had taken his measure straight away at the first parade, when Castricius had read out the imperial *mandata* putting them under Ballista's command. Regulus was not young. He had the broken veins of a drinker and the disgruntled air of a man who considered that life had treated him harshly. Perhaps, many years before, when he had joined up, he had imagined ending his career as *primus pilus* of a legion. Instead, he was the centurion in charge of a small river galley. It was likely his own fault. Clearly he was one of those officers who curried favour with those under him, mistakenly believing laxness would lead to popularity. The *Fides* needed to be got out of the water, her hull scraped and her seams caulked to ready her to take the expedition up the Borysthenes. Ballista had sent Regulus, with one *contubernium* of ten and the helmsman, rowing master and ship's carpenter, to see to it. The rest of the crew, twenty-eight oarsmen, had been assembled at first light in the *agora*.

To be fair, they had marched in step, formed line and doubled their line well enough. But when ordered to form a wedge, a square and a circle, it had ended in a shambles. Now, their weapon handling was proving little better. Obviously unused to the heavy wooden training weapons, they moved clumsily, finding the extra

74

weight a burden. There was no point in even thinking about ordering them to perform the *armatura*; the complicated and demanding dance-like arms drill would be utterly beyond them.

'Draw swords.'

There was a ragged scraping of wood on wood as even this was not performed as one.

'Attack.'

With little enthusiasm, the eight men hacked desultorily at the posts.

'The point, use the point,' Diocles yelled. 'You, cover yourself with your shield. Aim for the face, make the enemy flinch, make him fear you.'

Diocles was the only good thing. A big, tough, young Pannonian, given authority, freed from the negligent hand of Regulus, he might develop into a fine leader of men.

It was past noon. The spring sun was hot. The men were being treated like raw recruits, trained all day. It gave them another reason to resent Ballista. But they needed it. The passage up the Borysthenes was unlikely to pass without fighting. Ballista wondered if it would be advisable to put them on barley rations instead of wheat. Certainly their poor performance merited the punishment. Yet, while he had to instil discipline, it would not do to be too heavy-handed. They already had more than enough reason to hate him and the men with him. They needed discipline, but too draconian a hand might be counterproductive.

'Back in line. Next.'

Ballista went over to Diocles, told him to carry on.

Ballista, accompanied by Castricius, Maximus and Tarchon, walked back towards the inhabited part of Olbia. Once, the broad street had been a grand thoroughfare, flanked by luxurious houses. Now it was a narrow track, hemmed in by overgrown rubble from the long-collapsed dwellings of the Olbian elite. Off to the left, through the voids, where once had been peristyle and ornamental garden, the view swooped down to the river. Lush spring grass waved on slopes and hillocks where terraces had collapsed. Among the wildflowers, lines of cut grey stone indicated the transient hopes of the past. There were shrubs and trees. Here and there – like primitive squatters in the wreck of some higher order – rough, new buildings showed. A line of potters' kilns almost abutted the wall of the living town. Further out was a small foundry. The smoke from their industry was taken by a wind from the north-west out across the broad, islet-studded Hypanis. It further misted the low line of blue that marked the far bank some two or three miles distant.

'We are caught between Scylla and Charon,' Tarchon said in heavily accented, mangled Greek. 'If we are not teaching these sailor-fuckers to fight, they will be as women on our voyaging, and the tribes of the riverbanks will be killing us.'

'Charybdis,' said Castricius.

Tarchon ignored the interruption. 'But if we are teaching them, they will be turning on us in some unfrequented place. We are forging a sword of Diogenes.'

'Damocles,' corrected Castricius.

'Names are unimportant to a man with a sword hanging over his head,' Tarchon concluded with gravity.

'They lack the balls,' said Maximus.

'The Suanian has a point,' said Castricius. 'There are more than forty of them and just the four of us; it might give them encouragement. But Roman *disciplina* will bring them to heel.'

'I do not give a shite. There was a time in Hibernia – I was young then, still known as Muirtagh, Muirtagh of the Long Road – we were outnumbered by five, no ten to one . . .'

Ballista's attention wandered as Maximus launched into a lengthy epic with much hewing and smiting, many severed heads rolling and frequent digressions for scenes of violent sexual congress, their consensual nature not always evident.

They came to the gate. A cart was blocking it. A small herd of six head of cattle and its driver were waiting. On the instant Ballista turned away from the gate, looked all around for danger. Nothing. He turned, scanned every potential hiding place again. Even Maximus was silent. They were all looking. Still nothing.

Ballista studied the gate again. The cart was carrying furs. With the officiousness of his kind, a *telones* was checking every bundle – fox, beaver, wolf; each had a different customs duty.

Stepping off the path, Ballista climbed a low, grassy bank, which probably once had been the front wall of a house. He smiled at his reaction. It was a very old trick: get a cart to shed a wheel, break an axle, get wedged – anything to cause an obstruction which prevented a gate being closed – and from concealment men could storm into a town. Several examples from the 'Defence of Fortified Positions' of Aeneas Tacticus hovered at the edges of his memory. It had to be ten years or so since he had last read that book. He had been on his way to the Euphrates to defend the city of Arete from a Persian attack. He smiled again, ruefully. That had not turned out well. Despite all his efforts and all his theoretical and practical experience, the town had fallen. It was odd that of the very few who escaped death or enslavement, three were standing in this ruined street half a world away – Castricius, Maximus and himself. With that thought came another, far less welcome. Calgacus had survived the sack of that city, had survived so much else. But Hippothous had killed him, had left those who loved the old Caledonian to grieve, had left Maximus and Ballista himself, had left Rebecca and the young boy Simon. Ballista had written to Rebecca. It had been a long letter, difficult to write. But one day he would return to his house in Tauromenium on Sicily where they lived, and that would be much harder. He would give them their freedom, make sure they lived comfortably as freedwoman and freedman, but he doubted that would be much consolation.

The wind had shifted to the north. It was blowing the smoke of the kilns and furnace over the wall of the lower town, over the docks. Ballista ran his gaze over the wall from the water up to the gate. The wall was too low. It had no towers. He knew that, on the inside, houses were built up against it. The houses meant there were few accesses to the wall walk for the defenders, but they would aid an attacker jumping down into the town. The gate itself was too wide, and it had no projections to enfilade those approaching. A single felled tree – and there were several suitable growing close by – would be sufficient to smash it, if the men wielding it were determined, were prepared to take casualties.

This wall was the weak point of Olbia. The rest was good. The town formed an inverted triangle pointing south. The weak northern wall was its top. On its eastern side was the river; on its western a deep ravine. The citadel, at the tip of the triangle, was a fine strongpoint. It boasted massive stone walls built by the Roman army. They were studded with towers, each showing ports for artillery. It was true the walls had not been kept in good repair. Pocked with weeds, in places they were most shoddily patched with barely mortared, uncut stones. Yet nature aided their strength. On the river side, a cliff dropped nearly sheer down to the water. Opposite, the ravine was not so daunting. Indeed, it was planted with vines. There were even three wineries on narrow, cut terraces. But it was still not inconsiderably steep, and the cover the vines might give to an attacker ended in thirty paces of bare rock to the base of the wall. On the north side of the acropolis a deep moat separated it from the rest of the town. Unlike the main body of the city, the citadel was eminently defensible. Ballista wondered how it had fallen to the Goths some thirty years earlier. He would ask the *strategos* Galerius Montanus at the meal.

Finally, an armed guard told the *telones* to let the cart enter. The crack of a whip and it and the cattle were moving. Ballista and the others followed, watching their step to avoid the green, flat cow-pats which fouled the street. Inside, the buildings were close together. More kilns and granaries were wedged up against wineries, cattle shelters, small workshops, stores and houses. Near the gate was a shop which, inexplicably, appeared to sell nothing but tiny, carved-bone pins. The smells of cooking mingled with excrement, spices and packed humanity and animals. The streets were dirty. From what Zeno had said, presumably the *agoranomos* Dadag had much else on his mind.

They crossed the wooden bridge over the moat and walked under the arch of the citadel gate. Armed guards, fully equipped Sarmatian-style – pointed metal helmets, scale armour, bows and long swords – stood around in numbers.

The house of Galerius Montanus was just inside the acropolis gate to the right. Like all Greek houses, it showed a forbidding blank face to the world. They told the porter they were expected, and waited in the street. Maximus began to tell the old joke about the young prefect and the camel. He had changed it into something he had witnessed himself in Mauretania.

'Health and great joy,' Montanus greeted his guests.

'Health and great joy,' they all replied with formality.

They followed Montanus along a dark corridor which dog-legged and suddenly opened into a sunny courtyard ringed by Ionic columns. In the centre was a small pool with a water feature and ornamental fish. Couches were set for a meal in a room which opened off the far side. There was a mosaic underfoot – a straight-forward geometric pattern in black and white – and sweet-smelling plants in strategically placed pots. It was quiet – just the splash of water – and immaculately well kept. All very simple, yet an oasis of urbanity amid the desuetude of the town.

Montanus introduced them to his other guests: Callistratus, son of Callistratus, the first *archon*; Dadag, the *agoranomos*;

another member of the *Boule* called Saitaphernes; and the deputy *strategos*, Bion. This was a small town. Its society was limited, and – despite the outlandish names of some of the citizens – it was clearly one where provincial Hellenic ways were maintained. There were no freedmen or -women waiting to greet them.

When everyone had shaken hands and said, 'Health and great joy,' to everyone else, some several times, Montanus led them to their couches. Nine diners was a traditionally auspicious number.

Ballista was guided to the place of honour to the left of the host. A boy moused up with a pitcher and bowl. With downcast eyes, he washed Ballista's hands then removed the military man's boots; finally, placed a garland of flowers on his head. Ballista unbuckled his sword belt and settled himself down on his left elbow. In his youth, no one would have borne weapons into the dining room. Now it was quite normal, apparently especially at the imperial court among the *protectores* of Gallienus.

Montanus made a libation, calling on Zeus the Saviour, Apollo Prostates, Achilles Pontarches and Hecate the dark goddess to hold their hands over the city in this the two hundred and eight-eenth year of its Roman era.

Ballista noticed Montanus neatly tipped the wine offered to the gods not on to his mosaic floor but into the flowerbed. It saved any mess, and presumably the deities did not care where it landed.

Tables were placed close to hand and the slaves brought out the first course. The inevitable eggs were soft-boiled with a sauce of pine kernels. There was a salad of lettuce and rocket. The main dish of the course was grilled carp.

An older male slave mixed and poured out a tawny wine.

'A Lesbian,' said Montanus.

'The wine or him?' Maximus laughed.

Montanus looked disapproving – although Ballista was uncertain whether this was a result of the implication of oral sex or at the temerity of a freedman speaking out.

'He does not look like a cocksucker' – Castricius addressed Maximus – 'and being a Lesbian is no worse than being a Phoenician, and I am sure you have been down on more than a few women in your time.'

This was not playing well with the Olbians. Montanus looked more than ever like the bust of some stern old Roman from the days of the free Republic – Cato the Censor, or whoever, returned to upbraid modern frivolity and loose ways.

Ballista took a long pull at his drink. He was tempted to dismiss the censoriousness as backwoods prudishness. But had his *familia* been irrevocably coarsened by all the years in the army, or by the last two years among extraordinary barbarians? What did the Olbians think of them? Castricius would be none too unsettling, unless, as now, he was speaking in the language of the barracks, and provided they did not know that in his youth he had been condemned to the mines. But the rest of them were a different story: a Hibernian ex-slave with the end of his nose missing, a tribesman from the High Caucasus who mangled both Greek and Latin, often in the same sentence, and himself, a big northern barbarian with a veneer of civilization. Then – in one of those instantaneous flashes of insight – he knew that all that was only a minor part of the unease they created. How many men had they killed between them? Killing changes a man. It does something to the eyes. It was not always the same thing. Ballista had seen killers with eyes like cats in the sun, others with eyes like flat pebbles under water. He had no idea what his own eyes betrayed.

'The wine is good, both hot and dry on the palate.' Ballista spoke merely to move the talk on to less uncomfortable ground.

Montanus inclined his head at the compliment. 'You may not be familiar with the fish. It is only found in our northern rivers.'

Ballista laughed. 'And in the rivers further north of my youth.'

Montanus looked vaguely put out, more at Ballista's origins than any lack of tact on his own part.

'I read somewhere that carp are neither male nor female.' Castricius now spoke smoothly, in formal Attic Greek, no longer the rough soldier but the man of *paideia*.

'Indeed.' Montanus recovered enough to sketch a smile. 'They become so when in captivity. My own fish tanks are on the other side of the river.'

Conversation for a time became general on the subject of fish: the catching and keeping of, those good to eat, those less so, and the positively harmful varieties.

Bion, the young deputy *strategos*, cleared his throat. 'May I be so bold as to ask our honoured guest to tell us of his victories over the Persians? An opportunity to hear how you made the Persian king flee the field at the battle of Soli is not to be passed up.'

Ballista had no wish to talk about Soli, or the subsequent fight at Sebaste. He remembered little of them. It had been a bad time. He had been near out of his mind, believing his wife and sons dead.

'There was not much to them.' Ballista said no more.

The somewhat strained silence was broken by Callistratus. 'I wonder if we could prevail on you to put aside your becoming modesty and tell us instead how you saved Miletus from the Goths. It is a subject dear to our hearts. Miletus was mother city to Olbia, and many of us have connections there. I myself have the honour of being guest-friend of Macarius, the *stephanephor* of that great *polis*.'

That was a happier time, and Ballista acceded to the request. Apart from the Goths' lack of skill at siege works and the undoubted courage of those serving under him – Macarius notable among them – Ballista put it down to managing to cause panic among the attackers. The unexpected will often bring this about, and two stratagems had worked at Miletus: hidden stakes which the Gothic ships ran on to in the two harbours, and two hastily constructed siege engines unexpectedly raining down inflammable missiles. It was a carefully edited account, which omitted the underhand – if not treacherous – killing of the Tervingi leader Tharuaro.

The uncomfortable memory of his Loki-like trick made Ballista's final words less diplomatic than they might have been. 'Looking at the defences coming here, I was wondering how Olbia fell to the Goths.'

The brusque change of subject, on to what obviously was a delicate topic, seemed to instil a certain embarrassment among the Olbians. First Montanus, then Callistratus sought to remove their fathers from any blame. Both had been away. They had been campaigning across the estuary on Hylaea. Most of the fighting men of Olbia had been with them, the fathers of Dadag and Saitaphernes among them. The grandfather of Bion had been in Athens. A band of Goths had sacked the sanctuary of Hecate. It had been a cunning ruse to draw the militia out of the city. Olbia had been retaken almost at once.

To everyone's relief, the servants brought in the main course.

'Spring lamb, roast in the Parthian style,' Montanus announced. 'My grandfather served in the eastern wars of the divine Septimius Severus.'

As host, Montanus clearly thought it right he should hold centre stage, and guide the conversation back to where it reflected his family in a better light. Ballista was happy enough for it to be so. In this vein, he asked how they had become landowners and councillors in Olbia.

'My grandfather was a centurion with the XI Claudia. He was posted here after the Parthian wars. When those with the eagles were allowed to marry, he took to wife a woman of good local family.'

As Montanus's family history unrolled, Ballista enjoyed the lamb. It was in a pepper and onion sauce with damsons. There were peas in cumin, too, one of his favourites.

The peace of the afternoon was broken by noises from the other side of the courtyard. A man in armour burst from the passageway. He sought out Montanus.

'*Strategos*, the barbarians are in the old town!'

VII

OLBIA

After his Lesbian joke fell flat, Maximus concentrated on eating. The lamb was good, and the unfortunately named wine had been replaced with a local vintage. The drink tasted of elderberry, but Maximus had got used to that. Montanus, the local pretend general, was droning on about his family.

Maximus was not listening, his thoughts wandering with no idea of a destination. It was good they grew hemp here. He had grown to like inhaling cannabis the previous year out on the Steppe. He had missed it during the winter in Byzantium. There had to be a better way of smoking it than putting it between two knives, and you could not be building a tent every time like the nomads did.

Montanus appeared to be listing every individual who had ever been related to him by blood or marriage; and fine people they were in the telling. There was something about this meal that reminded Maximus of another occasion in another backwater, the town of Priene in the province of Asia. They had left that place to go to fight at Miletus. They had left Calgacus behind with Ballista's wife and sons in Priene. Maximus was surprised how much he missed the ugly old Caledonian. While he had been alive, Maximus supposed he had been fond of him – although not as fond as he would have been of a good hunting dog. But now it was different. In many ways, Maximus thought it would have been better if he had been the one killed. Calgacus had left the Jewish woman Rebecca and the small boy Simon. The old bastard had loved her, loved the slave boy like a son. It had seemed returned. There was nothing like that in Maximus's life. He must be getting old: he had begun to wish there was.

A man in armour was jabbering at Montanus. Everyone was scrambling off their couches. Shite, the Goths were in the old town.

Maximus hauled on his boots, then buckled on his sword belt as he bundled up the stairs after Ballista. From the roof you could see for miles. The house of the *strategos* was well chosen. To the west, beyond the ravine, the land rolled off into the distance, green and peaceful. Below, to the east, the river glinted through a veil of smoke. And, to the north, the remains of the old town stretched away. Maximus had good eyes. He saw the grey column of infantry skirting a still-standing tower, pressing on south down what had been the main street, towards the ancient *agora*.

'Hoist the signal for an attack.' Montanus sounded controlled. Maybe he was less of a joke commander than Maximus had judged him.

'Bion, get down and bar the northern gate. Make sure the bowmen are well spread along the wall. Callistratus, would you take your station down in the port. Dadag, assemble the reserve by the citadel gate; keep it open unless I give the order. Saitaphernes, keep a close watch from the acropolis walls. I will remain here. Let us remember our courage. Let us be men.'

'*Strategos*,' Ballista spoke urgently, 'my men are in the *agora*. If Bion shuts the gate, they will be trapped outside.'

'I am sorry, it cannot be helped.'

'There are nearly thirty fighting men out there – too many to sacrifice.'

'We cannot put the town at risk. There is no help for it.'

'Then we will go to them,' said Ballista. 'If we return, and are not hard pressed, have Bion open the gate.'

Montanus looked at Callistratus, who nodded. 'It will be as you wish,' Montanus said, 'but if the Goths are on your heels, you will have to take your chances.'

They turned to go.

'Wait,' said Montanus. 'There is a postern into the acropolis, the second tower on the west face, overlooking the ravine. Saitaphernes will tell the guards to watch. But if the Goths . . .' There was no point in him finishing.

Maximus ran down the stairs after Ballista. By the time he reached the street, he was out of breath: too much soft living. They pounded after Bion, under the great arch, over the bridge, between the crammed-together buildings. There were many in the streets, but to give the Olbians their due, there was little panic. Militia men ran to their posts – pulling on their arms as they went – women herded children and animals inside. Living surrounded by enemies taught a hard lesson.

At the gate Bion shouted orders, sending men up and along the wall walk. Maximus doubled over, panting; Ballista and Castricius likewise. Tarchon seemed in better condition. The Suanian was just a little younger. Gods, but Maximus was getting too old for this shite.

Ballista used Maximus to haul himself upright. 'Bion, would you get ropes?'

'Ropes?'

Ballista drew a couple of deep breaths, got the words out. 'If you have had to shut the gates, you might haul some of my men to safety. My *familia* can hold the Goths off for a time.'

'Where would –'

'The docks – use ship's cables, anything.'

The young officer smiled. 'I will see to it. You had better go. I am going to shut the gate.'

Outside, a boy was driving a herd of goats towards the town.

'Leave them,' Bion called. 'Run!'

The boy hesitated. He was a slave, and his owner would beat him if he lost the goats.

'Now!'

The boy sprinted past Maximus, sandals pattering on the road.

The gate slammed shut. The sound of the bar being dropped.

'Time to go,' said Ballista. They set off through the unconcerned goats.

As ill luck would have it, at that moment a family – a man and woman, two children – emerged from the ruins. They saw the shut gate and began to wail.

Maximus paused.

'Come on.' Ballista called over his shoulder. He was right. Maximus knew there was nothing they could do. Holding his scabbard out to avoid it tangling in his legs, he jogged off after the other three.

Running in the hot sun, a mailshirt dragging at your shoulders, a good meal and plenty of wine inside you, was never good. Castricius especially was suffering. Maximus had his breathing more under control. He overtook the little Roman.

More Olbians, caught out by the suddenness of the barbarian descent, appeared in the narrow path. Swerving around them, Maximus hoped Bion would exercise mercy, or that they would make it to the postern.

A largish body of men were fleeing down towards them. The crew of the *Fides*. They ran pell-mell, in no form of order.

'Halt!' Years of command had given authority to Ballista's voice.

They faltered, and stopped. Eighteen of them. They had thrown away the heavy wooden training weaponry. Maximus noted they had their real blades at their belts. No one had a shield or helmet. There was no sign of the *optio* Diocles or the others.

'Form columns of fours,' ordered Ballista. Most began to obey, until a large, shaven-headed soldier at the front gestured them to stop. Maximus knew him – Heliodorus, an Egyptian, particular friend of the two killed in the bar.

'Disobeying an order is mutiny. You know the penalty for mutiny,' said Ballista.

'Fuck you.' Heliodorus turned to the others and spoke in the Latin of the ranks. 'Are we going to take this from this prick?'

'The penalty is death,' said Ballista.

'This is our chance, boys; no one will know.' Heliodorus drew his sword.

Maximus found his *gladius* in his hand.

'Come on, *pueri*,' said Heliodorus. 'We can finish this here. There are only four of the cunts.' Five or six also drew their weapons. The others stood, hesitant.

The path was narrowed by rubble. There was only space for two men to wield their swords with any effect. Maximus moved up on Ballista's left shoulder. Castricius and Tarchon fell back a pace or two. They might be only four, but, unlike the mutineers, they wore mail. And, unlike the mutineers, they were all proven close to the steel.

In a fighting crouch, Maximus watched his opponent. Heliodorus faced Ballista. As ever, Maximus's chest felt tight and hollow at the same time. Out of the corner of his eye, Maximus saw Heliodorus lunge. He heard the ring of steel as Ballista blocked.

The man in front of Maximus came on, half turned, *spatha* held high.

Again the clash of steel to his right. The soldier in front was working himself up to strike.

'Do not kill him,' Ballista shouted over the noise.

Maximus's opponent cut to the head. Maximus took the blow on his *gladius*, rolled it over his head and thrust. At the last moment he remembered Ballista's instruction and pushed his strike wide. The man swung his sword back. Maximus had to scramble backwards. The edge hissed in front of his face.

Maximus regained his balance. This was all wrong. Only a fool fought and tried not to kill. It was unnatural, far from easy, just asking to get yourself struck down.

More clashes of steel on steel to the right – one, two, three, in quick succession.

The mutineer came in again, swung fast from left and right. A flurry of blows. Maximus parried them with precision. There was an opening each time. Maximus fought down his instinct to finish it. The battle calm was on him, the strange altered state where things moved slowly, where he had all the time in the world, where he could see the fight two or three blows ahead. He was laughing. Gods, but he knew himself to be a dangerous bastard.

The mutineer stepped back, breathing hard. Maximus risked a glance around. Some of the others were clambering over the debris on either side. He put them out of his mind. Castricius and Tarchon would deal with them. Most still stood, rooted to the spot.

The soldier feinted a low cut to the left ankle, withdrew and thrust at Maximus's chest. That was enough. Two-handed, Maximus forced the *spatha* to his left, stepped inside, brought his right elbow up and rammed it into the mutineer's face. A satisfying crunch as the nose broke. Maximus cracked the flat of his blade down on the wrist of his opponent's sword hand. The *spatha* clattered to the ground. He swung the pommel up and smashed it into the man's temple. He collapsed like a sacrificial animal. Stepping back, to avoid tripping over him, Maximus flicked the point of his sword up and out.

Heliodorus was also down, flat on his back, semi-conscious. Ballista stood over him, tip of the blade at his throat.

'Four of you pick them up. The rest form columns of fours.' Ballista's voice was calm, as if arranging some trivial point of detail.

As the troops shuffled to obey, Diocles arrived at the head of the remaining ten.

'All well?' Diocles asked.

'All well,' Ballista replied.

The men fell in.

'Ready to march?' There was little of a question in Ballista's words.

'We will do what is ordered, and at every command we will be ready.' The ritual response came back almost with an air of relief.

'The Goths are not here yet,' Ballista said. 'All should be well. Let us go.'

Back in safety, up on the roof of the house of the *strategos*, Ballista thought it could all have gone a great deal worse. The Goths had not come up with them during the retreat. Bion had opened the gate and let them into the town. Heliodorus and the other mutineer who had fought were now in chains in a cellar, and Diocles had most of the rest of the crew of the *Fides* at ease waiting in the street below. One *contubernium* had been sent to the docks to fetch the centurion Regulus and those who had been working on the ship, as well as to carry up all the shields and javelins.

From this point of vantage, it was obvious to what they owed their escape. While the Goths now had a force watching the town gate from well out of bowshot, and, judging by a concentration of standards and men, their leaders had established themselves on and around a large *kurgan* beyond the *agora*, most of the raiders were spread through the remains of the old town, looting whatever granaries, smithies and the like were to be found. Given the circumstances, Gothic numbers were difficult to estimate.

However, Ballista judged it a substantial war band – maybe about three thousand warriors.

Montanus was explaining the dispositions of the defenders. There were just under a thousand men under arms in the city: five hundred along the north wall, two hundred down at the docks, one hundred watching the acropolis, and the final two hundred acting as a reserve. The numbers were not exact. All had bow, sword and shield. About one in five had armour; all of those and quite a few more also possessed a helmet. While by no means first-rate troops – indeed, many were youths or old men – the exigencies of frontier life did mean that almost all would at least have witnessed combat.

Lost in thought, Ballista did not respond.

'Now we know why the Castle of Achilles upriver was deserted.' Montanus smiled ruefully. 'Also it explains why Gunteric, Chief of the Tervingi, did not appear to demand the usual tribute.'

Still Ballista said nothing.

'Perhaps the Goths had something to do with the slaves who are infecting Hylaea. In our fathers' time the city fell because the militia had been lured there.'

'Artillery?' Ballista asked.

'I am afraid not,' said Montanus. 'There is nothing behind the ports in the acropolis. When Gallus withdrew the troops, it went with them.'

'Horses?'

'Some two hundred of the militia can serve as cavalry.'

'I did not see any war galleys at the docks.'

Montanus shrugged. 'There are two. They have gone to watch the slaves on Hylaea. We can send a boat to recall them. But they are small; no more than fifty oarsmen on each.'

'Nevertheless, it should be done.' Ballista looked away across the broad river. 'Can your other settlements raise a relief force?'

'No.'

'There are wells in the town?'

'Yes, and in the citadel.'

'That is good. What of provisions? Zeno told me you were short of grain.'

'If the rich open their own reserves to the *polis* – and they will – we should have enough for five or six weeks; more with careful rationing.'

Ballista looked north to where he had been training his men. 'There was a granary by the abandoned *agora*. How much grain will the Goths have taken?'

'It is hard to say. There are other storehouses in the old town. Several of the members of the *Boule* prefer to keep their stores out there – less risk of fire.'

Less accountable in times of need, Ballista thought.

Callistratus politely, but firmly, spoke up. 'Marcus Clodius Ballista, you saved Miletus and Didyma from the Goths, Tervingi among them. What will they do?'

Ballista knuckled his eyes tiredly. 'I served under Gallus, before he was emperor, when he defended Novae. The Goths used rams, towers, ramps, even some artillery. They tried mining. It was believed Roman deserters taught them. They can do siege works, but they prefer other ways. They say they have no quarrel with stone walls. Unless they bring up boats and blockade the river, they cannot starve you out. Are there any within the town who might open the gates to them?'

'Never,' said Callistratus. 'Everyone knows the horror of the last sack.'

'Then it depends how badly they want what is in the town.'

At Ballista's words, Maximus looked sharply at him.

'Most likely tomorrow or the following day, they will assault the north wall.'

The Olbians stirred uneasily. 'What should we do?' Callistratus asked.

Ballista did not answer at once. He gazed in different directions, thinking hard; reckoning distances and lines of sight, estimating times and probabilities, weighing so many variables.

'*Dominus*.'

The voice broke Ballista's concentration. He turned, irritated.

'*Dominus*.' It was Diocles. 'Centurion Regulus and the *contubernium* with him at the quayside have taken the *Fides*. They have gone.'

For a moment Ballista had no idea what Diocles was talking about. When he realized, he was neither surprised or upset. In some ways, it might be for the best.

'He has deserted.' Diocles was outraged.

'He might have his reasons,' Ballista said. '*Optio* Diocles, by the authority invested in me by the *mandata* of the Augustus Gallienus, I appoint you centurion.'

Diocles snapped a salute. 'We will do what is ordered, and at every command we will be ready.'

'What should we do?' Callistratus failed to keep the edge of desperation out of his voice. 'We are outnumbered five or six to one.'

Ballista smiled. 'Nearer three to one. But you are right, it is bad. Your north wall will not hold. The kilns outside screen an enemy approach. The wall is too low, has no towers, no way of enfilading attackers. Can you withdraw into the citadel?'

'No!' The Olbians spoke as one. They talked over each other. It was unthinkable. The citizens would lose everything. There was not enough room in the acropolis. It would cause chaos.

'Then, when the Goths attack, you must withdraw from the gate. Barricade the streets behind, station warriors there and on the ground floor of the buildings – use the reserve and half the men from the docks – get the women and children on the roofs to drop missiles. You must pull the Goths into a prepared killing ground.'

The Olbians looked dubious. 'Will that be enough?' Montanus asked.

'Probably not,' said Ballista. 'It needs something else – something to sow panic among the attackers. I had thought to use the *Fides* – cast off tonight, conceal her on one of the islands in the Hypanis, when the Goths were committed tomorrow, land and attack their flank. But Centurion Regulus has removed that option. Although I think there is something else . . .'

VIII

OLBIA

'Everyone wants redemption.' The chains prevented Heliodorus from moving.

'It has to be earned,' said Ballista. It was dark in the cellar, hard to see.

'Releasing me will not make all the crew of the *Fides* love you.'

'Maybe not,' Ballista smiled. 'They all hated me – only you did something about it.'

'Back in Alexandria, my father – may the earth lie light on him – often said my anger would be the death of me.'

'I have much to do before tonight.' Ballista was brusque. 'Will you take an oath?'

'We will do what is ordered, and at every command we will be ready.' Heliodorus actually laughed. 'I swear by holy Serapis, and all my ancestral gods, that I will obey your orders.'

'Not seek to harm me or my *familia*?'

'Not seek to harm you or your *familia*.'

Ballista looked at the dark, motionless shape of the other chained mutineer. 'What about him?'

'Your Hibernian hit him too hard. He may not live.'

'If he recovers, and will take an oath, he, too, will be released.'

'And if the oath is too much?'

'The same as would have happened to you – his *commilitones* will beat him to death.' Ballista's tone contained no emotion. 'You will be one of them.'

'Is an oath extracted under compulsion binding?'

'If I were in your position, I would not raise such philosophical points.'

Again Heliodorus laughed. 'Do not be concerned. I will earn *my* redemption.'

The gentle touch of a fingertip just behind his ear: the accustomed signal. As he woke, silently and instantaneously, Ballista thought to see Calgacus. It was Maximus.

'Anything?' Ballista asked softly.

'No. It will be dawn soon.'

The abandoned winery was crowded, packed with recumbent figures, the air very stale. Ballista groaned slightly as he shifted. Sleeping in chainmail on a stone floor was not easy. Worse as you got older. He was pleased he had slept at all. But then, he had been very tired. There had been much to do.

Few hours of daylight had been left by the time the Olbians had acceded to Ballista's plan and put themselves in his hands. A semicircle of streets and alleys behind the north gate had been barricaded. Overturned carts, barrels, furniture and lumber had been roped together and pegged down to make them immovable – all except on the main road, where two large wagons, hastily palisaded, made a barrier which could quickly be opened. Rough holes had been knocked in the dividing walls between some of the buildings where the defenders needed to move about. The rear doors and the windows of others had been nailed shut or boarded over. Loop holes had been hacked in their ceilings, to turn the ground floors of these into killing traps. In those buildings which had flat roofs or thatch, old amphorae and stones had been carried up to the top. The tiles on the majority, as ever in urban combat, would make excellent missiles. The great general Pyrrhus of Epirus had been killed by one dropped by an old woman. The blacksmiths in the town had hastily produced some crude caltrops. They were to be thrown out into the streets when the defenders had withdrawn to the barricades. Although more effective against cavalry, in the confusion of the coming fight they should give the attacking infantry another concern. Knowing there were sharp metal spikes underfoot always preyed on the mind. Ballista had given strict and repeated instructions that they were for the side streets only; none were to be dropped on the main thoroughfare. This had to be kept clear; much depended on it.

The plan to draw the Goths into a prepared ground behind the gate could only hope to succeed if the adjacent walls were held. What could be done in the time had been. There were more than enough arrows. Stones, bricks, broken statues – anything that could hurt when thrown or dropped had been stockpiled along the wall walk. Pitchforks to dislodge ladders and axes to cut grappling lines had been distributed. After much thought, Ballista had ordered combustible material and metal cauldrons to heat oil – sand, when the supply of oil proved inadequate – placed at intervals. The locals confirmed his observation that the prevailing winds here were northerly or westerly. It was not in the defenders' favour. A fire would tear through the heavily built-up town. With luck, there would be no accidents, and hopefully the Goths would not resort to such tactics, fearing to burn what they had come to plunder. If the worst came to the worst, the outer town would burn but the dressed stone of the curtain wall of the citadel should act as a firebreak.

It had been full dark for at least two hours when the makeshift defensive works were near enough complete that Ballista considered he could leave them. Montanus had selected thirty well-armed militia men to act as cavalry the next day. Outside the *Bouleuterion*, Ballista had spoken separately to them. He had stressed the vital importance of their role, told them to see to both their horses and courage, pray to their gods, then get what rest they could. Tomorrow they must listen for the signal, obey commands and charge as one.

Ballista had walked back down to the house of the *strategos* by the citadel gate. Fifty more citizens under arms – these all volunteers – had waited for him in the street there. Diocles had them marshalled with the twenty-eight crewmen of the *Fides*. By the light of torches, Ballista had explained the plan, such as it was. Castricius and Diocles had inspected them, to make certain all had followed the instructions to carry only sword and shield – the next morning's work would be at close quarters, and bows would be just an impediment to their clandestine manoeuvres. They also checked that all had muffled their armour and boots, removed spurs, belt attachments and anything else that might make a noise, blackened their faces and hands, wrapped rags around metal helmets and donned dark cloaks. The latter had been no issue for the locals, who tended to wear them anyway. Most of the Romans had borrowed them. While that was carried out, Ballista, Maximus and Tarchon had had something to eat, relieved themselves, then had a final few words with Montanus and the other Olbian commanders.

Rejoining the men, Ballista had thought he should address them. He had felt too tired. But some sort of speech was always expected. Standing on a mounting block by the door, looking out over the quiet ranks in the guttering torchlight, he had kept it short. They were to observe complete silence and listen for orders. They were few, but numbers would be of no account.

The Goths would not be expecting them; surprise was everything. 'Let us be men,' he had ended. Like a religious response, they had returned the Homeric tag.

Ballista had embraced Castricius. The little officer's angular face was taut with concern. Ballista had run through the signals yet again: when Castricius wanted him to move he was to hoist a green flag alongside the red war standard on the house of the *strategos* and have three blasts on the horn sounded; if no signal had come from the town but Ballista himself judged the time was right, he likewise would have his *bucinator* blow three times; should those outside be forced to try to retreat back to the city, it would be four notes.

They had embraced again. Ballista was loath to leave him behind, but he needed someone he could trust both to take direct command of the barricades and the cavalry and to oversee the whole defence. The disposition of the Olbian leaders and troops had been altered. Callistratus remained at the docks, although now with only one hundred men. Bion held the wall to the west of the gate, and Saitaphernes to the east with five hundred men between them. The reserve under Dadag manned the barricades, with some two hundred and twenty men. The cavalry waited behind them. The acropolis, the very last line of defence, was garrisoned by one hundred under Montanus. They were all stretched thin, but if those at the gate fell back to join the men at the barricades and the women and children on the roofs played their part, the town might just hold.

Ballista had given the watchword: *redemption*. Most likely it was the Egyptian Heliodorus he had heard laugh, before being silenced by Diocles.

The torches had been doused, and in silence Ballista and his party had moved up to the postern in the west wall of the acropolis. As planned, the music and lights of a religious procession had appeared, moving along the north wall. The wicket gate –

carefully oiled in advance – had been swung open. Two Olbian scouts had slipped out, quickly but carefully descended the open slope beyond the tower, and been lost to view among the vines which covered the sides of the ravine.

Ballista had waited in the doorway. Time's arrow was held in its flight. It was about two hundred and fifty, at most three hundred paces to the third winery. The scouts had to go cautiously, but surely they had had time to get there and back.

It was a bright night. The moon was waning but not long past full. Thin, high clouds had scudded across its face. They promised little in the way of concealment.

Repeatedly, Ballista had fought down the urge to go outside and peer north around the tower. It would have done no good. The scouts would return opposite the postern, and anything ominous would be seen first by the watchers on the roof of the tower. Besides which, it would have undermined the pretence of calm assurance which he was trying against the odds to convey to those at his back.

With the suddenness of a twin epiphany, like the Dioscuri or some such divine pair, the scouts emerged from the vines. They had beckoned.

Ballista had touched Maximus on the arm and set off. Out of the shadow of the tower, the slope had seemed horribly light and exposed. It was steeper than it looked. Ballista had had to plant his feet sideways, encumbered by the shield in his right hand and his scabbard held away from his legs in his left.

The cover of the vines had been welcome. Wordless, one of the scouts had turned and led him across the first terrace and down on to the second. There he had turned right and Ballista had followed him north for about fifty paces. They had crouched down and waited for the others to catch up.

The noise had been terrible. Slithering, tripping footfalls, the creak of leather; despite everything, the clink of metal. One man had fallen, stifled a curse. Like eighty blind men blundering through a potter's yard. It had seemed inconceivable the Goths had not heard.

When all had been in position, Ballista had waited, listening. It was not too late to go back, abandon the dangerous enterprise. Ballista had closed his eyes, the better to hear. Not in motion, the men made next to no noise. There was the soft susurration of the breeze through the foliage. As if a door were opening and closing, snatches of the hymns being sung by the procession on the north wall had come to Ballista. Occasionally, more distant sounds – shouts, traces of music – had drifted down from the abandoned town, from the camp of the Goths. An owl had called, and far away another answered.

Ballista had got to his feet; everyone had done likewise. Ballista had wondered how many of the volunteers had come to regret their temerity. Too late now: the die was cast. The scout led them north through the speckled, shifting shadows of the ordered rows of vines. Every few paces there were fruit trees, their blossom strikingly pale in the blue-grey landscape. Now and then they had passed a henhouse, its occupants presumably gathered into the town. Ballista had always admired the resourcefulness of peasants, the way they made one plot of land serve more than one purpose. If some storm or blight took the grapes, the land would still produce apples, eggs or whatever.

They had passed two wineries before they had reached the one Ballista had selected. It was a big stone building. Inside were three presses and two reservoirs: all empty, with a sense of desolation. The air had smelt of must. Like a pack of animals, the men had huddled down for the night.

Ballista rubbed the sleep from his eyes. The atmosphere inside the winery was worse this morning: piss, shit and stale humanity. Forbidden to venture outside, in the night men had relieved themselves in the reservoirs. Painfully, Ballista struggled to his feet, and, following Maximus, clambered over prone bodies to the door. The air coming in smelt of early morning, clean and fresh. The ravine was still in darkness, but overhead the sky was lightening. All was quiet.

'You think you should have told the Olbians about you and the Tervingi?' Maximus whispered, his breath hot in Ballista's ear.

'No,' said Ballista.

Of course, it had crossed his mind. But what would it have served? Two years before at Miletus, Ballista had killed Tharuaro, the son of Gunteric, killed him with an underhand trick. Ballista had gone out to fight Tharuaro in a duel, but in Loki-like cunning had had the Goth shot down. The bloodfeud had been made worse, if such were possible, not long after, when he had also killed Respa, another son of the Tervingi leader. That had been in fair combat, but it made no difference. There had been no point in telling all this to the Olbians. The knowledge that the Goths held a bloodfeud with the man the citizens had entrusted with their defence would not have encouraged them. Maybe some among the magistrates and councillors of Olbia might have wondered if they could use Ballista as a bargaining counter, offering to hand him over to their besiegers in return for their own salvation, no matter how temporary.

A flight of birds blazed gold, like a handful of thrown coins in the risen sun. Somewhere, probably in the besieged city, a cockerel hailed the new day. The first incoherent sounds floated down from the Gothic encampment. There was a tang of woodsmoke in the air. The Tervingi would not attack on empty stomachs. It promised to be a long morning, a long and anxious wait.

Ballista put the bloodfeud out of his thoughts. He had given instructions that no one was to use his name. This day he would fight under the name of Vandrad. He smiled at the thought. It was the name he and his half-brother Eadwulf had used when they were doing the things wild youths will perpetrate and had not wished to be known as sons of Isangrim – not that he had given any explanation last night.

The baulks of timber that had regulated the flow from the presses to the reservoirs in the winery had been torn out and arranged against the wall as a makeshift ramp. With difficulty, and a shove from Maximus, Ballista scrambled up into the rafters. There was no ceiling. With care, and ignoring a certain amount of threatening creaking, it was possible even for a heavy man in armour to move around on the beams and rafters. Quite a number of tiles had already been missing, and others had been removed to allow something of an all-round watch. The west revealed nothing but the opposite slope of the ravine, the shadow sinking down it as the sun climbed. To the north and south were only the ordered lines of vines and occasional fruit tree, most still in shade. Things were less bucolic towards the east. Just above, at the lip of the incline, bright in the sun, a line of grassy knolls traced the long-abandoned defensive works of the old city. Off to the south-east, less than a hundred paces away, was the corner of the outer wall of the extant town; a squat and shabby thing it looked. The battlements of the towers and curtain wall of the citadel could be seen rising beyond, perhaps a hundred paces further. From this angle their dilapidation was not evident, and they made a more reassuring sight. Best of all was the sight of the roof of the house of the *strategos* and the Olbian battle standard, its scarlet bravely tinged with gold in the early light. As Ballista watched, flashes of silver marked the presence of armed men at its foot. Castricius would be up there now. He would remain until the Goths attacked; afterwards, Montanus would command there. The Olbian seemed sound enough. It was always imperative to have the hope of a viable way back to at least temporary safety.

The morning breeze brought the homely smell of campfires and, tantalizingly, the aroma of cooking. It was wafting down from the Gothic lines. Ballista's stomach was empty, his mouth dry. The Tervingi would take their time. Unlike the Greeks and Romans, all northerners appreciated the need for a good breakfast: fried steaks, bacon, hot bread, washed down with milk or watered beer. Ballista felt a twinge of the contempt, so deeply ingrained during his youth, for the men of the south. No wonder they were so small. If they ate at all first thing, it was no more than a few crumbs, fit for a sparrow. Some, through poverty or a misplaced asceticism, went as far as vegetarianism. No wonder they now went in fear of the tall, broad men from Germania.

Maximus swung up next to Ballista. As if he had read his thoughts, Maximus handed him some of yesterday's flatbread and a heel of cheese. With a flask of watered wine, they perched and ate in the companionable silence of men long accustomed to taking food together in strange places.

The sun penetrated down into the ravine. A shaft of light fell on Maximus's face. Its clarity gave an unusual delicacy to his features. Ballista watched his friend: the small, ever-shifting eyes, the bird-like motions, the scar at the tip of his nose. A hard man, brutal even, thoroughly addicted to sensual pleasures. But loyal to a fault, and, at times, a man of startling sensitivity, capable of love.

Ballista stopped eating. An almost physical fear rose in him. *Allfather, Death-blinder, let nothing happen to Maximus, let him live.* If he was killed, Ballista knew it would be his fault; just as it had been with Calgacus.

Two years before, Ballista had been in the Caucasus. There had been a woman. Not just any woman. Pythonissa was of the royal house of Suania, a priestess of the dark goddess Hecate. There had been an affair. Ballista had known from the start it would end badly. Perhaps the whining southerners were right: perhaps as a barbarian he lacked self-control, lacked the rational part of a man. Ballista had known from the start he would leave her.

He closed his eyes and the scene was before him. A lowering sky. Riding out through the muddy little village in the rain. Pythonissa standing in the gloom, hair unbound. Stretching her hands down to the earth, her blue-grey eyes on him, she had spoken the words. *Hecate, triple-formed, who walks the night, hear my curse. Vengeful furies, hear my curse. Kill his wife. Kill his sons. Kill all his family, all those he loves. Let him live – in loneliness and fear. Let him wander the face of the earth, among strange peoples, always in exile, homeless and hated.*

Ballista had loved Calgacus, and Calgacus had died out on the Steppe, died in agony, a sword through his guts. Ballista loved Maximus. *Allfather, Deep-hood, spare my friend. Allfather –*

'Men coming.'

The low-pitched words cut short Ballista's prayer, brought him back. Below him, the close-packed warriors – Romans and Olbians intermingled – were stirring. Tarchon was beckoning from the northern side of the rafters. Cramped and ungainly, his scabbard getting in the way, Ballista scrambled over to his side. A splinter pierced his right palm. The Suanian pointed through the gap in the roof.

At first Ballista saw nothing menacing, only the leaves of vines and trees shimmering as they shifted in the gentle wind, the patches of grey earth in their interstices. Swallows darted through the air. Below him Diocles hushed the rising murmur as the men readied weapons, whispered prayers.

A movement caught Ballista's eye. There, about a hundred paces away. Not caused by the wind. Not a bird. A shape glimpsed through the foliage, moving towards the winery. Another following. Maybe a third.

'Three of fuckers,' hissed Tarchon. 'Most untimely.'

Maximus laughed quietly.

No need to panic. Ballista had chosen the winery carefully. He had hoped its evident abandonment would deter looters. Yet it was well within effective bowshot of the town walls. The guards up there had been told to keep a sharp watch. Provided they spotted the Goths, and if the men in the building kept quiet, all should be well.

The three Tervingi were getting closer. Ballista sucked at the splinter in his hand. It hurt more than the half-healed cut on his left bicep. At the edge of his vision a cobweb fluttered. The three Goths were only thirty paces away, maybe nearer.

Something flashed very fast through the air. Another followed, then more. The Goths dived towards an apple tree. The bright fletching of arrows – red, yellow, white – quivered in the shade of the vineyard. There was something farcical, like a bad, provincial mime troupe, in the way the three Tervingi huddled together behind one thin trunk. Over their heads the spreading branches, already thick with white blossom, gave them more than enough shelter, and must have unsighted the archers on the wall. Arrows continued to drop around the tree intermittently. Surely it would be enough to deter further advance. There was unlikely to be much to loot in the shell of a deserted wine-making building.

From his vantage point Ballista could see the Goths clearly. Although their words did not carry, their beards were wagging. Obviously, they were conducting a fierce debate. At length, two of them jumped up and broke from cover. They diverged, running hard, bent over. Arrows fell thicker, some near them. Swerving among the vines, the men raced back the way they had come.

The third remained where he was. Ballista half heard the obscenity he shouted after his retreating compatriots. There was more humour than contempt in its tone. This was still little more than an exciting, dangerous game to him.

The two fugitives disappeared, unscathed. No more arrows came from the walls. Ballista cursed silently. From up there it might be the bowmen had seen only two of the Goths. What was this last one going to do? If he came closer, he must discover them. If that happened, he could not be allowed to return. Ballista worried with his teeth at the sliver of wood in his palm. He was a fool for not bringing some bows.

Surreptitiously, keeping the bole of the tree between him and the wall, the Goth started to move. The green of his cloak almost matched the leaves of the vines. He wormed through the plants until he reached the next terrace. He slid over it, and out of sight.

Hurriedly, Ballista scurried around the beams from one viewing place to another, like an ungainly primate in a cage. It was no good. Aiming for concealment from the watchers in the town, the Goth had got himself in a position where he was also invisible to those in the winery. He must be crawling on hands and knees close up against the side of the low terrace. Ballista was certain he would be heading towards their hiding place. Doubtless, the bastard wanted some trophy to flaunt; no matter how worthless, it would be something with which to taunt his friends for their nervousness.

Motioning those below out of the way, Ballista hung from a beam, then dropped as quietly as he could to the floor. Maximus and Tarchon landed beside him.

'Take command, Centurion,' Ballista whispered to Diocles.

The young Danubian officer nodded.

Not bothering with helmet or shield, Ballista went out of the door. Maximus and Tarchon accompanied him. The doorway faced east; the far side from where the Goth's approach was leading. Indicating Tarchon to skirt around the building to the south with a wave of the hand, Ballista demonstrated how he and Maximus were going in the other direction to cut off the Tervingi warrior from his camp.

Stopping, Ballista peered around the corner of the winery. Nothing moved. Without words, he told Maximus to go northwest, to a point just behind where he thought the Goth might have reached. He himself would go further north in case their quarry should avoid the Hibernian and double back. Maximus grinned. Ballista found he was smiling back. As one, they drew their swords, nodded and moved out of the lee of the building.

Ballista started to run. The fresh spring air, aromatic with blossom and tinged with cooking, was good after the stench of inside. The sun on him, his fatigue and the years fell away. He felt invigorated. When he remembered, he counted fifty or so paces and then pushed through the next gap in the vines. He crossed to the next terrace and leapt down. Landing, blade in hand, he looked south. There was no sign of the Goth, or the others.

In a fighting stance, taking short steps, feet close together for balance, Ballista went to the nearest cover. It was another fruit tree; not budding yet, probably a plum. Crouching down, he smiled. Now it was him seeking concealment behind something too small. He had left his dark cloak in the winery, but his mail was blackened and should not betray him in the patchy sunlight. He planted his sword between him and the tree. There was blood on the hilt from his palm.

Ballista waited, peering around one side of the trunk then the other, listening hard. The wind sighed through the foliage; birds sang. If the other two had already despatched the Goth and made Ballista look foolish by coming to get him, so much the better.

The sun was warm on his shoulders. It was going to be a hot day for so early in the season. A sudden sound of something big crashing through the vines came from not far away. It came again, from his right, the east, from somewhere below him. Ballista got to his feet, hefted his weapon. There, on the terrace below, a man in a brown tunic was running in his direction, long blond hair and green cloak billowing. He was only some forty paces away.

Ballista hacked through two lines of staked vines and jumped down the four or so foot to the next level. Regaining his footing, he brought his blade up. The Goth did not break stride. He lunged straight for Ballista's chest. A two-handed parry turned the point to Ballista's left. The Goth ran into Ballista with his shoulder. The momentum knocked the breath from Ballista, sent him back reeling. He collided with some close-tied vines behind him, half staggered forward again. The Goth swung at the left side of his unhelmeted head. Ballista blocked. The impact jarred up his arms. The young Tervingi warrior was good. In an instant, he had reversed his sword and cut down from Ballista's right. Another block. Again the juddering shock. Ballista gasped air back into his chest. The youth aimed a kick at his balls. Still part entangled in the greenery, Ballista twisted. The boot hit him high on the outside of his left thigh. A sickening surge of pain. He stumbled, fighting to remain upright. His leg was dead. It could give way at any moment.

The young Goth pressed his advantage. Feinting high to the left, he altered the blow and chopped down towards Ballista's ankle. Awkwardly, Ballista brought his own blade down just in time and desperately hobbled away from the tangling clutches of the vines. If ever he needed Maximus, it was now. Him or the demented Suanian Tarchon.

The Tervingi warrior stepped back, watchful but confident. He knew there was nothing his opponent could do to prevent him making his escape. He pushed the long fair hair out of his face and was about to turn to go when the recognition showed in his eyes.

'You – Oath-breaker, the murderer – Dernhelm, son of Isangrim. I saw you at Miletus.' He laughed. 'If Gunteric had known you were here, he would have come himself. Now I will take him your head.'

'His sons tried.' Ballista answered him in his own tongue. He had to buy some time. He flexed his left leg gently, willing the feeling back.

'Respa was a fool. But Tharuaro was a great warrior. You killed him with a low trick, the cowardly act of a *nithing*.'

'I am alive, they are dead.'

'You live as a slave of the Romans. Now you will die as a *skalks* at my hand.' The young warrior spat, changed his grip.

'Tharuaro was the fool.' Ballista went to shift his stance. His leg nearly buckled. Where in Hel was Maximus? 'No one can outlive what the *Norns* have spun. The gods had taken Tharuaro's wits.'

'Enough talk.' The Tervingi dropped into the Ox guard – half turned, left leg forward, sword held high, palm down, jutting out like the horn of an ox – good for outmanoeuvring an incapacitated opponent.

Ballista dropped into a defensive posture: side on, weight on his rear right leg, sword two-handed out in front.

The Goth stepped right then left. Ballista countered; slow, lame and favouring his good leg but never taking his eyes from the bright tip of the three foot of steel which sought to end his life. Almost all men make a tiny involuntary movement before they launch an attack. Where the fuck were Maximus and that halfwit Tarchon?

A slight tremor in the steel, and then the Tervingi cut down at Ballista's leading leg. A bad mistake fighting without a shield. Automatically, Ballista started to withdraw the leg and shape a riposte to the head. Allfather, his bad leg. Clumsily, Ballista checked, dragged his blade down and across. The ring of steel on steel. The pain was excruciating as much of his weight came on his left leg.

The Goth withdrew, reversed his blade and swung it underhand. Flat-footed, panting with distress, Ballista was driven nearly to his knees as he caught the attack a hand's breadth from his face. Instinctively, he flicked his own *spatha* at the young man's legs. Almost gracefully, the Goth leapt back out of reach.

Again they circled, the Goth driving Ballista this way and that. The Goth was moving well; Ballista badly. The Goth had age on his side. All Ballista had was his mailshirt and experience.

Ballista made a pass at the young raider's head. Not trusting his leg, he knew it would prove ineffectual, but it was important not to surrender all initiative. What was that sound?

'You suck cock like Tharuaro? You Goths are said to love it.'

The young warrior laughed. 'Insults will not help you, Oath-breaker.'

'Sucking cock and running like girls – you miss the northlands my grandfather chased you from?'

The sound again – running feet. The Goth heard it, too. His eyes flicked away. It was enough. Ballista lunged and jabbed to the face. The Goth flinched, instinctively covering himself with his sword. One-handed, Ballista slashed his sword down, almost vertical. It just caught the outside of the Goth's left knee. The young man howled, doubled up. Dropping his weapon, his hands clutched the wound. Ballista's leg gave. He staggered a few steps, righted himself and hobbled back.

The Goth looked up.

Maximus and Tarchon were nearly up with them.

The young Tervingi looked at his fallen sword, then at Ballista's blade, and abandoned the idea. 'I will see you in Hel.'

Ballista smashed the edge of his blade down into the face of the youth.

Maximus and Tarchon came to a halt, breathless.

'About fucking time.'

IX

OLBIA

'If I am remembering rightly,' said Maximus, 'you northerners will be going one of two ways when you are dead.'

Ballista shifted slightly where he was sitting astride a roof beam of the winery. He had been there a long time, and his leg ached. He made a vague noise of assent.

'You are either finding a good home with your gods, an eternity of fighting all day and drinking all night – and I think there may be women there to take care of your other needs – or you will be rotting forever in a dark, cold hall presided over by some hideous old hag.'

'Not eternity,' said Ballista. 'Nothing lasts for ever.' His eyes did not leave the red standard flying over the house of the *strategos* in Olbia.

'Maybe, but you will be in either place for a very long time.'

'Until the stars fall and the gods die.'

'Now, you get to the good place by dying in battle.'

Ballista rubbed his leg. 'I suppose if you died just before Ragnarok, you might only be in Valhalla or Hel quite a short time.'

Maximus, ignoring the line of speculation, continued with his own theme. 'So, your young Goth this morning was wrong. He died in battle, so it's the good place for him, and – no matter where you end up – he will not be seeing you in Hel.'

Ballista looked at the Hibernian in mock-despair. 'Have you spent all day thinking about that?'

'It passes the time. As your Greek wise man said: "The unconsidered life is shite."'

'I think you will find he put it as "not worth living".'

'Same thing.'

It had been hours since the death of the Goth. They had dragged his corpse back up to near the apple tree. Placing him face down, they had pulled the green cloak up to cover his ruined head and, taking three of the spent arrows, skewered them into his back. If his friends came back, with luck they would assume he had been shot while attempting to get away, and the bowmen up on the wall would deter them from coming too close.

While they had been about it, and on their return to the winery, Ballista had worried the archers in the town might mistake them for more Goths. He had seen too many men killed by their own side in the confusion of war. It had been an anxious time, but no shafts came. The young Olbian Bion held that sector of the defences. Thankfully, he must have good eyes. Either that or the commotion had drawn Castricius down to take personal charge.

They had waited. The sun ran across the sky in her relentless flight from the wolf Skoll that at the end of days will devour her. For at least four hours Ballista had perched under the tiles, always watching. Nothing of note had happened. Occasionally, he clambered down to relieve himself in one of the reservoirs. There were eighty-two men in that cramped confinement. The air was thick, fetid with their body odour and waste. Most had tied scarves around their faces. Ballista had done the same. It masked little of the stench, but it might serve another purpose. The young Goth had recognized him. It would be bad if others did in what lay ahead. Ballista's shield was propped against the door-frame. Its metal ornament of a northern bird of prey was still muffled from the night before. He would leave it that way. The motif was repeated as a crest on his helmet. Likewise, he would leave the rags tied around that. He had ordered that no one should use his names, neither Ballista nor Dernhelm. Today he would fight under the name Vandrad. If the Allfather was kind, the Goths might not become aware there was bloodfeud between themselves and the warrior who opposed them – at least not until some time after he and his *familia* had left for the north.

'Oath-breaker' the young Goth had called him. While Ballista had spoken no words when he went out to fight Tharuaro in single combat, the thing had been implicit. The young Goth was right. The killing of Tharuaro had been an act of no honour, the act of a *nithing*. Yet it had helped save the city of Miletus. When Ballista was young he had liked to listen to the *scops* who had come to the halls of his father. In their sagas the path of honour was always difficult, fraught with danger; frequently, it proved fatal. But most often it was clear. Since he had been taken into the *imperium*, Ballista had found honour and expediency often opposed.

Oath-breaker. The young Goth had been more right than he knew. There were many oaths Ballista had broken. When he had been hauled into the *imperium* he had taken the military oath to the emperor Maximinus Thrax. No sooner had he sworn the *sacramentum* than he had broken it. Just sixteen winters old and, on a warm spring day outside the Italian city of Aquileia, he had killed the man he had sworn to protect. The other conspirators – the ones who had forced Ballista to join them – had beheaded the emperor, left his mutilated body to be devoured by birds and beasts. Denied Hades, the *daemon* of the emperor was condemned forever to walk in this world. In the long years since,

Ballista had come to know well the nocturnal apparition; the dread as he woke, the smell of the waxed canvas cloak, the tall, grey-eyed figure grim in the dark of the night. Always the same words: *I will see you again at Aquileia. Oath-breaker.*

Julia often had tried to rationalize the thing away. Maximinus only appeared when Ballista was exhausted, under great stress. It was a figment of his thoughts running uncontrolled as he slept. Neither *daemons* nor gods existed. If they did, they had no care for humanity. She believed these arguments. Ballista did not. Unlike his wife, he had not been raised as an Epicurean. Besides which, bad dreams did not leave a lingering smell of waxed canvas.

Yet of all the oaths he had broken, that to Maximinus Thrax did not weigh most heavily. Four years before, he had been a prisoner of the Sassanid king. That ruler had sent him on an embassy back to the Romans. Before he left, Shapur had exacted an oath that he would return to captivity. The Greek words had not left him: *If I break my oath, spill my brains on the ground as this wine spills, my brains and the brains of my sons, too.* He had not returned to the throne of the Sassanid. The words ran together with those of Pythonissa's curse: *Kill his sons. Kill all his family, all those he loves.* He tried to put his fear for his family from his mind. Julia and his boys were safe in Sicily. Far from the frontiers, away from the campaigns of civil war, there was nowhere safer in the *imperium*. They could not be more secure than in the villa in Tauromenium. The tenants, freedmen and slaves of Julia's family were loyal. The few freedmen of Ballista who lived there were loyal. Isangrim and Dernhelm were safe; so was Julia. Nothing would happen to them.

'Movement!' said Maximus.

The first thing Ballista saw were more defenders appearing on the town wall. They ran fast along the battlements, ducking into shelter at their appointed stations. In the city, trumpets rang out, summoning the laggards. Ballista looked up to his left. On the crest of the ravine, dark against the sky, a body of Goths was assembling about a hundred and fifty paces from the wall, just out of effective bowshot. The Goths were packing together into a shieldwall. Ballista could only see those on the extreme right flank. They were six deep. Beyond that, it was impossible to judge numbers. There would be many more, though ; a solid mass of men facing the town, deepest opposite the gate. The phalanx would stretch all the way down to the river.

Time slowed. A strange hush fell. Nothing moved, except a black banner fluttering above the Goths. Now and then Ballista thought he could hear it snap in the wind. A bird sang nearby in the vineyard. Ballista looked back at the house of the *strategos*. The red standard still flew there alone.

A deep, low rumble came from above. Ballista knew it – the throaty growling of many northern warriors, the *hooming* sound of the massed Gothic *hansa* voicing its approval. Although invisible to him, Ballista could picture its cause. Individual champions, the gold bright on their arms, striding forward from the wall of shields.

A different sound, rhythmic, repetitive – two quick beats, one slow; two quick beats, one slow. Hundreds upon hundreds of warriors stamping, beating their weapons on the shields. Up there, out of sight, the heroes were beginning their war dance. The Woden-inspired among them were drawing down into themselves the awful power of the fierce beasts beloved of the one-eyed god; wolf and hound, bear and big cat.

Ballista wondered how many champions were dancing. Although few compared with the whole force, it was always important to know their numbers. Little heartened a northern war band more than seeing Woden the Terrible One move within many of those who would fight in the front rank. Experienced in war as Ballista was, trying to construct the preparations for battle from just noises and a few glimpses was disconcerting. Something from the philosophy he had been forced to study in his youth at the imperial court flickered in his thoughts.

Wild, high, individual howls came to Ballista's ears. In his mind's eye he saw the champions. Whirling, leaping, their long hair flying. Some were drooling, ropes of saliva in their beards. Baying at the sky, eyes dead to all compassion and humanity.

The *hooming* gave way to a rough, resonant roar. It grew and grew until it drowned out all else and then burst like thunder. The *barritus* faded, then rose again. Filled with wordless menace, the war chant reverberated back from the walls of the ravine. The strength of the *barritus* foretold the battle. Every northman knew that in his heart. As it echoed, distorted around the slopes, Ballista could not judge its true potency. It was like hearing the roar of the distant crowd rolling down one of the underground passageways of the arena, unable to guess its significance.

The Goths silhouetted at the top of the incline shifted into a shield-burg, the rear ranks roofing the formation with their linden boards, locking it tight, metal boss to boss. Hunched over like malignant troglodytes, they began to shuffle forward.

'Soon, the much killing start,' said Tarchon. The prospect did not seem to displease him.

'Tell me,' Maximus said, 'what do you think of dwarves?'

Ballista smiled. 'Ugly and misshapen, full of greed and lust, best avoided, so old Calgacus told me.'

'Sure, he would have known,' said Maximus.

'But no man is their equal at a forge. The goddess Freyja gave herself to the four Brisings in return for a necklace they had made.'

'Actually,' said Maximus, 'I meant midgets. I saw some exhibited in Rome once. Funny little fellows, they looked quite sad, although quite possibly full of lust and all the rest.'

The brassy ring of the trumpets of the defenders cut through further discussion of homunculi, mythical or real.

A dense cloud of arrows took flight from the walls. The visible shield-burg of Goths halted, seemed to contract. The *barritus* faltered. Ballista heard the awful *whisp-whisp* sound of the falling shafts. A few thunked into the close-lapped shields. The vast majority fell out of sight. Ballista could not see any Gothic casualties. The shield-burg edged forward. The *barritus* swelled again. Another volley came from the town. Again the shield-burg stopped, shrunk in on itself, then resumed its slow progress. This time, it left behind two of its number; one limping away towards the camp, the other motionless. Shooting from the walls became general. Hidden from Ballista's view, Gothic archers replied.

The advance of the Tervingi *hansa* was painfully slow. Again and again those that could be seen stopped; on occasion for quite a considerable time. After about a quarter of an hour they were directly up-slope from the winery, only about a third of the way to the walls. There was no evident reason for their sluggishness. The arrow storm on them was not intense; they had not taken many losses. Ballista conjectured that the broken terrain of the abandoned town was forcing the Goths to stop frequently to dress their line. Although, tantalizingly, it could be the result of some other development somewhere else on the battlefield. Certainly, now the *barritus* had faded to a murmur, he could hear confused shouting in the distance.

'Like being in the slave seats at the spectacles,' said Maximus. 'Lots of noise, but you can see fuck all.'

'Like being a prisoner confined from childhood in a dark cave, shackled so your only impressions of the outside world are shadows on the wall,' said Ballista.

'What the fuck are you talking about now?' Maximus demanded.

'It is an image in Plato's *Republic*.'

'I am not claiming to be a philosopher, but your love of wisdom might seem just a tiny bit intemperate.'

'*Intemperate?* You have learned some fine words.'

'Yes, I would not have you thinking I had wasted my time in the *imperium* on drink and women.'

There was a distant cheering. The Goths started to move faster. As they did so, their formation necessarily loosened. More arrows flickered out from the defenders. More Tervingi began to fall. Their advance now was marked by increasing numbers of their wounded and dead. Yet the *barritus* returned, as far as Ballista could tell, confident, if not exultant. The Goths were running; no longer in an ordered shield-burg but more of a pack. They were fast closing the town wall.

'Flag! Green flag!' Tarchon said.

There it was up above the citadel, alongside the red war stand-ard. No one had noticed it being raised. The triple blast of the *bucinator* must have been lost in the uproar.

'Now proper man-killing,' said Tarchon. He sounded relieved. To be fair, Ballista thought, in part the Suanian might just be looking forward to getting out of the malodorous winery. You could not blame him for that.

Cramped and stiff, Ballista clattered down to the floor. The young Danubian Diocles was waiting, his broad peasant face imperturbable.

'Draw the men up on the terrace, a column facing south, as we said, the Olbians at the head.' The majority of the townsmen who had volunteered were of high status. Most of them wore armour, mail or scale, cut to suit a rider. With the exception of Diocles, the crew of the *Fides* were protected only by helmet and shield.

'We will do what is ordered, and at every command we will be ready.'

Ballista slung his shield over his back. He fumbled with the laces of his helmet. Gods, but he was always clumsy at these moments, his fingers awkward with fear. He loosened first the dagger on his right hip, then the sword on his left; finally, he touched the healing stone tied to his scabbard. The smooth amber of the latter felt cool in the sun. The long-established ritual calmed Ballista a little.

'Maximus and Tarchon with me. We will reconnoitre.'

Followed by the other two, Ballista clambered up to the next terrace. It ended in a steep bank, about ten paces high. Pulling at the coarse grass, he scrambled to the top and looked over.

Gothic standards still flew over the tall mound of the *kurgan* away to his left. There were a few individuals left up there, more at its base. The latter were probably just non-combatants and the wounded. Across the plateau, through the ruins of the ancient upper town, a scatter of the injured limped back towards the *kurgan*. Many of them were supported by one or more evidently unhurt companions. Helping the wounded to safety was an excuse as old as Homer. Ballista felt his heart lift. Not every Gothic warrior was Woden-inspired. Better still, knowing there was no relief column that could come to save Olbia, the Tervingi had committed all their number to the storm. There was no Gothic reserve.

Off to the right, the assault was being pressed hard. The Goths were a thick, black smear at the foot of the wall, clotted more thickly where there were ladders or ropes. At one point to the east, near where the wall vanished down towards the river, some of them had got on to the wall. Nearer at hand, they had taken the gate. There, they flowed in like a turgid river being sucked down into a sink-hole. Apart from the one toehold on the wall, it was all as good as could have been hoped.

Ballista watched a moment longer. The Olbians were resisting with a ferocity born of desperation. A ladder was levered away from the battlements. Those on it fell, limbs flailing like insects.

'Time to go.'

The three slipped and slid down. Diocles had the men ready.

Several were fumbling with armour and clothing to take a last-moment piss. Ballista felt he could do with one himself, but there was no time. He knew the urge would pass. It was just nerves.

Ballista led them along the terrace for forty or so paces. He held up his hand, halted them, and then turned up towards the fighting.

They came up between two long, derelict buildings. The walls still stood to a few feet, and gave them an element of cover. Ballista paused, waiting for those behind to close up. Eighty-two men were very few to try to change the course of a battle, to break a force of perhaps three thousand. It all hinged on surprise and momentum. Above all, it depended on panic, and that was in the lap of the gods.

No time for a speech. If some historian from the *imperium* or *scop* from the far north recorded this battle, they would supply suitably stirring words: 'freedom', 'home and family', 'courage'. Ballista grinned. A Gothic bard would use other words: 'ferocity', 'bestial savagery', 'low cunning' and 'deceit'. Ballista unslung his shield. Adjusted his helmet, after the shield strap had caught on the rags masking its crest. Pulling the scarf tight up over his nose, he checked he was flanked by Maximus and Tarchon, that Diocles and the *bucinator* were at his back. Time to go. Do not think, just act. He drew his sword, flourished it above his head in the most martial way he could manage, and set off.

They emerged from the ruins, and there – a long javelin cast to their right – was the extreme right of the Gothic *hansa*. Lumbering figures in the haze of dust and smoke, hard up against the wall. A dark horde, flashes where helmet, shield-boss or blade struck the light. The Tervingi had their backs to the new threat.

Ballista ran at them, taking care where he placed his boots. The ground was humped, uneven, yellow-grey stones poking up through the grass. Not the moment to stumble or fall. His left leg still ached. A shout from somewhere near. More yells. The Goth ahead still unaware. Fifteen paces, ten.

Overhand from the right, Ballista brought his sword down. The Goth was unarmoured. The sharp, heavy steel cleaved his shoulder. Ballista pushed him away with his shield. The next was turning, mouth open. Ballista thrust the sword into his stomach, up into his chest, twisted and shoved him aside. The noise was deafening: screams, shouts; Tarchon was keening some savage, incomprehensible song.

Taken by surprise, assailed in front and rear, the courage of the Tervingi right wing ran away like water through a broken dam. In front, the unyielding wall and the rain of missiles; behind, grim-faced men wielding terrible steel. The Goths fled to the east, scrambling and fighting each other to get away from their imminent doom.

'After them! Drive them like sheep!' Ballista's shouts were muffled by the scarf. It did not matter. A Goth stood, rooted; arms wide in supplication. Ballista cut him down.

The fleeing Goths crashed into those to their left. Pushing, shoving, some using their swords; they sowed chaos among those still unaware of the new attack. Panic infected the next group of Tervingi. They, too, turned from the unseen, unreckoned danger, and ran.

Ballista chased them along the wall, as Achilles had chased Hector; swift-footed, remorseless, exulting. Along the battlements, the Olbians chanted: 'Let us be men. Let us be men.'

Ahead, a saffron war standard rose above the confusion, just short of the town gate. At its foot was a knot of Gothic warriors. They were not moving. The broken men sheered away from them, like so many waves from a cliff.

'Hold!' Ballista had to tear the scarf from his mouth to have a chance of being heard. 'Hold! With me!'

Ballista checked who was still with him. Maximus was on his

right shoulder; some Olbians beyond. Diocles and Romans were to his left. Jostling behind came Olbians and Romans together, Heliodorus the mutineer among them. Tarchon and the *bucinator* had vanished.

As if swept by the hand of a deity, an empty space had opened between Ballista and the Goths below the standard. Off to the left, the routed fled away through the wasteland that had been the antique city. Braids and cloaks swinging, many were throwing down their armaments, the better to run. But just beyond the saffron standard a dense throng of warriors continued slowly to shuffle and jam into Olbia through the shattered gate. Above and beyond that there were still ladders against the wall, and men still fought to gain the battlements. A few hundred men had been trampled or scattered like chaff, but the battle hung in the balance. If the Goths below the saffron standard held, the day was lost.

Ballista eyed these new opponents. Fifty or so tall men, clad in mail, gold rings on their arms. This was the hearth-troop of a war chief; a *comitatus* sworn to their *reiks*. Ballista could see the *reiks* in the third rank: a big man, gilded helmet and white fur cloak around his broad shoulders. If he fell, his *comitatus* had taken an oath not to leave the field alive.

Time was on the side of warriors beneath the saffron standard.

'Are you ready for war?' Ballista would have to take the fight to them.

'Ready!' The response at his back was thin. He had no idea how many were left. No time to make a tally.

'Are you ready for war?'

Fifteen paces to cross.

'Ready!'

Fifteen paces to a solid wall of hard linden boards, fifteen paces to sharp spear, axe and sword.

'Are you ready for war?'

The third ritual Roman response came and died away.

Do not think, just act. Allfather, Father of Battle, protect me.

'Now!' Ballista set off.

Bright patterned leather, glittering steel, hard eyes between helmet brow and shield rim; Ballista rushed at them.

A squall of arrows from the right tore down into the *comitatus*. Ballista saw at least two warriors fall. A flash of hope, dead in an instant. The rear ranks raised their shields; the *comitatus* did not flinch.

Just a few paces. Always go in hard. Ballista, shoulder in the belly of his shield, crashed into the man facing him. The collision cracked Ballista to a standstill. The Goth staggered back a pace or two, until brought up short by a warrior in the next rank. The man behind Ballista thumped into his back, driving him forward. Again he was shield to shield with the enemy.

The Goth tried to stab down over the locked shields. Ballista twisted and drove behind his shield. The blade skidded off and behind his mailed shoulder. Underarm, he tried to stab under the shields at the legs. The steel met no resistance.

A shield crunched into Ballista's back. At the same moment the Goth was pushed from behind. The pressure mounted as more men joined the maul. Trapped, squashed, unable to use their weapons, they were eye to eye. The Goth's beard and hot breath were in Ballista's face.

A sword jabbed over the Goth towards Ballista's head. He tucked his chin down. The edge of the blade clanged off the side of his helmet. His ears were ringing, a scrap of helmet covering was hanging over his eyes.

The pressure increased. The clatter and grunting as more and more strong men hurled in their weight; pushing, heaving. Half-twisted, Ballista bent his knees, dug in his right heel. He shoved with all his strength. No movement; no going forward, no going back. Trapped, near blinded, helpless; the pressure getting worse.

Someone sobbing in his ear. Hard to breathe, very hard to breathe. *Allfather, do not let me die here.* Pain in his chest. Too crushed to breathe. His vision greying at the edges. Bursting stars of light.

Suddenly, Ballista could breathe. With his sword hand, he tore away the material from in front of his eyes. The Goth was being hauled away by his companions. Ballista was tottering back, a hand on his shoulder guiding him, his legs all unsteady. Someone supporting him, as he gasped for air.

Seven or eight paces of trampled ground. Broken shields, a discarded sword, incongruously beautiful. Three ugly, trampled bodies. The Goths hefting their shields, steadying their line. The saffron standard snapping in the wind.

As if complicit in some unspoken rule, both sides stood, getting their breath back. It was quiet here; the noise of battle distant, oddly irrelevant.

Seven or eight paces. Ballista knew he could not cross that terrible space. There was no breaking these Goths. The *Norns* had led him to this place. He thrust the tip of his sword down into the ground, leant on the guard.

'Fuckers,' shouted Maximus. 'Arse-fucking cunts.'

Screened by his sworn companions, the big *reiks* threw back his white furs, lifted his hands to the skies. 'War-loving Teiws, thundering Fairguneis!' He called the gods of his people, offered his enemies to them. Deep in their chests, the Goths began the *barritus*.

'Vandrad!' Maximus was shouting. Diocles and others joined in. 'Vandrad! Vandrad!'

Ballista felt his spirit lift. Heart and courage. *Wyrd* will often spare an undoomed man, if his courage is good.

Ballista found himself yelling with the others. 'Vandrad!' He pulled his sword from the ground, raised his shield. In time with the swelling chant, he beat the flat of his blade on his shield-boss. 'Van-drad! Van-drad!'

The *barritus* opposite faltered. A tremor ran through the *comitatus*. Goths were looking over their shoulders, shouting incomprehensible things in alarm.

'Warhedge!' The hearth-troop was quick to obey. They shuffled to ring their *reiks* with shields. Already it was too late. A solid mass of warriors was surging back out from the town gate. Like a river in spate, it hit the half-formed circle of shields. Men were swept away from the rear of the *comitatus*. The flood rushed at those at the foot of the saffron standard. Their solid ranks checked it for a moment. Above the turmoil the proud banner swayed, eddied, looked to fall. The *reiks* held it aloft in one hand. With the other he pointed across at Ballista. The Tervingi chief was shouting, his words lost in the inhuman din of the rout.

Nothing human could withstand the torrent. The *comitatus* began to break up. Warriors disappeared beneath the stampede, their courage to no avail against the trampling feet. The saffron standard was borne away, bobbing like flotsam, glimpses of snowy-white fur beneath it.

'Shieldwall. Brace yourselves.' Ballista locked shields with Maximus and Diocles, thrust his blade out.

The tide of humanity veered away, fanned out over the plateau. The seven paces of trodden earth were transformed from a place of terror to a gods-given thing of safety, an invisible rampart. Ballista drew a ragged breath. His left leg hurt. There was blood on the hilt of his sword.

Beyond the rout, dreamlike through the dust and smoke, Ballista saw the last ladder topple away from the wall.

The tide of running men ebbed. The gate was blocked. The Goths' numbers were telling against them in that narrow space. Tripping and falling, they were clambering over their own. Maddened by fear and the proximity of safety, they turned their blades on each other.

As Ballista watched, a small group ruthlessly hacked their way through the human logjam. Again the horde spilled out. Now among them were men on horses, long blades slashing down. At their head was a slight figure in a Roman helmet. Like some vengeful *daemon*, indefatigable and awful, Castricius cut down the defenceless Goths.

Again Ballista leant on the crosspiece of his sword. It had worked. Pelted with missiles from the roofs, disordered and wedged in the confined street, the Goths had been unable to stand the charge of armed men on horseback. The battle was won. Ballista knew he should be exultant, but all he felt was weary.

PART TWO

Anabasis,

Spring–Summer AD264

THE HYPANIS RIVER

When the little boats paddled out on to the Hypanis river, Amantius the eunuch was surprised at his own reluctance to leave Olbia. He had felt no particular affection for the decrepit, backwater *polis* while staying there, and it had nearly been the scene of his death. If the barbarians had stormed the town, he had no doubt the ruins of Olbia would have proved his tomb. Apparently, they had come within a hand's breadth.

Amantius had seen nothing of the battle. When the Goths had arrived he had rushed to the lodgings of Zeno. The imperial ambassador was not to be found. His two slaves had gone as well. Scattered possessions testified to the hasty evacuation. Amantius's courage had failed. With his boy, he had fled through the narrow streets of the acropolis to the small temple of Hygeia. There he had kept vigil – through the day, the long night and the following interminable day – praying incessantly to the daughter of Asclepius. The close confines of the temple had been crowded. Women and children had moved and muttered in the incense-laden gloom; at times, they wailed. As far as they could, the women had kept apart from Amantius. They had scolded the children away from the eunuch; away from the exotic thing of ill omen.

The goddess was indistinct. Only her extremities were visible. Apart from face, hands and feet, she was festooned with dedications; swathes of material, and innumerable tresses of women's hair. For his safety, Amantius had offered her his precious things: his scarlet cloak of Babylonian silk, his golden rings, the ones set with sapphires and garnets.

The goddess may have been half hidden in the dark, but the Most High Mother had heard his prayers. Against all probability, the Goths had been routed. The pious saw the hand of a deity in it.

Many Goths had been killed. The gatehouse was littered with them. Several dozen, unable to escape that killing ground, had been captured. Somehow, Montanus, the *strategos*, had managed to cool the bloodlust of his fellow townsmen. After the initial euphoria of revenge, the corpses had not been further desecrated, and the remaining captives had not been butchered. They had been deployed in the negotiations which the first *archon*, Callistratus, had held with the Goths. For the return of both the living and the dead, and a substantial treasure as bloodprice for the latter, the barbarians had agreed to leave. They had not just departed but sworn great oaths to their unpronounceable gods not to return. Unless the annual tribute, now set at a substantially higher rate, was not forthcoming, the Tervingi would never again bear arms against the walls of Olbia. If they did, let the sky fall on their heads.

Even if they had set the payment at a rate that the Olbians could not meet – and Amantius strongly suspected that was the case– the point was that the Goths would not return for at least a year. Until next spring, Olbia was the safest place to be found in the wastes of *barbaricum* north of the Euxine. It seemed foolish to leave.

To someone thoughtful, such as Amantius, there was more to

it than just that: the implications ran deeper. Neither Ballista nor any member of the imperial embassy had taken any part in the negotiations. They had remained out of sight, and Callistratus said he had avoided all mention of them. Amantius did not know if the barbarians were aware of their presence. But, as they were recounted, it was evident that the oaths taken by the Goths only covered the city of Olbia. They did not preclude anything against those outside the walls, let alone anyone unwise enough to venture deep into the country along the rivers. The Tervingi could do what they liked to such improvident voyagers, with no fear that their angry gods would bring the sky down upon their heads.

Amantius looked back down the little boat, past the man on the steering oar and the up-curved stern post, past the rear two boats in the small flotilla. He saw nothing but an ephemeral safety to love in Olbia. The great expanse of scrub grass, wind-bent trees and dislocated stones where the Goths had camped. The low, stubby wall where many of them had died. The tangle of mean streets, some burnt out, down by the port where the defenders' fires for heating oil had got out of hand. The yet more congested acropolis, where Amantius had prayed and where he had been reduced to living like a slave in a tiny attic room.

Disparagingly, Amantius thought that Olbia might be less crowded in future. When the siege had been lifted and boats had returned to the docks, there had been an undignified rush of citizens booking passage south: to Byzantium, Chalcedon, Miletus, to any place of greater safety. At least the exodus had been of use. During his stay in Olbia, Amantius had not been quietly approached by a *frumentarius*. It was hardly surprising given the remoteness of the town and the confusion after the fighting. In the absence of an official channel for clandestine communication, there had been a wide choice of merchant vessels all leaving for the Hellespont. For discretion, he had entrusted the arrangement to Ion. A slave boy would have drawn less attention on the dockside than the distinctive figure of an imperial eunuch. Ion was a sensible boy. He had selected a reliable-sounding skipper, who, for a high fee, had promised to deliver the letter to a certain soldier stationed in Byzantium. From there the *frumentarius* could send it on to the Praetorian Prefect by the *cursus publicus*.

The missing centurion Regulus entered Amantius's mind. It was an unwelcome, even vexatious arrival. Amantius did not condemn him for his desertion. If opportunity had offered, and he had thought he could weather the consequences, he would have done the same. Presumably, Regulus would have taken the *Fides* back to her station on the lower Ister. He would have had to account for her unexpected reappearance, and for the absence of the imperial embassy and most of her crew. Amantius took pride in the veracity of the news he conveyed. It was likely that whatever exculpating tale the centurion had concocted might find its way to Censorinus. The safety of the sacred Augustus Gallienus – the very safety of the *imperium* – might often rest on the accuracy of the information available to the Praetorian Prefect. If the centurion's inventions cast Amantius himself in a bad light, the personal consequences might be serious. It might spell the end of his hopes to return to the Palatine and the imperial court. If the charges were grave, it would be much worse. There was never a public trial for those who failed Censorinus, but punishment was inexorable and draconian. The gods willing, Amantius's report would make clear the true turn of events. In any case, Amantius was sure, things would not go well for centurion Regulus.

The desertion of Regulus and the flight of the refugees had combined to pose serious problems for the embassy. After the departure of the Goths, three days after the battle, Zeno had strode into the *Bouleuterion* still clad in full armour. The *Vir Perfectissimus* recounted how he had taken up arms and made his stand on the wall. It was the duty of any man who wanted a name for virtue to do likewise for his friends. Zeno's rank and a level of tact precluded too close investigation of the claim or his whereabouts since. He had proceeded to rant against the cowardice of Regulus. He would see the centurion executed, and in the rigorous, old-fashioned way. The governor of Moesia Inferior, Claudius Natalianus, was a friend. He would see the thing was carried out, and in public, before the eyes of gods and men. The terrible execution would serve as an example to all. Yet, by all the gods, it could not remedy the fatal blow the coward had dealt to the embassy. The *Fides* was to have conveyed the mission to the north, and she was gone. All the ships in port were sailing for the south. There was nothing for it. The embassy would have to take passage back to Byzantium, and seek further instructions.

It had been a fine oration, possibly not quite as extempore as it implied, but powerful nevertheless. It was what one would have expected from a man of culture who had been *a Studiis* to the emperor. In his heart, Amantius could not have agreed more with its conclusion. Yet it had been undone in a moment. The first *archon* Callistratus had taken the floor. There were boats on his estates at the settlements on the other bank of the Hypanis. They were rustic things, but serviceable, good for shallow rivers. In fact, they were more suited for the portages of the Borysthenes than the *Fides* itself. As some small recompense for the services to the *polis* of Marcus Clodius Ballista and Gaius Aurelius Castricius, and of course Aulus Voconius Zeno himself, it would give Callistratus nothing but pleasure to present them to the embassy. He would not hear of accepting payment. Only what you gave to your friends was yours for ever. The councillors of Olbia had shaken back their cloaks and applauded. At once, unanimously, they had voted such extra crew as were required be seconded from the civic militia. The *strategos* Montanus was to select men suitable for the labours and dangers of the voyage.

Caught, like an insect in amber, there had been nothing Zeno could do but accept. The equestrian had made a reasonable stab at dignified gratitude. But Amantius suspected he was not alone in seeing behind the mask. Amantius knew himself lacking in courage. But he was a eunuch, and his kind were not as robust as others. Zeno was entire, and he was a coward. Spite and coward-ice often went hand in hand. Back in the rebellion instigated by Macrianus the Lame, Zeno had run from his province of Cilicia rather than face Ballista. It did not augur well for the two men travelling hundreds of miles in proximity, and it did not augur well for the success of a delicate mission.

Olbia slid out of sight behind a low, wooded island. The Olbian guide in the first boat had led the small flotilla between dank islands, oozing mudflats and treacherous shoals. They would take the far channel of the Hypanis down to Cape Hippolaus. The leading boat was turning south into it now. Splashes, laugh-ter, obscenities and shouted orders indicated they were making a poor fist of it.

Amantius shifted his soft haunches on the hard bench. He gripped the side nervously. The four boats had been a great disap-pointment. Narrow, low in the water, open to the elements, they were fragile-looking things. They reminded him of the *camarae* of his childhood in Abasgia, and that was not a good thing.

Each vessel had a local steersman and was paddled by ten men. The two bringing up the rear were crewed by Olbians, but the leading pair had the remaining men of the *Fides* at the benches. Used to rowing, the Romans were finding it difficult to adjust to paddling facing forwards. As the vessel on which Amantius was an unwilling passenger came about, it yawed and dipped alarm-ingly, the green water all too close to the edge. He clung on tighter, his chubby knuckles whitening.

The boats could take only four passengers in addition to their crew. The mission had been distributed among them. Ballista, Maximus and Tarchon rode in the first with the guide. Amantius had been assigned to the second with Zeno, the Danubian peasant Diocles and a slave. Castricius and the insolent-looking Egyptian soldier Heliodorus commanded the last two, each accompanied by two slaves.

Amantius was not just uncomfortable and anxious, he was simmering with resentment. Zeno had insisted Amantius travel with him, in case he should have sudden need of a secretary. The imperial envoy now lounged on a cushion at the rear by the helmsman, Diocles next to him in the place of honour. Amantius had been brusquely ordered to the front with one of Zeno's slaves. Amantius's own boy had been sent off to the last boat. It was as if Zeno were determined to remove the last shreds of *dignitas* from the imperial eunuch.

At least the weather was fine. Here the current ran smooth and strong, and there was little labour for the crew. Off to the right, in the creeks between the islets an unruffled calm prevailed, the surface as still and dark as polished wood. Trees grew out of the water, their bare trunks like the masts of a drowned fleet. The mudbanks were alive with wading birds, busy and completely indifferent to the passing boats. Amantius relaxed a little, his mind turning over ideas of the transience of humanity, its helplessness in the teeth of fate.

On the left the muddy shore slipped by, overgrown with reeds and trees. And there, at the river's edge, stood an enormous creature. Glossy black, it had the form of a bull, but was near the size of an elephant. Massive, double-curved horns overhung the water. Was this the auroch, the great beast of the northern forests of which Caesar had written? Amantius would have liked to ask, but he was not going to demean himself by calling down the boat to the steersman, let alone talking to the slave or soldiers at hand. As they passed, the beast lifted its head. Drops of water fell from its muzzle as it regarded the boats.

The Hypanis bore the boats along. The channel was broader here, other faster-flowing branches joining it from the right.

Behind Amantius, easy on their benches, the crew sang an obscene marching song about the needs of a young widow. The sun sparkled on the placid water. Amantius thought of the bull from the sea sent by Aphrodite to bring death to Hippolytus for scorning her mysteries.

A warning shout from ahead. The boat in front was turning hard to the left. The crew – urgent, but all out of time – thrashed the river with their paddles. The voice of the steersman came across the water, taut with anxiety.

Gods, the barbarians could not be upon them already.

Amantius was thrown sideways as the boat heeled to the right. His stomach hit the side. The water was no distance from his face. Fearing his own bulk would overturn them, he levered himself back. The vessel tipped the other way. Amantius found himself entangled with Zeno's slave. Water slopped around his slippers. In a lather of terror and fury, Amantius fought free of the servile embrace.

Back upright, he held on to the bench beneath his thighs for dear life. On an even keel, the boat was ploughing towards the eastern bank. The air was full of spray and grunted curses as the inexpert crew sweated to drive it faster.

Almost too scared to look, Amantius sought the peril from which they fled. At first he could not comprehend what he saw. It was as if the river god himself had turned against them. The channel running in from the east was full. A mass of timber stretched almost from bank to bank. Low in the water, but incalculably heavy and bearing down fast, it would crush the frail vessels in its path without pause.

Inexplicably, there were men standing on top of the logs. They had poles in their hands, and ran about like ticks on the hide of a hippopotamus. They were shouting and gesturing.

Amantius looked ahead. The bank seemed far away. He looked back at the monstrosity bent on overwhelming them. It was much nearer, travelling fast. The boat was going so slowly. How could Hygeia have spared him from the barbarians only to deliver him to this? Had the rings and the cloak not been enough? He would give more. Most High Mother, accept my last treasure. Take the bracelet, my last link to the sacred court of the Caesars. Spare my life. Save me from the fishes and a watery grave.

With no warning, the boat grounded. Amantius was hurled forward. His head cracked against a piece of wood. He sprawled on the floor. 'Hygeia, all the gods, do not let me die.'

Men were laughing. The crew were thumping each other on the back. The raft of lashed-together logs was drifting past. The men on it were polling it clear of the bank. They called out jokes.

'A hazard of navigating these rivers,' the steersman said. 'They float the timber down to the Euxine, sell it to merchants. Good timber. Good for shipbuilding.'

In the stern, Diocles was smiling, but Zeno was white-faced.

'We get going,' said the steersman. 'Follow them down.'

XI

THE ESTUARY OF THE HYPANIS AND BORYSTHENES

On that day the expedition encountered four rafts of timber being floated down to the Euxine. None was as alarming as the first. Apart from them, they had the river much to themselves all the way to Cape Hippolaus. There were fishermen out, but at the sight of four unknown boats, they rowed into overgrown creeks and were lost to sight.

Ballista enjoyed the journey. It was good to be on the water in a small boat very like the ones of his childhood on the shores of the Suebian Sea. The weather remained set fair. A gentle southerly breeze got up and ruffled the surface. It was warm in the spring sunshine. There were no clouds. In between the islands with their reeds and trees, the low, grey line of the western shore could be seen two miles or more away. There was a pale-blue band above it, straight as if drawn with a pencil; a white-blue sky above that.

The Hypanis was rich. Resting happily in the prow, Ballista saw perch, bream and carp. There were many catfish. Once, a huge pike, solitary in its ferocity, came to investigate the boats, before flicking away to find sanctuary under a bank. He had been told there were sturgeon, but he saw none. Great gaggles of geese and ducks bobbed on the water. The shallows and mudflats were crowded with waders; high-stepping, beaks darting, tireless in their endeavours. When the boats came too close, the birds took wing, filling the air with their noise.

The eastern shore was thick with reeds. Alder and willows grew among them. There were birch, oak and poplars behind. Animals moved through the vegetation, coming down to drink; herds of deer and wild sheep, lumbering bison.

Amidst this plenty the signs of man were few. They passed only two Olbian settlements. They were sited on high bluffs. They looked down on the river from cliffs which were banded with pink and grey rock. Both villages were small, circumscribed by ravines and heavily fortified in stone. Their inhabitants could not be blamed for such prudence. But Ballista noted the area of cultivation around them was narrow. There was little terracing, no vines and few domestic animals. When the boats approached, those cattle that were grazing were driven up towards the walls.

The water level was high. The lower trees were half submerged. Bleached branches swept downstream had tangled on promontories. The winter must have been hard further north in the cold interior of the continent. Ballista remembered the winters of his youth on Hedinsey. In the bleak midwinter the snow could drift so high that only the smoke of their hearths revealed the outlying farms around his father's hold of Hlymdale. In such a place it was easy to believe in Fimbulvetr, the winter of the world before Ragnarok, easy to believe the sun would never rise again, and that all except one man and one woman were destined to die.

They reached their destination at sunset. Cape Hippolaus

thrust out into the waters as sharp and firm as the beak of a ship. It was gloomy at the landing place. A broad cloak of clouds had formed and trapped the evening redness in the west.

There was no one to greet them. They hauled the boats out of the water, took out what they needed, and set a guard. In near-darkness they climbed the broad stone steps.

At the top the gate was shut. No torches burned, but men could be sensed watching from the wall. There was the sound of metal scraping on stone. Some of the Romans shifted uneasily, their hands reaching for the reassurance of their sword hilts.

A voice challenged them in Greek: Who came in the dark to Cape Hippolaus and the Temple of Demeter?

The Olbian guide announced himself, detailed those with him and what they were about. The names of the first *archon* Callistratus and the *strategos* Montanus were well received.

Inside, torches flared, and at no long interval the gate swung open. Men in leather and horn armour emerged.

'Health and great joy.' The headman introduced himself and those considered of note in the village. He seemed predisposed to make much of Ballista and Castricius. News of the heroic defence of Olbia had not long reached Cape Hippolaus; it was an honour to welcome the saviours of the city. Zeno intervened. With the barest nod to civility, the imperial envoy demanded entrance. By the *mandata* entrusted to him by the most noble Augustus Gallienus, and in the name of Claudius Natalianus, governor of Moesia Inferior, within whose province this place lay, food and lodgings should be provided, suitable in both quantity and quality.

Ballista thought there were many things that were dislikeable about Aulus Voconius Zeno. Some, above all his cowardice, were damning. Others, such as his endless, often inapposite quotations from Homer and his pretence of contempt for all later Greek literature, let alone anything in Latin, were merely tiresome. But his sanctimonious pomposity could put all the rest in the shade.

Back in Cilicia, Zeno had abandoned his province and run like a deer. But he had left Ballista a letter whose carefully crafted sentences stressed how the departed governor's actions had been dictated by good faith, piety and devotion to duty and should be emulated by others. Years later, the phrases still rankled.

They were led through alleys so narrow they had to walk in single file. They came out into a tiny square. The torchlight revealed a small temple on one side, what probably passed for a *Bouleuterion* opposite, and a stone-built house on each of the others. The council chamber and one of the houses were made over to the expedition, the occupants of the latter being summarily evicted. Ballista thought there were winners and losers in politics in this remote village, just as there were in the imperial *consilium*.

The headman, who rejoiced in the title of *Archon*, invited Zeno, Ballista and Castricius to dine at his home, which turned out to be the other house facing on to the square. Provisions and firewood would be sent in to the rest. There was a well in the square.

Between the inevitable eggs and apples – respectively hard-boiled and dried this time – the meal was made around a none too large, cold leg of mutton with cold, once-dried peas. The bread was from the day before. But there were fresh, plain, grilled fish.

They drank a little well-watered wine from clay beakers and ate off a mixture of pottery. Most of the crockery was red; some pieces grey. Not all had been turned on a wheel. Ballista noticed the rings on the fingers of the locals were iron or bronze; their brooches were inlaid with beads of glass or paste. Most striking were the tallow candles – there was not a lamp anywhere.

Conversation was uncomfortable. Zeno made no attempt to speak or hide his disdain. He seemed to take the poverty of the villagers of Cape Hippolaus as a personal affront. Given the air of suspicion with which he regarded everything around him, including every morsel he ate and those who offered them to him, it was possible he thought it all subterfuge. Perhaps he thought the villagers secretly as rich as Croesus, with caches of treasure buried under the floors. Perhaps he resented them passing this poor fare off on him, certain they had hidden larders groaning with delicacies.

Ballista and Castricius put themselves out to be charming. They responded at length, although with some modesty, to the hosts' questions about the siege. Unsurprisingly, this did nothing to improve Zeno's mood.

The end of the dinner brought little in the way of relief. Zeno had taken the *Bouleuterion* for himself. The secretary Amantius was to attend him; their slaves would look after them. Zeno required no more than a bodyguard of ten of the Romans commanded by Diocles. Even with six men watching the boats, it left more than thirty crammed into the requisitioned house. When Ballista and Castricius returned, they found a small area of floor had been reserved for them to sleep. A slave had made Ballista a bed of almost clean straw.

Ballista knew he would not rest easy. He had always had a horror of confined spaces. One by one, the others started snoring. Ballista lay in the dark, tired but tense. Iron-eyed, sleep rejected his embrace. He should have checked the defences. The headman had told him a watch was always set, but he should have checked. Ballista imagined the Tervingi out there in the night; blades in their hands, revenge in their hearts, they scaled the wall, slid through the alleyways.

Most men would have been unable to leave the crowded house without a commotion. Ballista, like most sons of warriors in the north, had been brought up partly by his maternal uncle. Heoden was King of the Harii. They were night fighters. Thanks to Tacitus, their skills were known even within the *imperium*. Stepping quietly, feeling with the outside of each foot before putting his weight down, Ballista left. At the click of the latch, a couple of men stirred, but none woke; not even Maximus. Outside, Ballista slung his sword belt over his shoulder.

The moon was low, but the eyes of Thiazi and the other stars shed enough light. It was quiet up on the walls. Ballista saw no sentinels. There were cliffs on three sides of the village. Good walls of unmortared stone at the top. The citadel was tiny. On its landward side the wall was fronted by a deep ditch. A wooden bridge crossed over to the lower settlement. Down there the dwellings were much wider spaced, more like farms than townhouses. Another deep ditch and similar walls encircled them. Motionless, Ballista peered through the darkness at the outer wall. There was a chill to the wind. He should have brought his cloak.

A movement on the wall. Gone as soon as he saw it. Opening his eyes wide to admit all the light there was, Ballista looked a little to one side of where he had spotted the movement. His own breathing filled his ears. There it was again. Now he had it. A man walking the rampart. Without hurry, and with no attempt at concealment, the figure moved along the battlements. Ballista watched until he was certain it was a watchman. He relaxed. There should have been more than one, but it was good the guard did not carry a torch.

Ballista thought of walking the palisades at Hlymdale with his half-brothers, Froda and Eadwulf. They had been older; Froda by nine winters, already a man. He remembered the creak and jingle of Froda's war-harness.

A noise, close at hand. Ballista turned, drew his sword. A footfall in the dark, a croaking raven, a chance encounter with your brother's murderer – Calgacus had been fond of listing things not to be trusted. It had done the old man no good. Ballista's blade glinted cold in the starlight.

Soundless, like some dark elf or dwarf, the short, hooded figure approached.

'Who walks the night?'

'A friend.' Castricius pushed back his hood. 'Sleep eluded me, too.'

They leant on the parapet, watching the stars slip their moorings and race to their doom.

'How long is it since we met?'

Ballista thought. 'Coming on ten years. We were young then.'

'Already old in the ways of the world.'

Ballista laughed softly. 'Maybe you more than me. Why were you in the mines?'

'It is a long story, for another time.'

'Ten years is a long time.'

Castricius turned his small, sharp face towards Ballista. 'The *daemon* that watches me has been strong. Yours, too.'

'My people do not have that belief. Three old women – the *Norns* – spin our fate.'

Castricius smiled and turned away. 'Back in Arete there was much talk before you arrived. The men of Legio IIII Scythica said our new barbarian commander had been born in a mud hut.'

Ballista said nothing.

'We knew you were a hostage, but we had no idea of the power your father wields in the north.'

'Most inhabitants of the *imperium* know little of the world outside. All barbarians are much alike.'

'Your family rule over many peoples. They must be fine warriors.'

'The north breeds hard men.' Ballista shrugged. 'But much of the rise of the Himlings was down to love, or at least marriage.'

Castricius looked back at Ballista, waiting for more.

'There were rival families, but we have held the island of Hedinsey time out of mind, since the first Himling, Woden's son. My great-grandfather Hjar took a Waymunding woman for his first wife. She brought him the island of Varinsey. His second wife was from the Aviones, and he married his sister to the chief of the Chali. It brought him influence on the mainland, on the Cimbric peninsula. His son Starkad extended that. He married women from the Varini and the Reudigni, and gave his sister to the king of the Farodini.'

Ballista stopped. 'These are just strange names, meaningless to you.'

'We are bound for the north. I am not Zeno. My *daemon* will protect me, but it is good to know the sort of people I must move among,' said Castricius.

'My father Isangrim has had many wives; a Langobard, a Bronding, a Frisian. My mother is from the Harii. Many peoples of the islands and shores of the Suebian Sea pay him tribute.'

'All that without fighting?'

Ballista grinned. 'No, there was much fighting. Hjar sailed east and never returned. Starkad died in battle. But the most important fighting was not in the north. About a century ago the divine Marcus Aurelius wore the purple. In the great wars, when the Marcomanni and other tribes crossed the frontier, the emperor offered Hjar friendship. Hjar sent warriors south to fight for the Romans along the Ister. Hjar himself attacked the lands of the emperor's enemies from the north. In return, Marcus sent Hjar money and swords. You could say the emperor created the power of the Himlings.'

'And now one emperor wants to turn that power against another,' countered Castricius, grimly.

'Yes,' said Ballista.

'It will be good for you to see your family,' said Castricius.

'Some of them,' Ballista said. 'Some are no longer there for me to see.'

XII

ROME

The bride stepped over the threshold out from her father's house. It was a blustery evening, the wind whipping up from the Tiber. The whitehorn torches guttered. In their light her tunic was dazzlingly white, her scarf and shoes a hectic red. She looked beautiful, and very young, no more than her fourteen years.

Gallienus thought she looked both relieved and apprehensive at the same time. He imagined the relief would have come from having negotiated the archaic ceremonies inside without faltering. She had remained motionless as her hair had been parted with a bent iron spearhead, rusty with the blood of a slain gladiator. She had been seated on the fleece of a freshly slaughtered sheep, eaten spelt bread, salt cake and other unaccustomed things. She had spoken the ritual words – *ubi tu Gaius, ego Gaia* – the meaning of which eluded the speculations of those better educated than her. The mistress of the ceremonies had placed her right hand in that of her husband, and the guests had repeatedly wished the newly-weds good luck: *Feliciter, Feliciter.* Finally she had offered a pinch of incense and a libation of wine to the *lares,* and so said farewell to her household gods. The cause of her apprehension was obvious to all. Her old nurse, all the women of the household, would have told her, reassuring or teasing in their intent, what would happen to her later.

The girl was taken from the arms of her mother. A young boy took each of her hands, supporting her on either side. Gallienus thought he could do with some support. He had been drinking hard inside the house. A different wine in every glass. His head was buzzing, inappropriate thoughts insinuating themselves. The will of an emperor is law. He could do as he likes. It was all too easy to imagine a Caligula or Heliogabalus pulling the wives of other men from the dining couches, taking them out, having their pleasure, then returning to discuss their performance with their stony-faced husbands. Gallienus felt a stirring at the perversity of the thing. He pushed the thought down. He was not a Caligula or Heliogabalus, if for no other reason than the brevity of their reigns. Both had been killed after but a brief season of misrule, and no one could say their killers acted unjustly. Gallienus had worn the purple for well over a decade. Virtue was more than its own reward.

The band struck up. As the procession set off, the throng lining the street raised the shout: *Talasio! Talasio!* Well fed, full of free wine; the plebs' ignorance of its meaning was no impediment to their enthusiasm.

Gallienus took Salonina's hand. Together with his wife, he promenaded at the head of the family, just behind the bride. Weddings made everyone think of sex. Perhaps there would be time to claim his conjugal rights before he left tonight. Recently, on the few occasions he had visited her bedchamber, Salonina had been reluctant. She had paraded the Platonism of the teachings of Plotinus: the body was a prison, its pleasures to be scorned as demeaning and unworthy. Things might improve now the aged sage was deep in Campania spending Gallienus's money making the *Laws* of Plato a living reality in Platonopolis. Anyway, to Hades with the lukewarm joys of the marital bed. Gallienus's German concubine Pippa waited for him in Mediolanum. Pippa, his glorious Pippara, only feigned reluctance to heighten the pleasure. He would take the bitch bent over a table, as soon as he arrived, still in his riding boots. The journey north would take several days. If his needs became too insistent, there was always Demetrius. Beautiful as he was, the Greek youth was really too old now. Perhaps instead there was that new, slut-eyed little Syrian boy who helped him dress.

Having descended from the Palatine, the procession had made its way through the Forum Romanum. It halted at the Temple of Concordia Augusta. Beneath the marble gaze of Pax, Salus and Concordia herself, the newly-weds offered a libation and prayer to the harmony of the imperial house.

Gallienus thought the symbolism could not be missed. The marriage of the son of the emperor's half-brother Licinius to the daughter of his cousin Flaccinus made public demonstration of the unity of the house of the Caesars. In fact, Gallienus had always considered his half-brother rather slow. But Licinius had done well enough when the Alamanni had reached the suburbs of Rome itself the other year. He was reliable. That was more than could be said for Flaccinus. On a routine punitive raid to burn a few villages, his cousin had been captured by one of the tribes north of the Ister. Clementius Silvius, the governor of the provinces of Pannonia, had done nothing. It had been left to a young tribune called Probus to rescue a member of the imperial house from the savage Quadi and restore something of the *dignitas* of Rome. The initiative had been well rewarded; Probus now rode in the imperial entourage as one of the *protectores*.

Whatever the shortcomings of some of its men, the stability of the dynasty was exhibited to the world by this marriage. No matter what further trials it might undergo at the hands of a malignant fortune, it was well stocked with heirs beyond young Marinianus, the emperor's one remaining son.

Tears pricked Gallienus's eyes. Outside Greek tragedy, had any family been so afflicted? Gallienus's father remained in eastern captivity. Reports said Valerian was shamefully treated. Whenever the Persian king came out to ride, the frail old man who had been emperor of Rome was forced to his hands and knees. There in the dirt, Valerian was forced to hear vile words and to take the boot of his conqueror on his shoulders. The cruel gods had reduced the ruler of the *Oikoumene*, their own vice-regent on earth, to no more than an animate mounting block. Yet it was not that which brought the tears to Gallienus's eyes. His eldest son, Valerian the Younger, had been on the Ister in the care of the *protector* Ingenuus when he died. The doctors had blamed a fever. Rumours had whispered of darker causes. The subsequent rebellion of Ingenuus lent them credence. No doubt shrouded the fate of Gallienus's second and favourite son. No more than a terrified child, far from home he had been betrayed, hauled out and butchered. His body desecrated, the shade of Saloninus could know no rest. The cruelty of the gods was infinite. As he did every day, almost every hour, Gallienus tried to force away thoughts of the last moments of his son.

The procession retraced its steps through the forum, between the tall, shadowed façades along the Sacred Way.

Hymenaee Hymen, O Hymen Hymenaee.

So far the nuptial songs were seemly enough. This one had been composed for the occasion by Cominius Priscianus, *a Studiis* to Gallienus. Of course, it had been previously performed in private for the approval of the emperor. It was a reworking of a poem by Catullus; the story of Theseus and Ariadne, with a more uxorious hero, and a happier outcome.

Henceforth let a woman believe a man's oath, let all believe a man's speech can be trustworthy.

Its conceit barely stood up to public scrutiny. Despite repeated betrayal – despite Ingenuus, Regalianus and all the others; despite even Postumus – Gallienus wanted to believe the oath of at least some men could be trusted. He had given charge of the eastern provinces to Odenathus the Lord of Palmyra, had given him the high office of *Corrector Totius Orientis*. The Palmyrene had sworn oaths of loyalty. He had taken the war to the Persians, had burnt their capital, Ctesiphon. Now despatches from the *frumentarii* claimed Odenathus's wife, Zenobia, was urging him to strike for something higher. Gallienus had sent imperial *mandata* east. The governors of Syria Coele and Egypt, Fabius Labeo and Theodotus, were to return to the imperial court. Virius Lupus was to move from Arabia to replace Fabius Labeo. New governors had been sent from Italy to govern Arabia and Egypt. If Odenathus acknowledged imperial authority and allowed the appointments to go ahead, probably all was well. If not, next year the field army would have to march east, and the long-meditated revenge on Postumus would be postponed yet again. Another two campaigning seasons would have passed and Saloninus remain unavenged. Gallienus prayed to his special companion Hercules, to all the gods, that Odenathus remain true to his word. In the chill wind, the emperor's tears were cold on his face.

As the procession snaked up to the Palatine, mannered verses gave way to traditional songs; ripe figs were plucked, fields ploughed and swords found their sheaths. Attendants threw nuts to the crowd and the choir sang of the joys of the night, the daring joys of the next day. The contest awaited: Eros was the umpire, Hymen the herald, the bed the wrestling ground.

Bawdy songs failed to return Gallienus's thoughts to pleasures of the flesh. Postumus had sent an agent to Rome to suborn Placidianus, the Prefect of the *vigiles*. Placidianus had remained loyal. When Gallienus had first come to the throne, what happened in the cellars of the palace had turned the young emperor's stomach. The years had hardened him. The previous night he had watched the torture of the agent with an equanimity approaching pleasure. On the wooden horse, under the terrible steel claws, much had been revealed. One thing had been most providential. It was common knowledge that Bonosus, the commander of the rebel Legio III Italica Concors in Raetia, was a notorious drunk. Yet Bonosus was trusted by the usurper Postumus because he was a Spaniard. Now Gallienus had learned the Spanish estates of Bonosus were all mortgaged, his patrimony squandered. In the dead of night a cloaked horseman had ridden north. Venutus was said by Censorinus to be the most resourceful centurion among the *frumentarii*. Dressed as a sutler, or wine merchant, Venutus would approach the impecunious Spaniard. If Venutus failed, most likely he would find himself at the mercy of Postumus's torturers. His agony would yield nothing – Censorinus had given assurances the centurion knew nothing of grave importance – and his mere presence might serve to sow doubts in the mind of Postumus about the loyalty of his commanders in Raetia. And that would be most timely. For, although next to no one knew it, Gallienus and his field army would be in Raetia within two months. Postumus traded in treachery, and – the gods willing – treachery was the coin in which he would be paid. The evidence extracted in the cellar implied Bonosus was not the only supporter of the child murderer whose loyalty might not be above suspicion. Even Postumus's Prefect of Cavalry, Lollianus, might repay discreet blandishments.

They had reached that part of the palace given over to the

household of Licinius. The torch which had led the procession was thrown. Sparks streamed as it tumbled through the night air. A bold onlooker caught it and gained the promise of long life. The bride wreathed the door posts with wool and rubbed them with oil and wolf fat. The latter was hard to obtain, but Gallienus had declared the traditions of the ancestors should be observed at an imperial wedding and parsimony was out of place.

Attendants carried the bride over the threshold. While she was taken off to touch fire and water in her new home, Gallienus led his wife into the atrium. The other guests followed. They stood around the marriage bed set for the *genius* of the bridegroom and the similarly incorporeal *juno* of the bride. A slave offered drinks to the imperial couple. Chosroes of Armenia presumed upon his royal status to approach and speak to Gallienus. He had been expelled by the Persians more than a decade before, but the last king of the Arsacid dynasty was a useful bargaining tool. Politics might dictate Chosroes was treated as if he were a reigning monarch, but the Roman emperor felt under no obligation to listen at all closely to his platitudinous conversation in oddly accented Greek.

Gallienus gestured for another drink. He sensed the disapproval of Salonina and felt a flash of anger. What cares did the woman have to carry? How to spend money? Which philosophical sect to patronize? It was as if she had forgotten the existence of their murdered son. Gallienus had not forgotten, drunk or sober. The gods willing, this summer the first acts of his revenge would fall on Postumus. They would fall on the child-killer both in Raetia and at the same time from a less expected direction. Admittedly, the previous expedition Censorinus had sent into the far north had disappeared without trace. But the centurion Tatius had not impressed Gallienus, and the titular leader of the mission, a fat equestrian called Julianus, a collector of amber, had been like an actor in a bad mime. Ballista was a different proposition.

Although some in the north may not welcome his return, Ballista was a *princeps* among his own people. Gallienus had known him since they were young, knew his capabilities. Things would have been easier if the previous mission had not failed, but Gallienus could imagine no one more likely to succeed among the Angles than Ballista.

Gallienus found he had a different cup in his hand. The world was getting a little off-set. Chosroes was still talking. Gallienus smiled benignly at the Armenian. His thoughts remained among the Hyperboreans.

Zeno would hate it beyond the north winds. The Greek was not without his own capabilities. He had been more than conscientious as *a Studiis*. His knowledge of Greek literature, especially the earlier writers, was admirable. When invited to attend the *consilium*, at first he had spoken out cogently and with frankness on whatever issues were discussed. There was nothing wrong with that: Rome was not an oriental despotism like Armenia. Measured freedom of speech was to be allowed. But then Zeno had gone further. He had begun to criticize Gallienus's military appointments. Repeatedly, at inapposite moments, the Greek had inveighed against what he called barrack-room upstarts. He had dared to announce that the *mos maiorum* demanded that high commands should be reserved for senators. The presumption of claiming to know the ways of the ancestors better than his emperor had been bad enough, but also it had raised questions of motive and integrity. Zeno was neither senator nor soldier. Although the *frumentarii* detailed to investigate had unearthed no evidence, Gallienus was convinced some disaffected faction of senators – the gods knew there were enough of them – had bribed the pompous *graeculus*. Zeno had been dismissed, and got out of the way as part of a diplomatic mission that crossed the lower Ister. That the embassy had failed could not be held against him. There had never been a realistic likelihood of turning the

Tervingi, Gepidae, Carpi and Taifali against each other or their allies. But Gallienus was not ready to let the impudent little Greek return. Zeno had been particularly virulent against Ballista. He would watch the northerner like a hawk. That was good. Ballista was not above suspicion. Once their bias was filtered, Zeno's reports might prove useful. Gallienus wondered if vanity and prejudice would blind his sometime *a Studiis* to who was really leading the expedition. Still, if the *graeculus* hampered the mission, Ballista carried something from Gallienus that would make the position clear.

Loud applause brought Gallienus back from the frigid north. There was no relief about the bride now; nothing but naked anxiety. With her husband, she was brought before Gallienus. Her eyes kept flicking to the bed in the atrium. No doubt, her thoughts ran to the other one, the one inside to which not her *juno* but herself would be taken. It was time for the *epithalamium*. Gallienus handed his drink to a servant. Holding the hands of the bridal pair, he recited the verse he had composed:

> 'Come now, my children, grow heated together in deep-seated
> passion,
> Never, indeed, may the doves outdo your billings and cooings,
> Never the ivy your arms, or the clinging sea-shells your kisses.'

The rest slipped his mind. Another couple of lines; something about playing … watching . . . the lamps.

When the wedding guests realized there was no more to come, they voiced their appreciation.

Gallienus watched the girl being led away. She was beautiful and very young. It was fortunate for her the ways of the ancestors had changed and the bedding was no longer public. She looked terrified as it was. Still, at twenty-six, Licinius's son had a certain experience. He was not an unkind man. Out of concern for her timidity, her hymen would remain intact tonight. Of course, he would make up for his forbearance by buggering her, and tomorrow he would fully enjoy his new wife. Such consideration was to be admired.

XIII

THE BORYSTHENES RIVER

The entrance to the Borysthenes lay between the Temple of Demeter on Cape Hippolaus and the grove of Hecate on Hylaea. The connotations could hardly have been less auspicious. The awful curse of Pythonissa, priestess of Hecate, terrifying, triple-headed goddess of the dark, had occupied Ballista's thoughts. *Kill his sons. Kill all his family, all those he loves.* Demeter had lost her child, snatched away to the underworld.

It was impossible to tell where the river began and the great estuary it formed with the Hypanis ended. From the height of the village, innumerable islets, reed banks and mudflats had spread out, creating a green labyrinth of channels and creeks, the open water often betrayed by only the glint of the sun. Down in the boats, hemmed in by feathery walls of reeds, visibility had seldom been further than a javelin cast.

To minimize the chance of any encounter with the once-servile pirates infecting Hylaea, the Olbian guide had kept as much as possible to the bank on their left. He had had no time to talk. The silt shifted the shallows day on day. Each year, the river presented a fresh map of dangers and dead ends. Alert as a hunting dog, he had peered over the bow, calling directions to the helmsman in the stern. Ballista had sat behind him, silent with bad thoughts. *Kill all his family, all those he loves.*

The first day had been calm. In the creeks, the current was imperceptible. But in their winding course, they made few miles. They had spent that night in another village. Mean dwellings packed behind ditches and ramparts, only the absence of a temple to Demeter distinguished it from the one at Cape Hippolaus.

In the next four days they paddled against a headwind as well as the more noticeable flow of the river. Progress was slow. They passed more villages. These, they avoided. The cracked walls and smoke-blackened roof beams jagged against the sky marked them as places of tragedy and ill omen. Some of the burning was recent enough to leave its reek on the air. Three nights they camped on muddy islands, and once on a stinking peninsula full of cormorants and gulls.

Despite the threats of barbarians and pirates, they were not alone on the river. Fisherfolk in dugout canoes slunk off into the shallowest backwaters at their approach. Four small trading vessels travelling in convoy and several rafts of logs being poled down to the Euxine had no option but to approach. They did so cautiously. The crews of the boats were armed and looked prepared to fight, even against the odds. Those on the timber were few, near naked, and ready for flight. A short swim and they would be hidden among the thick vegetation of the banks. As the distance narrowed, Greek voices were not enough – whatever their origins, the runaway slaves on Hylaea would know Greek – but the names of the great men of Olbia reassured. *Health and great joy.* The voyagers exchanged news. The gods be praised, no one had encountered anything worse than the mundane hazards of riverine travel. *May the gods hold their hands over you.* Both sides parted a little heartened, but somehow more isolated on the river after the meeting.

The sixth day out, the guide took them over towards the bank on their right. The only channel of any reasonableness was there. The slaves from Hylaea had never been seen this far upriver. A hard day, and tonight once again they could sleep easy behind the walls of a strong village, where the inhabitants would keep watch.

Practice had improved the paddling of the Romans. They were nearly as fluent as the Olbians. The wind had backed to the south-west. The sun shone, and the four boats sped along.

There were redshanks and kingfishers. High above, Ballista saw a pair of sea eagles. Some way up the river, from beneath a weeping willow, a heron took wing, its long legs trailing. Ballista's mood had lightened a little, but still ran on his family and death. Not his wife and sons, but his family in the north. 'Some are no longer there for me to see,' he had said to Castricius. His half-brothers Froda and Eadwulf would not be there. Froda was dead, and Eadwulf eating the bitter bread of exile with the name Evil-Child.

Ballista, or Dernhelm as he was then, had known just fourteen winters. He had stayed with his father. Although sixteen, Arkil had remained at Hlymdale as well. The older sons of Isangrim had led the Angle longboats east against the Heathobards. There had been hard fighting and little booty. The Heathobards were renowned warriors. Yet the Himlings had the glory of the day. That night, in the tent of Froda, the brothers had celebrated as men of the north will. Oslac, always the quietest and most thoughtful, had left early enough to walk unaided. The others had drunk more, much more. Morcar and Eadwulf had quarrelled. None of the brood, except his full brother Oslac, cared much for Morcar. He was brave and clever, but always aloof and quick to sneer. Eadwulf had a temper; the slightest insult was known to enrage him. He had roared insults and threats at Morcar. Froda, the eldest, had told him to get out, come back when he was old enough to hold his drink. At the commotion, Eadwulf's friend, Swerting, had rushed in and dragged him back to the tent they shared. Morcar had stormed off in the other direction. Froda was left alone.

In the morning Froda was dead. His body was cruelly cut, and in the shambles was Eadwulf's sword. Eadwulf was still unconscious when they came for him. Taken back to Hlymdale in chains, Eadwulf had sworn his innocence. He remembered nothing after returning to his tent. He would never have harmed Froda. Some enemy had taken his sword, left it to incriminate him, to bring dissension to the Himlings.

Many believed Eadwulf. He and Froda had been close. But when questioned, at length Swerting had said he had got up in the night to relieve himself, and Eadwulf had not been in the tent. Having lost one son, the *cyning* Isangrim would not order the death of another. Before his seventeenth winter, Eadwulf went into exile, and men had started to call him Evil-Child.

Ballista had worshipped Froda. Eadwulf had done the same. Open and kind, Froda had been a man when they were still little more than children. Eadwulf had a temper, but Ballista had never believed him guilty.

Ahead, a flight of duck clattered up from the reed beds. Ballista idly watched them circle and stream away. The river was quiet when they had gone. There were no waders busy on the mudflats. Nothing but the splash of the paddles, and the water running down the sides of the boat.

Eadwulf and Froda were gone, but there were others Ballista had waited more than half a lifetime to see again. The resentment he had felt when his father had sent him away into the *imperium* had long dissipated. Since then, Ballista himself had been forced to make hard decisions. His father would be old now, as would his mother. A sharp stab of anxiety came with that thought. It took a long time for news to travel down the amber roads from the north to the *imperium*. Given the outlandish places where Ballista had served in the last two years, it was no wonder he had heard nothing from the Suebian Sea. Allfather, let them both be alive. Other faces swam into view – nothing could have happened to Heoroweard. His friend was indestructible. Always stocky, after Ballista had left he was said to have grown very fat, earning himself the name Paunch-Shaker. And then there was Heoroweard's sister. Kadlin would not be a girl any more. She was the same age as Ballista. Not a wild girl of sixteen winters, a girl with a look in her eye. She would be a mature woman. Twice married, with Starkad, her son by her first husband, and a son and daughter by Oslac. If Ballista had remained in the north, most likely he would have married her. It would be strange to see her as wife to his half-brother, more than strange. Oslac might not welcome his return. For different reasons, Morcar certainly would not.

Ballista watched the willows slip past, their long fronds weeping down into the water, making dark caves along the bank. He wondered if any of the Angles would really welcome his return. He had been away a long time. Twenty-six winters in the *imperium* had changed him. He smiled. They were sailing past the woods of Hylaea, according to Herodotus, the scene of a particularly unhappy homecoming. Anacharsis the Scythian had gone south, travelled the world. He had lived in Athens, discussed philosophy with Solon. Although a barbarian, Anacharsis had been reckoned one of the seven sages of Hellas. On his return north, he had stopped at Cyzicus on the Hellespont. There he had witnessed the worship of Cybele. If the goddess granted him a safe journey, he had sworn to perform her mysteries in his native land. Back among his own people, Anacharsis had slipped away into Hylaea. Drum in hand, he had danced in honour of the Great Mother. His strange rituals had been observed. The Scythian king himself had killed Anacharsis. The moral was not hard to find.

A movement among the trees, not an animal. A creak, not a rubbing bough. Ballista threw himself sideways with an incoherent yell. As he hit the bottom of the boat, the arrows hissed through the air. One took the Olbian guide in the arm. He started to topple off the prow. Ballista grabbed him, hauled him back. Shouts and screams from the rear. A loud splash. More arrows, gouging white furrows from the gunnels, thumping into flesh.

Ballista snatched his shield, got to his knees. Scrabbling over the floor, he brought the linden boards up. Barking his shins, he swung the shield out to cover the man on the bench behind him. More arrows whipped around them. At least two men were down. No one was paddling. The way was coming off the boat.

'Keep paddling. Get us clear.' Ballista realized it was his voice. 'Paddle!'

The small craft tipped to the right. Maximus and Tarchon were alongside him, their shields forming a ragged wall. The man at the steering oar was gone. The boat was dead in the water, listing badly.

'Maximus, take the helm.'

The Hibernian scrambled into the stern. An arrow plucked at his tunic.

'Paddle, you fuckers! Get us out of here!'

Ragged, with no cohesion, the crew stabbed the water. One misjudged his stroke, missed the surface, fell forward. A shaft slammed into Ballista's shield, snapped his jaws shut. He bit his tongue, spat blood.

'Paddle!'

Maximus had the steering oar, shield held awkwardly across himself. The boat was moving, picking up speed. The arrow storm was easing. Ballista looked around his shield. Figures among the branches. Not many of them. A tall man in a white cloak, shouting. The following boat was almost up with them. Now the shafts swarmed around it, flicking up the water, sprouting from shields and woodwork.

'Ahead!'

Two low dugout canoes were pulling out from under a canopy of willows. Five men in each. Four dark men at the benches in tunics, one armoured man in the bows. Ballista scanned the surroundings. Nothing. No sign of another vessel. Just ten men – odds of four to one against them. They must be insane.

'Maximus, take us straight at the first one.'

The leading canoe had paddled out to block the channel. Its crew were bringing its bows around. Its companion was a little way behind.

'Diocles, take the second.'

The young Danubian shouted something back. His boat was clear. The bowmen had switched their aim to Castricius, the third in line.

'Ram them.'

Ballista hauled the wounded Olbian guide back, braced himself in the prow. His sword was in his hand. He had no memory of drawing it.

The boats met bow to bow. The dugout was driven back, half under the surface. Shield up, the warrior at the front leapt for the larger vessel. Ballista surged up, brought his blade down, weight behind the blow. The shield shattered. Off balance, a foot in each boat, the warrior tried to thrust at Ballista's stomach. Ballista smashed the metal boss of his shield into the man's face. He fell into the river. His long blond hair fanned out as his mailshirt dragged him down.

The other four had abandoned the waterlogged canoe. They swam like otters back towards the bank. Tarchon reached past Ballista, and fended the canoe away.

'Paddle. Keep going.'

Ballista looked back. The other dugout had thought better of it, and was nearly back at the shore. Now Heliodorus's boat in the rear was running the gauntlet of the arrows, but would soon be clear.

XIV

THE BORYSTHENES RIVER

After the ambush, they paddled hard for at least an hour. They would have stopped sooner, but all the landing places were on the bank to their right. Eventually, there was an island in midstream, still marshy, but solid enough to disembark.

Maximus accompanied Ballista as he moved through the men. It would have been worse if there had been more archers, much worse if their attackers had possessed more than two dugout canoes. But it was still bad. Two crewmen were dead: a Roman from Ballista's boat and an Olbian from that of Castricius. Ballista's steersman was gone. If he was not dead when he hit the water, he was either drowned or captured. Nine had taken serious wounds; the guide and eight paddlers, four of them Roman and four Olbian. A couple of the latter looked certain to die. The uninjured did what they were able: hurriedly buried the dead, washed and bound the wounds of the living, gave them alcohol, spoke encouraging words. The barbed arrowhead embedded deep in the arm of the guide would have to wait until they reached the fortified village.

166

Ballista rearranged the crews as best he could. All the five slaves were drafted to the benches. It remained to be seen how useful they would prove. One each of the Olbian paddlers from out of the boats of Diocles and Heliodorus was assigned to that of Ballista. The more experienced of the two took over the steering oar. It left nine men to propel the boats of Diocles and Heliodorus, and eight those of Castricius and Ballista. In the latter, Maximus and Tarchon volunteered to help. No one, least of all themselves, suggested Zeno or Amantius might help.

In less than two hours they were ready to return to the boats. There was some debate about wearing armour. The fate of the warrior from the dugout weighed against the obvious protection. Maximus told the tale of his maternal cousin Cormac. Hard pressed by his enemies, Cormac had swum a loch in full war gear. It was not just any loch either, but one of the great ones on the west coast; a good mile or more. Ballista said not every man had the stamina or the limitless breath of a Hibernian hero, and Maximus had agreed that was true. Possibly influenced by the deed of his cousin, those with mailshirts – Ballista, Castricius, Tarchon and Diocles – had joined Maximus in donning them. This time, every fighting man made sure both shield and bowcase were to hand.

Back on the water, Maximus felt a little put out. He thought he had managed the steering paddle well. If you could sail a coracle, as he had in his youth, you could handle any vessel. Admittedly, it was a bit smoother with the Olbian at the helm, but it was just a matter of a bit of practice. Maximus seldom thought about his home. Muirtagh of the Long Road he had been called then, not with any great seriousness. In those days he had not travelled far, but he had always told a fine story. Sure, he had travelled long roads since the cattle raid had gone wrong and he had been captured. Of course, if he had not been knocked unconscious, he would never have been taken. He had been sold to a Roman slaver, shipped to Gaul and resold into a gladiatorial troop. The latter had not been a bad time. At first he had been a boxer, then fought as a *murmillo*. He was good at killing, and the adulation of the crowd was good – that and the women it brought. He had won a fight in the great arena in Arelate the afternoon Ballista had bought him. The Angle had been on his way to Hibernia and needed an interpreter and bodyguard. Maximus had taught Ballista his language and fulfilled the latter function ever since. Back in Hibernia on that journey, he had seen High Kings made and overthrown. Indeed, he had near killed one himself. But their path had not led him to the far west. He would like to return home one day; not for ever, not even for very long. Just for long enough to kill his enemies, burn their homes and rape their women.

They made slow progress. All were tired. The two slaves of Zeno and the eunuch's pretty boy were of but little use. After no more than a quarter of an hour, they had been drooping, their paddles trailing in the water.

It was near full dark, just a residual glow on the water, when they reached the village. Mudflats made the approach to the landing stage difficult. To give the guide his due, he remained at his post, and conned them through, despite the pain from his arm.

The settlement was on the bank from which the ambushers had struck. But it was well fortified, and, on receipt of the news, the villagers mounted a good guard. Ballista, Zeno and the other men of any account among the mission were invited to dine with the headman.

As there was no doctor, Maximus remained with the guide in the barn assigned as their lodgings. By candlelight, with care and much gentleness, he sawed through the shaft of the arrow, removed the fletching. As it was barbed, the arrowhead could not be withdrawn. Maximus gave the injured man drink and a leather belt to put between his teeth. Two Olbians held him down.

Considerable force was needed to push the arrowhead through the arm to the other side. It was not a thing that could be hurried. Maximus had to make first one, then another incision to grip the arrowhead and work the slimy thing out. When it came free, the blood flowed fast. The guide grunted a few times, but bore it well. If he did not die from loss of blood, infection or some malign fate, this Olbian – Hieroson by name – could be thought a man of some regard.

The meal was all but over when Maximus entered the house of the headman. The diners were talking over nuts and dried fruit.

'If there had not been so many of them, they would never have dared such an attack.'

Zeno sounded drunk. No one corrected his estimate of the numbers.

Maximus was passed some food Ballista had saved. There was more to drink here than at Cape Hippolaus or the other place. Maximus still had some cannabis in his bag. If there were women later, reasonably clean women, this could all be fine.

'The pirates have never been known so far upriver,' said the headman.

Ignoring the local, Zeno began to recite some Greek poem:

'A howling . . .
That brought tremendous Laestrygonians swarming up
From every side – hundreds, not like men, like Giants!
Down from the cliffs they flung great rocks a man could hardly
    hoist
And a ghastly shattering din rose up from all the ships –
Men in their death-cries, hulls smashed to splinters.'

'There were not many of them,' said Maximus.

Zeno rounded on Maximus. The Greek's eyes were unfocused, as if there were a different thought behind each of them:

'One man . . .

Who knew within his head many words, but disorderly;

Vain, and without decency.'

Keep going, thought Maximus; every day takes us further from your *imperium*.

Ballista interrupted Zeno's recitation. 'I had a friend who looked more like Thersites than Maximus here does. Old Calgacus's skull went up to a point, sparse hair covering it.'

Everyone, including Zeno, regarded Ballista in silence. Maximus wondered if the Angle also was drunk.

'Our ambushers were not just the runaway slaves turned pirates,' said Ballista.

Maximus could tell Ballista was sober.

'Back in Olbia,' Ballista said, 'Montanus and Callistratus thought the Goths might have established the runaway slaves on Hylaea as a diversion. The warrior in the dugout, the one who drowned, was a northerner; most likely a Goth.'

'A Goth?' Much of Zeno's bluster had vanished. 'How can you be sure?'

'The leader on the bank wore a white fur cloak, like the Tervingi *reiks* outside the gate at Olbia.'

Maximus nodded. 'And a gilded helmet – the same man.' His eyesight had always been good.

'Why would the Tervingi pursue us?' Zeno sounded as if he wanted reassurance that such a thing was unlikely.

'Perhaps they covet the gifts you carry from Gallienus to my people. Perhaps they would like revenge on the men who defeated them at Olbia.' Ballista raised his cup towards Zeno. Maximus decided he might be drunk after all.

Tarchon joined the discussion. 'Why fuckers be attacking with so few fuckers?'

'My guess,' Ballista said, 'is the *reiks* rushed on ahead with a couple of men, collected those pirates he could find, and was using them to delay us, while the rest of his men caught up.'

'How far behind are they?' This was all surprising, and very unwelcome to Zeno.

Ballista shrugged. 'The gods know.'

'How long before we are out of the territory of the Tervingi?' Zeno asked.

'The lands of the Grethungi begin at the rapids,' said the headman.

'How far is that?'

'Five, maybe six days rowing upstream at this season,' said the headman. 'You will be safe from the Tervingi there.'

In the morning, one of the severely hurt Olbians was dead. Less expectedly, so was one of the Roman crewmen. Ballista arranged for their burial. The wounded were to be left at the village. As they had seen, convoys of trading boats still ran to Olbia occasionally. Those that recovered could take their chances on one of them. From Olbia, the Romans should be able to get passage back to the *imperium*. They were to tell the captains of the ships they would be paid by the army at their destination. Ballista wrote a letter for each man authorizing the payment. He admitted to Maximus they might not be honoured, but he would not leave the soldiers money. They would just spend it on drink. Maximus went with Ballista to visit the wounded. Money passed hands here, from Ballista to their hosts, generous provision being made for their care.

As the morning wore on, Zeno fretted and complained. They had been entrusted with a sacred duty by the most noble emperor. The mission was of greater account than any individuals. The importance of the mission could not be overstated. Nothing should be done to endanger it. Gallienus would hear of any who did so. Time was of the essence. They should leave at once.

As far as he could, Ballista ignored Zeno.

171

Maximus had asked Ballista who was this Thersites from the Greek poem the night before. The answer – an ugly rabble-rouser among the men before Troy, justly beaten by his betters – had not further endeared Zeno to him.

Finally, through the headman, Ballista had called for volunteers from the village to fill the benches of the boats. Not one man had come forward.

Just before midday, when they went down to the boats, for the first time Zeno and Amantius had eagerly helped stow their own belongings.

For three days they journeyed north. Knowing the river well, Hieroson the Olbian guide had refused to be left behind. He led them back and forth from one bank to the other to use the ebb flows and as far as possible avoid moving against the main stream. The Borysthenes here had cast off the aspect of a marsh and revealed itself as a great river, although still filled with obstacles. They paddled around and between green flats that broke the surface, great rafts of lily pads and floating islands of pale reeds like misplaced fields of wheat. In the distance, hills came and went, but the banks never changed, an endless screen of reeds with mud at their feet, walls of dark-green trees beyond.

The majority of the paddlers fell into a rhythm. It was a rounded, smooth motion – reach, stroke, pause and twist the blade free – not too hard, soothing in its monotony. In the rear, the crew of Heliodorus's boat was not so good. The two slaves, Amantius's boy and one of Zeno's, still splashed and floundered, contributing little but confusion.

The boats glided upriver. The Romans sang softly. The marching songs of the legions easily adapted to the tempo of these labours. They sang old songs about Caesar, Gaul and whores, but often they returned to a newer one in honour of Ballista's friend the great general Aurelian.

Thousand, thousand, thousand we have beheaded now.
One man, a thousand we have beheaded now.
A thousand drinks, a thousand killed.
So much wine no one has as the blood that he has spilt.

Maximus knew both the song and its subject well. Such adulation was dangerous. Sometimes, he thought, only an outsider could see things clearly. In Rome there were only two places the love of the soldiers could lead: to the throne, or the suspicion of the emperor and an early death.

The first two nights they slept safe behind the walls of inhabited villages. The third, where the Borysthenes made a great bend to the east, they camped on a headland. The beach here was sandy, littered with pines fallen from the eroded cliff above. They made beds from the boughs. It was quiet. The river slid past. In the evening light its water had the thickness of milk.

As the sun came up they pushed out from the shore. Once on the river they saw their pursuers. The distant boats looked black, glimpses of white where the prows cut and where the paddles broke the surface. There were eight of them, about a mile downstream.

Maximus had been expecting them. He had never doubted the Tervingi would learn the identity of Vandrad. He had never doubted they would follow, do all they could to kill Ballista. It was a bloodfeud. The Romans knew all about revenge. They held *ultio* as a duty. But it was a pale shadow of a northern bloodfeud. They did not sing songs about it, did not pass it down generations beyond number. If these Tervingi killed Ballista, his father and his half-brothers must take vengeance, or each become a man of no account in the eyes of the world, a *nithing* in their own eyes. When Ballista's sons came to manhood – if they were not too Roman – they, too, must seek out their father's killers, them and their families. The sagas of the north were punctuated with the flames of burning halls.

There was no singing now. They paddled east. For the twelve hours of daylight they did not cease. They ate at their benches. They shat over the side, their buttocks bare to the wind and the cold slap of water. Their humour did not desert them. When the eunuch had to defecate, they called out: show us your prick, mind the fish do not get your balls. They hooted and jeered when Zeno had to haul up his tunic.

Maximus paddled with the rest. Blisters soon formed on his palms. They burst, and blood and clear pus smeared the handle of his paddle. His shoulders and arms felt as though they had been wrenched on the rack. He put it all from his mind as of little importance. Through the long morning he watched the bank, studied the river. On the water nothing but low islets of vegetation. Once he saw a herd of wild horses crashing away through the reeds on the shore to his left, but no convenient tributaries.

On the broad face of the Borysthenes there was nowhere to hide. By mid-afternoon Maximus was numb with repetition and fatigue. His whole body felt as though it had been flayed. He saw nothing but the shoulders of the man in front. At the end of each stroke this man half toppled forward. But he never fell. None of those at the benches despaired. Ballista and the helmsman reassured them the Tervingi were not gaining. Soon the night would take them in its embrace and conceal them.

As the sun went down it turned the river to molten metal, edged the shoulders and head of the man in front with fire. Maximus had assumed they would stop when darkness fell. They did not. Ballista worked his way down the boat, talking low to each man. Keep going, just a little longer. The Tervingi would expect them to stop. The Goths would make one final effort to overhaul them. Just keep going a little longer.

Maximus kept paddling. It was just another example of life being a bastard. Reach, stroke, pause and twist the blade free; over and over, without cease, like some eternal punishment.

Ballista reached the front, hunched there with the guide. Heads close together, they whispered. Sounds carry a long way on the water.

The moon rose. It changed the river into the silvered fur of some nocturnal beast. There was a slow swell, like the breathing of an old wolf. Dead trees stood stark on the bank, like dead men rising from the ground. Their blind eyes and thin, fleshless arms reached towards the moon. They were the dead men the river had taken. It was a ghastly corporal resurrection, the hideous final day longed for by insane sects, prayed for in locked, darkened rooms by outcast priests.

Ballista was talking to the man on the bench in front. The man put down his paddle, slumped over. Ballista was talking to Maximus. Take us in to the islands. Maximus did not break stroke. Ballista was behind him, muttering instructions to the helmsman, the boat heeling on to a new heading.

Dark-blue water, a black tree line, a steel-blue sky, the moon dragging its tail from the depths. They nosed through reeds and overhanging branches. Ballista reaching out to tie a mooring rope around the trunk of a half-submerged tree. The other boats bumping against them. Maximus dropped the paddle, bundled his cloak as a pillow and curled up on the bench. He heard men groan, felt the boat shift and was enveloped in a more profound darkness.

A light touch behind his ear and Maximus was awake. Ballista smiled down at him. For a moment Maximus was fine, then the pain came. Every muscle was locked. A white agony in his shoulders and arms. His palms had been skinned. The tiniest movement brought more pain. Gingerly, he unfolded himself from the hard bench, dragged himself upright, took the flask Ballista held out, and drank. The unwatered wine was harsh in his throat, sour in his stomach. He managed not to be sick. Panting with discomfort, he ate the flatbread he was handed. Ballista moved on.

Maximus dug out some dried beef from his wallet, forced himself to chew. It was hard to swallow, but he would need the sustenance.

The sky was lightening. Around them the trees were emerging from the dark, taking on more definite shape. They must cast off soon. His breathing harsh as a torn cloth, his limbs clumsy, Maximus hauled up his mailshirt and tunic, dropped his trousers and got his arse over the side. The tension, then the relief. The foul stench of shit, soon lost in the pervasive smell of mud, dead leaves and decay.

Out on the water it smelt better, cleaner. Once he had worked through the pain and his muscles were warm, Maximus slipped back into the rhythm as if he had never known anything else: reach, stroke, pause and twist the blade free.

The sky was layered with purple and gold. As the sun came up behind a distant hill it threw a long, raking light through the trees out on to the river. The blaze faded, and the clouds showed high and white. It was going to be a fine spring day.

They had rowed for perhaps two hours when a long vista revealed the pursuit. The Tervingi boats were dark specks, a good deal further behind than the day before, but still there, hateful in their remorselessness.

The river narrowed. Its flow increased. Leaves and small branches slid by fast. The paddling became harder. The previous day had sapped the stamina of the men at the benches. The boats laboured upstream.

Ballista had gone to sit with the guide. They squatted in the prow like a pair of demented ferrymen leading damned souls to the underworld. A coin would not pay the fare; this crew must work their passage, get a taste of the punishments to come.

The river narrowed further. It was less than a bowshot wide. The Borysthenes was surging against them, as if set on sweeping them back to their fate. Every advance was hard won. The banks inched past. The men were sweating, gasping with the effort. And Ballista and the guide sat and talked. As they talked, they gestured upriver, waving their hands here and there. Maximus found it hard not to hate them.

'Not far now.' Ballista was standing. He raised his voice to reach the other three boats strung out behind. 'Another mile and you can rest. We will be safe.'

There was no telling how long it took to win through the narrows. Suddenly, the shores receded and there was open water all around. Ballista laughed with the guide, then waved for the other boats to follow them over to the right-hand bank.

Away from the main stream, the water was very still. It was bliss no longer to have to fight the river. The boats glided in towards a huge raft of timber moored by a lumber camp. If there were loggers there, they hid themselves from those approaching. The boats ground to a halt against the floating logs.

Maximus was unsure how this represented safety.

Ballista stepped on to the raft. He and the guide had worked out a plan. The gods had been kind. He told them the plan. Certain, it was very simple. It might even work. If not, Ballista said, each boat should make for whichever bank seemed good. The final Olbian settlement was not far upriver on an island in the river just below the rapids. They should scatter and try to get there overland, each man for himself.

Maximus half expected Zeno to object. What of the mission? What of the diplomatic gifts, the gold? But the imperial envoy sat motionless in the stern of the second boat, seemingly overwhelmed beyond speech.

The logging camp was well sited. A slight ebb flow helped the four small boats tow the massive expanse of floating timber away from the side, then an eddy pulled it out towards the middle of the river. The main stream took it. Keeping upstream, there was no more to do than use the towing ropes to guide its progress.

As they came to the entrance to the narrows, they pulled up against the raft. Four men from each boat climbed out. Only two had axes; the others would have to use their swords.

The logs were trimmed, with three or four tied together and then lashed to the next group. They dipped alarmingly as Maximus trod on them. He moved with great caution. If your foot slipped between the logs, most likely you would lose your leg.

In the mouth of the narrows the man-made island began to pick up speed. There were sixteen men widely spaced along its leading edge. The Tervingi were not yet in view, hidden by a bend. Ballista gave the signal.

The rope securing the first three logs did not part at Maximus's initial blow, nor at the second or third. His fourth missed, bit into a log. The bobbing footing made it difficult. He wrenched his sword free. This was going to do it no good at all. He struck again. The rope parted. With the flat of his blade, he pushed the detached logs away. He moved back behind the next float.

Maximus worked without pause. He had untethered five or six lots when he heard the scream. One of the Romans from the boat of Diocles had slipped. His leg was trapped between two logs. As the raft moved, the logs ground against his thigh. He sobbed for help. Ballista called for two men from his own boat to try to free the man. Everyone else continued to work.

Maximus went on cutting ropes: seven lots free, eight. After a time the screaming stopped.

'Here come the fuckers.'

The Tervingi were in sight. They had rounded the bend. It was much nearer now, not above five hundred yards.

'Keep working,' Ballista shouted. 'Just a few more.'

Ignoring the pain in his back, ignoring everything but the labour in hand, Maximus swung his notched sword.

'Enough. Back to the boats.'

Maximus sheathed his sword. With the greatest care in the

world, he stepped back over the remaining logs and dragged himself into the boat and back down on to his bench.

'Cast off.'

Maximus took up his paddle. Its handle was polished with his blood and sweat.

'Paddle.'

Reach, stroke, pause – his whole body rebelled as he set to the horrible work again.

He saw nothing but the back of the man to his front, until the steersman angled them across towards the bank opposite the lumber camp. His curiosity could not be denied. He stopped paddling and stood up. Finally able to look downriver, what he saw was good.

Already the main logjam was a distance away, moving at great speed. The river beyond it was full of bobbing baulks of heavy timber. From almost one bank to the other they were swept fast downstream. They surged and clashed together, threatening inexorable destruction to anything in their path. Tervingi boats paddled desperately towards the banks. As Maximus watched like some curious god detached from the sufferings of humanity, one of them disappeared beneath the onrushing doom.

XV

THE RAPIDS ON THE
BORYSTHENES RIVER

Ignominy and discomfort had been piled upon danger, Mount Pelion heaped upon Ossa. The whole journey had been one of constant humiliation for Zeno. Yet this day was the nadir. He found it difficult to imagine how things could get worse.

After the barbarians had been scattered by the timber sweeping down on them, the expedition had reached its next temporary haven in a few hours. The island seemed secure. It was set in a broad expanse of water. There were cliffs on three of its sides. The mooring place was on the fourth. The village, the very last Olbian settlement, was encircled by a deep ditch and tall rampart topped with a rustic but strong-looking stockade.

Great oaks grew on the island and in the centre was a sacred grove with a bucolic temple dedicated to Achilles. Zeno had left his slaves to attempt to make his accommodation vaguely fit for him to occupy. Ballista could deal with the barely Hellenized locals headed by a sly slave trader called Potamis. As Zeno made suitable offerings to the hero for their deliverance, there was a certain equanimity in his mind. He was even toying with the idea of immortalizing their journey in dactylic hexameters, a Homeric epic for a modern *Odyssey*. It could be titled the *Borysthenetica*. Perhaps Achilles might appear to suggest the stratagem of the logs, or Borysthenes stir from his watery sleep. The river god could shake his weed-tangled locks and dash the impious barbarians to destruction – although too much divine intervention might detract from the role of Zeno himself. He knew he had displayed admirable *andreia*; showing quiet courage as others dashed about in near-panic.

The calm of mind necessary for literary composition had been shattered when Zeno had returned to the village. He had found all the expedition drunk; some sleeping, some still gorging themselves with food. All discipline abandoned, they had made swine of themselves with no need for the sorcery of a Circe. When Zeno had remonstrated, Ballista had said the men needed to recover after their exertions. There had been no civility at all in his words. Of course, the barbarian himself had been half drunk, his eyes drooping. Worse yet, Ballista had announced they would not be leaving for three days. He had tried to cloak the innate indolence of his kind with some words about the demanding nature of the river ahead.

When the expedition belatedly pulled out, the first day of travel had not struck Zeno as too daunting. Admittedly, the Borysthenes had narrowed again. There was a ford no wider than the Circus Maximus. But the difficulties of those paddling had more to do with their hangovers than the flow of water against them. Any lingering frowziness was dispelled when they had come to the first rapids. There the majority of the crews had been compelled to strip and get in the chill water to manhandle the boats through. Having been advised they were now in the territory of the Grethungi, a tribe of Goths well disposed to Rome, at least temporarily, Zeno had risked – all alone, with just one of his slaves – taking a bracing walk along the cliff path. It had been amusing to look down from the heights at those below. The men still in the vessels had wielded poles like inexpert acrobats; of those in the water, no more than their heads and shoulders could be seen. Their cries had floated up to him like the calling of seabirds. That evening they had made camp on a small islet. The lapping of water had lulled Zeno to sleep.

The second day there were two more sets of rapids which had to be negotiated in the same fashion. These had been less pleasant. There were no convenient footpaths. To avoid a lengthy detour, with its concomitant risks of going astray or having unwelcome encounters with wild animals and supposedly friendly barbarians, Zeno had been compelled to remain in the boat. As it was hauled forward, the boat had lurched and pitched. He had clung tightly to the thwarts, almost like Odysseus tied to the mast. Twice at the second cataract the clumsiness of those in the water had let the vessel yaw sideways, nearly overturning Zeno into the turbulent river. Needless to say, his cloak and tunic had been sodden. When they pitched camp, it was discovered water had got into his baggage and his changes of clothing were almost equally damp. Zeno had beaten both his slaves, although, mindful of the dangers of loss of self-control, he had first called for his stick and not in any sense given way to anger.

Yet all that had been as nothing compared with the degradation of today. They had come to another run of bad water. The noise was appalling; a constant deep roaring which drowned out all else. The river was nothing but white water and spray seething over jagged rocks. The local Ballista had got to accompany them from the village on the island had called it the Pelican, although Zeno could not imagine why. The shifty-looking fellow had said there was nothing for it but they must unload the boats and carry first them and then the cargo overland.

The portage was no less than three miles. Naturally, Zeno was prepared to make the march. Had his ancestors not tramped the dusty road from Arcadia to Boeotia in full armour to face the Persians and secure the freedom of Hellas at Plataea? Had he ever spared himself as governor of Cilicia? In all weathers he had ventured deep into the mountains to bring justice and the majesty of Rome to boorish and ungrateful villages of goat herders. But this thing today was beyond all reckoning.

The boats had been emptied and a number of small pines felled and trimmed. Ballista, flanked by his two vicious-looking familiars – it was hard to conceive of barbarians uglier than the Hibernian and Suanian – had walked up to where Zeno was sitting pondering the precise metrical requirements of Homeric verse. The barbarian had announced that all hands were needed. If they were to make the portage in one day no one could be exempt – not Zeno's slaves, not even the imperial envoy himself. So unexpected and outrageous was the demand, Zeno had been unable to reply.

At least he had been spared the hauling of the boats; even Ballista had not dared suggest that. It was backbreaking labour, fit only for a slave. They had to make two journeys, moving two vessels each time. Ropes had been tied to the prows and were then turned around trees uphill to act as pulleys. Some men had heaved on these; others lined the gunnels, leaning into the slope, while two unfortunates put their shoulders under the stern of each boat. The fate of the latter, should the weight prove too much, was almost too horrible to contemplate. Zeno had tried to disassociate himself from the whole wretched business by returning to the technical challenges of composition in the Homeric style. Yet even his trained mind had not succeeded. Both times, the squealing of the keels on the pine rollers and the gasps of the men as they dragged each boat a few feet forward, paused and then did it again had proved impossible to ignore until they were almost out of earshot.

It had taken the better part of the day before men made their way back and said that the last boat had been slid into the water upstream of the obstruction. The contents remained to be portaged. Zeno stood by the pack one of his slaves had made. How had his life come to this?

'Time to go,' Ballista announced.

Zeno slipped his arms into the straps and stood up. The pack was very heavy, but he would not be bowed down by it; not in front of his inferiors. He eased the weight on his back, trying to look unconcerned. Inwardly, he was furious with those slow getting to their feet – their laggardliness meant he must bear this burden a fraction longer than otherwise.

'Forward!' Zeno called. He walked around those still struggling to master their loads. The sacred *autocrator* Gallienus had appointed him the leader of this march upcountry. Piece by piece, Ballista had usurped his position. Zeno had to reassert his authority as head of this *anabasis*.

Zeno set off. Obviously, he had not accompanied the two trips hauling the boats, but it was impossible to go wrong. The portage way was marked by scoured earth, trampled vegetation and broken runners.

The slope was not steep but he was encumbered. The wrapped diplomatic gifts and his books bumped awkwardly against his back. Soon the straps were tearing into his shoulders. Zeno suspected the slave had deliberately distributed the weight badly. Tonight, if he had the energy, he would wield his stick until the whipling confessed.

The incline was never-ending. Sweating and panting, Zeno laboured on, leaning his weight on his walking stick. His world had narrowed to the beaten earth just in front of his shambling feet. He was dimly aware of others passing him. He did not care. It was not a race. If he survived this journey, on his return to Rome he would sacrifice an ox to Achilles, and to all the gods. He would feast his friends, and some of his neighbours, clients and freedmen. Garlanded, the blanched skull would be hung in the atrium opposite the doorway, a visible sign for gods and men of his courage and piety. He missed his home. Not his wife. It had been a good match – she had come with a sizable dowry, and her brother had been adlected among the ranks of the *quaestors* by the late emperor Valerian in person – but she was a shrew. It was best when she stayed in the women's quarters or went to visit her prattling friends. He missed his son. The boy had come of age two years before. Zeno had taken him to Delphi to dedicate his lock of hair. Zeno had bought him a pet jackdaw there. The little bird looked so brave hopping about, the miniature shield attached to his leg, the tiny helmet strapped to his head. What Zeno would not give to be at home, to be at ease in his comfortable dining room, the one with the tapestry embroidered with Alexander defeating the Persians. It would be so good to be there, discussing Homer with a few men of culture, possibly playing dice. He felt a great longing for the smooth feel of his dice, the ones made from gazelle horn.

Zeno had to stop. He was finding it hard to breathe. The portage was three miles long. He had to keep moving, like an ass turning a mill wheel. How *had* it come to this? He was a eupatrid. None in Arcadia would dispute his birth. He had done nothing wrong. He was not one of those Hellenes who sneered at Rome, let alone one of those madmen who tried to stir up the ignorant hoi polloi with wild talk of past freedoms and apocalyptic revolution. Some Romans were boorish. Their often-parroted Virgil was a tedious parody of the divine Homer. But the best of the Romans had other virtues. Not culture but the governance of empire was their province. They knew how to humble the proud and spare the vanquished.

More men were passing Zeno. Gripping his staff, he stumbled forward. He did not deserve this cruel exile from all he loved. He had never impugned the *maiestas* of Rome. He was proud to be an equestrian, a *Vir Perfectissimus*. He had served Rome all his life, served her to the best of his ability. He had never let a word be said against the emperor, not even in the homes of his senatorial friends. If he had spoken out too strongly in the imperial *consilium*, it was for the best of motives. He was proud to be friends with men like the great consulars Nummius Faustinianus and Nummius Ceionius Albinus, or the young Patrician Gaius Acilius Glabrio. They were right: the high military commands should not go to ignorant peasants and barbarians risen from the ranks. Rome had grown great when her armies were led by men of *virtus* from the Senatorial *ordo*. Certainly, they should never be under the orders of a hulking barbarian like Ballista. Even his name was uncouth.

'Form on me!' Ballista was bellowing like a bull.

Dazed with his exertions, Zeno leant on his stick, bemused by the sudden commotion. Everywhere, men threw off their loads. They snatched up their weapons and ran unsteadily, stumbling over each other, as if maddened by poisonous honey.

'Get in line!' The pinch-faced midget Castricius was shouting. How could that urchin from the Subura have ever become an equestrian? Now Castricius and the other officers were physically pushing men into place.

Zeno lowered his pack to the ground. He eased the cloth of his tunic away from his raw shoulders and looked about. When he saw the cause of the frenzy, he cursed himself for a fool. He had tempted fate when he imagined things could not get worse.

In the slanting evening light, a solid phalanx of barbarians was drawn up about a discus throw ahead. A huge banner depicting an animal devouring itself floated over the centre of their line. They were fully armed, bright painted shields, metal helmets, sharp spearheads. Big men, blond-bearded – there were hundreds of them. They stood on the flat ground at the crest of the portage, between the expedition and its boats.

As quickly as his stiff limbs and his *dignitas* allowed, Zeno walked up to where Ballista was standing. 'You assured me the Tervingi would not venture as far as the rapids.' He did not try to hide his anger.

'They are Grethungi.'

'But they are meant to be friendly to Rome.'

'Yes, they are meant to be.'

'What are we going to do?'

'That really depends on them.'

Infuriated by the laconic insolence of the barbarian, Zeno choked on the recriminations he wanted to voice.

'Fucking here come fuckers,' said Ballista's Suanian cut-throat in a barbaric almost-Greek.

Unarmed though he was, Zeno was not going to let himself down, not here, surrounded by barbarians. He stood very still and grasped his stout Spartan cane. The twisted wood was slick in his hands. 'Let us be men,' he muttered to himself. 'Let us be men.'

Three warriors walked across towards the expedition. They wore shiny mailcoats and seemed to be wearing the property qualification of an equestrian in gold. Like all barbarians, they were arrogant when fortune favoured them.

Ballista stepped out to meet them. Zeno forced himself to follow.

The foremost Goth said something in their incomprehensible language. He sounded angry.

Ballista said something in reply.

'What did he say?' Zeno spoke in Greek. He was determined to take charge here.

'He said he was Tuluin, son of King Tulga of the Grethungi, and who the fuck was wandering across his father's lands?'

'Tell him I am Aulus Voconius Zeno, envoy to the far north of the noble *autocrator* Gallienus.'

'He knows that.'

The big Goth said something else.

'He says there is a toll for using the portage.'

Zeno felt his anger rising. 'The greed of these barbarians is outrageous. Money was sent to them from Byzantium. Our passage has been paid.'

'They might consider it impolite not to give a gift, and they are in a rather better position than us.' Ballista seemed unconcerned. 'The silver dinner service with the hunting scenes might be well received.'

'That is intended for the king of the Angles.'

'My father has many plates and bowls. He will not miss a few more.'

Zeno looked round to tell one of his slaves to bring the precious things. They were already dragging them out of his baggage. Yet more annoyingly, as they did so they were tossing his treasured papyrus rolls anyhow on the ground. Zeno would let them feel his displeasure later.

The tall Goth called Tuluin examined the embossed huntsmen, hounds and beasts cursorily, passed them to the others. He said something else.

'What?' How could Zeno be expected to conduct diplomacy with people so savage they spoke neither Greek nor Latin?

'He has invited us to a feast. He says our boats make excellent fuel.'

'The boats!' Zeno exclaimed.

'I think he is joking.'

Tuluin smiled. 'Health and great joy,' he said in good Greek.

XVI

GALLIA NARBONENSIS

A gust of wind took the purple hangings, and, before an attendant gathered them, it gave a glimpse outside. Beyond the forum, the emperor Postumus saw the theatre built into the side of one of the hills at the eastern end of Colonia Vienna. It was a fine morning. Briefly, he heard the sounds of the port, and could smell the water.

It would be good to be out on the river. He had always found fishing soothing, ever since his childhood on the Rhine. After the ordeal of the day before he needed to be soothed.

The heavy curtains back in place, a reverent silence and gloom was restored. There was nothing to smell but the incense burning on the sacred fire.

A morning of leisure – fishing, hunting or just staying at home – was out of the question. Postumus was emperor, and an emperor had little leisure and no home. There were always demands on him; he was always in motion. Postumus had arrived only three days ago. Colonia Vienna was one of the leading cities of the province of Gallia Narbonensis, and thus one of the most important communities in his *imperium*. When an emperor arrived, everyone clamoured for justice.

The will of the emperor was law. He could make new laws, ignore, alter or abolish old ones. No jurist would demur. Yet no one was more constrained by the processes of law. This was the first of four days Postumus had set aside to sit in judgement. The *curia* of the town council had been transformed into an imperial courtroom. Postumus sat as judge, the senate as his assessors. They had already heard two cases: a boundary dispute and the unpaid inheritance of an orphan. At least the one before them now was more amusing. It was the sort of thing that pleased Postumus's son. The boy sat forward on his bench, jotting notes.

The son of a local worthy had put on the rough cloak and staff of the Cynic philosophers and taken to their ascetic lifestyle in public. The father had disowned him. The son had brought a case for wrongful disinheritance. The father was speaking in his own defence, upbraiding his son.

'Why are you embarrassing me by begging food from other people when you have a home and a father? Are you training yourself against fortune? What worse can happen? Do you suffer cold and hunger for fear they may happen some day? You and your kind have a new type of ambition – you seek veneration for misery.'

Having ended on a note of righteous indignation, the father glowered across the *curia*, the very embodiment of outraged provincial decorum. Hairy, straggle-bearded and rather dirty, the son stood on the other side, as if virtue itself arraigned. In order of precedence, the assessors murmured their advice. Postumus listened with all signs of attentiveness before delivering his verdict.

'Not all philosophy is hostile to the *mores* of Rome. True lovers of wisdom, those who honestly seek virtue, are at one with the spirit of our age.'

Actually, Postumus had no time for any of them, but an emperor was expected to be a man of culture. It was the sort of thing he should say.

'Philosophy concerns itself with the highest good, the soul of man. Material things it rejects as irrelevant and unworthy of consideration. Therefore, by bringing this case the son has shown he is not a philosopher at all. In which case his father's argument that he has adopted these ways as a form of ambition has validity. The Cynics are the most debased of false philosophers, always yapping against their betters and the established order, outraging public decency. The son should either welcome the removal of the distraction of worldly goods and become a philosopher in reality, or take himself to the baths, put on respectable attire, comport himself according to the station of his birth and seek reconciliation with his father. Having consulted my *consilium*, I dismiss the case.'

As the plaintiff and the defendant were removed, the assessors voiced decorous approval. Postumus regarded the senators benignly. He had never had any intention to invade Italy and attempt to seize Rome. Civil war was to be abhorred. Having been forced to take the purple, he was content to rule over those the gods had allotted to his care. But to have legal authority, an emperor must have his powers voted to him by the senate; without a *Lex de Imperio*, there was no legitimacy. There had been enough senators serving as magistrates or living on their estates in the west for Postumus to constitute his own senate.

Postumus had never hidden his humble Batavian origins. But, unlike Maximinus Thrax, the first emperor to have risen from the ranks of the army, he had no desire to be seen as a military autocrat at odds with the traditional elite. With Gallienus ever more estranged from his own senators, conspicuous respect for rich landowners might bring advantage.

There were more than forty toga-clad senators on the benches around Postumus. The governor of Gallia Narbonensis, Censor, sat on his right hand. The governors of two neighbouring provinces, Honoratianus of Gallia Lugdunensis and Aemilianus of Hispania Tarraconensis, were on his left. All three had held the consulship since Postumus's accession. The *curia* of Colonia Vienna paraded a fine spectacle of loyalty.

As the previous day had shown, loyalty could never be taken for granted. Lollianus was an old friend. He had commanded Legio XXX Ulpia Victrix when Postumus had defeated the Franks at Deuso. He had counselled Postumus to take the purple. His rewards had been vast: money, land and promotion to Prefect of the Imperial Cavalry. No one had stood higher in the regime. Postumus had not wanted to believe the treachery, but the evidence left no doubt. Lollianus had approached an officer, Probinus, in his command. This Liberalinius Probinus had reported everything that Lollianus had said. Postumus was a half-barbarian usurper. He must be struck down, and the west restored to the rightful ruler, Gallienus. Worse yet, Lollianus – the very man who had proposed the horrible deed – had condemned Postumus as the cold-blooded killer of a defenceless child. Lollianus had urged Probinus to think how Gallienus would thank those who brought him the head of the man who had murdered his son, Saloninus.

It had been terrible to watch, but Lollianus had incriminated himself under torture. A man had come to him from Rome. Although dressed as a civilian, Lollianus had known him for a soldier. The *frumentarius* had handed over a letter from Rufinus, the *Princeps Peregrinorum* of Gallienus. It had contained many promises: the consulship, command of Gallienus's *comitatus*, admission to the ranks of the *protectores* and five million sesterces would be granted to Lollianus when he had killed Postumus. As the claws tore his flesh, Lollianus had sworn his innocence. Fear of unjust suspicion was what had stopped him reporting the approach. He had destroyed the letter. The latter was damning. It had been a relief to Postumus, as well as the bloodied hulk of the man on the rack, when he ordered Lollianus executed. The body had been disposed of discreetly.

Haloed by sunshine, the dramatis personae of the next case were ushered into the courtroom.

Gallienus had no monopoly on underhand means. Postumus reflected that his own attempts to suborn Gallienus's supporters continued. Admittedly, the consul Saturninus had feigned incomprehension when approached, and nothing could be expected there. Equally, nothing yet had been reported of the sounding out of the *protector* Carus or the *Praefectus Vigilum* Placidianus, although, in time, things might develop. But, at Mediolanum, the net around Proculus, the commander of the detachments of the Pannonian legions, was cunningly laid. Knowing the reputation of Proculus for lechery, the *frumentarius* had travelled there well disguised as a merchant, with a beautiful woman posing as his wife. Sure enough, Proculus had begun an affair. Now it remained for either the woman to draw Proculus into betrayal or her supposed husband to threaten denunciation to the authorities. Adultery was a serious crime. Gallienus might indulge in it himself, but he could not be seen to condone it in others.

The hangings cut off the light, and the gold-gleaming, perfumed shade of imperial sanctity was restored. Postumus welcomed the interruption to his murky thoughts.

Unlike those earlier, this case involved a capital offence. In fact, there were two conjoined: sacrilege and treason. Faustinus, a Roman senator with wide estates spreading across Narbonensis and Lugdunum, was accused of cutting down a sacred grove and erecting imperial images where corpses were buried. Given the seriousness of the potential consequences for both accused and accuser, depending on the outcome, and the high status of the former, the facts had been carefully scrutinized.

The man bringing the charges performed adoration and answered the formal questions: Name? Race? Free or slave? The water clock was turned, and the accuser began his speech.

Postumus did not need to give it his full attention. He had been thoroughly briefed. The evidence around the *maiestas* charge was ambiguous. The portraits of Postumus and certain past emperors deified for their goodness – Augustus, Trajan and Pius – had been set up in a small building next to a cemetery. But both were surrounded by the same wall. The charge of sacrilege was straightforward. Faustinus was guilty. He had ordered the trees sacred to the gods chopped down. His sole defence would be ignorance.

Faustinus was a rich man from an established family, kin to many senators present in the courtroom. He was not yet bound to the Gallic regime. Postumus had no wish to bend the law to favour the influential, but sometimes the greater good demanded a *clementia* beyond the statutes. Now Lollianus was dead, imperial *mandata* had gone north summoning Lepidus, the governor of Gallia Belgica, to take command of the imperial cavalry. Postumus was minded to appoint Faustinus to the vacant province.

The most pressing of the new duties of Faustinus would be to send detachments of troops south. The gathering of forces on the north Italian plains left no doubt that Gallienus would strike this summer. Postumus considered Gallienus would follow his previous invasion route over the Alps via Cularo down into Narbonensis. Postumus would await him here in the Rhodanus valley at Colonia Vienna. Detachments were being summoned from those provinces currently least threatened by barbarians: Hispania Tarraconensis, Gallia Belgica and Britannia Superior. Should Gallienus take the only other viable route, north into Raetia, Postumus would force-march north and east by Lugdunum, Vesontio and Augusta Raurica. The governor of Raetia, Simplicinius Genialis, would have to hold out as best he could.

The only reinforcements Postumus had been able to spare him were the thousand or so Angles from his German bodyguard. As noble warriors, all Arkil's men were experienced horsemen. Postumus had issued the Angles with mounts and watched them ride off into the mountains. The thought of them made Postumus glance at his bodyguards by the curtains: big, tough Franks. It was strange the ways by which these northern warriors ended up in the heart of the *imperium*. The Franks had come by the terms of a treaty imposed after defeat in battle, the Angles as a result of the treachery of one of their own.

The accuser finished his speech. The water clock was turned again and Faustinus began his defence. Naturally, the senator had not been told his acquittal was a foregone conclusion. Considering he was on trial for his life, Faustinus was making a good showing: weighty, calm and without histrionics. Postumus was impressed. Faustinus had no military experience, but, as the composition of Postumus's bodyguard showed, currently there was nothing to be feared from the Franks and Angles. With only civilian tasks, Faustinus should do well in Belgica.

The acquittal of Faustinus would bring another problem. What to do with his accuser? Bringing a malicious charge on a serious matter – and what could be more serious than sacrilege and treason? – laid a man open to a countercharge of *calumnia*. A jurist had advised Postumus that the penalties for *calumnia* were exile, relegation to an island or loss of status. Postumus had no doubt the accusation had been motivated by money. Avarice most likely lay at the heart of the majority of *maiestas* charges. If a man was convicted of treason, his accuser stood to gain a quarter of his property. That the imperial *fiscus* got the rest was a standing temptation to impecunious and unprincipled emperors. Postumus needed money, never more so now war threatened, but he would not act the tyrant. Besides which, the accuser came from a landed family of equestrian status and was related to several senators loyal to his regime, including his *amicus* Volcatius Gallicanus.

Faustinus timed his oration to perfection. It ended moments before the water clock ran out. The senators gave their opinions. Postumus stroked his beard and listened, for all the world as if he were Pius or Marcus Aurelius. '*Clementia*' was the word most often on the lips of his assessors. Clemency would reign for both parties. Faustinus was exculpated because the sacred grove had fallen into disuse, which might have an element of truth. His accuser was guilty of nothing except excessive loyalty to his emperor. Faustinus would be appointed to Gallia Belgica, and Postumus would have Volcatius Gallicanus assure his kinsman that the failed prosecution had not brought any imperial disfavour; in fact, any reasonable petition he might wish to bring might well be granted. Postumus knew it was hardly the justice Marcus Aurelius might have dispensed, but times were hard. Disaffection had to be avoided with civil war looming and treachery everywhere.

XVII

THE HEADWATERS OF THE VISTULA RIVER

The Grethungi had treated the expedition well. Ballista had liked Tuluin, the son of King Tulga. They had exchanged gifts as between equals: heavy gold arm-rings, cunningly wrought. After a round of feasts, when he had finished entertaining them, Tuluin had accompanied them upriver to the neighbouring Venedi. That people wore clothes like the Sarmatian nomads, but spoke the language and observed the customs of Germania. Their king, too, had shown them hospitality, and then led them on to the lands of the various tribes of the Lugii. Here they had come first to the Helisii, where they had left their boats drawn up on the banks of a tributary of the Borysthenes and continued on horse-back. From there they had traversed the territory of the Naharvali, whose priests dressed as women, and the Manimi, who were more conventional in their religion. Finally, thirty days after the portage of the great rapids, they had reached Mirkwood and the headwaters of the Vistula.

Ballista dismounted before the high-gabled hall of Heoden, the king of the Harii. Without asking permission of anyone in the courtyard, he ordered his men to stable the horses. The guards looked down from the surrounding palisade, and children peered around outbuildings. Ballista stood with Zeno and the eunuch Amantius, and waited. Nothing could be heard from inside the hall, but smoke issued from the smoke holes in the roof. When his men returned, Ballista led them to the iron-bound door of the hall and pushed it open.

The hall stretched away. It was lit by torches and the fire that burned in the central hearth. Long tables and benches ran down both sides, the high table along the far end. The throne behind the latter was unoccupied. Men sat at most of the benches. They were all dressed in black, silent and watchful. It crossed Ballista's mind to wonder what the Greek Zeno behind him was making of all this. Possibly he saw himself as Orpheus or some other hero stepping into the underworld. It was all very familiar to Ballista.

Enough space had been allocated on the left-hand benches for Ballista and those who followed him. Up near the high table, it was an ale-bench of sufficient honour. Ballista led them through the hall. Their boots thumped on the boards of the floor, their spurs and war gear jingled. At the table they remained standing.

An elderly warrior got up from his seat at the foot of the empty throne. He addressed Ballista in formal tones. 'Is this the Dernhelm son of Isangrim who left this hall as a boy of fifteen winters? Despite the beatings we gave him, he remained stubborn and full of boastfulness. Even the famed night-fighters of the Harii could not teach him how to set an ambush, how to move in the dark. He seems little changed except for his years. We heard that, undissuadable by friend or foe, his pride urged him to seize the throne of the Caesars. Once perched there, he found the eminence too high, and threw himself in the dust before a statue of the emperor, sobbing and begging for mercy. Despite that humiliation, he looks around now as if the hall of his foster-father Heoden is beneath him.'

A low *hooming* of approval came from the black-clad warriors of the Harii.

'Gifeca,' said Ballista, 'the drink lends eloquence to your tongue; although your wife always said it unmanned you in other ways. She could tell you how I moved in the dark all those years ago. No wonder she told me that a sober youth was more use to her than a drunken man.'

The Harii snorted into their ale.

Ballista had not finished. 'No whisper has ever reached me of any deeds of Gifeca of the Harii among distant enemies, no perils or ambushes survived by daring swordplay. He has killed a few bare-arsed local tribesmen, but at the mere mention of the red-crested legions of Rome or the fierce Persians, it is said, old Gifeca reaches for more drink or shits himself with fear.'

Now the Harii laughed, banging the tables. Gifeca himself grinned, walked across to Ballista, and enfolded him in his arms. 'It has been a long time, you little shit.'

Finding it hard to speak in the bear hug, Ballista grunted in assent.

The formal flyting over, servants brought in more drink. Ballista got little of it, as many of the Harii who were companions in his youth or were kinsmen of his mother wanted to talk.

No sooner was there a lull than Ballista had to get back to his feet as the king entered the hall. Heoden led his queen by the hand. He stood in front of the throne, she by his side. His hair was white; hers golden. He looked over the hall, and the ale-benches fell silent as he began to declaim.

'Tonight in the hall of the Black-Harii, the Walkers-of-the-Night, we celebrate the return of Dernhelm, son of Isangrim, my sister's son, my foster-son. Since his time among us, no man of the north has travelled further or won higher renown among distant peoples. Like the Allfather his ancestor, he goes by many names. The Romans know Ballista, the Persians tremble at the name Nasu, the Tervingi run from Vandrad. And we feast his Battle-companions. From the way they carry themselves, I am thinking it is not exile but adventure and boldness of spirit which brings them here. They will have many tales to relate as we feast. At no other time is the heart so open to sincere feelings or so quick to warm to noble sentiments. Let the soul of every man here be laid completely bare in the freedom of friendship and festive surroundings.'

As the Harii roared, Heoden seated himself on the dark, rune-carved throne.

Ballista thought the king had pitched far too high the praise of the ill-assorted Romans and Olbians who followed him. The eunuch Amantius had never shown himself possessed of much of an adventurous disposition. Still, the words might well have pleased Zeno, if he had been able to understand any of them.

The queen took the feasting cup, and, as was only right, offered it first to her lord, the guardian of the people. The *theoden* tasted the mead, and pronounced it good. She passed among each part of the hall, offering the treasure-cup to every man according to his rank. After the *eorls* of Heoden had drunk, she came to Ballista.

'Greetings, Dernhelm, son of Isangrim. I give thanks to the gods that my wish has been granted to meet the nephew of my lord.'

Ballista put the cup to his lips. The mead was bright and sweet. The girl was good to look at, her arms very white. She was young, this Myrging princess, Heoden's new wife. Ballista thought of Julia.

The queen looked into Ballista's eyes. 'All hold you in honour, even to the cliffs at the world's end, washed by ocean, the wind's range. As you remember the benevolence of my lord in your youth, so I am sure you will repay answerable kindness to the young sons I have given him, and guard them honourably.'

Ballista said he would. Like his own father, Heoden had married several times. The king of the Harii had older sons from his previous wives. Everywhere in the world where one man ruled, inheritance was a problem. It could not be otherwise, unless by custom the eldest took power, and then an unworthy man might sit on the throne.

Servants brought in food: great platters of roast meats, hot bread. Ballista drank from a silver goblet with scenes of men assaulting a city on it, most likely the seven against Thebes. A thing of great worth, made by a Roman craftsman, it was filled with local beer.

As the drink went round, the warriors became boisterous. Crude jokes and outrageous boasts were joined by hard words. Drinking vessels and fists slammed down to give weight to what was said. A bone was thrown, then another.

The target was an ill-favoured warrior seated at the end of Heoden's hearth-troop near the door. The first missiles went wide, and he tried to ignore them. Those near him edged away. His tormentors were his own companions among Heoden's men. A beef bone caught him on the shoulder. A roar went up. More things were thrown. The victim ducked and tried to fend them off.

Lithe as an eel, Maximus vaulted the table. He caught a bone in mid-air, turned and hurled it back. The warrior who had thrown it was too surprised, too slowed by drink to move. It hit him in the forehead. He crashed backwards like a felled ox.

There was silence in the hall. Warriors got to their feet, reaching for their weapons, outrage in their movements.

Ballista climbed over the table, stood between Maximus and the men on their feet. 'My friend Muirtagh has a good arm and a good heart. The odds seem unfair. It is unseemly for many to persecute one.'

Castricius and Diocles came to stand by Ballista. A moment later, Heliodorus joined them. As the latter moved, the other Romans and some of the Olbians got to their feet. No one had yet drawn a blade, but violence was only a moment away.

'Hold. There will be no fighting in my hall without my word.' Heoden stood. Despite his age, he stood straight and tall. All eyes were on him.

'Your actions show your courage and the nobility in your souls. But you do not know the reasons for this thing. The man you protect swore his sword-oath to me. He was not the least among my warriors. Many times I rewarded his bravery in battle. But Rikiar stole from one of his companions. Now he must sit in the lowest place and endure their taunts until such time as I declare his punishment over. It is that or he must go into exile, sorrow and longing his sole companions.'

Rikiar rose from his place at the foot of the table. 'I was drunk. It was no more than a jest. This dishonour has lasted too long.'

Others of the hearth-troop hissed their disapproval. It was not for Rikiar to speak. They did not trust this outsider, this Vandal. Let him endure or go into exile, a lordless man, a *nithing*.

'Lack of trust, dissension in a sworn-band is a terrible thing. It undermines the shieldwall.' Ballista pitched his voice to carry to the furthest recesses of the hall. 'There is another way. We must travel a long road before we reach my home. We must pass by the Aestii and the Heathobards. They are enemies of my father. The Rugii pay him tribute, but they do not love me. Another sword in our company would be welcome. If Heoden, the Master of Battle, will release this Vandal from his oath, and, if Rikiar is willing, let him swear a new oath to me, here in this hall, in the sight of all.'

'I am willing,' said Rikiar.

'To release a man from his vow is no light thing,' said Heoden. 'But let it be as Dernhelm wishes.'

As it will when men are drunk, the mood changed in a moment. The Harii shouted praises of their lord, of Dernhelm, even of the recently reviled Rikiar: the Vandal might be light-fingered and ugly, but he could fight. Bring out the gift-stool. Do it now. All would stand witness.

Ballista drew his sword. He sat on the gift-stool and laid his blade across his knees. It was notched from its hard use on the Borysthenes.

'Wait,' said Heoden. 'It was in my mind to welcome my foster-son with a gift. Bring me Battle-Sun.'

Gifeca took the sword down from where it hung with the others behind the throne and passed it to his king.

Heoden unsheathed the steel. 'This blade was forged in ages past by the Brisings. It was won from them by Wade, the sea-giant. The hero Hama wielded it at Fifeldor and Bravoll. From his hand it was given to Helm, the founder of my line. Now I, Heoden of the Harii, give it to Dernhelm, my sister's son. May he carry it with heart and courage.'

'Heart and courage!' the warriors bellowed.

Ballista sheathed his own blade and put Battle-Sun across his legs.

Rikiar knelt, his head against Ballista's knees, his hands on the sword. Ballista put his hands over those of Rikiar.

'By this sword, I, Rikiar, son of Rikiar of the Vandals, swear my oath to you, Dernhelm, son of Isangrim of the Angles. As I eat at your hearth, so I will follow you into terrible battle, among the perils where renown is won. I will defend and protect you. If you fall, I will not leave the field alive, or suffer lifelong infamy and shame.'

After the oath, Ballista led Rikiar back to sit among his men. Much more drink was taken, but the feast proceeded in the most amicable fashion. It was as if every man saw how narrowly violence had been banished from the hall, and none wished it to return. Sometimes it was better to eat and drink than to fight.

When men were beginning to reel and put their hands on the serving girls, Heoden summoned Ballista. The queen had retired to her bedchamber. Heoden waved Ballista to sit by him.

'You look well, boy.'

'As do you, uncle.'

The king grinned drunkenly. 'You have got better at lying among the Romans.'

Several Harii *eorls* on the high table laughed.

'How is my mother?' Ballista asked.

'Old, like me. But she is well. As always, she keeps your father's hall in Hlymdale. Your father still moves between there and his Frisian wife at Gudme. Now he is even older than me, he travels less. Last year he did not go to his *eorls* on Latris. It is two summers since he went to the mainland. He should take another young wife to keep his bed warm, like me.'

'It will be good to see them.'

'Good to see Kadlin . . .'

Ballista felt light-headed from the mead and beer. 'That was long ago.'

Heoden looked at Ballista over the top of his drink. 'That first husband of hers – the one she married straight after you left – pity he took an Aestii spear in the guts. She has been married to your half-brother a long time now.'

'Hmm.' Ballista took another drink.

'Oslac will not be overjoyed to see you return.'

'We were very young – a long time ago. I never had a problem with Oslac.'

Heoden pulled a wry face. 'Not long enough for him to forget who took the virginity of a girl who is now his wife, all those winters ago.'

'How –'

'I did not know – not until right now.' Heoden smiled, pleased with himself. 'You do not hold the throne of the Black-Harii without some low cunning.'

The black-clad *eorls* laughed indulgently.

Ballista raised the silver goblet to the king.

'Morcar always had a problem with you – with Froda, Eadwulf and you.'

'Yes.'

'Take no offence, but Froda was the best of you.'

'I always thought so.'

Heoden put his arm around Ballista's shoulder, pulled him close. 'I was going to talk about this tomorrow, when we were sober, but . . .' The king shrugged.

'The Persians discuss great matters twice: first drunk, then sober.'

'You have been in many places.' Heoden squeezed Ballista's shoulder. 'Do not talk about it too much now you are back. Men do not care to be reminded that others have won greater renown.'

Ballista nodded in acknowledgement.

Heoden leant in, the fumes of his breath sickly in Ballista's nostrils.

'Things are not good in the realm of the Himlings. Gallienus has sent no gold since your half-brother Arkil and his men swore their swords to the other Roman emperor in Gaul.'

'I know this. The emperor Gallienus told me in the letter ordering me home.'

'There were Roman soldiers where none should have been. It is said Arkil was betrayed.'

'Who?'

'Old wives' tales. No one knows.' Heoden paused as a girl filled their cups.

'Postumus sends your father no gold. It is said the Gallic

emperor has none to spare. Why should he open his treasure hoard, when he holds a thousand Angles hostage? Your father is old. Isangrim has less gold to give, less swords at his command. The Himlings' grip on the Suebian Sea has weakened. The Brondings of Abalos follow a new leader, a fearsome, masked warrior from overseas. This warrior Unferth has cast off your father's authority. The men of the islands – the Wylfings of Hindafell, the Geats of Solfell – have hailed him Amber Lord. Unferth's longships raid where they will around the shores. Last summer Unferth's son descended on the Heathobards. But those loyal to the Himlings – the Farodini, the Dauciones – they have suffered with the rest. I fear this will be a bitter homecoming for you.'

PART THREE

Hyperborea,

Summer AD264

XVIII

THE VISTULA DELTA

Escape from the river was not easy. The Vistula reached the Suebian Sea in a wide delta. It twisted and turned, dividing and redividing into any number of channels. They were hard to distinguish from the narrow creeks which coiled away, turning back on themselves, to end in mudflats or vanish into impassable reed banks. Ballista had been here before, but that was no help. It had been more than twenty years, and the navigable waterways had shifted out of all recognition. There were no discernible landmarks. Visibility was limited by the reeds and half-submerged trees. The open stretches of water frequently were obstructed by fish traps and weirs. The passage was slow going. It demanded skilled handling of the boat, much patience and faith in the taciturn river pilot they had taken onboard at Rugium. The last was somewhat hard to maintain, as they seemed to spend as much time going in every other direction as towards the north.

As the dawn mist lifted, Ballista saw a beauty in this strange landscape, where fresh- and saltwater merged with land, where sand martins and tern darted and bitterns boomed.

'Another fucking great marsh,' said Maximus.

The journey down had not been particularly quick. It was twenty days since they had left the hall of the king of the Harii. But almost all of it had been easy, pleasant even. Heoden had given his foster-son a longboat, well founded and packed with supplies. Two warriors of the Harii had asked permission to accompany them. Wada the Tall and Wada the Short were brothers; Ballista had known them in his fostering. They were amiable company. Both knew well the upper and middle courses of the river, and they had sailed the sea beyond.

Even in the spring – it was now late May – the Vistula did not run particularly fast. But until the delta it was usually a single broad stream, and posed no problems. It had borne them along in great sweeps. The weather had been kind. There had been some grey days, when the water and sky had the same colour, but once they had emerged from Mirkwood on to the less forested great plain of northern Germania the scale of the purpled sunrises and sunsets had never failed in their majesty.

They had travelled through the territory of several tribes: Ombrones, Avarini and Frugundiones. Always Wada the Tall and Wada the Short had secured them generous hospitality. In each settlement Ballista had found himself the object of much curiosity: the son of Isangrim the Himling, the warrior at bloodfeud with the Goths of both the Tervingi and Borani, the northerner who had defeated the Persian king and who had briefly raised himself to the throne of the Romans. In one hall a *scop* had gone so far as to compose and sing a heroic version of his travels, almost unrecognizable even to Ballista himself. All the interest, bordering on adulation, had not been completely uncongenial. He was returning to his world, although such attention had showed that world now regarded him as something strange. He was no longer wholly part of the north.

Another thing slightly unsettling Ballista's equanimity had been the foul mood of Maximus. The Hibernian had said it was just the watersnakes. There had been a surprising number of them in the Vistula, long, grey and shiny. They left a curved, overlapping twin wake when they swam, their black heads cocked evilly out of the water. Ballista knew the snakes had not been explanation enough. Despite their continual bickering, Maximus had got on well enough with Calgacus. The old Caledonian Calgacus had been with Ballista for ever. And over the years, Maximus had welcomed the Greek *accensus* Demetrius, Castricius and the demented Suanian Tarchon into the *familia*. But clearly he resented the rekindled intimacy from Ballista's youth with the brothers Wada. At times the Hibernian was like a child – albeit a very dangerous and often very drunken child with a strong liking for cannabis. In many ways he had not been quite the same since old Calgacus died. Perhaps none of the *familia* would ever be quite the same.

The only place where the welcome had been less than wholehearted had been at Rugium, the last port of call before the sea. The Rugii were vassals of the Himlings of Hedinsey. They had not chosen that allegiance. The last time Ballista had been in Rugium it had been as part of an Angle-conquering army. In the sack of the settlement twenty-six winters before, Ballista had behaved no better than might be expected of a half-drunk youth who had just fought his way over a stockade into a now-defenceless town. He wondered what had happened to the girl. It would have been both tactless and pointless to ask. He had not known her name. It had been in one of the longhouses in the centre. Her clothes had marked her of high birth. Perhaps there had been a child. That would not identify her; that day, far too many women had been taken against their will.

To be fair, the Rugii had done their duty by their overlord, Isangrim. They had feasted his son and the men Ballista brought with him for two nights, although they had offered not much drink and no women or gifts. They had provided the river pilot. Yet things had not been convivial. The king of the Rugii had complained at length of the depredations of Unferth of Abalos. Late last autumn the masked warrior and his son Widsith Travel-Quick had led their Brondings, along with Wylfings, Geats and Dauciones, along the coast. They had killed, enslaved and burned. Early this spring, just after the ice had gone, one of their ships had been sighted scouting the delta. It was the obligation of Isangrim, if he wished to remain the Amber Lord, to protect those, like the Rugii, who paid him tribute. If Ballista reached his father, he should tell him these things.

Ballista sat in the prow, looking at a heron picking its way near the bank. He had not cared for the message of the king of the Rugii: not its unwelcome news that the Dauciones had joined those who had cast off their allegiance to the Himlings, not its implicit threat, and not its conditional nature. *If he reached his father . . .*

The heron took wing, implausible in its forward-weighted profile, yet oddly graceful. *If he reached his father . . .*

They rounded a bend, the starboard oars almost touching a line of stakes holding a fisherman's nets. The surface was getting choppier. The banks fell back. At last, they must be nearing the open waters of the gulf which gave on to the sea.

'Ahead.' Maximus did not need to raise his voice. He was proprietorily next to Ballista.

'There,' said Wada the Short, pointing.

Maximus glowered at him.

Ballista stood, held the prow and climbed on to the freeboard.

Ahead, the water sparkled in the sun. It widened out into a bay. There were two low islands between them, and the gulf beyond.

And moored by the islands were two longships. The dark, curved and double-prowed profiles left no doubt.

'Stop rowing.' Ballista spoke quietly, even though the warships were almost a mile away. 'Take the way off her with your oars.' He turned to the pilot. 'Whose are they?'

'I do not know.'

Ballista stared at him. The boat lay dead in the water.

'They could be Brondings.' The Rugian licked his lips, his eyes evasive.

As Ballista went to study the ships, the pilot spun around, took two or three scrambling steps and hurled himself over the side. He landed clumsily in a fountain of spray.

Without thinking, riding the sudden rocking of the boat, Ballista shrugged his baldric over his head, unbuckled his sword belt. Scabbards and belts clattered to the deck. He went to the gunwales. Stopping, he dragged off his boots. There was a splash as someone else dived.

The pilot was swimming for the larboard bank, about fifty paces away.

Ballista dived.

The river was still very cold. He came up spluttering, swallowed some water and, coughing, struck out after the Rugian pilot.

The fugitive was near the shore. Another swimmer was almost up with him. Ballista concentrated on swimming. He was strong in the water, but his sodden clothes hindered him, dragged him back.

The Rugian was wrestling with someone, thrashing wildly. Ballista caught the Rugian's hair, pulled his head back, under the surface. In the struggle they both went under.

In the green, dark world the man's face was pallid. His eyes were wide. Weeds clutched at them. The man clawed at Ballista's eyes. Forcing the hand aside, Ballista tried to get a grip on his throat. The man had him by the arm. Twisting, entwined together, they sank to the riverbed. Clouds of silt billowed up around them. Ballista's lungs were hurting, his ears throbbing.

Another shape in the gloom. The hold on Ballista vanished. He shot up, broke the surface, sucking in air. The head of the Rugian appeared. It was twisted in pain. Maximus surfaced behind him, closing in again.

'Do not kill him!' Ballista shouted.

Maximus enveloped the pilot, driving him back under. Ballista was unsure if the Hibernian had heard.

Ballista took a deep breath and prepared to dive again.

Maximus bobbed up. He had the Rugian. The latter was curled, not fighting. Maximus spat and grinned. 'He will not die. I just gave his balls a little squeeze.'

Wada the Short swam to them. Maximus stopped smiling. Together they got the Rugian back to the boat. The crew hauled them aboard, the Rugian roughly.

'Tie his hands.'

Water sluicing off him, Ballista went to the prow. Both long-ships were pulling towards them. Brondings or not, their intention was obvious.

'Reverse positions.' Ballista retrieved his boots, sat to pull them back on.

The helmsman had already got the steering oar at the stern inboard. He rushed past, slotted the other one into position. The rowers reversed their places on the benches.

'One, two, three – row.'

The blades bit the water. The boat seemed to hesitate, then edged forward. With the second stroke, it gathered way. In moments they were gliding fast away from the threat. It was one of the beauties of a double-prowed northern warship.

'Bring the pilot here.' Ballista walked to the new prow, strug-gling back into his sword belt.

Maximus thrust the bound Rugian to his knees. Wada the Short gave the captive a clout around the head.

Ballista leant down, took hold of the man's chin, tipped it up. With his other hand he drew his dagger, ran it across the man's throat with just enough pressure to cut the skin. He held the bloodied point just in front of the man's left eyeball.

'I want there to be no misunderstanding between us. If they catch us, you will be the first to die.'

The Rugian said nothing.

'Take us back into the delta. Find us somewhere to hide. You know these waters; the Brondings do not.'

Ballista touched the eyelid with the dagger. 'Will you do this?'

'Yes.'

'Tie him to the prow. Diocles, watch him. Maximus, help me arm. Those with mailshirts, make your choice whether to wear them.'

The pursuing longboats were still about half a mile behind when the boat slid around a bend and they were lost to sight.

The marsh closed around them. The green water ran down the sides of the boat. There were no sounds of pursuit, just the splash of their oars in the water, the creak of the rowlocks, the breathing of the rowers. The pilot conned them, just loud enough to carry the length of the boat to the helmsman.

Perfidy aside, the Rugian knew his calling. Watching the colour of the water, he guided them this way and that, ever deeper into the labyrinth of the delta. At length, he had them pull towards what looked to be a solid bank. The keel scraped through mud. Parting the hanging branches of two willows, they emerged into an isolated backwater. Midges were thick in the air. Black vegetation wrapped itself around the blades, weighting them down. Some duck flapped up off the surface and wheeled away. After fifty or so strokes, the channel forked. The pilot guided them to the left. The little channel dog-legged, then opened into a still, black pool.

There was a dilapidated hut. They ran the boat up next to it. Castricius, Tarchon, Rikiar and the Wada brothers swarmed ashore. The rowers and steersman reversed positions. Ballista and Diocles jumped out, ready to push off. They waited, tense, as the landing party searched the hut and its surroundings. Maximus kept a blade to the throat of the Rugian.

Satisfied there was no one in the vicinity, Castricius waved them ashore. There was no need to tell anyone to be silent, not even Zeno, Amantius or their slaves.

Ballista sent Tarchon and Rikiar struggling back through the mud and undergrowth to keep watch where the channel divided, and posted Wada the Tall and two of the Romans as sentries away from the water. When they were in position, Ballista got out of his war gear and soaking clothes. Maximus and Wada the Short did the same. Naked, they towelled themselves down and put on dry things from their chests. Nothing else was unloaded from the boat.

The sun arced up across the sky. The duck returned. There were moorhens on the pool as well.

Ballista went and spoke to the Rugian. 'Your king betrayed us to them?'

'Perhaps. I do not know. There are several passages to the gulf. He told me to use that one, take my time getting there.' He stopped abruptly, as if reluctant to say more.

'What?'

'If I tell you, will you spare me?'

'That depends.'

'The news of your coming ran long before you. There was another Angle here. He left just two days before you arrived.'

'One of my brothers?'

'No. A tall, thin warrior. He wore a hood. I did not talk to him. He did not dine in the hall. He spoke with the king alone. Then he left in a small boat. But there was a longship out in the roads.'

Ballista mulled this over, but could make little of it.

'Will you let me go?'

'This is what will happen. We will lay up here until dark. Tonight you will take us out by unfrequented ways. There are many channels out of the delta. The Brondings cannot be watching them all. If we get clear, I will put you ashore somewhere to the west.'

'If not?'

'Use the daylight to plot our course.'

'If we run into them?'

'You will die.'

XIX

THE VISTULA DELTA

Snakes were everywhere on this river, big fuckers, absolutely fucking everywhere. Maximus knew he should get some rest. There would be none to be had tonight. But in this dismal marsh it was hard to find a place where a snake could not get at you. Most of the crew had stretched out on the bank near the hut, dozing in the sun. That was just asking for trouble. The snakes could swim, and the boat had a low freeboard, so that was no good either. The idea of a pointed black head, forked tongue flicking, eyes full of malice, sliding over the gunnels, thick, grey body coiling after, slithering up while you slept, all defenceless, was too horrible to contemplate. Fuck, he hated snakes.

Maximus could not settle. He went and sat with Ballista. One of the half-witted Harii, the taller one, was droning on about one of his relatives who was a shape-changer. When the fellow went to sleep his spirit roamed the woods in the form of a bear. Absolute fucking nonsense. Perhaps the Greeks and Romans, like that little shite Zeno over there, were right and northern barbarians were stupid beyond belief. Of course, the southerners did not know much about Hibernians. Not many of them came to the island, and quite a few that did had not been alive to leave.

Some cannabis would have been good. But with the gods knew how many longboats full of Brondings combing the delta there could be no lighting a fire. Cold food and no cannabis: it was going to be a long day. It seemed an eternity since he had had a woman. Now the other of the Harii, the short-arsed one, was talking about another relative. Apparently this one wore women's clothing to help him communicate with whatever benighted gods haunted the forest. It appeared that holding a horse's severed cock helped the process. Maximus had had enough of this.

Saying he would stand watch, Maximus left. Having collected some things from his pack on the boat, he made his way to where the creek divided. It was hard going, mud sucking at his boots. He used his sword to probe the reeds for snakes. You could never be too careful.

Rikiar thanked him, and went back. At least the Vandal did not yap like an old woman; not like those Harii. Actually, he was too quiet. He needed watching. If he stole anything from Maximus, it would be more than a few mutton bones around his ears the fucker would be getting.

Maximus hunkered down with Tarchon to watch. The Suanian took his duties seriously and was quiet. The water was still, black in the sun. The reeds meant you could not see far. It was more a matter of listening.

From nowhere came a feeling of loneliness. Maximus missed Calgacus. Odd, he never had when the miserable, ugly bastard was alive. The old Caledonian might have moaned the whole fucking time, but you could trust him. Not like a light-fingered Vandal or a couple of superstitious Harii. It had been better when the *familia* was just the three of them: Maximus, Calgacus and Ballista.

Chewing some air-dried beef, Maximus fished out the one book he owned, Petronius's novel, *The Satyricon*. He unrolled the bulky papyrus at random. It was the dinner of Trimalchio, the part where the host tells the story of the midnight hags stealing the body of a baby. It reminded Maximus of something. He scrolled back. Yes, there it was: the story of the soldier who was a werewolf. Gods below, the Romans were no better than a bunch of Harii barbarians from a forest in the middle of fucking nowhere. At times Maximus wished he had never had to leave his own people.

In the mid-afternoon, Maximus and Tarchon were relieved. Back at the boat there was much to be done. Ballista had ordered the oars muffled and the rowlocks greased. The men had to stow all the metal ornaments from their gear and wrap rags around the fittings of their scabbards and bowcases. They were to wear dark cloaks, hoods pulled up over their helmets and blacken their faces and hands. The order was inclusive. Maximus enjoyed watching Zeno and the eunuch Amantius having river mud rubbed into their delicate skins by their slaves.

The sun was low when they set out. The boat glided from shadow to shadow through bands of golden light, hazed with insects. The water was thick with blown leaves, solid like amber. Beyond the screen of willows, they turned south.

Maximus crouched by the pilot. He kept the short sword below the side of the boat, but let the man see it. Ballista was on the other side of the Rugian, the latter once again tethered to the prow.

The sun went down, and they threaded their way in near-darkness. The smells of rotting vegetation and wet mud lay over the tallow and pitch rising from the boat. It was deathly quiet, every slight noise amplified: the run of water down the sides, the soft splash of the oars, the scuttle and plop of night creatures taking to the river, and the hiss of the breeze shifting the reeds. At the pilot's whisper, they turned now left, now right. Lost, unsure of their heading, Maximus was far from trusting the Rugian. He felt the smooth leather of the hilt, reassuring in his hand.

A light showed through the trees ahead. A yellow-orange fire flickering just above the water level some way off. Maximus readied himself to kill the Rugian without sound. No one else seemed concerned. He looked again. It was the moon, enormous, just past full. Moving branches made its light into dancing flames.

Time lost all meaning. The carved head on the prow led them onward, like a stern deity guiding them to some unalterable fate.

The moon had risen free of the trees. Its light made the shadows along the banks impenetrably black. But when they emerged they could not have been more exposed.

Maximus smelt the open sea long before the guide murmured for utter silence. One more turn and they would be at the mouth of the channel.

Keeping to the shallows, tight against the shore, the boat nosed around the bend. A soft indrawn breath from those at the prow. Ballista gestured back down the boat. The noise of the oars in the water was fearfully loud as they stopped the boat.

Not a hundred paces ahead were two moored longboats.

Maximus covered the pilot's mouth with his left hand; with his right he brought the blade to the man's throat.

The warships had their awnings rigged to shelter their crews as they rested for the night. No sound came across the water. But low on the mast of each a lantern burned. In the bright moonlight there could be no sneaking past if so much as a single one of the Brondings was alert.

The boat drifted slightly. Maximus felt the pilot's breath hot and damp in his palm. His own breathing rasped in his throat. They were near the edge of the moonlight. Ballista had to make the decision now.

As Maximus watched, one of the lanterns blinked as a figure

crossed in front of it. Ballista had seen it as well. Quiet as a wraith, the big northerner moved back through the boat, motioning to the men on the benches.

Every creak sounded like thunder as the rowers, with all the care in the world, pushed against their oars. Maximus's eyes never left the darkness on the longship where the moving shadow had vanished. The man had to hear their blades leave the water, slide in again.

Slowly, slowly, the boat inched sternwards. No alarm rang out. As they gathered a little momentum, the noise increased. The best oarsmen in the world could not back a boat without making a sound. Still no alarm. The deck heeled a little as the steersman brought them around.

A bank of reeds slid across the view of the warships like a curtain. An all too audible sigh of relief, hurriedly shushed.

There would be thumps and bangs if the crew reversed their positions. Instead the starboard oarsmen braced their blades in the water, while the larboard ones rowed circumspectly. With the steering oar hard over, the boat came about in a little over its own length. They stole away south again like thieves in the night.

In the contingent safety of the delta, they pulled into a sidewater and brought the vessel to a halt. They did not anchor or go to the bank. They rested on their oars. The water lapped at the sides.

Ballista did not threaten or bluster. He spoke to the pilot as if they were old comrades-in-arms, this just the latest of many desperate ventures they had shared. Was there another obscure channel to the gulf, one the Brondings might have overlooked, one which they could reach before daybreak? The Rugian pondered the proposition. To give the man his due, he was calm, took his time, gave it his full consideration. Yes, there was one further west, but coming to it involved several detours. They would be lucky to be there before dawn. It was both shallow and narrow, thus little frequented except by a few marsh-dwelling fishermen. At this time of year there should be just enough clearance for the boat. But there could be no guarantee the Brondings did not know of its existence. If they were aware of it, everything would depend on their numbers – if they had sufficient ships to blockade it as well as the more obvious places.

Decisions are easy, Maximus thought, when there are no real alternatives.

Like neophytes of some gloomy and clandestine sect, they followed the wooden idol carved on the prow through the marsh again. They moved through an unchanging landscape. The water was glossy and black. The drops from the oars shone like jewels in the moonlight. On either side, reedbeds slid past, the stalks bone-white, the feathery heads black and clear as if etched in metal. Down at water level, the wind had dropped. Up above, clouds chased across the haloed moon.

Again, time had loosed its moorings, drifted away into something immeasurable. The rhythmic creak and splash of the oars, the water slopping down the sides of the boat, lulled Maximus into an altered state. It was like the calm that came over him in battle, but less urgent and more reflective.

If they were alive and not captured, this time tomorrow, Ballista would be well on his way home. The Harii Wada brothers were drawing him back into that world. But Maximus was concerned it would not go well for his friend. All those years in the *imperium* had changed Maximus. They would have changed Ballista, too. And, leaving aside the nonsense about amber, there was the mission. The Angles were now allied to Postumus. Ballista was tasked with turning them against him, bringing them back into friendship with and obedience to Gallienus. Given the hostages held in Gaul, Ballista's father and remaining half-brothers were unlikely to welcome that idea. Ballista had said nothing on the subject – the time in the *imperium* had taught him discretion – but Maximus had little doubt that if the king of the Angles refused to alter his allegiance, the imperial *mandata* ordered Ballista to replace him with someone more amenable. In Sicily, Ballista's wife and sons were in the power of Gallienus. There could be no question of Ballista ignoring the *mandata*. If it came to overthrowing his father, there would be blood. A terrible burden came with patricide.

The mist rose just before dawn. At first, thin tendrils coiled up, then banks lay across their path. As the sky lightened, they voyaged through an opaque cloud. Beads of moisture stood on the men's hair and clothes. The pine of the prow was damp to the touch. The trees floated above, unconnected to the earth.

'We are there,' the pilot whispered.

The boat shifted as it quickened to the patterns of the wider waters.

The familiar presence of the enclosing treetops faded astern. They rowed in silence through the clinging whiteness. Everyone was taut, straining their senses against the enveloping fog.

A skein of geese flew overhead, wings whirring, calling their eerie calls. After their raucous passage, the oars were loud in the surrounding quiet.

Off the starboard bow, above the mist was a tree that was not a tree. Tall, straight, with a crossbeam, shrouds hanging down. With no order, Wada the Short at the steering oar swung them to the left away from the mast.

With infinite caution, they rowed on.

Another mast, dead ahead, no more than fifty paces. They curved back to the right.

If the gods were kind and the mist held, they might yet pass undetected between the ships.

Maximus could hear nothing but the gentle slop of the oars and the harshness of his own breathing. They crept forward. Slowly, slowly, the masts fell behind.

The wind came out of the north. It snatched the fog away.

They were alone on a sparkling sea. The great wall of fog was retreating towards the land.

'Pull!' hissed Ballista. 'Full pressure.'

Suddenly, as if formed from the fog itself, the two longships appeared astern, their carved, painted figureheads turning towards the fleeing vessel as the wind swung them on their sea anchors.

The deck lifted under Maximus's feet as the boat surged forward. Foam creamed up from under the bow.

The Bronding warships had striped awnings, red and blue, bright in the sun, furled sails in the same colours aloft. Two men stood on the prow of the nearer one, no more than a hundred and fifty paces away. But their backs were turned. They were watching the fog bank recede towards the land. It would be a fine thing, Maximus thought, if they escaped unseen after all.

A hoarse shout. A man on the further ship had half climbed the prow. He was pointing, hallooing. The sentinels on the nearer one spun around. They stood as if unable to comprehend the apparition of the ship to seaward. Then pandemonium broke out. Men swarmed over the Bronding decks. Horns rang. The awnings began to be hauled down. It would take them a time to get ready, win their anchors, but Maximus knew their lead would be slight.

Ballista was calling orders. The *Warig* was a ship with twenty benches. The thirty-two remaining Roman and Olbian crew had filled only sixteen of them. Now Ballista sent the Vandal Rikiar, Wada the Tall, Tarchon and the five slaves to take the empty places. As they unshipped their oars – some of the slaves with no great dexterity – Maximus joined Diocles in doubling up on the two bow oars.

Beyond the rising and falling stern, Maximus could see the Brondings. While the further one had yet to move, the nearer had already run out its oars and was getting under way. The improvident bastards must have slipped their anchor. It was a big vessel, probably thirty or more benches. If they had additional warriors aboard, they could put two men on some of their oars. Most of the Brondings would have slept. The crew of the *Warig* had been rowing all night; not hard, but they would soon tire. Pulling into the wind, the chase could not last long.

Over his shoulder Maximus could hear both Zeno and Amantius muttering prayers where they huddled among the stores in the bow: 'Athena . . . Achilles . . . Zeus . . . Poseidon.' Hieroson, the injured Olbian guide, who had been with them, hobbled past, and settled to give what help he could to another oar. Maximus had been right to judge that he was a man of some account, unlike the Greek and the eunuch.

At the prow, Ballista and Castricius were talking to the Rugian. The urgent invocations and promises in Greek prevented Maximus hearing what was being said. 'Grey-eyed Athena, hold your hands over me. Swift-footed Achilles, turn your anger aside. To Zeus, an ox for my safety.' Sure, all gods liked to be offered things, but Maximus thought they were more likely to aid those who helped themselves. And it would be good if Zeno and Amantius sought divine intervention on more than just their own behalf. Actually, a local deity or two might be more use. It could be the Greek gods did not spend much time up here in Hyperborea. From what he understood, they spent most of their time drinking, fucking and squabbling among themselves anyway; all that, and abducting pretty boys and girls. A feckless crew from which to seek salvation.

The man next to Maximus on the larboard bow oar was the Egyptian Heliodorus, the mutineer Ballista had nearly killed. Once Maximus had got into time, he looked down the boat, out past Wada the Short on at the helm. The big Bronding longship was not much more than a long bowshot away, maybe three hundred paces. It was coming on in unpleasantly fine style, its banks of oars rising and falling all together, like the wings of a grey goose.

If there were any comfort to be drawn from the view, it was the other Bronding. The yet bigger warship – fifty benches at least, a huge vessel – had still to move. The useless fuckers must have fouled their anchor. Unless they cut or slipped the rope and abandoned the thing, they would soon be out of the reckoning.

Ballista walked the length of the boat to stand next to the steering oar. He stood, feet wide, hands hooked in his sword belt, riding the rise and fall. His long blond hair streamed out from under his helm and his black cloak whipped around him. His dark mailcoat shimmered in the sun. He looked a proper warleader, the sort men would follow.

'Boys' – Ballista spoke in Greek. He shouted into the wind but his voice carried easily over the noises of the boat – 'there are some islands up ahead, about a mile. The Rugian says there is one small channel through them. The *Warig* has a shallow draught. We should make it. The Bronding will have a tougher time. If they cannot follow us, it is a long way around. Either they get stuck fast, or they give us a lead of an hour or two.'

Ballista repeated the news in the language of Germania.

Despite their efforts in rowing, the crew gave a low cheer. Maximus hoped it carried to their pursuers. No one cares to know that their enemy are in good heart.

'The pilot says the prevailing wind here is easterly. When it shifts later in the morning, we can hoist the sail and test my foster-father's claim that the *Warig* can out-sail anything in the north, and you delicate girls can take a rest.'

Again, Ballista repeated it for those who did not have Greek. Again, it was well received. Maximus thought the crew in good spirits. If only the two *Graeculi* would shut the fuck up, things might not be too bad.

The northerly breeze competing with an easterly current was beginning to raise a choppy, cross sea. Some of the slaves down towards the stern were making a balls of it, but Heliodorus was a skilled oarsman and Maximus got into a good rhythm with him.

Gouts of cold water broke inboard, soaking Maximus and the foremost rowers.

'It is warmer in the Mediterranean.' Heliodorus timed his words to the stroke. 'I should have joined the Alexandrian fleet.'

'They have a good reputation. I doubt they would have had you.'

'It is true; there were one or two misunderstandings in Alexandria.'

Out of the corner of his eye, Maximus could see the big, shaven-headed Egyptian was smiling. A good man in a corner; maybe it was as well Ballista had not killed him.

The rear benches of rowers jeered. Maximus did not know why, until he saw a bowman on the prow of the Bronding. The man drew and released. The shaft went wide and well astern. They had closed to about two hundred and fifty paces, but from a pitching deck it would take the gods' own luck to hit anything at that distance. There were more jeers from the *Warig*.

'Save your breath, boys,' Ballista called. 'Nearly there.'

Careful not to break stroke, Maximus took a look over his shoulder. They seemed to be racing directly towards a belt of trees growing straight out of the sea. He hoped that fucking Rugian knew what he was about, was not playing them false. Still, he was only a couple of steps away. He would not have long to get any pleasure from treachery.

The surface was calm in the lee of the island. The *Warig* shot forward. Trees appeared on either side, closing in fast.

'Full pressure,' Ballista said. 'Keep the rhythm.'

They were rushing down a narrow creek, the oars almost brushing the banks, weeds festooned around the blades. The breeze did not play through here, and there was a foul stench of decay and dead fish.

The *Warig* heeled, as Wada the Short put the helm over. Maximus saw the Bronding. Throwing a fine bow wave, about two hundred paces astern, it had no intention of breaking off and going around the islands. The *Warig* took the bend, and the Bronding disappeared.

A tremor ran through the hull. Another stroke, and the *Warig* shuddered to a stop, as if clutched by an invisible hand. Maximus was thrown off the bench. He landed in the bow in the lap of the eunuch. Amantius screamed like a girl. Cursing, Maximus struggled to get up. The length of the boat, men were doing the same. Maximus gave the eunuch a shove for good measure.

'Stay at your places. Silence.' Ballista was vaulting the benches towards the bow.

Maximus got back on next to Heliodorus and gripped the oar. Taut ropes ran to the prow from poles in the water pulled out of true by the impact. The *Warig* had run into fishing nets strung right across the creek. So close to escape, and now this. It really was, Maximus thought, an absolute fucker.

'Castricius, Diocles, Heliodorus, cut us free.' Ballista was heading back to the stern. 'Maximus, Tarchon, Rikiar, Wada the Tall, with me.'

Maximus ripped off his cloak, grabbed up his shield and, drawing his *gladius*, clattered aft.

The five warriors clustered around Wada the Short at the steering oar. Ballista pointed at four on the rear benches. 'Get your weapons. With us.' The three Romans and an Olbian obeyed.

The bend in the channel was thirty or so paces astern. The Bronding was not yet in sight. Those at the prow were hacking at the stinking tangle of ropes and nets.

Nine armed men, four of them unarmoured; it was not many to hold the Brondings. Still, the narrow creek meant the enemy could not come alongside. It would be close work, stern to prow.

'How is it coming, Castricius?'

'Getting there.'

Neither Ballista nor Castricius betrayed any emotion, beyond an understandable urgency.

'The rest of you, ready to row on command.'

The tall, curved prow of the Bronding came around the bend. Her crew howled. Warriors rushed forward, thick on her deck.

'Get ready,' Ballista said. 'We will take the fight to them.'

A last glance back. Swords flashing, slimy ropes being hauled free and cast into the water. Tense faces staring up from the benches.

The figurehead of the Bronding loomed above. The bearded, implacable face sliding towards the left of the stern post of the *Warig*. Wada the Short hauled the steering oar onboard.

A Bronding leapt before the ships closed. Wada the Tall swung a great two-handed blow into his shield. The wood split. The warrior was knocked aside. Arms wide, he fell into the water. The prow-idol forced him under his own keel.

The deck bucked under Maximus's boots. He staggered back a step. Wood ground against wood. The longship's gunwales were a foot or two higher than the *Warig*. The Bronding stopped six paces beyond her stern. Maximus gained his balance, stepped forward, gathering himself to jump.

A Bronding slammed into him, shield to shield. Maximus was driven down on one knee. The Bronding brought his sword down overhand, like a man chopping wood. Maximus got his shield up at an angle, jabbed the point of his blade out low at shin level. The inside of Maximus's shield crashed down on to the top of his helmet. His head rang, his arm dead with the impact. The Bronding was on one leg, the other bright with blood. Maximus surged up and forward under his own ruined shield. He thrust the steel under the hem of the mailcoat, into the crotch. The warrior fell half on him. He shouldered him aside.

Ballista was on the prow of the Bronding longship, the enemy all around him. Maximus went to cross over to help. A sword sliced at his face from the left. Still numb, his shield arm was too slow to block. Desperately, he brought his blade up and across. The hilt took the blow a hand's breadth from his nose, drove his own fist into cheek. Rolling back on his right foot, with his left he kicked the man in the left kneecap, then whipped his *gladius* around and down into his assailant's left shoulder. Sharp cracks as rings of mail broke. A grunt of pain and surprise. The wound was not deep. Maximus dropped nearly on to his right knee and cut into the Bronding's left calf. As he doubled up, Maximus straightened and finished him with a neat blow to the back of the neck below the helmet. Fuck, he had been careless; fucking lucky to get away with it.

Maximus checked the situation. Shouts. Screams. Boots stamping on the deck. Steel on steel. Steel on wood. Too many men fighting in too small a space. As the battle calm descended, Maximus could take it all in, order it correctly. Four Brondings on the deck of the *Warig* fighting five men. Ballista and Wada the Tall on the prow of the enemy longship preventing more warriors getting to the *Warig*. The Brondings jostling each other trying to get at the Angle and the Harii. Their numbers must tell in the end, but now they were hindering.

A sidestep, four balanced steps forward, and a jab into the back of a distracted Bronding's thigh. Maximus twisted the blade, withdrew it and danced clear. Make that three Brondings fighting on the *Warig*. Maximus grinned. Some men could understand philosophy, others interpret a poem, but Maximus could read a fight, the most difficult text of all.

Maximus went to the side of the boat. His left arm was still numb, the shield dragging it down. Better without the thing. He dropped it, hoping it would be there later. There were some expensive ornaments on its face. He waited until Ballista attacked and moved forward a little. Shifting his *gladius* to his left hand, with his right Maximus grasped the gunwales of the longship and swung up.

Landing on the balls of his feet, he took a two-handed grip on his sword. A gap opened to the right of Ballista. A Bronding moved to get at the Angle's flank. Maximus lunged at the warrior's face. Instinctively, the Bronding flinched back. Maximus took his place at Ballista's shoulder.

The warrior opposite Maximus did not lack courage. You could see it in the many bright rings on his arm, the set of his face and the way he came on again. Maximus parried a cut to his right shoulder, then his left. The steel shivered and rang. He riposted with a downward slash to the leg. As the Bronding drew back, he collided with the warrior behind. Seeing the advantage, Maximus thrust to the stomach. The man managed to drag his shield into the way.

They drew apart, just beyond sword reach, panting and watching each other. Behind Maximus, someone was shouting. Ballista was still fighting. Wada, also, beyond him.

Maximus stamped his right boot, feigned to lunge. The warrior with the arm rings brought his arms up to block. In the brief time he had won, Maximus glanced over his shoulder. Tarchon was yelling something incomprehensible from the stern of the *Warig*. Further away, Castricius was beckoning from under her prow-idol.

To his left the warrior matched with Ballista pressed home an attack, swinging furiously. Steel flashed in the sunlight. The Bronding reeled back and across the one facing Maximus.

'Jump!' Ballista shouted.

With no hesitation, Maximus spun around and, one boot on the gunwale of the big ship, vaulted down into the *Warig*. The deck was unsteady under him. He staggered a few steps. Someone landed heavily behind him, crashed to the deck. Maximus ran into Rikiar.

'Row!' Ballista was roaring from down on the deck. 'Row for your fucking lives!'

Maximus felt the ship stir as the oars fought the resistance of the water.

'My brother!' Wada the Short had dropped the steering oar. He moved to the side.

Tarchon grabbed the Harii, held him fast. Ballista was scrabbling along the woodwork towards the abandoned helm.

Wada the Tall was trapped on the prow of the Bronding, ringed by warriors. His sword was weaving intricate patterns.

'My brother!' Wada the Short fought to get free of Tarchon's embrace. Rikiar leapt to help restrain him.

'All bad with him. Too late,' Tarchon said.

A tortured scraping of wood against wood, and the *Warig* pulled free from the longship.

Wada the Tall was surrounded. He staggered. His blade was still moving. A Bronding tottered back, clutching an arm that looked nearly severed. The others closed in. Wada took a blow, then another. Wada fell. Swords arced down over the space where he had stood.

'He die brave,' Tarchon said. 'Much honour.'

Wada the Short stared out over the widening gap of water. He said nothing.

'To your places.' Ballista had the steering oar. 'Get down, let me see the prow. Maximus, Tarchon, get the dead over the side.'

There were six Brondings – four dead, and two who needed finishing off – and three dead Roman crewmen. There was no time to search them. Friend or foe, Maximus and Tarchon just cut the wallets from their belts, removed any still-sheathed blades and threw them all in a pile. Gripping the dead by the feet and under the armpits, they hauled them over. As the last splashed in, Maximus noticed the mailcoat of the previous Bronding shining through the disturbed silt. He was only about four feet down.

The channel ran straight for half a mile or more. The Brondings were slower getting back to their benches. But, all too soon,

Maximus saw the oars lift and dip. They had no intention of giving up.

No one spoke. There was nothing to say. A wounded Olbian who was whimpering was told to shut the fuck up and be a man.

Wada the Short had not moved. Motionless, he looked back at the Brondings.

The *Warig* had a slender lead, no more than a hundred paces. She was well within bowshot. No sooner had the thought occurred than the first shafts sliced down. Maximus snatched up a discarded shield and crouched over Ballista, covering them both.

The Brondings' aim was wild. They were not shooting in volleys, but men on benches can neither jump aside nor shield themselves. Inevitably, an arrow found its mark. An Olbian screamed. He fell back off his bench. He was not dead. The shaft in his chest quivered obscenely with his breathing. No one went to help him.

Another scream. Another man down, a Roman this time. The oarsmen anxiously watched the sky. It was affecting their timing. With each stroke, one or more missed the surface or caught the bed of the creek, their wake streamed grey with silt.

Maximus peeped around the shield. The scowling Bronding figurehead was only a heavy javelin throw behind; twenty-five paces at most. An arrow came straight at Maximus. He ducked back. It whickered past.

The *Warig* shivered the length of her hull. The speed dropped off her. There was a slithering, sucking sound. Her keel was grounding.

'Pull! Pull, like never before!'

Maximus jumped to the nearest bench, added his weight to the next stroke. As they brought the oars back, the *Warig* was almost stationary, almost held by the mud. The oars fought to keep her momentum. For a moment the opposed forces seemed in balance. Then, with a surge, like wine out of an upended amphora, the *Warig* was free, rushing ahead.

'Get back in time.'

Maximus was not listening to Ballista's orders; none of them were. They were all gazing with wonder over the Angle commander's shoulders. The Bronding ship had come to a shuddering stop. Her mast swayed – once, twice, a third time – then, ropes cracking, went by the board. Warriors threw themselves clear, splashing into the shallow, muddy water. Not all made it in time; screams came from the inboard.

A ragged, exhausted cheer. The crew of the *Warig* held their arms aloft in relief. Oars skewed this way and that.

'Keep rowing. Bend those oars, you lazy bastards. That longship will be here a time, but there are other Brondings out there.' Despite trying to sound fierce, Ballista was grinning in almost disbelieving delight. They had won free. The Suebian Sea lay before them: the way north was open.

THE ISLAND OF VARINSEY

Oslac looked out over the northern sea. His mind was troubled. He loved his wife, but knew she did not love him. She loved both their children, and so did he. It was a bond. They got on well enough. Oddly, they had got on better since her son Starkad, his stepson, had been taken hostage in Gaul. But Oslac knew she did not love him. When she was young, Kadlin had loved his half-brother, and now Dernhelm was coming home.

Desperate events demanded desperate responses. Yet Oslac was not sure he was doing the right thing. Would Pius Aeneas have done the like? After duty, family had been everything to the Trojan. He had braved the horrors of the underworld to talk with the shade of his father. Surely, if her ghost had not appeared to him of its own volition, Aeneas would have ventured the same for his wife. Oslac steeled himself. The Himlings were descended from Woden, but Aeneas was also in their ancestry.

It was time. Oslac turned away from the sea and walked back to where two of his hearth-companions waited with the horses.

They had not wanted to come with him. He did not blame their reluctance; only a desperate concern had urged him to make the journey. In the winter it was the practice of the *wicce* to travel from one hall to another. She would have come to him. Yet it was better it was springtime, better he had been constrained to go to her. In the hall everyone would have heard what she said, not that he could have asked the questions he needed to ask, not in front of an audience, not with Kadlin there.

The previous evening had gone well enough. It had been a long day's ride from Gudme to this desolate place on the northern coast of Varinsey. They had brought the things the aged *wicce* always wanted: the hearts of various animals, freshly slaughtered. Oslac had watched her cook and eat them with a gruel made from goat's milk. She used a brass spoon, and a knife with a walrus-tusk handle bound with two rings of copper; the blade had a broken point. She had told him to return the next day at sunset. Not wanting to spend the night near her dwelling and the pond with its guardian, Oslac had decided they would ride to the shore and camp there. He had had a vague idea that the clean wind off the sea would dispel any taint.

One of his hearth-companions, the tall one, held his bridle, the other gave him a leg-up. They did not speak. He waited while they swung up on to their own mounts. His horse tossed its head and sidled. Calming the animal made him feel better. He knew he was a good horseman. The creak of leather and the jingle of the bit were part of his world. He was a warrior, an *atheling* of the Himling dynasty. He would not let this ritual unman him.

They set off at a walk. The day was overcast. Oslac could not have kept this journey quiet. The cook had butchered the animals. Why else would she have thought that he had wanted the hearts? She was a good-natured woman, but talkative; the news would have spread from his hall to the others: soon all Gudme would have known what he was about. This in mind, Oslac had announced he was going to consult the *wicce* about Unferth. It might have seemed unusual, but not out of all expectation. The situation was grave, the future uncertain. Already since the thaw, longships full of Brondings, Wylfings and Geats had harried the lands of Himling vassals on Latris. Worse, there had been warriors from the Dauciones among the raiders. The rumours had proved true: they, too, had cast off their allegiance to the Angles. Things were so bad his father had even talked of opening the tomb of Himling and bringing out the great terrible-forged sword Bile-Himling. It was said that in the direst times Bile-Himling would save the Himlings from certain defeat. Perhaps, Oslac thought, his brother, Morcar, was right. What the Himlings needed now was strong leadership, not supernatural aid. Their father was old. Perhaps it was time Isangrim stepped aside.

They came to the pond. It was fringed with black poplars. The hut of the *wicce* stood in their shade. They dismounted. The sun was not yet touching the horizon. They waited.

Oslac felt badly about himself. Aeneas had loved the Carthaginian Dido, but he had deserted her for the destiny of his people. Much as he groaned and felt shaken at heart by the great force of love's power, nonetheless Aeneas followed the gods' commands. Oslac was not as pious or as dutiful. Long before, he had taken the opposite, less worthy course. When Dernhelm had gone to be a hostage, Oslac had sent his young wife back to her people, the Wylfings; all in the hope of marrying Kadlin. His father had been furious. Kadlin had been married off instead to Holen of Wrosns, to secure the allegiance of the islands of Latris. Only when Holen was killed, and she was a widow, had Isangrim relented, and let Oslac wed Kadlin. All these years later, Oslac again could not help but put love over duty. It was not about Unferth and the fate of the Woden-born Himlings he was here to ask.

As the sun began to go down, the *wicce* emerged, very old and crooked, leaning on a brass-bound staff. She beckoned Oslac.

Before he followed, he told his men to retire out of earshot. They looked both relieved and suspicious as they led the horses away.

Inside was warm and surprisingly well-lit, with a brazier and two gleaming lamps of Roman manufacture. Despite the warmth, the *wicce* was dressed as he had seen her before: in a blue mantle adorned with stones to the hem. Her face was half hidden by a black lambskin hood lined with the fur of white cats. On her feet were hairy calfskin shoes, and more white cats had been killed to make her gloves.

She seated herself on a low stool, not the high seat of prophecy he would have provided in his hall. Oslac remained standing.

> 'War-father picked for her rings and circlets:
> He had back wise tidings and wands of prophecy;
> She saw widely and widely beyond, over every world.'

Oslac acknowledged her words by passing over a brooch unfastened from his cloak. She turned it over in her gloved hands. The garnets were like blood in the lamplight.

'My half-brother, Dernhelm, the one the Romans call Ballista, returns home. I would know his fate.' Oslac stopped. It was hard to force the rest out. 'Will my wife leave me for him? Will she betray me?' There, it was said.

The old woman snorted, as if once again confronted with damning evidence of the vain pride of men. She took some powder from the purse at her belt, sprinkled it on to the brazier. Leaning over, she shut her eyes and inhaled deeply. While she crooned softly, her gloved hands fondled the staff obscenely.

It was close in the room. Oslac wished he was somewhere else.

When the crone opened her eyes, they were bleared. 'The guardian of the pool is present. Many things stand revealed to me which before were hidden both from me and from others.'

Her voice trailed off, her eyelids drooped. Her body twitched.

Oslac wanted to leave, but did not dare. He had to hear the prophecy. He dreaded what might be revealed.

She wrenched open her jaws and yawned deeply.

> 'She saw there wading through heavy currents,
> Men false-sworn and murderous men,
> And those who gull another's faithfullest girl;
> There spite-striker sucks the bodies of the dead
> – a wolf tore men – do you know yet, or what?'

She stopped, head lolling.

Oslac stood; rooted, sweating.

Her mouth gaped wide, her breathing harsh as torn sailcloth.

> 'Brothers will struggle and slaughter each other,
> And sisters' sons spoil kinship's bonds.
> It's hard on earth: great whoredom;
> Axe-age, blade-age, shields are split;
> Wind-age, wolf-age, before the world crumbles:
> No one shall spare another.'

The *wicce* shivered, and came back. The lamps guttered. Now all Oslac could hear was his own breathing.

'Do you want him cursed?' Her voice was near normal.

Oslac was sweating. Dernhelm was his half-brother. He did not love him, but he did not hate him. It was not Dernhelm's fault. Oslac could not curse his brother, but he could not lose Kadlin. Fleeing from Troy, Aeneas had failed to look back. He had lost his wife. Aeneas had left Carthage, and Dido had killed herself. Oslac would not lose his wife.

'Curse him.'

The *wicce* nodded, as if she had already known his answer, and it saddened her.

240

'Dernhelm, son of Isangrim, you will receive only ill fortune from me. You have become famous through your deeds, but now you will fall into outlawry and killings. Most of what you do will now turn against you, bringing bad luck and no joy. You will be made an outlaw, forced always to live in the wilds and to live alone.'

XXI

THE SUEBIAN SEA

The gods had been capricious, Ballista thought as they ran the boat out from the desolate shore. At first, they had smiled. When they had won clear of the islands off the Vistula, there had been no Bronding longships bearing down. In fact, there had been no vessels of any sort in sight. But the Rugian pilot had been wrong: as the morning went on the wind had not moved into the east. Now and then it had shifted to the north-east, but it had soon backed. Most of the day it had gusted from the north.

Wada the Short had retaken the helm. 'Only a slave takes vengeance immediately, but a coward never,' he had announced, as he settled to his task.

They had had to tack, mainly on an easterly heading. It was frustrating when their course and safety lay to the west, but they knew they had to clear a long spit which stretched down south-eastward from the westerly tip of the gulf. On each tack Wada had the yard braced round until it ran from bow to quarter, bringing the windward sheet forward of the mast. Late morning, when the wind picked up, and the bow had begun to dig into the waves, he had them lower the yard about a third of the way down the mast. Not only had it made the boat plane the water better, it had had the advantage of making their sail harder to see from a distance. Unlike the gaudy spread of the Brondings, it was a plain, tan, weather-stained thing; which was all to the good in trying to avoid pursuit. In the afternoon the wind had risen again. Wada had ordered the canvas abaft the mast brailed up and the weather sheet tightened. With the sail almost triangular and the forward yardarm dragged down, the *Warig* had sailed as well into the wind as any ship could.

Ballista had much admired Wada's seamanship. He would have done the same himself. But it was many years since he had sailed these northern waters, and he was happy to let the Harii take charge. Except when tacking, and apart from a few men bailing intermittently, there had been no task demanded of the crew. The majority had attempted to sleep, huddled and damp beneath their benches. Ballista had gone from bow to stern, always scanning the sky and sea; trying to judge their progress, guess the turn of the weather, and ever, ever looking for the sight of a sail. Twice he glimpsed a smudge of white far to the north. Otherwise, the grey sea remained empty, nothing but gulls soaring above.

After a time, Maximus had stopped shadowing Ballista and had curled up like a dog and gone to sleep at the helmsman's feet. But Tarchon had not left Ballista's side. Sometimes the Suanian had muttered things in his native language. Mostly inaudible, the few words Ballista both caught and understood were dark, involving gods, honour and bloody revenge. After Ballista and Calgacus had saved Tarchon from drowning, the Suanian had sworn to protect them with his life. Out on the Steppe he had failed Calgacus. It sat heavily on Tarchon. Ballista knew its weight.

The sun was getting low when they had finally won the searoom to clear the spit. As they turned, as if to mock their previous progress, the gods had set the wind to blow steadily from the east. Ballista had been tempted to stand out well from any sandbanks and sail through the night. But the men were cold, wet and cramped. Despite having taken what rest they could, they had still been exhausted. They had needed hot food, the chance to stretch and sleep ashore. They were not as far as he would like from the Vistula delta and the Brondings, but Ballista had asked Wada to take them in.

The spit was a low beach of white sand, backed by timber. It was an exposed anchorage in anything other than a southerly wind. With nearly their last reserves of strength, they hauled the ship half out of the water. They had unshipped only what was absolutely necessary, and made the *Warig* ready for a hasty departure. In the glooming they had gone to gather wood. The trees formed a narrow belt, with open water on the far side. Their lower trunks were bare. As there were not many fallen branches, the crew had gathered driftwood as well. It was all damp, but with perseverance they had got the campfire burning. As the flames sawed in the wind, they had warmed themselves, and cooked a stew of disparate contents. Ballista had been one of those who had taken first watch. After an hour, another had taken his place, and he had rolled himself in his cloak by the embers of the fire and fallen straight into a deep sleep.

The morning was overcast. The wind was still in the east, but it had fallen. Sky and sea were united in sullen grey.

The *Warig* came alive as her keel ran free. The men launching her clambered over the stern, and went to their places, their boots slapping wet and noisy on the deck. The bow oarsmen were already pulling her out. Maximus touched Ballista's arm. The Hibernian flicked his eyes to the east. Ballista looked but could see nothing. He gripped the prow and swung his boots up on to the gunwale. Swaying with the rise and fall, he peered out into the greyness. His eyes smarted with tiredness and the salt. He thought he saw something. It was gone before he could tell what. He wiped his streaming eyes. There it was again. A patch of solidity in the shifting air and water, a hint of colour.

'Two sails,' Maximus said quietly.

'The same two?'

'I have good eyesight, I am not a fucking magician.'

Wada pointed the prow-idol to the west. The men got the oars inboard, squared the yard and shook out the sail so the following breeze fell on both sheets simultaneously. Ballista and Maximus moved to the stern. There was no point in sharing their fears until they were certain.

The rising sun struggled to make its presence felt from behind the leaden clouds. Yet it was enough. Distance was hard to judge in the monochrome world, but perhaps two miles astern were two sails. They were black in the dim light. They could be any colour, belonging to any two ships. Many vessels plied the Suebian Sea. But Ballista had no doubt as to their identity.

Wada the Short received the news calmly. He turned the *Warig* to starboard to get the wind on her quarter. Then, as she heeled and forged out into the open sea, he had Ballista take the steering oar. Wada moved purposefully through the ship. He felt the tautness of the lines, slackened off those towards the prow and took in those towards the stern. Taking the steering oar again, he brought the wind first a little more abeam, then a bit astern, feeling the run of the ship. Announcing he needed to bring her head up a fraction, he shouted for some of those to the fore to move back down the boat.

Ballista managed not to grin as he watched a bedraggled Zeno and Amantius shuffling towards him. There was something pleasing in those one-time inhabitants of the imperial court being used as ballast in an open boat in a northern sea.

The rearrangement complete, Wada grunted his satisfaction.

The improvement seemed small, but it might be significant. Despite the light airs, the water lapped white down the larboard side.

Ballista looked back to the east. In the gathering light, any lingering uncertainties were resolved. The two ships had altered course in pursuit. Their sails were red- and blue-striped. At least they seemed no closer.

'Persistent fuckers,' Maximus said. 'Given the other one in the delta, there may be more following.'

'We die before them take you,' Tarchon said. 'Best you dead too.'

'Sure, he does have a point. From what we hear, your Bronding lord Unferth would love to be getting his hands on a son of Isangrim.'

Ballista was finding little enjoyment in this conversation. 'They are heavier ships; in a gentle wind we should outrun them.'

Within the hour, Ballista regretted his words. Usually he was careful to tempt neither gods nor fate. The wind got up, raising white caps on the waves which now rolled out of the east. The *Warig* began to pitch and slide slightly as she rode the sea. The motion brought no danger, but both Zeno and one of his slaves were violently sick on the deck where they huddled. Men roared at them to get to the leeward side.

Ballista took the Rugian guide to Wada the Short in the stern. All three knew the Suebian Sea. They agreed it would be madness to try to sail direct to Hedinsey. It would be a run of at least two days and a night. Even if they had the supplies and the crew still had the stamina – neither of which was the case – the Brondings would overhaul them. 'A heavier ship for heavier weather,' Wada announced. There was a storm coming, the Rugian said, a bad one. The tall, black clouds piling up on the eastern horizon made this hard to gainsay. They must look to find shelter from both weather and pursuit.

As they brought the ship around to the south-west, the first shower swept over them. With that and the spray coming inboard from the rougher sea, men had to be set to bailing regularly. It kept the men with the scoops warm, and, Ballista thought, it gave the whole crew the impression they were more than passengers being delivered helpless to their fate. *Wyrd will often spare an undoomed man, if his courage is good.*

They ran the whole day, angling first towards the shore then standing out again. The coastline here was flat, remarkably featureless, with little offer of refuge. It would be difficult to beach. There were frequent sandbanks offshore, the surf breaking on them. The beaches themselves were often studded with jagged, half-submerged tree stumps and drift wrack, which might tear the bottom out of a boat. They did pass inlets. Only dire emergency would force them to turn into one. The lack of landmarks meant they were unsure how far they had travelled. But they had left behind the known shoreline of the Rugii. Any channel might be nothing more than a dead end. They were a long way yet from the territory of the Farodini, who were allies of the Himlings. This inhospitable coast was held by the Heathobards, and they were friends to neither Angles nor Rugii.

Wada was getting the best out of the *Warig*. She was a weatherly craft. Clinker-built, her lashed planks flexed and creaked, but she was not taking much water and sailed taut and responsive to the helm. Through the drizzle, the Brondings did not seem to have narrowed the distance. Ballista took turns at the stern-rudder and at bailing. The steering gave Wada a chance to check the rigging, bolt some cold food and snatch a little rest. Their commander bailing was intended to hearten the men.

In the gloom, night succeeded day with no great show. In the first hours the rain blew over, but the wind did not slacken. Weary, cold and soaked to the skin, they raced on over a silver sea, the shore black to larboard, the sky between the tattered clouds a strange, threatening yellow. In the glinting light among the rushing shadows the dark shapes of the Brondings could still be seen.

In the dead of night, when the moon and stars were obscured, Ballista was bailing. He filled the scoop, handed it up to Maximus, who threw the contents to the wind, handed it back down, and Ballista filled the scoop again. Over and over: the repetition numbed the mind. The screws and pumps of Mediterranean vessels were equally monotonous and hard work. But you did not have to crouch, were not actually in the water. They should not be hard to fit on a northern longboat. Ballista came out of his daze. The water was slopping around his boots. It was gaining. Telling Tarchon to take over bailing, he got to his knees. The water was cold on his legs. In the darkness, he ran his hands under the surface along the bilges. The wood seemed sound. As he worked along, he found no cracks, no holes. Perhaps it was nothing.

The *Warig* came down the leading edge of a wave, bottomed out in the trough. A jet of water hit Ballista's forearm. Carefully, not wanting to trap a finger, he felt the overlaps between the side planks. He found the wadding. A clump of it came out in his fingers. The material was still sticky, but it came apart in his hands. Whatever it had been treated with was being washed out by the seawater. As the ship flexed more water squirted through.

They bailed in shifts. There were only three scoops. The others bailed with their helmets, bowls, whatever would hold water. Some mutton fat was produced from the supplies. Rikiar and Heliodorus rubbed it into torn-up strips of clothing. Down below the waterline, working by touch, Ballista and the Rugian pilot packed it into the overlaps where the water seemed to be coming in worst. They hammered it home as best they could with wooden mallets. It was cold, filthy work. Time and again Ballista swore as the mallet caught his numbed fingers. After an hour or so, the water stopped rising, even fell. But there could be no stopping the bailing.

248

In the dawn, they were about half a mile offshore. The gods had not been kind. The Brondings were still there. They were closer, much less than a mile astern. The sun played on the water between. But behind them a great curtain of lurid purple-black cloud stretched across the eastern horizon. Lightning flickered in its heart.

'This will be bad,' Wada said. The evident profundity of the oncoming danger banished all fatigue. The crew leapt to lower the yard halfway down the mast. Wada had them brail up the sail so that there was only enough showing to keep steerageway. Back on the benches, the men feverishly tied their oars to the thole pins ready to be run out. Eight men were kept bailing.

With terrible speed the Brondings disappeared behind the outlying squalls.

The noise of the wind in the rigging rose to near a scream. The sun vanished.

A gust of spattering rain, then the storm was on them. It smashed the stern of the *Warig* to the right. She heeled, her starboard gunwales in the water. Men crashed from their benches. Wada was fighting the helm. Ballista scrambled across the sloping deck to help. The *Warig* was near side on to the sea, a tall wave bearing down. Ballista threw his weight on the steering oar. Agonizingly slowly, she began to come around, get her stern to the storm.

The wave towered over them, green and immense. The *Warig* shifted, heeled even further. Somehow, she did not tip but climbed crabwise up the wave. At the crest, she twisted, righted herself and slid down the far side.

The following wave was looming. Ballista and Wada strained. Her prow began to turn. The wave kicked in under her stern, throwing it high. Her bows lost in white water, again slantwise she rose up the awful incline.

A crack of wood, loud even in the uproar. The steering oar

suddenly limp in Ballista's hands. A moment of blank incomprehension.

'Out oars!' Wada was bellowing.

The steering oar had broken just below the handle.

'Row! Larboard side, row hard. Starboard steady. Bring her round.' Wada's voice carried.

Ballista scuttled across the moving deck, grabbed an unused oar, hauled it back. Together with Wada, he shoved it over the side. The force of the water near tore it from their hands. The impromptu stern-rudder was far from effective, flimsy and likely to break any moment, but it was something to help control the ship.

'Keep her stern to the waves.'

The rowers needed no urging. They bent their backs to the fraught task. The makeshift rudder groaned ominously. The wooden idol on the prow crept around to the west. The next wave hit, but now the *Warig* lifted as it drove almost square under her stern.

Ballista yelled to Maximus to lash two oars together to make a better rudder to steer them to shore.

'It will break,' Wada shouted in his ear.

'If we just run – the men cannot row and bail – she will water-log and go down,' Ballista shouted back.

The rain fell hard now. Lightning hissed and threw fleeting hard-edged illumination.

Maximus and the Rugian lugged the ungainly thing they had created to the stern. They lashed it to a thole pin.

'Rowers ready to turn to larboard. On command, starboard side full pressure, larboard easy.'

Ballista and Wada ran out the slender, inadequate-looking double oar.

'Now.'

In the maelstrom, some blades missed the surface, others dug far too deep. One snapped altogether, flinging its rower down. Ballista and Wada braced the lashed-together oars. They kicked and struggled in their hands. Water streamed through the boat. The air was full of it. Yet little by little their head came around and they pushed across the storm.

Ballista realized he was praying. *Ran, do not take me with your drowning net; spare me the cold embrace of your nine daughters.*

'Breakers!'

Ballista could not see anything. Unable to let go of the steering oar to wipe his eyes, he shook his head, trying to blink the spray out of them.

A line of white straight ahead. A dreadful roaring, like a hundred mill wheels.

The *Warig* surged into the wild water. She trembled, paused in her way. The deck vibrated under Ballista's boots. A long way to the beach. She was on a sandbar. The next wave lifted the boat, threw her forward. She raced through the surf until her keel rasped into the sand. A big wave pushed her further in. The backwash began to drag her out. Another wave crashed clean over the stern, grinding her forward half clear of the water.

All discipline gone, men hurled themselves over the prow.

'Anchor out!' Ballista shouted. He was largely ignored. Slipping, Ballista joined Maximus and another figure wrestling with the awkward, heavy iron. As soon as it was over the side, they all followed, running and falling in their anxiety to get to safety away from the hideous sea.

There were men all over the beach. None of them was moving. Most stood, some were on their knees, a few, despite the wind and rain, had thrown themselves down as if to sleep. Ballista pushed his hair out of his face. It was stiff with salt. His hand came away filthy. His things were still on the boat. He should get them ashore. Waves broke around the stern of the *Warig*. Beyond, the sea raged. It seemed impossible that anything could live out there. The boat might survive, or the storm might yet break her up. Ballista was too tired to care.

Allfather, what was he thinking. 'Diocles, get the men on their feet. Get a rope around her prow. We need to pull her clear of the water.'

No one moved. Fatigue fired Ballista's temper. Diocles was a few paces away, staring away from the ship. Ballista marched over. 'Centurion, I gave you an order.'

'*Dominus.*' Diocles pointed inland.

The beach shelved up for about forty paces. It ended in a low, crumbling cliff of sand. At the top, back from the edge so only their heads and shoulders could be seen, were warriors. At least a hundred of them, helmeted, carrying weapons. Heathobards.

Zeno felt like Ixion bound to the wheel. First he had been raised up. He had prayed to Zeus and Poseidon, promised each an ox and other fine things. They had heard his prayers, nodded in acceptance. When all seemed lost, they had rescued him from the howling, daemonic gale. The gods had cast him up on shore. Filthy, cold and exhausted, he had been saved. Honest earth under his feet, rather than treacherous, shifting planks, the retching sickness had receded.

With no pause, the wheel had begun its downward turn. Strange warriors had sprouted from the cliff, like barbaric sown men. Heathobards, someone said. In the face of this new threat, all courage and resource had deserted Ballista and the others. They had stood as if themselves rooted to the ground. They had dropped their weapons, and with no resistance let these seeming autochthonous warriors take them all captive.

The wheel had dipped still lower. With the unthinking arrogance and brutality of barbarians, the Heathobards had manhandled their prisoners into a rough line. Two huge, hairy warriors had seized Zeno. They had tied his hands and put a halter around his neck. A rope ran from his tether to that of Amantius in front and to the oarsman behind. At a stroke, Aulus Voconius Zeno, *Vir Perfectissimus*, had become part of a slave chain; an Abasgian eunuch in front, a *pleb* behind.

In the slanting rain, the Heathobards had driven them up a narrow, slippery path which climbed the cliff. Zeno had found it difficult to keep his footing. Each time his boot skidded or he hesitated, the shackle had tugged him forward, the rough hairs of the rope burning his neck. At the top they were herded for what seemed an eternity across an open, storm-blasted heath. They had trudged through the downpour to a stockaded settlement on a rise in the distance. On arrival, they had been led down a muddy lane between mean timber buildings. Water dripped off the thatch. Grimy barbarian children and huge women, as pale and monstrous as their menfolk, had come out in the rain to stare at them.

Their prison was a large, empty barn. The halters had been removed, but their hands remained bound. When the door was shut, it was dark. A heavy bar thumped into place.

Zeno sat, head in his bound hands, his back against the log wall. As far as he could tell, the others had flopped down to sleep like dumb beasts. Certainly some were snoring. Zeno did not sleep. Like Odysseus in the cave of the Cyclops, his mind kept weaving, weaving cunning schemes. Physical escape was impossible: they were bound, it was too dark to see, the walls were stout, and he had seen that the ceiling was high. If they got out, they were in the middle of the territory of their captors, the boat miles away, most likely damaged, and probably guarded. Brute force and violence would not win their freedom.

Escape would take intelligence and cunning. It would take words. Zeno was skilled with words. That he had acquired only an inconsiderable smattering of the language of Germania on this ghastly journey need not be an insuperable barrier. His hands were eloquent, and his slaves had learnt more and could interpret for him. From what he knew, the tribe of the Heathobards had never had diplomatic dealings with Rome. Simple appeal to her *maiestas*, as reflected in his own person, her envoy, was unlikely to be effective. Yet while they might not be predisposed towards Rome, they might not be intensely hostile. They would have seen what her *imperium* could achieve. Roman gold and Roman-made swords had raised the Angles to wealth and hegemony among the barbarians of the far north. It had been said the Heathobards were not friends of the Angles. If they did not already know who they had captured, Zeno could offer them Ballista. A son of the king of the Angles should make a useful bargaining counter in the politics of the Suebian Sea. And Zeno could go further. He could offer them what the Angles had been given: Roman money and weapons. If they let him return south to win them the friendship of the emperor, they could keep Castricius and the others as hostages. Of course, out of imperial favour as he was, it was most improbable he could achieve anything of the sort. But that was no great matter. Once safely in the *imperium*, the whole course of the embassy could be recast in a very different light.

Outside, the bar was lifted. The door opened. Warriors with torches stood there. The light shone on their helmets and mail-coats. One of them spoke. Ballista and the Harii called Wada got to their feet and went to the door. Their wrists were untied. Zeno followed them. The Heathobard who had spoken before said something to him; from its tone, a question. Zeno gave him his full name and rank, trying to make the Latin sonorous and impressive. He announced his mission, repeating 'envoy' and 'emperor' in what he thought were the Germanic words. The Heathobard grunted, and unbound Zeno's hands as well. He gestured for them to leave.

'I need one of my slaves,' Zeno said to Ballista.

'We are going to talk for our lives, not to the baths.' Ballista turned and left. Zeno had no choice but to follow.

It was difficult to tell the halls of northern kings apart. Outside, enormous beams set at unexpected angles and overhanging thatched roofs; inside, they were gloomy, always smoky despite their height, the benches packed with fierce-looking warriors. The hall of the Heathobards could have been that of the Rugii, the Harii, or any of the other oddly named tribes through whose territories they had passed. Zeno had plenty of time to study the interior. The talk was entirely in the northern tongue.

The king of the Heathobards was elderly. He spoke for some time, his tone neutral. First Ballista answered, Wada afterwards. Then two councillors, each of an age with their king, spoke. There was disagreement between them. One appeared not unkindly disposed. Zeno noticed him smile at Wada. Finally, the king made a brief pronouncement.

A Heathobard brought Ballista his sword, the barbaric blade the chieftain Heoden of the Harii had given him. The Angle unsheathed it. Placing the flat of the blade in his left palm, and holding the ring at the end of the hilt in his right, he delivered a solemn monologue.

The king drew his sword. He unclipped one of the golden rings on his right arm, slid it on to the point of the blade and held it out. Ballista put the tip of his sword against that of the king. With a rasp, the precious thing slid down on to Ballista's weapon. He took it, and slipped it on to his arm.

The Heathobards *hoomed* their approval.

'What happened?' Zeno tried to sound as if he were back in the imperial court, questioning an underling about a meeting he had been too busy to attend.

'We are free to go. The Heathobards would show us their hospitality first. They will help us repair the *Warig*.'

'Why?'

255

Ballista smiled. 'The enemy of their enemy has become their friend. The Brondings were here last year. It seems they hate Unferth and his son now more than the Himlings.'

'You took an oath.'

'Yes.'

'What did you swear?'

Ballista gave him a sharp glance. 'It is of no concern to Rome.'

Zeno looked at the great, hulking, dirty barbarian. Now was not the moment, but he would bring this impertinent savage to heel. Fabius Cunctator had overcome Hannibal by patience, had won his cognomen through provident delay. Zeno would wait, but in the fullness of time, when the moment was right, he would reassert his command of this expedition, would bring Ballista down.

XXII

THE ISLET OF NERTHUS, SOUTH OF VARINSEY

Kadlin thought about Dernhelm. To begin with, in the first months after he had gone, he had been in her mind all the time. She had thought she would go mad. She had been very young, her life in confusion: the hastily arranged betrothal to Holen, leaving her family to live over the sea, her pregnancy, the painful birth, nursing the infant Starkad, trying to adapt to the role of mistress of a strange hall. All those things had played their part, but not accounted for the whole. *It was wanting you that made me sick . . . the hollowness at heart.* Over the many subsequent winters she had thought of him less often. His memory had become like an heirloom or the image of a household spirit; most of the time it remained locked away in a cupboard or dowry-chest. Now and then she had taken it out, turned it over and viewed it from different angles, each time to be surprised almost by its powers of evocation. Now he was coming home.

The lowing of cattle announced the approach of the goddess.

Men and women laughed, children played in the sunshine. The festival of Nerthus was a time of rejoicing, a time of peace, when all iron was locked away. It was a moveable feast. The priest in charge of the sacred grove had announced the epiphany more than a month in advance. It gave time for the news to travel, for celebrants to journey from far away to the tiny holy island. There were Aviones, Varini, Myrgings and others from the Cimbric peninsula. Farodini and Langobardi had travelled from the mainland, Hilleviones from Scadinavia. There were many Angles, of course. And there were a few Brondings, Wylfings and Geats, all men. Unsurprisingly, Unferth and his son Widsith had not appeared, but it would have been hard to turn away the people of the tribes which had fallen under their rule. Time out of mind, those on the islands had worshipped the goddess. With everyone else, they had handed their weapons over to the priest. Morcar had argued that if they were to be allowed to participate at all – a thing he opposed – they should be searched. Oslac had said that submitting them to such indignity would be unprecedented. In the absence of their father, the *cyning* Isangrim, the decision had been made by the priest. The island was inviolate; no man could be so sacrilegious as to think of bearing arms in the sight of the Earth Mother.

The cows could be seen, dappled coming out of the shade of the grove. The chariot they drew flashed with gold and silver. A cry went up as the goddess was seen. She shimmered, glorious in silken vestments. Kadlin felt her heart lift. It was impossible not to accept that the deity inhabited her statue. It swayed slightly as the chariot rumbled along, as if animated from within. Men and women raised drinking horns, called out things of good omen. Children ran, squealing. Only the slaves walking behind the procession remained sombre, as well they might. Later, when Nerthus returned to her grove, the slaves would wash her in the lake. And then they would die.

Kadlin was soothed by the presence of Nerthus, the bringer of all good things. The goddess had brought much that was good into Kadlin's life. Her first husband, Holen of the Wrosns, had been a good man; tactful enough not to question his new wife's virginity, strong enough to ignore the rumours about the paternity of the infant she had given birth to in his hall. Holen had treated Starkad as his own. Kadlin smiled. Holen had been strong in other ways. She had appreciated his vigour in their bedchamber, and not just there. At the one Nerthus ceremony they had attended, he had led her away from the crowds. In one of the woods nearby, he had hauled up her skirts and taken her, fast and urgent, against a tree. The danger of discovery had added to her excitement. Their time together had been all too brief. When the news came that Holen had fallen fighting the Aestii away in the east, her grief had been unfeigned, as deep as when Dernhelm was sent away.

On Holen's death, despite her unhappiness, she had done what was right. Starkad was only three winters old. The talk about his paternity would always have cast a cloud over his rule of the Wrosns. Having sought the *cyning* Isangrim's permission, Kadlin had sensibly arranged for Holen's brother Hrothgar to take the high seat.

Kadlin had had little desire to remarry. Holen had been generous. Along with the traditional oxen, bridled horse and shield, spear and sword, he had included several estates in her dowry. With those and the lands settled on her by her father, she could have lived independently in comfort. She could have raised Starkad. As a woman of means, if discreet, she could have taken lovers of her choice.

The position of her family had demanded she remarry. The Wuffingas stood second only to the Himlings on Hedinsey. Her late father and the *cyning* Isangrim had decided the two families should be more closely bound together. Conscious of her duty, she had raised no objection to marrying Oslac.

Kadlin looked across to where Oslac stood with her brother, Heoroweard, and her sister, Leoba. They made a striking group, all tall and blond, but very different. Oslac was powerfully built but slim. Heoroweard was vast and fitted his nickname, Paunch-Shaker. Leoba was the most unusual, a tall young woman dressed as a man. Kadlin got on well with her sister, but made no pretence of understanding her. What made a girl renounce the pleasures of men to become almost one of them as a shield-maiden was inexplicable to her. Kadlin had never had any ambition to fight. Her place was running a well-lit hall, decorously moving through the benches, acting as a peace-weaver. She liked jewels, fine things, pleasure. She wanted a man in her bed.

Oslac was a man in bed, every bit as enjoyable as Dernhelm or Holen. And Oslac was considerate in many other ways. He was open-handed, and he loved her. Yet he was not Holen, let alone Dernhelm. Oslac had always been in the shadow of the other sons of Isangrim: the beautiful, doomed Froda, the capable and strong Arkil, the wild young Eadwulf and Dernhelm, and his own full brother, the overbearing Morcar. Oslac was the quietest of the *athelings*; always thinking, reading Latin poetry and always consumed with worry.

Kadlin had been faithful to Oslac. She had given him no cause for concern. He had given her the son and daughter who stood by her. At nineteen winters, Aelfwynn was a beautiful girl, radiant like the sun, and Aethelgar, just a year younger, was already a fine young man, a proven warrior. The marriage had lasted, could be considered a success.

With the news that Dernhelm was travelling the Amber Road, much had changed. She knew Oslac was troubled. Much of the time he was yet more attentive, making love to her with something like desperation. But at others, he was withdrawn. Too often he was away, closeted with Morcar and his brother's sinister familiars Glaum, son of Wulfmaer, and Swerting Snake-Tongue.

And all the time, Dernhelm was coming. She had to accept he would have changed. He would be older, much older. News travelled slowly up the Amber Road, but she knew he had two sons by his Roman wife. What would she do when she saw him? What would she say? Would she say anything? How could she tell him he had another son, and then in the next breath tell him that Starkad was a hostage far away in Gaul? Kadlin longed to tell him. She longed to see him. But she knew if she were given the choice, it would be Starkad coming home, not the father he had never met.

Sudden shouts through the sounds of merrymaking. A flash of steel. The screams of women and children. A man with a knife in his hand running towards her. Aethelgar stepped in front of Kadlin. The man thrust at him. Aethelgar failed to catch his wrist. The blade cut deep into her son's arm. His blood was bright in the sunshine. Her daughter was screaming. Aethelgar doubled up, defenceless. The man drew back for the killing blow. He reeled sideways. Leoba hit him again with the heavy metal drinking cup. He went down. Leoba landed on top of him. Again and again she brought the cup down, smashing his face to a bloodied pulp.

Men were fighting. Others were running with the women and children. The chariot of the goddess had come to a halt. Her slaves were fleeing, seizing this opportunity to escape the terrible fate which awaited them.

Kadlin struggled to make sense of the confusion. The Brondings and the others subject to Unferth were massively outnumbered, but they had knives. Four of them surrounded Heoroweard and Oslac.

'Get Aelfwynn to the boat.'

Kadlin struggled to take in what her son was saying.

'The boat – you and Aelfwynn get to the boat. There are guards there.'

Leoba got up from her horrible handiwork. She had the dead Bronding's dagger. She moved to help their brother and Oslac.

'You are hurt,' Kadlin said to Aethelgar.

'Go, now!' The youth sounded angry.

Kadlin put her arm around Aelfwynn's shoulders, turned her to go.

Aethelgar wrapped his cloak around his left arm, and picked up the metal cup Leoba had discarded. When he was sure his mother and sister were moving, he ran after Leoba.

At the edge of the timber, Kadlin looked back. They were still fighting. She could see Aethelgar and Leoba. Oslac was still on his feet. But her brother Heoroweard was gone.

XXIII

THE ALPS

'A coin for a shave, *Dominus?*'

Gallienus smiled down at the bearded soldier standing near his horse, and held out his hand for Achilleus, his *a Memoria*, to place a coin in it. A recollection came to the emperor. 'You were at Mediolanum.'

'I was, *Dominus*. We whipped those hairy fucking Alamanni.'

'We certainly did, *Commilito*, and we will win again.' Gallienus raised his voice. 'Today we will beat Simplicinius Genialis and his rabble of Raetian levies. Next year we will crush his master, the Batavian bandit who pretends to be an emperor. Today we start to dismantle the foul, murderous tyranny of the half-barbarian Postumus.'

Gallienus flipped the coin through the air. 'Good luck.'

The soldier caught the coin. 'May the gods grant you victory, *Imperator.*'

Others called out. '*Dominus*, over here. Me, too, *Dominus.*'

Gallienus held up his hands, palms empty. He waited for the

clamour to die down before speaking. 'There will be little plunder today, although the baggage of Simplicinius Genialis I give to the troops. When we have won, you will not find me ungenerous. If you Cantabrians chase those northern peasants off this hillside, your donative will be doubled.'

The auxiliaries cheered. *'Io Cantab! Io Cantab!'*

Gallienus saluted them, and, nodding to his entourage to follow, turned his horse.

Riding back to where the horse guards waited behind the main line, Gallienus wondered about the loyalty of the Cantabrians. The unit had been raised in northern Hispania. But they had served with his *comitatus* for many years. There could not be many Spaniards left in their ranks; not many in whom the call of home and family might have been played upon by agents of Postumus to lead to thoughts of desertion.

The opening moves of the invasion of Raetia had gone smoothly enough, the result of long planning. Gallienus had left a sizable force in northern Italy; eight thousand infantry and six thousand cavalry under the Prefect of Cavalry. Aureolus may have started life as a Getan shepherd, but now he was a senior officer long experienced in independent command. He had orders to block the Alpine passes to the west. The infantry to be employed would be commanded by four other experienced *protectores*: the Danubian Claudius, the Egyptian Camsisoleus and the Italians Domitianus and Celer. Should Postumus break through, his counterattack would be met by the cavalry on the wide plains where they could best manoeuvre. As deputy, Aureolus had another *protector* in Marcianus. If all should fail, the towns of the region were being put in readiness for a siege by yet another *protector*, the siege engineer Bonitus, assisted by a capable officer called Julius Marcellinus. It was hard to think what more could have been done to protect the rear.

An order had long been issued that on the day Gallienus left

Mediolanum, troops from the province of Noricum would begin their advance through the high country to the river Aenus to threaten Raetia from the east. The governor Aelius Restutus was capable. There was no reason to think it had not been carried out.

Gallienus and the *comitatus* had marched due north from Mediolanum to Comum. They had taken the road on the western shore of the lake, advanced as far as Clavenna, turned first east, then west, and negotiated the Julier pass. In the mild early-summer weather, the mountain road was not too hard for a lightly equipped expeditionary force. The slopes reached up on either side; dark green where there were trees, lighter on the high Alpine meadows. Mist hung in the valleys and folds in the mornings until the sun burnt them off, leaving odd clouds anchored to the distant bare rock peaks. They had just passed a perfect, still, little lake where the road clung to a precipice, when the scouts had come back with the unwelcome news.

Simplicinius Genialis had done well. There was only one other practicable route for an army from Mediolanum up through the mountains into Raetia. It started at Verona and ran east of Lake Benacus, up through Tridentum, on the Via Claudia Augusta. Unfortunately, both routes came together far to the north at the town of Cambodunum. Gallienus had known Simplicinius Genialis had based his army at that strategic place. What had surprised the emperor was the alacrity with which the governor of Raetia had moved to meet him down the path he had chosen. Gallienus was still some fifteen miles short of the small mountain settlement of Curia, a very long march south from Cambodunum. Obviously, the secrecy of the imperial *consilium* had been broken. Although it was probably otiose, Gallienus had instructed his *Princeps Peregrinorum* Rufinus and his junior Praetorian Prefect Censorinus to conduct investigations.

For a fat, small-town equestrian with a civilian career behind him, Simplicinius Genialis was turning out to be something of a general. Some four years before he had defeated a force of Iuthungi and Semnones returning from the great Alamannic raid into Italy. Now he had selected an excellent defensive position for an army vastly outnumbered in cavalry. The road ran uphill through a highland plain about a thousand paces wide. Steep, heavily wooded slopes reared up on either side. These precluded not just cavalry but the movement of any formed body of troops. There was a small stream running along the tree line under the western escarpment, but Gallienus thought it was likely to prove of little consequence.

Simplicinius Genialis's dispositions showed equal skill. He had drawn up his heavy infantry, six deep, in close order across the plain, filling it from slope to slope. Legio III Italia Concors, about four thousand men under the Spaniard Bonosus, held the centre. On their right were *vexillationes* from two legions from Germania Superior, VIII Augusta and XXII Primigenia, amounting to about a thousand shields. The left consisted of something less than a thousand Germanic warriors. They were on foot, but handlers held their horses a little way to their rear. Gallienus's *frumentarii* had informed him recently that Postumus had despatched these Angles to Simplicinius Genialis.

Close behind the main battle line stood the provincial militia. Their numbers were harder to judge; by their very nature, they were ad hoc units. They looked to almost equal the total of those in the front. Raetia was a beleaguered frontier province, and its levies would have more experience of fighting than most. They had been a part of the recent victory over the barbarians. But militia could never stand up to regular troops in close combat. It had to be assumed they had been stationed there to hurl missiles over those in front. Should they want to, the amateur soldiers of Raetia would find it difficult to run. Some twenty paces to their rear were posted what Gallienus already knew were all the two thousand regular auxiliary archers in the province. Most likely, apart from shooting at the oncoming enemy, the latter also would have been given orders to shoot any of the militia who turned tail.

No reserve was to be seen, except, much higher up the road and thus well to the rear, almost back with the baggage, two *alae* of cavalry. At a distant glance it was evident that these were far less than the thousand riders which should have been on their muster rolls. Judging by the mounted messengers coming and going, Simplicinius Genialis himself probably was with them.

The array was completed by some regular auxiliaries on the extreme flanks armed with javelins and swords. Some of them could be seen now and then precariously scrambling between the trees on the vertiginous slopes. Given the terrain, despite the words he had spoken to the Cantabrians on his right, Gallienus considered it most improbable that troops there would have any influence on the outcome.

The emperor had had plenty of time to study his opponent's order of battle. Simplicinius Genialis had chosen his ground well and set out his forces with acumen. Yet he had surrendered all initiative. For the past two days the imperial field army had watched the rebel forces. Each morning the army of Raetia formed up in good order, and each night posted adequate numbers of advanced pickets. The latter had little effect on the deserters. In the dark, men crossed from one side to the other, as was the way in any civil war.

Both days, the imperial army had remained in camp. They could not stay where they were indefinitely, because their supply line was too long and tenuous. They could not retreat, because that might prove fatal to imperial prestige. The troops were restless. Despite the advantageous position of their enemy, despite the terrible casualties that would come from plunging missiles, they were eager to advance. In part to curb this impatience, on the first day Gallienus had made it known he had sent two columns on flank marches to come around behind the enemy. One thousand Dalmatian horsemen under the Egyptian Theodotus had retraced their steps through the Julier pass all the way to Clavenna, where they were to take a parallel route north through the mountains to Curia. At a conservative estimate it was over a hundred and twenty miles along a narrow road easily blocked. If they arrived at all, it was unlikely to be any time soon. Another thousand cavalry, Moors commanded by the Danubian Probus, had followed a local shepherd who claimed he knew a sheep track passable by horses which snaked off to the east and came out to the north of the enemy. The existence of this path was dubious.

Several factors, all in the lap of the gods, had encouraged Gallienus to delay. The omens had been ambiguous, and there had been portents.

When they were in Clavenna, bees had swarmed around one of the standards. The priests had produced specious positive interpretations: bees laboured together for the common good; they never failed to obey the sole ruler of the hive. But Gallienus remembered the same had happened to the standards of the emperor Niger shortly before his army had been defeated by that of Severus.

Back in Comum, a priest of Jupiter had announced a dream he had said was sent by the god. In it a man in a toga had forced his way into the emperor's encampment. He had been accompanied by two *lares*, the household divinities easily recognizable by the short dog-skin tunics they wore and the cornucopias in their hands. Near the *praetorium*, in front of the imperial standards, the *lares* had vanished. Left alone, the toga-clad figure had been beaten to death by the soldiers. The priest had produced his own exegesis of the dream. In every domestic shrine, the *lares* flanked the togate image of the *genius* of the household. Genialis was the adjective of *genius*. After initial success, the governor of Raetia would be deserted by the gods and killed.

Gallienus was unconvinced by this oneiromancy. For thirteen years his own *genius* had been worshipped across the *imperium*. The gods abandoning the *genius* chimed too closely with a thing that had been preying on his thoughts. Not since that day at Platonopolis with the old philosopher Plotinus, when his soul had been taken to these very Alps, had Gallienus sensed the presence of his divine companion. The emperor was sure Hercules had not left him for ever – like Antony in Alexandria, he would have heard the music – but the god was not with him now.

Amidst these supernatural concerns, Gallienus had been waiting for something else, something akin to divine intervention. It had appeared in the dead of the previous night in the form of the *frumentarius* called Venutus.

As dawn's rose-red fingers lit the sky, Gallienus had led his army out to battle. His dispositions largely mirrored those of the enemy. A phalanx of heavy infantry was massed across the plain. On their right were four thousand drawn from all the four legions in the two Pannonian provinces. This mountain battle should hold nothing out of the ordinary for their commander, Proculus. He had been brought up in the Alpes Maritimae. Next to Proculus stood the veteran Prefect Volusianus with two thousand of his Praetorians. The left was held by Tacitus with a thousand shields drawn from the Italian Legio II Parthica, and another thousand from Legio V Macedonica marched west from Dacia. Like the enemy, they were all in six ranks, except on each wing, where the additional numbers allowed a formation packed twice as deep.

To provide covering shooting, the second line consisted of every one of the three thousand auxiliary foot archers the imperial field army possessed. The young Narbonensian *protector* Carus had charge of them.

The battle would be decided by the infantry, but not all the cavalry was without use. Gallienus had formed a third line of eastern horse archers to augment the storm of arrows. There were a thousand Persians. They were among those who had surrendered some years before at Corycus in Cilicia. They were still led by their original Sassanid commander, the *framadar* Zik Zabrigan. They were joined by five hundred Parthians. Ironically, these had fled to Rome to escape the Sassanids even longer ago. As he was a scion of their ancient Arsacid royal dynasty, Tiridates, son of the exiled Armenian king Chosroes, had been set over them.

The Cantabrians had been sent clambering up the cliff to the right; another five hundred auxiliaries were doing the same on the left. The remainder of the army was the reserve of two thousand horse guards with Gallienus.

The emperor surveyed the field. All was ready. He had military men around him: the *protectores* Aurelian and Heraclian, the junior Praetorian Prefect, Censorinus, the *Princeps Peregrinorum*, Rufinus. Somewhat apart were the heads of the imperial chanceries. Quirinius, the *a Rationibus*, Palfurius, the *ab Epistulis*, Cominius, the *a Studiis* and the others looked very civilian and more than a little out of place, but wherever an emperor went, the commonplace business of the *imperium* followed.

It reminded Gallienus of the morning before the battle of Mediolanum. But there was a difference. At Mediolanum the divisions had been commanded by senators as well as *protectores*. Today the latter provided all the high command. However, he had senators in his entourage. Some were there because he liked and trusted them: Saturninus, the consul; Lucillus, the consul-designate; Sabinillus, the philosophic friend of Plotinus. Others were in attendance for the opposite reason. It was best not to have men like ex-prefect of the city Albinus or the wealthy Nummius Faustinianus out of his sight.

Gallienus looked up at the standards flying behind him: the red Pegasus on white background of the horse guards, and his own imperial purple *draco*. With the serried ranks of steel-clad riders and horses below, they made a brave sight. It was a pity he did not feel the tension in the air, the tightness in his skin, that told him his divine *comes* was with him. But, with or without Hercules, he knew he would acquit himself with courage. Was he not descended from both the Licinii and the Egnatii? *Virtus* had never been lacking in those two ancient Roman families.

There was no reason for further prevarication. Gallienus drew his eagle-hilted sword. Freki the Alamann and another of the German bodyguard closed up on either side of the emperor they had sworn to die protecting.

'Are you ready for war?' Gallienus flourished the sword.

'Ready!' The cry spread out through the army.

'Are you ready for war!'

As the third response echoed off up the hillsides, Gallienus told the *bucinator* to sound the advance.

The brassy notes were picked up by trumpet after trumpet through the army. The thing was in motion, and there could be no stopping it now. With the tramp of measured tread, the infantry moved forward. The cavalry walked after, the hooves of their horses crushing the yellow flowers which carpeted the valley.

The Raetian army waited, dense and immobile. The only movements were the flags fluttering above.

Gallienus transferred his sword to his hand with the reins while he wiped the sweat from his palm on his thigh. He prayed silently, his lips barely moving: *Hercules, Guardian of Mankind, Overthrower of Tyrants* . . .

The tide of the imperial *comitatus* slowly flowed up the slope. Twice, parts of the line halted to let the rest catch up. They dressed their ranks. There, Gallienus thought, that was the advantage of professional officers over senatorial amateurs. No wild charges like the uncontrolled pursuit unleashed by that young senator Acilius Glabrio at Mediolanum. Here, Gallienus's *protectores* had their men well in hand.

When the front rank closed to within four hundred paces, trumpets rang out from the Raetian lines. Their standards inclined to the fore. Like a great vessel slipping its moorings, their whole force moved downhill.

Gallienus's spirits soared. His men were within ballista range. Simplicinius Genialis had no concealed artillery. And the Raetians were moving. They had not sown the ground in front of them with caltrops. They had not dug those concealed pits with stakes at the bottom the soldiers called lilies. Simplicinius Genialis had had the time to prepare the battlefield. Perhaps the portly equestrian had not been metamorphosed into such a man of war after all.

At about two hundred paces, just outside effective bowshot, the imperial army halted again. 'Testudo!' – the call came back to Gallienus from dozens of centurions – 'Testudo! Testudo!' Big shields swung up, locked together, and the heavy infantry roofed and walled themselves against what must come.

Gallienus felt a dip of disappointment. The Raetian troops had halted. Their front ranks, too, were going into testudo. Of course, they were Roman regulars as well. It was only to be expected. Gallienus noted the Angles on the enemy left were going into their version of the formation. What was it Ballista had said they called it? A shield-burg, something like that. It was strange to think he would never see the friend of his youth again. In his report, the centurion Regulus who had fought his way out had said he had not seen Ballista's body but made it clear there was no possibility he had survived the Gothic sack of Olbia.

Like sentient siege engines created by some latter-day Daedalus, massive artifices made of men and wood and steel, the leading edges of the two armies ground towards each other. There was no moving fast in testudo.

As if choreographed at a lavish imperial spectacle, trumpets simultaneously sounded from both sides, to be followed on the instant by a myriad twanging bows and the awful sound of thousands of arrows slicing through the air. They fell like squalls of dark, evil rain. Thunking into wood, glancing off steel; all too many found a place in flesh, human and equine. Men and beasts screamed. Horses, maddened with pain, reared and bolted among the eastern horse archers in front of Gallienus. Most of the victims in either army were in the rear ranks. Warded by their shields, in the gloom, the inhabitants of each *testudo* shuffled and nudged ahead.

Gallienus watched the eagle of Legio III Italia Concors. The gilded bird advanced steadfastly over the *testudo* of Bonosus's rebel legion. Arrows began to fall among the imperial party. It was good. As Gallienus had thought, the purple *draco* was too tempting a target. He was drawing the aim of the Raetian archers away from his fighting men at the front. Gallienus called for a shield. Freki the Alamann gave him a surprised glance. Let him look. It had been a long time since Gallienus had entered battle without his divine *comes*. There had been no need for a shield when Hercules had wrapped him in the skin of the Nemean lion; it was proof against iron, bronze, stone.

The armies were closing. The gaze of Gallienus switched between Bonosus's eagle and his own heavy infantry. '*Now!*' he whispered. '*Surely now, Proculus.*' As if the thought caused the deed, the imperial front ranks halted. Not as neat as on a parade ground, but not too ragged or bowed. On the left, the column of legionaries commanded by Tacitus kept going. But there was no movement on the right. Had something gone wrong? Why was that wing stationary? What was Proculus doing?

With relief, Gallienus saw the two thousand on the right resume their advance. Proculus might be a whoremonger, but he was a fine officer. And he was loyal. Gallienus found himself grinning. It had been an inept attempt by the *frumentarius* of Postumus to entrap Proculus. The whore masquerading as wife to the *frumentarius* had admitted everything without torture. Gallienus had had her whipped anyway. Her pain – the livid stripes – had added to his pleasure when he had taken the bitch himself. Afterwards, he had been merciful; merely giving her to Proculus's men. It might be doubted if they had exercised much *clementia*. The *frumentarius*, of course, had died slowly.

A roar brought Gallienus back. The Angles on the rebel left had burst from their Shield-burg into a wedge. They raced forward. Fleet of foot, they caught Proculus's men by surprise. They crashed into the legionaries before the Pannonians had a chance to shift out from their *testudo* into a fighting formation. Gallienus could see Angle warriors actually climbing on top of the locked shields of the legionaries. They hacked down with their long-swords, like crazed roofers demolishing the structure beneath their feet. Only the twelve-man-deep formation of the Pannonians, the constant pressure from the rear, was preventing them from being swept away.

Away to Gallienus's left, the Roman legionaries of both sides were more circumspect. The big shields swept down, the men jostled further apart to allow them to wield their weapons. They exchanged javelins, drew their swords and then both sides charged. The clash echoed back from the hillsides. The advantage of the slope on the rebel side and the greater numbers on the imperial cancelled each other out. But it was an equilibrium purchased with men's lives.

As the wings engaged, Legio III in the middle of the rebel line came to a standstill. There were perhaps thirty paces between it and the stationary centre of the imperial army. Gallienus stared at the rebel eagle, willing it to move. '*Hercules, Saviour . . .*' He prayed desperately, mouthing the words aloud, unconcerned if mortals overheard. Deliberately, the eagle inclined forward. *By all the gods, no.* The eagle tipped further, swept right down to the ground. All the other standards followed. The legionaries put down their shields, reversed their swords, raised their right arms in salute.

'*Ave Imperator* Gallienus!' The men of Legio III chanted his name. *Imperator* Gallienus. It had worked. The deep-laid plot had worked. Venutus had achieved what he had claimed. The blandishments of gold had won over the spendthrift Spaniard Bonosus, and he in turn had brought his legion back to its right and proper allegiance.

Enfolded in hot battle, the men on the wings fought on, unaware of events in the centre. Things were different for the Raetian militia. Seeing themselves betrayed, as one they turned and sought safety in flight. The auxiliary archers, far from shooting them down, looked to get away first.

Gallienus looked up the valley, beyond the fleeing mob. The standards above the horsemen were turning, moving away. Simplicinius Genialis was enough of a commander to see the day was lost. The cavalry *alae* began to canter back towards the baggage. They would get through, but it would be difficult for the thousands on foot. Their numbers would hinder them, the carts and tents get in their way, and the hills on the right came round close to those on the left, leaving but a narrow passage.

'Sound the recall,' Gallienus said to the *bucinator*.

The call was picked up across the valley.

On either wing the combatants stepped apart. Tacitus could administer the *sacramentum* to the legionaries from Germania Superior on the left. Proculus could do the same to the Angles on the right.

Gallienus handed back the shield, sheathed his sword. He tried to think of an epigrammatic saying suitable to the moment of success; something modest, stern but memorable. Nothing came. He did not care. He had won. He had proved to himself he did not need divine aid. Why should he? Was he not worshipped as a god himself? In time, he would slough off his mortality, and take his place on Olympus.

A rider clattered up from the left. The men of Legio VIII

Augusta and Legio XXII Primigenia had sworn the military oath to their rightful *Imperator*.

Ordering just his German bodyguard to accompany him, Gallienus rode across to the right.

'I give you joy of your victory, *Imperator*.' Proculus saluted.

'What is the delay?'

Proculus shrugged. 'The barbarians are reluctant to give their oath. They are too stupid to see their position is hopeless.'

Gallienus looked out over the crests of the legionaries. A big Angle chieftain stood out in front. Standards flew over the wall of shields: a white horse on a green field, various *dracones*, one white, another red.

These were Ballista's people. The big, middle-aged chieftain even looked like him. Gallienus knew some words of their language. But it was unbecoming for an emperor to use such a tongue. He spoke in Latin, slow and clear.

'Your leader has fled. The battle is lost. Give me your *sacramentum*, and you will serve in my *comitatus*.'

The tall Angle replied in decent Latin. 'We gave our oath to Postumus, not to Simplicinius Genialis. Postumus has our word and our treasure.'

Gallienus unlaced his helmet, hung it on a horn of his saddle. Diplomacy should always be conducted with an appearance of confidence, and with an open hand. 'Give me your word, and I will give you new treasure.'

'We are not Alamanni. We do not break our word.'

Gallienus stilled his bodyguard Freki with a gesture. 'I know the good faith of the Angles. I grew up with your *princeps* Ballista.'

At the name, the ranks muttered.

'Ballista has served me for many years. Now, on my instructions, he travels to your homeland to bring your king and the peoples he rules back into my friendship. Swear your oath to me, and the Angles will be reunited.'

'I must consult my *principes*.' The warrior stepped back, and was surrounded by a group of mailed warriors, each as large as himself. They talked, low and earnest.

Gallienus sat his horse. It would not have been politic to tell these barbarians the truth, that Ballista was dead in the ruins of Olbia.

A different noble came out of their ranks. An older, grizzled man, his mail was clotted with blood.

'You have not shown Ballista honour. We keep our word. We will leave this place.' The chieftain moved back. The shields of the front ranks snapped together. The rest turned. Under the white horse banner and the white *draco*, they ran off towards their mounts. Those that remained beneath the red *draco* began to edge away.

For a moment, Gallienus was too angry to speak. A roar swelled up from the legionaries.

'Kill them!' Gallienus shouted. 'Kill all of them, do not let one of them escape!'

XXIV

THE ISLAND OF HEDINSEY

Ballista walked down the gangplank. Maximus, Tarchon and Wada the Short followed him on to the dock; the rest remained on the *Warig*. He went up to the warriors. There were fifty of them, in full war gear. He did not recognize any of them. Under their helms, their eyes were unfriendly. Their spears were levelled. A dozen archers, bows drawn, stood off to one side, covering the ship. It was not quite the homecoming he had imagined.

A young warrior spoke the ritual challenge.

'Strangers, you have steered your steep craft through the seaways, sought our coast. I see you are warriors, you are dressed for war. I must ask who you are. I will have your names now, and the names of your fathers, or further you shall not go.'

Ballista unlaced his helmet, took it off. 'I am Dernhelm, son of Isangrim. It is with loyal and true intentions I have returned to Hedinsey. My bench-companions are from many lands; Romans and Olbians from the south, a Vandal, two Heathobards, a

Rugian. Tarchon here is from Suania in the Caucasus, Muirtagh of the Long Road from Hibernia, Wada the Short is from the Harii.'

There was a stirring in the ranks, but the young warrior did not unbend. 'If you are who you claim to be, I was a child when you left.' He gestured.

An older warrior stepped forward, peered at the newcomer. Ballista peered back.

'Ivar Horse-Prick.'

'Dernhelm, you little fucker.' Encumbered by shields and weapons, they embraced. 'It is him, even uglier than when he left.'

A cheer came from the warriors. Not all joined in.

'Why have you come?' The young warrior's tone was still unwelcoming.

Ballista looked at him measuringly. 'I do not know you.'

'I am Ceola, son of Godwine. The *atheling* Morcar has entrusted me with the defence of this shore. Your father is not here.'

'I know that. If you will give me a horse, I will go to see my mother in Hlymdale. When I return, we will sail to Varinsey to see my father at Gudme.'

Ceola considered this. 'Your men will remain here. They will cause no trouble, or you will answer for them. Ivar Horse-Prick will accompany you.'

Ballista and Ivar Horse-Prick rode knee to knee through the open, gently rolling countryside. The sun was warm on their backs. Cattle grazed in the meadows, the winter wheat was just showing green. Their path wound inland past wet depressions fringed with alder. The mounds of the burial ground loomed on the horizon. Ballista had recounted his long journey from Olbia to the Heathobards helping to repair the *Warig*, and two warriors of that people joining the crew. Nothing had happened in the final two days' sailing to need comment.

'It has always been the way,' Ivar said. 'Young warriors with a name to make want to follow a war leader of reputation.'

Ballista smiled. 'Young Ceola did not seem in a hurry to join my hearth-troop.'

'He is your brother's man,' Ivar said. 'Your father is old; Morcar makes many appointments. Ceola is too young to be among the *duguth*. His father the *eorl* Godwine is a good man. You remember him?'

Ballista grunted.

Ivar Horse-Prick laughed. 'I forgot. Godwine did not approve of you or Eadwulf Evil-Child. And he was jealous of Froda. We were all jealous of Froda.'

Men were working among the burial mounds. Ballista reined in to watch. The chamber was nearly finished. The long sides had been revetted with overlapping vertical planks, shored up by struts. The labourers were forming the short walls by fitting horizontal timbers behind the ends of the construction.

'Heoroweard,' said Ivar.

'How?'

'Of course, you would not know.' Ivar shook his head. 'At the Nerthus ceremony. Some Brondings, and a few Wylfings and Geats – Morcar said they should be searched, your brother Oslac and the priest argued against it – they had concealed knives. Paunch-Shaker died fighting. He will be in Valhalla.'

'Who else?' Ballista's chest was very tight.

'Two young warriors; you would not know them. A few others took wounds, Oslac among them – nothing serious. Two of the Brondings were taken alive.'

'Was Kadlin there?'

Ivar gave him a sharp look. 'Yes, she got to the boats.' Ivar looked away. He seemed to be choosing his words carefully. 'Her son Aethelgar fought well. Oslac's boy is growing into a fine man.'

Ballista looked down into the grave. 'I had hoped to see Heo-roweard Paunch-Shaker this side of Asgard.'

As they came near Hlymdale, much was the same, as if the years had counted for nothing. Smoke rose from the halls. That of his father stood far the largest. They dismounted inside the stockade. Grooms led their horses to the stables. The piggeries still stood to the left; the thatch of their roofs slumped, as he remembered, lines of green moss growing across them where the ties ran. Swine snouted, busy in the sunshine. As in his child-hood, the mud was flat, closely pocked by their sheds, rougher, more churned further out by the wattle fences.

'Come,' said Ivar Horse-Prick. 'You have not travelled all this way to look at pigs.'

They walked up past the forge. There were new buildings, but, sensibly, none had encroached on the domain of the smith. The grass was springy under his boots, again as Ballista remembered. The wind whistled through the lime, beech and hazel of the wood backing the settlement.

The great hall of the *cyning* Isangrim was empty except for a couple of serving women. The lady was not expecting visitors. She was with her women in the weaving hall.

The day was mild, and the door was open. It threw a rectangle of bright light into the building. There was the click and shuffle of the looms; the smell of wool and charcoal. Ballista stood, wait-ing for his eyes to adjust. The women formed themselves in his vision from the gloom. They sat on their stools before the frames, their fingers paused as they regarded him.

His mother's hair was grey. Otherwise, she looked unchanged. She sat, tall and stately among her women. A brooch gleamed with garnets and gold at her breast.

Ballista knelt before her, put his hands on her knees. 'Mother.'

She put her hands over his. 'Dernhelm.'

He looked up. Her face had more lines, yet was the same. Her eyes were moist, nevertheless she smiled calmly. His father had often said she was self-controlled beyond other women, far beyond his other wives. Ballista thought of his own wife. Julia had the same quality.

'You are filthy from the road.' She told one of the women to bring water. 'How old are your sons now?'

Ballista had to think. 'Isangrim has twelve winters, Dernhelm five.'

'Do they look like your Roman wife?'

'No, they are fair.' Ballista felt like crying.

'They are well?'

'Yes, the last time I saw them.'

'When was that?'

'Two years ago, in Ephesus.'

His mother had to swallow, marshal herself before she could speak again. 'It is hard to be far away from your children. You left your family safe?'

'In Sicily – safe, the gods willing.'

'The old Caledonian slave Calgacus?'

Ballista had to fight not to break down. 'Dead. Killed last year.'

'You avenged him?'

'Not yet.'

The woman returned with a bowl and towel. Ballista washed his face and hands, and dried himself on the middle of the towel. His mother took it from him. 'How uncouth you have become. Others will have to use this towel. You are not among the Romans now.'

Ballista acknowledged the mild rebuke with a dip of his head. He knew then how much he had changed.

'You will be hungry,' his mother said. 'You always were. When you have eaten, we will talk.'

They ate in the great hall. Ivar Horse-Prick consumed an immoderate amount, even for a northerner. Ballista told his mother how her brother Heoden did, how things went among her people, the Harii. She admired Battle-Sun, her brother's gift to his foster-son. Afterwards, Ballista and his mother retired to the privacy of his father's chamber at the rear of the hall, upstairs under the eaves. There were different wall hangings, a couple of new chests. The rest was the same: the huge, dark-wood carved bed, some of his father's favoured weapons. Ballista threw open the shutters, letting sunlight flood the room.

Suddenly, his mother hugged him fiercely. Stroking his hair, she sobbed. Ballista held her, his own tears hot on his cheeks.

She stepped away, drying her eyes. 'It has been a cruel parting. Twenty-six winters. I prayed, but often doubted I would see you again. You are bigger, your teeth and nose have been broken, but you are much the same.'

Ballista went to speak, but his mother silenced him.

'Pull the chairs to the window.'

He did as he was told. Side by side, they sat and looked out over the palisade at the trees stirring in the wind.

'You have come back at a bad time,' she said. 'You will know about this Unferth and his son, Widsith. No one knows where they came from: some say they are from the south, others that they are not human. The father always goes masked. They gave their oath to the king of the Brondings, ate at his hearth, then – two years ago – murdered him, and took his throne. The Wylfings, Geats and Dauciones have cast off the rule of the Himlings and acclaimed Unferth the Amber Lord.'

Ballista carried on looking at the moving branches. 'Your brother told me all this. The kings of the Rugii and Heathobards said the same.'

His mother made a slight gesture of impatience that he remembered well. 'You will not know how things are here. Your father has become old beyond his years. Sometimes he comes here; mainly he stays in the hall at Gudme. In most things, he lets Morcar rule. With you a hostage among the Romans, Arkil the same

283

with the Romans in Gaul, and Eadwulf long in exile among his mother's people in Frisia, there is no one else.'

'Oslac?'

'He does nothing except read Latin poetry and brood over his wife.' She paused. 'Kadlin's eldest son, Starkad, is with Arkil in Gaul.'

'Kadlin is . . .'

'She is mourning her brother.' Again, the little movement indicating impatience. 'Your father is surrounded by Morcar's creatures: Swerting Snake-Tongue; Glaum, son of Wulfmaer. Either Morcar or one of them is always there. Unferth and his men have burnt outlying farmsteads on Latris, even here on Hedinsey. They kill our people, raid our allies, and the Himlings do nothing. Morcar is a great warrior, but it is as if he is reluctant to fight Unferth.'

'Everyone is afraid of someone,' Ballista said.

His mother laughed. 'Whatever Morcar is, he is not a coward.' The laughter went from her. 'Nor is Oslac. Neither will welcome your return.'

The Island of Varinsey

Morcar looked up towards the severed horse's head on the pole. It was too much. It could not be ignored.

The village of Cold Crendon through which he walked had been a quiet place, its inhabitants farmers and fishermen. Now it was a reeking shambles. Two of the cottages must have been well alight before the rain came. Only their beams remained, shimmering with the fire still in their core. The thatch of others smoked wetly. It would have to be raked off. If there was anyone left to do it, and they had the heart to start again.

Bodies lay in the mud. Men, women and children, old and young cut down indiscriminately. Some were naked; their heads had been hacked off and placed by their buttocks. Morcar felt their shame. These were his people. This was too much.

Morcar walked up to the headland. The rain had blown away to the west. Just a few thin clouds raced after it. The north coast of Varinsey was spread out, its low islands and lakes deceptively peaceful in the gusting wind and returned sunshine.

Rock thrust through the soil up here. The hazel pole had been wedged into a cleft. The horse's head had been turned to face inland. There was writing cut into the pole. Morcar read the runes.

Here I, Widsith Travel-Quick, son of Unferth, set up this Sorn-Pole and turn its scorn on the *cyning* Isangrim and the Himlings, and I turn its scorn upon the spirits that inhabit this land, its groves, springs and marshes, sending them all astray so that none of them will find a resting place by chance or design until they have driven the *cyning* Isangrim and the Himlings from this land.

'The fuckers are taunting us,' said Swerting. 'They mean to drive us out, kill us all. No matter what Postumus the Roman says, we have to fight.'

Snake-Tongue was right, Morcar knew. It had been bad enough before. Now Unferth's son had burnt a whole village, and on Varinsey, deep in the heart of the empire of the Angles. The mutilations, the Scorn-Pole; it was all a direct challenge to the rule of the *cyning*. The Himlings needed strong leadership now. They needed it as they had not since the coming of the Heruli then the Goths in the days of the *cyning* Starkad. Morcar knew it fell to him. His father had fought in every battle at Starkad's side driving out the Goths, but Isangrim was old now, his fighting days were done. Morcar's brother Oslac would not answer. Oslac was brave, skilled at arms, but always he had thought too much and done too little. Oslac did nothing but dwell on Latin poetry – how would Virgil's Pius Aeneas have acted? – and worry about his wife. Since Arkil had gone into Gaul, there was no one to lead the Himlings but Morcar himself.

Yes, Snake-Tongue was right: if this went unavenged the Himlings would not have an ally left. The Rugii, Farodini, Hilleviones – even the Aviones, Varini and Reudigni, all the tribes of the Cimbric peninsula – would follow the islanders in deserting to Unferth. With them gone, it could only be a matter of time before the Himlings fought their final defeats on Hedinsey and Varinsey, before their great halls burned like this village of Cold Crendon.

Morcar knew well in his heart that he must take the fight to Unferth. But the problem remained. Postumus was their ally, and the emperor in the west had been unequivocal in his orders: he would not countenance the Angles attacking the new Lord of the Brondings.

Morcar turned his face to the sea, let the wind lift his long hair, play on his face. The thing was out of his hands. His father was still *cyning*, and Isangrim had decided to consult the gods about war. One of the Brondings taken after the Nerthus ceremony had been uninjured. Isangrim had announced that the Bronding would fight a champion's duel against an Angle warrior. The gods would show the outcome of the coming war in the result. As the duel was inevitable, Morcar had demanded he fight for the Angles. He was not much afraid. When the Hilleviones had rebelled, he had defeated their champion before both armies and returned them to their allegiance with no further blood spilt. He had won four judicial duels among his own people. He did not know how many men he had killed in battle. It was not arrogance; he knew he was as good with weapons as any in the north.

'Swerting, take the boat from Hronesness. Go to Postumus's governor of Gallia Belgica, explain why we have to fight Unferth.'

Snake-Tongue nodded.

'If you think it necessary, go inland to Postumus himself. Leave now.'

After the tall figure of Snake-Tongue had gone, Morcar turned back to the sea. He closed his eyes, let the wind buffet him. It did not clear his mind. Like a dog with a bone, his thoughts returned to worrying at his problems. From the first, he had known the Angles must ally themselves with the breakaway Roman regime in Gaul. It was not the trade, and not just the clandestine money he received. It was simple geography. The mouths of the Rhine were but a short sea journey. The Angles were separated from the lands still ruled by Gallienus by innumerable miles of forest and plain, by many other peoples, many of them hostile. Postumus held Arkil and some thousand Angles. When Postumus heard the Himlings had gone to war with his other ally, Unferth, he might execute his hostages. The deaths of the others would be a pity, but that of Arkil would be far from a concern to Morcar.

There was a much worse aspect. Postumus, of course, knew fine well how Arkil and the others had come into his power. Apart from Morcar himself and Swerting Snake-Tongue, among the

Angles no one else knew; not even Glaum, son of Wulfmaer, or Morcar's own son, Mord. There was no worry about Snake-Tongue. He had been part of a yet worse thing, and held it close in his heart for twenty-eight years. Swerting was trustworthy. Which was more than could be said of any Roman. How many Romans knew? Obviously, Postumus himself; Lepidus, his governor of Gallia Belgica; Celer, the *frumentarius* who had arranged the thing – any one of them could have told any number of others. Morcar felt like a man standing on a bastion already undermined by his enemies. At any moment, they might light the wood and pork fat. Would there be any sign – telltale wisps of smoke, a slight tremor; something which would give him time to get clear – or would the whole edifice crash down without warning?

And now Dernhelm was coming home, with money and false promises from Gallienus. Morcar opened his eyes, looked at the wide sea, and smiled. Oslac thought no one knew he had paid the witch to curse Dernhelm. Perhaps when that failed, Oslac would turn to more practical measures. Oslac was mad with love for that slut Kadlin. What lengths would he go to if he happened to find her with Dernhelm? . . . Morcar had arranged more difficult things.

XXV

THE ISLAND OF VARINSEY

Ballista reined in on the last rise, and looked at the home of the gods. The young tended to accept their surroundings as natural and immutable. Ballista had never dwelt on the meaning of Gudme. Now, seeing the place again, somehow, it was evident. The settlement was set in a sacred landscape. The lake of the gods and their springs marked its western border. From up here, he could see the Hill of Sacrifice a mile or two to the north, the Hill of the Gods beyond the lake, and the Hill of the Shrine off to the south. When his great-grandfather Hjar had taken control of the island of Varinsey – over a century before – he had realized that he needed more than his marriage into the ruling Waymunding dynasty, more than his success in war. He had needed the authority of the gods. Hjar had built his hall here at Gudme, the home of the gods, overlooked by those he had claimed as his divine supporters.

Hjar had been no fool. For three generations, the gods had been kind. Gudme had flourished. Now it seemed to stretch for miles. There must have been sixty – a hundred – individually fenced farms. They were gathered in groups on the low hills, fields and meadows in the lowland in between. To Ballista's eyes, long accustomed to the towns of the *imperium*, it was strange. It had a centre in the great hall of the Himlings, but no other civic buildings; no central *agora* with council house and temples. Some of its paths were paved, but they followed no pattern, were flanked by no porticos, no statues. There was not a stone building to be seen, not a tiled roof. No wall encircled Gudme. Apart from the lake, it possessed no real boundaries, nothing to mark the urban from the rural.

The lack of an enclosing wall did not mean it was indefensible. Each farm had its own palisade. They were sited on the higher ground. An attacking force would get split up in the meadows. There were dead ends, natural killing places among the inter-locking fences and buildings. In such an environment it would be difficult to keep control of the men. Best to start at the east, take one hillock at a time, move methodically through to the great hall. If you had artillery, site it on the neighbouring rise, use it to keep the defenders' heads down until just before each assault. If time was short and you were unconcerned about plunder or what happened after, you could attack with the wind behind you and use fire; the thatched, wooden buildings would burn unless the weather was very wet.

'Big, is it not?' Maximus said. 'Has it changed?'

'Not really.' Ballista was glad of the interruption to his line of thinking. After all these years, he had returned to the seat of his family's power, was looking at Gudme, the home of the gods, and in his mind he was weighing up ways to destroy the place.

'It has no wall,' Zeno said. 'Like ancient Lacedaemon, its safety must lie in the courage of its men.'

Ballista inclined his head at the implied compliment. 'Yet when the Spartans took chains to enslave the men of Arcadia, they were the ones who wore them.'

Now Zeno gracefully accepted the flattering reference from Herodotus to the courage of his ancestors.

Ever since they had been among the Heathobards, the demeanour of the imperial envoy had changed. Perhaps, Ballista thought, Zeno had come to realize how things really lay in this embassy. With luck, Ballista would be able to spare the feelings of the Greek, and not be forced to produce the secret imperial *mandata* from his baggage.

Ballista checked over the column. The five slaves were with the beasts of burden and baggage at the rear. In front of them were twenty-eight armed men on foot, Romans and Olbians mixed together. The Rugian pilot was with them, having chosen to give his oath to Ballista, rather than be left among the Heathobards. The other ten were mounted with Ballista at the front. Discounting Zeno, the eunuch Amantius and the slaves, there were thirty-seven fighting men. Drawn from different peoples, it was a respectable hearth-troop for the return of an *atheling* to Gudme of the Himlings.

Things had gone better the day before, when the *Warig* had beached at the port of Gudme, than they had back on Hedinsey. The defence of Gudmestrand was in the hands of an older *eorl* called Eadwine. Ballista had half remembered him from boyhood. Eadwine had provided lodgings and a feast. They had drunk with his warriors. There had been no fights. Ballista had given an arm ring to Eadric, the son of the *eorl*. In the coming days, it would be important to have men well disposed to him among the leaders of the Angles. A tangible expression of Eadwine's goodwill were their mounts and the baggage animals.

Ballista gave the signal, and, with Zeno at his side, led them into Gudme. As they crossed the final bridge, its guard blew a long blast on his horn. An answering note came from the great hall far ahead. They went between the farms and workshops. Women and children came out to point and stare. Skilled craftsmen – workers in gold, silver and steel, bone and wood – put down their tools to watch. They climbed north up the hill to where the hall of the *cyning* stood, the smaller halls of his chosen warriors beyond. Like the Allfather's *Gladsheim* with Valhalla beyond, Ballista thought; Gudme, where Hjar of the Himlings had re-created Asgard on Middle Earth.

Even to one who had seen the Forum of Trajan, the scale of the hall was still not unimpressive. More than fifty paces long, the ridge of its thatch roof dominated the skyline. To those who had never left the north, it was simply the biggest building in the world.

Ballista and the others dismounted in its lee. A large black bird regarded them from the roof. *When the ravens leave Gudme, the Himlings will fall.* The horses, baggage animals and slaves were taken away. The doorway was at the midpoint of the long wall. It was surmounted by the gilded prow-beast of a longship which the *theoden* Starkad had taken from the Heruli.

Throwing his travel-stained black cloak back over his shoulder, Ballista adjusted the roseate brooch which held it in place. The brooch of gold and garnets had been a parting gift from his father. The *cynings* of the Himlings gave out few of the distinctive orna-ments. Wearing one declared a man either one of the dynasty, or an important, highly favoured ally, lord of his own people. Bal-lista checked the gilded things on his belt: the battered bird of prey which his mother had given to him when he left the north, and the Mural Crown, the original of which he had been awarded by the emperor Philip the Arab. He took off his helmet, tucked it under his left arm, pushed back his hair.

Zeno came and stood to one side, and a little behind. His white toga with the thin purple stripe was badly creased. It was an impractical garment in which to ride. Futilely, the envoy attempted to smooth its folds.

'It looks fine,' Ballista said. 'Time to go.'

Battle-Sun hanging with the dagger on his right hip, and the old, unnamed sword he had carried all the years on his left, Ballista walked into the hall of his ancestors.

In the cavernous interior, the massively thick pairs of oak posts marched away on either side. Shields and spears hung from the roof. Isangrim, son of Starkad, *cyning* of the Angles, was enthroned opposite. On either side of him sat Oslac and Morcar. Many *eorls* and many of the *duguth* stood around. Off to the left were leaders of many of his allies.

Ballista walked forward and knelt before the throne. He placed his helmet on the floor, then his hands on Isangrim's knees. The hands that covered his were spotted with age. There was a slight tremor in one.

Ballista looked up. His father wore a jewelled diadem around his brow. His long hair was plaited back. It was silver. His face was clean-shaven as before, but the cheeks were sunken. His father looked old, tired and careworn. The very pale-blue eyes were rheumy. Yet there was still some light in them.

Isangrim stood. He pulled his son up with him. The old man was surprisingly strong. His arms came around in a bear hug.

'Dernhelm,' he whispered. 'My gentle, beautiful, long-lost boy.'

'Father.'

Isangrim stepped back, let go one of Ballista's hands, lifted the other high, turning him to face those assembled.

'My son is returned.' The voice of the *cyning* carried to the furthest reaches of the hall, out through the still-open doors to the crowd that had assembled. 'The youngest, but far from the least of my sons. Dernhelm, the much-travelled. Dernhelm, whom the Romans call Ballista. Dernhelm, the Angle who defeated the Persians and who overthrew an emperor and took the throne of the Romans.'

While the cheering continued, Isangrim gestured for Oslac to move along, so Ballista could sit beside the throne. Ballista scooped up his helmet, placed it on his knee, tried to look impassive. The *cyning* remained standing.

'My people, our allies, the Allfather has brought the *atheling* Dernhelm back for the coming war. Have the duelling-ground prepared. Let us see which side the gods will favour.'

A cloth, six paces by six, was spread on the level ground before the hall. Its edges were pinned down with sprigs of hazel. It was ringed with armed warriors.

The Bronding had been given full war gear. The other prisoner taken at the Nerthus ceremony helped him prepare.

One of the men assisting Morcar was bald, but Ballista recognized him as Glaum, son of Wulfmaer. Morcar had aged better than his friend. The other was very young, well short of twenty winters. It had to be Morcar's son, Mord.

'What are you doing here?' There was no friendship in Oslac's question.

'A man has to be somewhere,' Ballista said.

Morcar and the Bronding stood on the cloth. Each had a sword and shield.

The crowd was still with expectancy.

As was right, Morcar, as the challenger, waited for the first blow.

The Bronding leapt forward, swinging a mighty blow. It cut through the leather rim of Morcar's shield, splitting the linden boards to near the boss. As he staggered sideways with the impact, Morcar violently twisted his shield, hoping to pull his opponent's sword out of his hand, if not break it. The Bronding hauled his blade out and swung again. A thick wedge of wood flew from Morcar's shield.

'Stop! New shield!' Morcar shouted.

Convention just held. With evident reluctance, the Bronding drew back, lowered his sword point to the cloth. A warrior took Morcar's ruined shield, handed him a new one. Like the last, it had a red cover and a spiked metal boss.

As soon as Morcar hefted the shield, the Bronding surged in again. This time Morcar met it with his shield at a different angle. The steel merely scraped away some dyed leather and a few splinters.

The Bronding pressed home his attack. His sword moved so quickly it was as if there were three in the air. He drove Morcar this way and that. Yet every time Morcar was almost trapped in a corner, he riposted and stepped clear. Soon Morcar's shield was so hacked he had to call for another.

Both men stood panting as Morcar's third and final shield was brought. Some in the crowd murmured unhappily at the passivity of their champion. Others said he was letting the Bronding wear himself out. Ballista was not sure that was the case. Defending was tiring also. More likely, Morcar was playing with his opponent's thoughts, exhausting his hope. Again and again the Bronding attacked, but he had yet to land a blow.

Morcar lifted the new red shield. The Bronding launched another full-blooded swing. It went differently this time. Morcar moved inside the blow, and past. His sword flicked out, caught the Bronding's exposed left leg. A line of blood appeared.

If Morcar had been quicker, he could have finished it then, while his opponent's back was unguarded. The Bronding rallied. They went at it again. Now Morcar attacked – thrusting, jabbing, cutting – working his man around the cloth. In one of the exchanges Morcar nicked the Bronding's sword arm. When the foreigner attacked, sometimes Morcar watched the blade, did not move his feet but just swayed back out of harm's way.

'Rest,' called the Bronding.

Morcar backed off.

A new shield was passed to the Bronding as they paused. He nodded. They fell to again.

The Bronding was moving heavily, but he was not done yet. He smashed a cut, rending Morcar's shield. The Angle reeled back. His sword stayed up, but he flexed his shield arm as if it were troubling him. The Bronding saw his advantage. With renewed vigour he closed in, cutting left and right. Morcar gave ground, meeting the blows with his blade, shield arm hanging near immobile.

With skill the Bronding took a thrust on the edge; steel rang. He rolled his wrist. Morcar's sword was forced wide, leaving his chest open for the killing blow. Before it came, as if miraculously cured, Morcar's shield arm whipped up. The iron spike of the boss punched into the Bronding's face. Almost too quick to follow, Morcar sank to one knee and cut the man's thigh open to the bone.

The Bronding was down, curled in his pain and blood. Morcar stood over him.

'Victory!' Morcar shouted. 'This is the will of the gods.' He lifted his blade to the sky.

The crown roared their approval. 'Out! Out! Out!'

A lone voice cut through the chanting. 'Finish him!'

The noise of the crowd faltered.

Isangrim stepped on to the cloth. 'Finish him.'

With contemptuous ease, Morcar killed the Bronding, flicked his blood from his sword. It rained on the stained, crumpled cloth.

'The gods favour our cause,' Isangrim said. 'The other Bronding can take the news to Unferth.'

The *cyning* held up his hand to cut off the renewed celebration.

'This will be a cruel war. It may be a long war. Let no one enter into it lightly. No move is to be made until it has been discussed by the Himlings and the *eorls*, and approved by me. Any man who endangers his companions, endangers us all, by acting without my sanction will be outlawed.'

The Angles accepted the prudent words of their *theoden* with silence.

'Before the war council, we must return to Hlymdale, and bury the noble Heoroweard.'

The Island of Hedinsey

Kadlin stood with Heoroweard's family: his widow Wealtheow, his son Hathkin, his younger sister Leoba, and her own children, his nephew Aethelgar and niece Aelfwynn. It was a gentle, early summer's day. The air smelt of recently turned soil, fresh-cut wood, and woodsmoke.

The funeral procession emerged between the great, grassy barrow of Himling and the empty cenotaph of Hjar. Smoke rose from the treasure-fires which were always tended on top of the mounds under which the *cynings* lay.

Everything had been done properly. That morning Kadlin had gone with Wealtheow to the house of the dead at the edge of the cemetery. The body had been washed and dressed, placed in the oak coffin. The physical work had been done by slaves. Heoroweard had been dreadfully cut about, and he had been dead for some time; directing their ministrations had not been easy. Wealtheow had been strong. With no hesitation, she had placed in her dead husband's cold mouth the hacked piece of gold that would pay Heimdall, so that the watchman of the gods would allow Heoroweard passage across Bifrost to Asgard.

Everything was ready. The grave was well furnished with expensive things from the *imperium*: two buckets and a ladle in bronze, two fine glass cups, one with the image of some imaginary big, spotted cat, and a wallet of coins bearing the heads of long-dead emperors. The grave goods were suitable for a warrior of the Wuffingas. They would have been quite acceptable for one of the Himlings themselves.

Heoroweard had never cared particularly for material things. Wealtheow had added things more to his liking: a leather bag stuffed with lamb chops, flatbread and apples; next to it, a big flask of mead.

Allfather, but Kadlin would miss her brother.

The coffin was shouldered by ten men. Paunch-Shaker had been a big man. Behind the deceased came the *cyning* Isangrim, then the rest of the Himlings: Oslac, Morcar with his son, Mord, and then, a little apart, Dernhelm.

Kadlin would not think about Dernhelm now. To do so would somehow tarnish her grief.

The cortège reached the grave.

Dernhelm had been Heoroweard's friend. It was right he was here, but Kadlin wished he was not. She had not looked at him yet. What did it matter how he had changed? Her brother was dead.

The bearers, all strong young men, were struggling to lower the coffin into the grave. The ropes tore at their palms. The coffin swayed in its descent.

'Just as awkward in death,' Wealtheow murmured.

All the family smiled, except Leoba. Perhaps, Kadlin thought, a woman has to suppress too much to become a shield-maiden. Or it could be her sister blamed herself for not saving their brother. All at once Kadlin both pitied and envied her sister. It would be good to be a shield-maiden and take revenge on those who had set the murderers on her brother.

The coffin was in the grave. The bearers had retrieved the ropes. The family were on one side, the spoil from the digging on the other. Isangrim, the Himlings and their followers stood at one end. The other mourners – his hearth-companions, more distant relatives, friends and, finally, free tenants – drifted around the heap of earth to the other.

'Allfather, listen to the request of your descendant.' Isangrim seemed to have shrugged off something of his age. 'Heoroweard died a heroic death, fighting barehanded against murderous men with sharp steel in their hands. He fought to protect his loved ones and his people. He did not die like a dog in the smoke of his own hearth. No straw-death, but the death of a hero. Send the Choosers of the Slain. Let them take him to Valhalla. He was my *eorl*, let him become yours.'

There was something awful about these Himlings, Kadlin thought. They naturally saw themselves as akin to the gods. A couple of clicks of the *Norns'* spindles those years ago, the Wuffingas would have ruled, and the Himlings served them.

'Heoroweard was . . .' Isangrim moved into a lengthy speech of praise, no doubt heartfelt enough.

There was movement in the people behind Isangrim. Two strangers were working their way to the front. Kadlin's irritation turned to alarm when she saw the gryphon-head brooches which proclaimed them Heathobards. Allfather, not again. Not like at the Nerthus ceremony.

The Heathobards stopped by Dernhelm. One of them whispered to him. He made a gesture that said, 'Later.' The Heathobard took his sleeve, spoke urgently. Dernhelm nodded. He blew a kiss to the coffin, looked at Heoroweard's family, and bowed. For a moment his eyes met Kadlin's. Then he turned. Followed by a shorter warrior with the end of his nose missing, Dernhelm walked away.

Kadlin could not have been more angry. A typical Himling, putting his own concerns before everything, even a funeral. The same selfishness as before. He had taken her virginity, fathered her child, and left; all without caring. Now he could not even wait until the end of his friend's funeral. If she had to speak to him at the funeral feast, she was not sure she could contain herself.

In her fury, Kadlin had not noticed Isangrim had stopped speaking. The *cyning* took a gold band from his arm and dropped it into the grave. Hathkin was first of the family to make a last offering: an amber gaming piece. It was heart-rending to remember father and son sitting together playing. When it was her turn, Kadlin dropped in the bone comb Heoroweard had seldom used as a child. Her brother had always been untidy. Wealtheow was last. She gave back the ring Heoroweard had given to her.

As they moved off to the feast, above the muted talk Kadlin could hear the awful finality of stones and soil rattling on the lid of the coffin.

XXVI

THE OUIADOUA BANK OFF THE SOUTHERN SHORE OF THE SUEBIAN SEA

Maximus kept close behind Ballista and the Heathobard who was guiding them. It never failed to surprise him how quietly the big Angle could move in the dark. By contrast, those following behind were like a herd of bullocks. Still, the wind from the sea was loud in the trees. It would take the noise off behind them, away from the men they were approaching.

It had been a wild thirty-six hours since the Heathobards had brought them the news. They had slipped away from Heoroweard's funeral and ridden down to the port. While Castricius had rounded up the crew, got the *Warig* fitted out for the sea, Maximus had gone with Ballista to see Ceola. It had not been an easy meeting. The young *duguo* charged with the defence of the coast was Morcar's man. He had been sitting drinking with his father Godwine. The old *eorl* was not close to Morcar, but it was evident he had no great love for Ballista either. As luck would have it, Ivar Horse-Prick was drinking with them. In the end, Horse-Prick had made them see the urgency. Isangrim would be caught up in the funeral feast for the remainder of the day. It could not be discussed in the council of the *cyning* until the next morning. By then the opportunity would be lost. *Eorl* Godwine had announced that neither he nor his son would hinder their departure. Weightily, he had pointed out the threat of outlawry they were bringing on their heads. He and his son might feel the displeasure of the *cyning*, but it would pass. Isangrim was a fair ruler. He had said nothing specific about those who failed to stop men who acted without his sanction.

Ivar Horse-Prick had accompanied Maximus and Ballista to the ship. When the three had gone aboard, they had found that Castricius had her ready. Food and water had been stowed, all clutter cleared away. The men were armed and waiting at their benches. Zeno, Amantius and the slaves had been left ashore. With no commotion, they had cast off, and soon left the coast of Hedinsey behind.

The wind had shifted that morning and set in the north. It had blown steadily on their larboard quarter as Wada the Short held their course to the south-east. They had sailed the rest of the day and through the night. At some point the next day they had sighted the chalky cliffs of Cape Arcona. Knowing the rocky spit which ran below the surface to the east, Wada the Short had given Arcona a good berth. The light had been failing when they reached the great Ouiadoua Bank, pulled into one of its many inlets and hauled the *Warig* up on to the fine, white sand.

The Ouiadoua Bank was a desolate place, a disputed march between the Heathobards and the Farodini. The Heathobard had led them away from the sea, around in a long detour, to come up from the south on their prey. They had been walking through the darkness for at least three hours. Maximus had slept only a little on the voyage. He knew he should feel tired, but he did not. The prospect of action was on him. Nowadays he found it banished not only weariness but thoughts he did not wish to entertain: grief for old Calgacus, a certain emptiness that had come with his own advancing years, the suspicion of a lonely old age.

The Heathobard held up his hand. The column stopped. Through the trees, at the bottom of the slope, dark in the moonlight, they could see the longship. They had not known if it would still be there. Five days before, the Brondings had raided a village to the east. In a small boat, the two Heathobards who had arrived at Heoroweard's funeral had tracked it to this isolated mooring. Although they had said the Brondings had taken much drink and some women, until this moment Maximus had been half sure the raiders would have moved on. Carelessness or arrogance – maybe both – had left Widsith, the son of Unferth, with just one boat in this lonely place.

The longship was not beached but close moored to the shore by its stern. It lay in the shelter of a small, projecting cape. Its benches could not be counted because its awnings were rigged. But it was big; a crew of up to a hundred, Maximus thought. They watched it for a time. Nothing moved. No lights showed on the vessel. The embers of a fire on the beach pulsed in the wind. The Brondings must have eaten ashore, then gone back on board to sleep in shelter.

Ballista passed the word for them to gather round. He outlined his plan. They would divide into four groups. One – himself, Maximus, Tarchon, Ivar Horse-Prick, Wada the Short, Rikiar the Vandal, and the Rugian guide – would wade out to the prow. When Castricius saw them climb on to the boat, he was to lead six of the Romans and all sixteen Olbians in the main attack from the beach on to the stern. At the first alarm, all four Heathobards – the two newcomers and the two who had joined the hearth-troop earlier – were to board from the water on the starboard and cut the ropes securing the awnings, while three Romans led by Diocles were to do the same on the other side. The Egyptian Heliodorus said it would be better if he replaced Diocles leading the Romans in the water, otherwise, if Castricius fell, there would be no one to take over command of the main force. Ballista checked this with Castricius, who agreed.

They crept down the incline, keeping as far as possible in cover. The wind soughed through the branches, and pine needles cush-ioned their footfall. They halted at the tree line. Maximus looked back. The men were blackened, as they had been outside Olbia. No one had drawn his weapon yet. The banded moonlight broke up their outlines as they squatted, waiting like a band of malevo-lent dwarves risen from under the ground to take vengeance on mankind for some primordial wrong. The smell of resin was strong, sickly. The sound of splashing water, as nerves prompted first one then another to empty his bladder.

Ahead, thirty paces of open beach, the sand almost blue in the moonlight. Little tongues of white flame occasionally flickered in the ashes of the fire. Beyond, the dark boat sat on a coal-black sea. Its mast rocked gently against the sky. Torn, high clouds rushed across the moon. Logs ticked in the fire, water lapped the shore. Still no sound or movement to indicate anyone was awake.

Ballista stood. With the creak of leather, Maximus and the others did the same. They all waited, their breathing shallow. Once this was begun, there could be no stopping.

Ballista moved off. Maximus went behind his shoulder. Neither looked back. They crossed the beach at a careful jog. To begin with, the sand gave under their feet; then it was compacted and hard.

They slowed to a walk as they reached the water, wading in gently. At first the beach shelved steeply. The water was very cold as it lapped over the top of Maximus's boots, up to his knees. They went past the gangplank. The bottom levelled out as they went in the lee of the longship to their right. Shallow draught, clinker-built; each overlapping plank was underscored by a black shadow.

Level with the mast, halfway to the prow, the water rose to their chests. Shield above his head, with exaggerated high steps, Maximus pushed against the resistance of the water. If the beach shelved more, the water would be over his head before they reached the prow.

'Get up!' A shout from the stern. 'We are being attacked.'

'Come on,' Ballista said. No point in silence now.

The thunder of boots on the gangplank. The first clash of steel.

Half running, half swimming with his right hand, Maximus floundered through the sea. Muffled thumps and shouts from inside the hull.

A splash as a body fell from the stern.

Even before the prow swept up, they could not quite reach the gunnels. Ballista passed Maximus his shield, told Wada to lift him. Maximus handed both shields on to Rikiar. Hands gripped under his armpits hoisted him. He got a good grip on the top plank, but his sodden clothes and mail dragged him back. There was a huge shove from under his arse. Ivar Horse-Prick grinning up at him.

Maximus slithered over the side. The quickest of glances showed the fight raging at the afterguard. Forward, the awnings were still drawn, no immediate threat. Maximus leaned over the side. Rikiar was passing the shields up to Ballista. Maximus reached down, and helped Wada aboard.

'On me,' Ballista said. He gave Maximus his shield. They stood shoulder to shoulder with Wada. Water sluiced off them, pooled around their boots. It was very cold. The sounds of the other four clambering up the side.

The awning was pulled back. A man came out, blinking foolishly. Ballista stepped towards him, Battle-Sun in his hand. A backhand to the shoulder, a howling forehand to the head. The man crashed away to the far side.

Maximus could see other faces, pale under the awning. They hung back.

The fight at the rear was fierce. Men falling underfoot, another off into the water.

Men swarmed over both sides. Their blades shimmered in the moonlight. They moved along the gunnels, swords sweeping in great arcs, ropes parting. Towards the stern, the awnings sagged and collapsed on to the crew. Yells of consternation and fury. The warriors on the sides were striking down at movements under the canvas, like men killing rodents in a sack. Maximus could see the bald pate of Heliodorus; the blacking must have washed off in the sea.

Somewhere, women were screaming, and what sounded like a child.

In front of the mast someone had taken charge of the disconcerted Brondings. The awnings were being hauled aside, before they could entrap the men there. The warriors wedged into a tight shield-burg, leather-bound boards facing in all directions. Maximus thought there must be about thirty of them.

'Break them, and it's over,' Ballista said. 'On three.'

'One, two . . .'

They shrieked down the deck. The warrior in front of Maximus tried to flinch. Close-packed, there was nowhere for him to go. He jabbed, with no real conviction. Maximus watched the blade, punched it aside with the boss of his shield, thrust down overhand. His sword plunged down over both shields, caught on the man's chest, slid, slicing down his front.

The wounded man dropped his weapons, stood tottering, impeding those behind. Maximus leapt high, bringing his sword down on a man in the second rank. The heavy edge cut down into his skull.

'Rally!' Ballista called.

Maximus fell back to his friend's right shoulder. Horse-Prick was to his own right, Rikiar the Vandal behind.

'Surrender!' Ballista shouted.

The Brondings huddled, indecisive, almost overwhelmed by the magnitude of the surprise.

Heliodorus loomed above and behind them on the rail; bald, streaked with blacking, like one of his bestial native deities. At the stern, the massacre continued.

'Surrender!' Ballista demanded again.

'Never!' A tall young warrior emerged from the Brondings. 'Never.' He was unarmoured, his arms bright with gold. His hair was long and black; a man from the south. He had a blade in each hand.

'Widsith Travel-Quick, I will give you the lives of your men.' Ballista spoke almost conversationally.

'I will not take them from you, Oath-breaker.' The son of Unferth spat, then yelled at his men. 'Clear the prow. There are only seven of them, many more of us. Follow me.'

Widsith leapt forward. Only one warrior, off to Maximus's left, came with him. In a second the latter was dead, impaled on Wada's sword.

Ballista took the first blows on his shield, giving ground. Sharp fragments of wood spiralled through the air. Widsith drew back. As he went to pounce again, Wada's sword bit into his right arm. The weapon in that hand clattered to the deck. Too late he brought up the blade in his left. Ballista, his whole frame twisting behind the blow, sheered Widsith's left arm off below the elbow.

The young son of the Amber Lord staggered sideways, until the side of the ship brought him up. He stared at the blood pumping from the stump.

Ballista went after him, stepping carefully on the slippery deck. 'No need to look, it's just as you think, the arm is gone.'

Battle-Sun blazed in the moonlight. It nearly severed Widsith's neck. The young leader collapsed half over the gunnels. Ballista raised his blade. It took two more blows before Widsith's head came away from his shoulders. Ballista rolled the body into the water. Gripping the long, black hair, Ballista held the grisly trophy aloft. 'Surrender.'

It had gone beyond that, beyond reason. The Brondings tried to throw themselves over the sides. There were men everywhere, hacking at them. There was no holding the bloodlust.

Maximus went and stood by Ballista.

The killing spilled over into the shallows. Perhaps some got away.

Rikiar came back to Ballista and Maximus. The normally taciturn Vandal spoke:

> 'The warrior's revenge
> Is repaid to the King
> Wolf and eagle stalk
> Over the King's son
> Widsith's corpse flew
> In pieces into the sea
> The grey eagle tears
> At Travel-Quick's wounds.'

Maximus looked at Rikiar in surprise.

Rikiar said nothing, then took the head from Ballista.

When the killing was done, and the looting underway, the cost was counted. Two Romans and two Olbians were dead, one of the former and two of the latter badly injured. One Heathobard was missing, and could only be assumed lost in the sea. Given the odds, and the unaccounted slaughter among the Brondings, it had been a low price to pay.

Maximus walked the length of the boat with Ballista. The dead still lay underfoot, grotesque in their attitudes. Six captive women sobbed near the stern. Two had bad cuts. Near them lay the bodies of two children: boys, no more than twelve winters.

Ballista stared down at them.

'Some things just happen,' Maximus said.

XXVII

THE ISLAND OF HEDINSEY

Ballista watched the men digging down into the largest barrow in Hlymdale. They had come well prepared with picks, shovels, buckets and barrows, ropes and ladders. The treasure-fire on top of the mound had been extinguished. The men had been working for some time. Only their heads and shoulders could be seen now. Already a path had been worn in the grass to where the pile of excavated earth was steadily growing. Soon they would need the ropes to draw the buckets of spoil to the surface. It would not be long before the tomb of Himling was disturbed. Suitable offerings to appease his shade were ready.

The *cyning* Isangrim stood off to one side with his court, Ballista among them. Ballista had been uncertain if he would return to Hedinsey in time. After the killing of Widsith, they had spent the following day burying the corpses that could be found, their own and those of the Brondings. Maximus had been evidently upset when it had come to interring the children. The Heathobard women they had released had said the boys were servants brought with Widsith. No one admitted to their killing. Most likely they had come by their death blows in the chaos of the slaughter under the fallen awning.

Ballista had been in two minds about the burials. Loitering on the deserted strand had brought disaster to the son of Unferth and his followers. Ballista had no wish that the same fate should fall on himself and his men. There were said to be other Bronding longships in those waters. He had been tempted to honour their own fallen, bury the innocent and leave the enemy for scavengers. Yet to do that would have been only one step removed from what Widsith had done at Cold Crendon. Many men found it hard to fight unless they believed their behaviour better than that of their opponents.

After a night on the beach, at first light they had heaped stones in the Bronding boat, until her sides were only a hand's breadth above the water. They had taken her out into the deep. They had smashed holes in her hull. The coal-black water had poured in, and the longship had gone to the bottom. The rest of that day had been devoted to another act of decency. They had taken the Heathobard women back to the settlement to the east from which they had been abducted. The wind had shifted into the east, and it had involved hard rowing.

The *Warig* had moored there for the night. In the morning the Heathobard who remained of the two that had come to Ballista on Hedinsey had asked to join the other two of his tribesmen who were already followers of Ballista. Four more warriors from that place had made the same request. Ballista had counselled them to remain and see to the safety of their village. Cruel war was coming to the Suebian Sea. Brondings or other sea raiders might return. The Heathobards had not been swayed. The northern code of blood vengeance was too strong in them. If he would lead them against Unferth and his followers, they would gladly die for him. Ballista's hearth-troop needed men, and he had accepted their sword-oaths.

311

The wind had stayed in the east. The *Warig* had raced across the whale road. They had made Hedinsey the previous night after two days' fast passage. Their reception had been mixed. Isangrim had not been minded to forget his threat of outlawry. He had spoken terrible words from his high seat. His sons and their followers were as bound by his commands as any other of his *eorls* and warriors. As outlaws, Dernhelm and his men could be killed without recompense. From a leather bag, crusted with the salt in which it had been packed, Ballista had produced the head of Widsith Travel-Quick. The *cyning* had smiled. Glaum, son of Wulfmaer, had whispered in his ear. Isangrim had waved him away. Morcar and Oslac had glowered. In this one instance, the *cyning* had said, no penalty would be enacted. Let no other flout his words, but Dernhelm and his hearth-companions had done him a great service. They had earned their place back in his favour.

Rikiar had taken it on himself to give thanks on behalf of all of them:

'Ugly as my head may be,
The cliff my helmet rests upon,
I am not loath
To accept it from the King.

Where is the man who ever
Received a finer gift
From a noble-minded
Son of a great ruler?'

The Vandal had come to them as a thief. He was ill-favoured, and in many ways kept apart from their fellowship. He remained an object of suspicion. Yet no one could deny his skill with verse.

And now a shout came from the top of the grave mound. The

labourers had dug down to a row of timbers. It would not be long before they broke through these rafters.

This would be the third time the Angles had turned to their long-dead hero in time of need. Starkad had first opened the tomb of Himling when the Heruli came. As a youth, Isangrim had been with Starkad the second time, before they led the alliance that drove the Goths from the north. Like war itself, it was not a thing to be entered into lightly.

'Sure, it must be a fine sword your great-grandfather used, to go to this trouble, the digging and the disturbing the dead and all, to get it back,' Maximus said.

'Great-*great*-grandfather,' Ballista said. 'He never carried the sword. It was made after his death. Himling is the sword.'

'Your dead man *is* the sword?'

'When Himling was killed by the Wuffingas . . .'

'I thought they were your greatest friends.'

'It was a long time ago. Unlike you Hibernians, we are not terrible people for holding grudges.'

'For a man who has been there, you maintain an incredible ignorance about my people. If the people of my homeland were not much given to reconciliation, would you think either of us would have left Tara alive – given all the killing and the like?'

'Possibly not.'

'Your grandfather's sword?'

'*Great-great*-grandfather. After Himling was cremated, the smith put some of his bones with the charcoal in the bellows pit when he forged the blade. A part of Himling's strength, spirit and luck passed into the steel of Bile-Himling.'

'What happened to the rest of him?'

'The rest of his bones are in the barrow. Hopefully, as he died in battle, his shade is in Valhalla, not waiting in there with the sword and the other bones.'

A hail from the summit of the mound told them the tomb was

open. Looking up, Ballista saw the ladders against the sky, before they were lowered into the pit.

Everyone waited on Isangrim. The *cyning* leaned on his staff, eyes focused on things the others could not see. Perhaps, Ballista thought, his father was remembering the previous times he had been here, half a century or more before. Bile-Himling had granted Starkad victory over the Goths. But, ignoring dire warnings, Starkad had not returned the blade to the tomb. Things had not gone well for him after that. He had carried Bile-Himling two years later against the Langobards. It had done him no good. It had fallen from Starkad's hand when the Langobards had cut him down. Isangrim had returned Bile-Himling to the dark, before he had made peace with the killers of his father, taken one of their sisters as his first wife.

'I will not go into the tomb,' Isangrim said. 'I am an old man, too old to wield Bile-Himling. My sons will make the descent. They will bring Bile-Himling to me, and I shall decide which of them will carry the blade.'

With his brothers, Ballista took up the offerings and walked up to the top.

Morcar stepped between him and the ladder. 'A newcomer will not go first.'

Ballista stood back to let them go down first.

It was dark inside the pit, just the light from above, and not altogether sweet-smelling. The scattered bones of a horse lay underfoot. Gold and precious things glowed dully at the edges of the darkness. There was an urn on the seat of the throne, the receptacle of those remains of Himling that had not been used by the smith. Above it, resting across the arms of the high chair, was a heavy, single-edged sword.

Ballista placed the silver bowl he carried on the floor. He went to the throne, put out his hand towards the sword.

'No,' Oslac said. 'You will not carry Bile-Himling.'

'I have done more since I returned than you did in all the years I was away,' Ballista said.

'You should have been outlawed.'

Both had their hands on their hilts.

Morcar stepped between them. He turned to Oslac. 'Most of what you do will now turn against you, bringing bad luck and no joy.'

Oslac recoiled as if struck.

Ballista wondered what this was between the two of them.

'As the eldest, Oslac will take the thing to our father.' Morcar spoke smoothly.

Oslac stood for a time, as if still shocked, then picked up the blade and went to the ladder.

Back above ground, in the land of the living, Oslac had recovered. He held Bile-Himling aloft. The assembled *eorls* and warriors *hoomed* in awe. Oslac offered the weapon to the *cyning*. Isangrim did not take it.

With sudden insight, Ballista wondered if after all these years Isangrim blamed the sword for his father's death, or perhaps himself.

'A time of war.' Isangrim raised his voice. It was cracked with age, perhaps emotion. 'Unferth will come and seek revenge for his son Widsith. If he does not, his followers would count him a *nithing*. They would desert him, and he would leave the north as he arrived, an outcast. He will come, and we must be ready.'

All there – the gold-bearing men of violence, the three or four shield-maidens – nodded.

'It will happen like this,' Isangrim said. 'My son Dernhelm will defend our allies on the Cimbric peninsula. My son Oslac will hold Varinsey. I will take my stand here in our home of Hlymdale. My son Morcar will be here with me on Hedinsey. Latris and the islands of the south will be in the charge of Hrothgar of the Wrosns. Let all of you, all our allies, summon the fighting men.

Let the war-arrow travel throughout our realm and summon men to cruel war.'

Everyone waited.

'Bile-Himling, the blade forged from our ancestor, has returned to the light. It will be wielded by my son Morcar.'

With no expression on his face, Oslac passed the weapon to Morcar.

Amantius put the stylus and writing block down on the ground next to him. He wiped his hands on his fleshy thighs. His back rested against the rough wall of a byre. Cattle regarded him from the other side of a fence. Gods, how low he had sunk. A eunuch of the imperial court sunk to the level of a banausic slave hiding among the beasts. But no other privacy was to be found in the sprawling barbarian settlement of Hlymdale.

He picked up his writing things again.

Publius Egnatius Amantius to Lucius Calpurnius Piso Censorinus, Praetorian Prefect, *Vir Ementissimus*.

If you are well, Dominus, I can ask the gods for no more.

Amantius could think of nothing else to write. There was nothing to report about the embassy. As secretary, four times he had accompanied Aulus Voconius Zeno into the presence of Isangrim, the senile, petty kinglet of this squalid and insignificant Hyperborean tribe. The ambassador had uttered a few courtly platitudes – his pleasure in standing before the ruler of the Angles, his prayers that the favour of the gods would continue to fall on such a noble father of a harmonious house – all of which Amantius presumed had been translated. Not once had the imperial envoy mentioned the amber which was the ostensible cause of this hideous odyssey. There had been not so much as a hint of their true purpose. Even such diplomatic gifts as had survived the journey had not been handed over. It was as if Zeno had reneged on the sacred duty laid on him by the Augustus Gallienus. The charitable might decide Zeno was exercising discretion, biding his time until the moment was auspicious. Amantius was not of that mind. He had observed Zeno during their tribulations. Zeno was weak, a coward. Amantius knew himself little better. But he was a eunuch, and everyone, including himself, knew eunuchs did not possess the constitution of other men.

If you are well, Dominus, I can ask the gods for no more.

The words mocked him. Already he had asked the gods for much. There were no rings on his hands, no bracelets on his wrists. He had given all his fine things to the gods for his safety. Now he must ask for more.

It all made sense. At the outset, the storm in the Euxine that had driven them to the island of Leuce had been divinely ordained. It had been a test, and they had failed. They had not put their trust in the gods and gone back aboard the warship. They had defied the divine prohibition and spent the night on the island. They had brought down on themselves the implacable anger of Achilles. It all stemmed from that: the murderous fight in the bar, the attack on Olbia, nearly being crushed by the raft of logs on the Hypanis, the Goths on the Borysthenes, the Brondings off the Vistula and the tempest in the Suebian Sea. Time and again souls had been snatched from the midst of life, those without the coin to pay the ferryman condemned to wander for eternity.

Amantius knew the anger of Achilles was not played out. It would fall on them again when Unferth came for his revenge. Amantius's possessions had all gone to the gods. Desperate need had made him bold. Eunuchs were always suspected of peculation. To cover his tracks he had hidden a few of the coins he had taken from the diplomatic gifts in the possessions of the Vandal called Rikiar and in the paltry things of one of Zeno's slaves. The former had the reputation of a thief, and Zeno habitually thought the worst of his servants. Amantius had made the offering in the lake, the nearest thing he could find to a place he recognized as sacred. To salve his conscience, he had included both of them in his prayers.

Publius Egnatius Amantius to Lucius Calpurnius Piso Censorinus, Praetorian Prefect . . .

What did it matter? There was nothing to say. There was no way to send the report anyway. No one would ever know the things that happened on this doomed embassy.

Amantius got up, secured the writing materials to his belt. He smoothed down the barbarian tunic and trousers he was reduced to wearing. It was time to get back for the leaving feast.

Ballista waited outside in the dark under the low eaves of the hall. They had followed the old custom and drawn lots for who sat where at the feast. The lots had not been kind. Still, he had been surprised when the slave-girl whispered her message.

'Kadlin.'

She stood in the light from the doorway. She was as he remembered her: tall, slender, standing very straight. Her long hair framed her face, her very dark eyes.

'Over here.'

She looked back into the hall, and quickly all around, before stepping into the dark passage between the wall and the over-hanging thatch.

He took her hand and drew her further away from the light.

They stopped behind a pile of stacked logs. He let go of her hand. She moved a little back from him. Her face was a pale oval in the gloom, not much lower than his own. He had forgotten just how tall she was.

'It has been a long time,' he said.

'A very long time.' He sensed as much as saw her smile.

'You look well.' After all these years, he found nothing but banalities to say.

'Your have broken your nose and teeth.'

She moved towards him. She was very close, almost touching. He could smell her perfume, her breath, the warmth of her body.

'Did you . . .' What did he want to say? *Did you miss me? You know I did not want to go. Do you still love me?* He could not say any of them.

Her hand came up, touched his face. She was smiling again, her eyes bright in the gloom. 'How long have you been waiting out here?'

'Long enough.' He was smiling, too. 'You took your time.'

'What?'

'The slave-girl, your message.'

She stepped away. 'I sent you no message. Quick, we must go back.'

As he followed her into the light, Oslac came out from the hall.

Kadlin half turned to Ballista. 'Thank you for escorting me.' She spoke formally. 'I hope we will have a chance to speak before you leave tomorrow.' She turned back to her husband.

Oslac stood very still, his eyes moving between the two of them.

'Kadlin.' Ballista nodded to his brother. 'Oslac.'

Ballista could not make out Oslac's words as he walked back into the hall, but the tone of interrogation was unmistakable. Oslac was a jealous man; all the Himlings were. If he harmed her, he would answer for it.

XXVIII

THE INLET OF NORVASUND ON
THE CIMBRIC PENINSULA

The forest was full of the sounds of axes biting into hardwood, the smells of fresh-cut timber, disturbed earth and animal dung. Ballista walked down towards the inlet of Norvasund. Sixty men were employed cutting down trees. They had been working in shifts for three days. Every draught animal, all the plough horses and oxen from miles around on the east coast of the Cimbric peninsula, had been gathered. Harnessed in teams, they hauled the felled trees. Ballista stopped to watch one begin its short but laborious journey to the water. The mighty oak lay entire and untrimmed on the ground. Its crown fanned up to the sky, the leaves still green and vigorous. Stout ropes lashed around the severed trunk and lower branches ran to the complicated harnesses of the twenty waiting bullocks. The man in charge gave the command. The long whips of the drovers flicked out. Bellowing with pain and effort, the oxen strained against their traces. For a moment, the trunk did not move. The whips snapped again, and

320

men shouted. With a deep rending sound, punctuated by the sharp cracks of breaking boughs, the huge oak inched forward on to the waiting rollers. Dust billowed up from the dragging foliage. The gentle incline was with them, but it would take hours before the oak reached the water.

Ballista went on down to the strand. The inlet of Norvasund ran north-west into the Cimbric peninsula. Some way inland from the sea, a promontory on the western side, the far side from where Ballista stood, narrowed the water to less than four hundred paces. He surveyed the progress of his defences. The seaward line of some hundred vertical poles already stretched all the way across, hammered down hard and roped together. The first dozen oaks were braced to them, in a row, their crowns all to the east. Two longboats were towing the next into position. The crew of another vessel were working along, fixing the inner poles, roping the whole barrier together. The final two boats were further out. Their task was to drive individual sharpened stakes in at an angle.

It would be a formidable obstacle to attack from the sea when finished. Some enemy ships should run foul of the outlying stakes, perhaps even tear their bottoms out. The oaks floated low in the water, no more than a foot or so of their trunks above the surface. But their branches would hinder any attempt to ride over them. With archers on both shores and on the five defending longships deployed inside the barrier, any attempt to sever the many binding ropes and breach the structure by towing trees away would bring large numbers of casualties. It would be a formidable obstacle, if it was finished before Unferth arrived. Ballista estimated it would take at least forty oaks. They were only a third of the way there. And it would be as good as useless if the land defences on either side were not completed.

'Food, *Dominus*?' Diocles said.

'What have you got?'

'Re-heated stew; not sure what is in it. I think there is some rabbit, some chicken, and definitely cabbage – very good for you, cabbage. There is bread from yesterday.'

'If there is enough, thank you, yes.'

'It is not Lucullan, but there is plenty.'

There were eight men, Romans and Olbians together. With Maximus and Tarchon, his two constant shadows, Ballista joined them. The firewood and kindling had already been gathered. Diocles fished out his fire-making kit. He took tinder from a pointed oval wooden case. Using a firesteel, he angled sparks from a special striking stone. With the ease of long practice, he had the fire going in no time at all.

As the food heated, they sat and watched the activity on the water.

'It is good your father has so many grown sons, *Dominus*,' Diocles said to Ballista. As with everything he did, the young Danubian gave his words a great seriousness.

Ballista made a noise which might have been interpreted as assent.

'There are enough leaders he can trust to defend several places at once.'

Ballista made no reply, just gazed out over the water.

Diocles stirred the stew, his brow furrowed with earnestness. 'It has never been that way in the *imperium*. If a general does well against some barbarians when the emperor is elsewhere, that general's soldiers insist he takes the purple. It leads to civil war. No matter who wins, the frontiers are stripped of troops, and more barbarians seize their opportunity. If a local Roman commander does well against them, it all starts again.'

Ballista and the others agreed.

Diocles went on. 'No imperial dynasty has had enough men to cover all the frontiers. Take Valerian. Before the Persians captured him, he could hold the east and Gallienus one of the frontiers in the west. But that left either the Rhine or the Danube in the charge of a child. If Saloninus had not been so young, would the revolt of Postumus have succeeded? Perhaps our emperors should marry several women, breed more sons.'

'You Romans would have to change your ways,' Ballista said.

'As everyone says, it is an age of iron and rust. Perhaps it demands change, even from the *mos maiorum*.' At times, Diocles was weightiness personified.

'In my countries Suania,' Tarchon said, 'brother often killing brother, fratricide very good, very popular.'

'And,' Maximus interrupted, 'there is no telling the son will be half the man the father was.'

'There could be another way,' Ballista said. 'If the emperor could find a man to really trust, he could share his power. Then each of them could adopt a younger man of abilities. Four men holding imperial power: one for each of the Euphrates, Danube and Rhine, and one in Rome or somewhere else. They would form something like a *collegium* of emperors.'

'Not a fuck of a chance that would last,' Maximus said.

Diocles said nothing, but looked more serious than normal.

'You so sure the arse-fucking-cunt Unferth come?' Tarchon had developed a rare talent for creating compound obscenities in different languages.

'Yes,' Ballista said.

'Come here for fucking sure? Not other fucking Angle place?'

'No,' Ballista said. 'Not other fucking Angle place. No other fucking Angle killed his son.'

'Fuck, indeed,' said Tarchon.

'Yes, fuck, indeed,' said Maximus.

After they had eaten, Maximus and Tarchon rowed Ballista over to the other side in a skiff. Mord, son of Morcar, and Eadric, son of *eorl* Eadwine, were waiting. They made their reports. The work was progressing. Nothing too bad had happened that morning:

two broken limbs and a near-drowning. With over a thousand men doing heavy work in a desperate hurry, accidents would happen. So far, no one had died.

They walked past the big stacks of planks and up to the low hill where the village had been. Half a dozen other young Angle nobles stood there. In all, twenty had accompanied Ballista. The glamour of serving the war leader who had killed the Roman emperor Quietus with his own hands, who had briefly worn the purple himself and who had now beheaded Widsith Travel-Quick, was strong. Ballista wondered whether the adulation of these young warriors would seem more natural to him if he had spent his life in the north.

Eadric asked if there was anything they could do. Ballista said it would be good if they could all draw back, create a ring around him and by intercepting any messengers give him some time to consider the defences.

Neither Maximus nor Tarchon withdrew, but Ballista was so accustomed to their presence, they did not impinge on his thoughts. He sat in the sun on a pile of wood. Three days before, there had been a village here; now it was a lumberyard. The women, the young and the old had been sent inland to find shelter among the other settlements of the Angles, Chali and Aviones. The able-bodied men had participated in the destruction of their own homes. Now they were labouring at the defences; when Unferth came, they would fight as part of Ballista's war band. Unlike the young nobles, they had not been trained almost exclusively for war. Many of them would die.

The low, round hill commanded a fine view over the inlet of Norvasund: the still, inner waters to the left and the choppier outer ones to the right which led to the Little Belt between the Cimbric peninsula and the island of Varinsey, and on to the wider ocean. From up here Ballista could see the ships working on the sea barrage, and the vestigial defences appearing on either shore.

The plans for the latter were simple. Where the floating barrage came to the shore on the far, eastern side, it would be protected by a semi-circular low ditch and bank, the latter topped by wooden stakes. From the sea barrage a palisade would run forward to meet the earthworks, thus enfilading the former from the land. If anything, the defences on the eastern side were even more basic. A simple palisade running out from the barrage along the waterline – again letting archers shoot along the face of the line of oaks – before snaking back to the hill, where here at the top another palisade would block access to the headland. The demolished houses of the village had provided excellent ready-worked wood.

Ballista worried at a shred of meat caught in his teeth. Water was not an issue. A stream ran into the Norvasund just inland of where the eastern palisade would stand. They were collecting food, but it should not be a problem. Unless completely surrounded, they would be able to draw supplies from the hinterland. They were stockpiling weapons which could kill at a distance – arrows, javelins and stones to throw – and incendiary materials. If there were time, refinements could be added. Sharpened stakes could be concealed in the ditch of the eastern fortlet, and maybe below the water on the west. When the blacksmiths had finished making arrowheads, they could turn to producing caltrops. Both Castricius and Diocles were familiar with torsion artillery. There were skilled carpenters among the Angles. If there were time, perhaps they could build two or three very simple artillery pieces, something similar to the ones he had designed and used a couple of years before when defending Miletus from the Goths.

If there were time . . . It all returned to that. A chain of beacons stretched across Hedinsey and Varinsey. Ballista had men out in small boats in the northern and southern approaches of the Little Belt. They would have warning: several hours, perhaps as much as two days. Yet that would mean little if the defences were incomplete. If Unferth came now, the plan was for the longships to defend the as yet unblocked section of the Norvasund, the men with Ballista here in the west to make a stand on the hill, and those in the east to force-march around the inlet to join them. If Unferth came now, the plan would allow them to die with honour.

Even if there were time, these defences would not hold for ever. Still – Ballista made an effort to cheer himself – they should not have to hold for long. Oslac's ships from Varinsey could be here in a day, two at the outside – unless Unferth came with numbers that Oslac could not hope to defeat with just the aid of those already here. In which case, the defences at Norvasund would have to manage until Morcar could sail from Hedinsey to join Oslac. That meant at least two days; at the outside, no more than four. Ballista worked free the bit of gristle, spat it out. Four days; more if the weather was unseasonal.

Mord was walking up around the post holes of a destroyed cottage. The young *atheling* had his big hunting dog with him.

Tarchon barred Mord's approach. The dog bounded ahead to Ballista. It had got used to him quickly. It wagged its tail as Ballista rubbed behind its ears.

'Young prick-arse wants talking,' Tarchon called.

Ballista waved Mord up. Perhaps he would have to talk to Tarchon about his linguistic inventiveness.

The hunting dog was a fine hound. It looked like a Maremma from the *imperium*. Morcar must have imported it for his son from the Roman provinces on the Rhine.

'I am sorry, Uncle,' Mord said. 'I know you did not want to be disturbed.'

He was far from a bad youth. Ballista wondered what his half-brother thought of his son asking to join this force.

'Do not worry. What is it?'

'A man has come in with a prisoner.'

'What man?'

'He gave his name as Vandrad.'

Ballista's chest felt hollow. 'What does he look like?'

'Tall … hard to tell. He would not remove his hood.'

Could it be, after all these years?

'He would not let me search him either.'

That sounded right. An exile caught in Angeln could be killed as an outlaw. He would not let them disarm him or see his face. Surely it could not be him? Even he would not take such a risk. 'Let him come up, with his prisoner.'

Ballista's eye was caught by the prisoner. Unlike the others approaching, he was bound, and he stumbled. He was barefoot, and his tunic was in shreds. He had been beaten, probably tortured. If he could stand straight, he would be tall and thin. Despite the dried blood matted in his blond hair and caked on his face, he looked familiar, like someone not seen since childhood.

Then Ballista saw the hooded man. He was tall and broad enough. None of his face showed beneath the deep hood. He had a fine blade on his hip. The way he walked was right, well-balanced, a slight swagger.

'Dernhelm,' the hooded man said.

Twenty-eight winters, but Ballista knew the voice, knew it like his own. 'What are you doing here?'

The voice came from under the hood. 'Some things just happen. And I have to be somewhere.'

XXIX

NORVASUND

They came in the night. No beacons flared. Ballista was awake, but the first he knew of their arrival was the northern picket boat flying in from the Little Belt, her crew hailing wildly.

There was a certain chaos as torches flared, horns rang and leaders shouted. Men bundled out of tents and shelters to rush to their posts. The five longships were run out. Maximus helped Ballista arm. Around them, in the guttering lights on the top of the hill, members of the hearth-troop did the same for each other. Riders were despatched north and south to light the warning signals further up and down the coast. Others spurred away inland to bring word to the tribes of the Cimbric peninsula.

Over the black waters Bronding warships stole down into Norvasund. Ballista counted six or seven. Maximus saw eight or nine. More moved out in the darkness of the sea.

The lights and commotion on the waterfront would have told the enemy that surprise was not with them. Nevertheless one ship slid to within long bowshot of the sea barrage. Volleys whickered out from the two nearest of Ballista's boats. The arrows could be heard, but their fall was unseen in the dark. The enemy vessel backed, turned and followed the others out again.

In the greyness of pre-dawn Ballista ate porridge and waited for their return. The enemy had come up the inlet and moored against the eastern shore no more than half a mile away. Some around him – Rikiar the Vandal, Mord, son of Morcar, and the Heathobard known as Dunnere Tethered-Hound – had urged an attack from the land. Ballista had overruled them. The numbers of the *fiend* were unknown. Night attacks were notorious for confusion. The defenders would hold to their plan.

The light was gaining. Ballista put the bowl aside. It was always difficult to eat before a fight. He stood to study the disposition of his forces.

Across the water Castricius had about four hundred men under arms. Should the little Roman fall, Diocles was to take over. The defences there were incomplete. To their rear was nothing except the shallow stream.

Ballista ran his gaze over the inlet. The sea barrage was finished, more than forty great oaks lashed into place. The five warships, the *Warig* among them, each crewed by fifty Angles, were under the orders of Ivar Horse-Prick. Ballista had appointed Eadric, son of *eorl* Eadwine, as the second-in-command there. He was young, but he showed good sense, and both he and his father were held in high regard by the Angles. For this section of the defences the only thing lacking was that the line of sharp stakes concealed below the waterline ran only halfway across the sound from the eastern bank.

On this side, below where Ballista stood, the palisade was complete. Behind it were just over three hundred warriors commanded by Wada the Short and a Heathobard called Grim. Up on the hill, things were less good. The defences had not even been started. In the course of the night, since the alarm, a rough barricade had been thrown together from baggage, stacked timber and what remained of the village. Running along the crest, it would somewhat hinder any enemy advancing out along the headland. Ballista had kept most of his hearth-troop around him: Maximus and Tarchon, Rikiar and the Rugian pilot, the *atheling* Mord and six more young Angles of the nobility, Dunnere Tethered-Hound and five other Heathobards, fifteen Olbians, and eight Romans, including the bald mutineer Heliodorus. It amounted to only forty-one shields, but, the young Angles aside, they were all proven warriors. The men from the south had acquired much equipment from the Brondings of Widsith. Clad in this northern armour, intermingled with the others, there was little sign that they were from the *imperium*.

It had been eight days since the coming of the hooded man and his prisoner. Another two or three, and the defences would have been accomplished. Four or five more and there would have been caltrops, hidden traps, perhaps even artillery. Still, as the Greeks said, it was no use crying over the stubble on a pretty boy's cheeks. When some things are gone, like youth, they are gone.

After the man calling himself Vandrad had spoken, Ballista had sent everyone except Maximus and Tarchon away. He had listened to what the captive had been forced to say. Then, his deep hood still hiding his identity, Vandrad had departed.

The prisoner, now masked as well as bound, was being guarded by the maimed Olbian guide Hieroson and a Heathobard called Vermund. They were to remain out of the fighting. Should the day go badly, they were to get their charge away. A rowing boat was ready. They were to go inland to a village of the Chali. From there they were to skirt back to the coast, get a boat from the Aviones, and take the captive to *eorl* Eadwine on Varinsey. It would be a heavy task, but the *eorl* would know what had to be done. Hieroson and Vermund had taken great oaths. They would do this or die in the trying.

Ballista waited. It was hard enough to face what might be the end, even without the waiting. But, always before battle there was the waiting, the awful time when fear crept into a man's heart, tried to steal his courage. He thought of his sons, the awfulness of never seeing them again. He thought of his wife, and of Kadlin.

The sun had not yet crossed the horizon. To the east the sky was a smooth band of purple-gold. Arching back from there its vault was ribbed with darker purple clouds. In the distance the tiny black dots of a flock of crows fluttered north-east towards where the enemy lay.

'What if they put some ashore elsewhere?' Mord asked. 'If they attacked from inland as well as from down Norvasund it would go badly for us.'

Ballista leaned down and fussed Mord's dog. 'They may not have the numbers.' He spoke reassuringly, for all those standing about to hear. 'And they do not have the time. They know Oslac and your father will be here soon.'

Was that true? Ballista did not know. Neither Oslac nor Morcar had any love for him. Oslac had looked like he wanted to kill him outside the feast, when he saw him with Kadlin. But surely Oslac would not sacrifice this many of their people out of personal animosity. And Morcar was with their father. He would have to be seen to do the right thing.

The sun was still not up. The colour had leached out of the morning. The westerly breeze had shifted the clouds, bringing a trail of white smudges against the blue sky overhead. It was going to be a fine day.

The call of a horn. The deep echo of a drum. The whole of Norvasund was filling with ships – sixty, seventy, still more. Soon it was as if a man could walk dry-shod from shore to shore.

'Allfather!' someone muttered in the hush.

As the sun rose, it picked out innumerable standards above the fleet. The bull with silver horns of the Brondings of Abalos, the double-headed beast of the Geats of Solfell, the gold-on-black lion of the Wylfings of Hindafell, the killer and the slain of the Dauciones; each banner repeated again and again. The islands and eastern Scadinavia must have been stripped of fighting men.

In the centre, shielded on all sides by his vassals, flew the enormous black standard with the wolf Fenris picked out in silver, the sign of Unferth, the man who would be Amber Lord of the North.

Ballista's eyes flicked here and there, trying to count the ships, estimate their size, calculate the numbers. At least three thousand men, most likely yet more; perhaps as many as four thousand. There had not been an armada like this on the Suebian Sea in his lifetime, not since Starkad and Isangrim defeated the Goths. If only there had been time to build artillery. The slaughter it would have brought down in these confined waters on those close-packed ships.

Achilles, hold your hands over us . . . Allfather, turn your baleful grey eye on them . . . Different prayers rose in divergent tongues. Even the toughened men of the hearth-troop were shaken.

'A lot of the fuckers,' Maximus said. 'Makes them hard to miss.'

Men laughed, some immoderately because of the tension.

'The Hibernian is right.' Ballista pitched his voice to carry, tried to make it exude confidence. 'Every missile will find a home. They cannot all fight at once. They will get in the way of each other. Their ships will foul each other. And they will burn. Light the fires!'

Fuck, this is not good, Ballista thought. One thousand men against four times that number, with only a few stakes and a flimsy barricade to even the odds. Even if they survived the first onslaught, Oslac and Morcar would have to get here soon. But Ballista still wondered whether they would come at all. The former had reason to hate him, and the latter had sacrificed as many before. Ballista looked at his own white *draco* writhing above his head. How many men would Unferth send up here to avenge his son? Would this be the end? A stand with forty men on this windy little hill?

Across the water, the sound of the horn rang out again. The drum beat a different rhythm. Slowly the enemy fleet opened up, like the carapace of some massive water insect. The ships flying the standards with the killer and the slain man nosed into the eastern bank. The small figures of Dauciones warriors could be seen jumping ashore. Ballista reckoned there to be about a thousand of them. Castricius and Diocles would have much to do to hold out. Further away down the inlet, ten longships carrying the bull with silver horns of Abalos – half the Bronding contingent – moved to the nearer bank. These warriors would have a longer march to come to the base of the headland where Ballista stood.

As the warriors disembarked on either shore, the rest of the fleet advanced in two divisions. First came twenty longships of the Geats, the double-headed beast of Solfell fluttering above each of them. They were in line abreast filling the water, rowing straight for the sea barrage. Behind them were another twenty vessels. These flew the rampant lion of Hindafell. In two ranks, these Wylfings were angling towards the palisade at the foot of the hill held by Wada the Short and Grim the Heathobard.

Ballista looked for the largest battle standard with the silver wolf on black. Unferth himself with ten longships remained further out as a reserve. Briefly, and with no real hope, Ballista scanned beyond, towards the two tiny islands and the mouth of Norvasund. As he expected, the sun shone on empty water. There was no realistic chance of any relief for at least another day, maybe more, as the beacons had not tracked the approach of the enemy.

The enemy had come down the Little Belt from the north. They must have slipped through the Sound between Hedinsey and Scadinavia the night before last and spent the previous day lying up somewhere on the west coast of Scadinavia. It had been a dark night when they made their passage through the Sound, but it was strange they had not been seen by any of Morcar's watchers on Hedinsey. A dreadful foreboding gripped Ballista. Even Morcar could not have added such a greater betrayal to his earlier treacheries.

Ballista pushed his fears to one side. Long ago, at the siege of Novae, his old commander Gallus had taught him that an essential aspect of command was to ignore what cannot be altered. There was more than enough to worry about here in Norvasund today.

The Geat longships were picking up speed, their oars rising and falling, white water curling from their prows. As they came into range, volleys of bright fletched arrows shot out from the five guardships and fell on and around them like swarms of wasps. Some oars swung dead in their wake, but their speed did not slacken.

Ballista stared at the deceptive surface about twenty paces from the barrage where the stakes were hidden. Surely they were there? Now; it must be now. With a wonderful suddenness, a Geat ship juddered to a stop. Another veered sideways. Even from such a distance Ballista could see the planks torn from its side, men thrown into the water. Over near the far bank, a third crashed to a halt, then a fourth. Three others banked down hard, the water creaming as their oars fought the water to bring them to a standstill.

As the rest closed with the barrier, Ballista saw what they intended. At full speed, just before impact, their crews scrambled towards the stern. For four or five, it did no good. They ran bow on into the oaks or tangled in the untrimmed branches. The raised prows of the others slid up over the floating trunks. The warriors piled forward. For a couple the momentum was not enough. They slid backwards. Three more stuck fast. Men jumped out on to the treacherous, shifting barrage. As they hauled at the ships, from both banks arrows sliced among them.

Three of the Geat ships scraped over the obstacle. Ballista's five longships were alongside in moments, men pouring over the gunnels. One of the Geats held out for a time, but when surrounded by four vessels its end was inevitable.

With fire arrows from Castricius's men on the far bank arcing down at them, the remaining Geat longboats attempted to pick up men from the wrecked vessels and pull back some way down Norvasund.

There was no time to celebrate. The boats of the Wylfings had reached the palisade on the nearer shore. They ran into a storm of missiles. Using the rising ground, Wada's three hundred men shot and threw everything to hand without cease. The plunging shafts and stones swept the decks. Flames blossomed briefly, before they were stamped out. The frontage allowed only ten longships to come prow on to the wooden defences. The bravest Wylfings hurled themselves at the rampart. Some got over; most were hurled back into their boats or down into the shallows. Those who made it inside were surrounded and hacked apart. Soon, those in charge had had enough. The boats backed water. Missiles flew back and forth, smoke trails coiled through the air, men still suffered and died, but it could bring no decisive result.

Ballista gazed over to the far side of Norvasund. Those under Castricius were not yet engaged. But things did not bode well. Whatever his orders from Unferth, the leader of the Dauciones was exercising more discretion than the other tribal chiefs. He had formed up the majority of his warriors in a shieldwall just out of bowshot. The backs of a smaller group could be seen disappearing into the trees. Ballista had no doubt they were setting off on a flank march which would bring them around behind Castricius's position, where there were no defences apart from a shallow stream. Attacked from all sides except the water, there would be no salvation for Castricius's men. The professional in Ballista could not help admire the unknown leader of the Dauciones.

'They are coming,' Maximus said.

The Brondings were about three hundred paces away. They were jostling into a shield-burg at the base of the headland. Behind their overlapping shields, numbers were difficult to judge. Exactitude mattered little. Ballista's hearth-troop had to be outnumbered by something like ten to one. A slope and a makeshift barricade would make no difference. This could only end one way.

Ballista searched around for Hieroson and Vermund the Heathobard. They were down near the rowing boat with the prisoner. Ballista considered sending them away. He could join them, row to safety with Maximus and Tarchon. He dismissed the *nithing* thought. He would not run, and if he sent anyone away now, it would undermine the fragile morale of the hearth-troop. Things would have to play out as the *Norns* had spun.

Rikiar the Vandal raised his voice:

> 'Let us make our drawn swords glitter
> You who stain wolf's teeth with blood;
> Now that the fish of the valleys thrive,
> Let us perform brave deeds.
> Here before sunset we will
> Make noisy clamour of spears.'

The warriors *hoomed* their approval, slowly beat their weapons on the linden boards of their shields. Ballista felt tears prick his eyes with pride at being one of this brave, doomed band.

Mord's hunting dog was baying. Ballista spoke gently to the youth. 'Are you content with this? I forgot your grandmother was a Bronding.'

The boy grinned. 'My mother is from the Eutes, and my father is an Angle. I am a Himling *atheling*, like you.'

Ballista grinned back.

The Brondings were advancing. When they came in range, Ballista shouted for those with bows to shoot. It did little good – the shields of the Brondings soon quivered with shafts – but the hearth-troop had more arrows than they could use today, and they would not need them tomorrow. It made them feel they were doing something.

The shield-burg came on slowly, but to those waiting it took all too little time.

Twenty paces out, the shield-burg broke open. With a roar, the Brondings rushed forward. Now arrows found their mark. Men were snatched backwards, as if they had run into an invisible rope. But far too few to break the charge.

Ballista carefully weighted then threw a stone the size of his fist. He saw it smash into a shield. Its owner staggered, but came on. Ballista dragged out Battle-Sun.

A warrior grasped the barricade with his shield hand, swung himself up. Ballista back-handed his blade into the man's leading leg. He collapsed at Ballista's feet. Another hurdled the obstacle. Ballista got Battle-Sun into his guts. The dying Bronding fell into him, driving him back. Ballista took a blow from an unseen assailant to the right shoulder.

All along the line the Brondings were swarming over. Ballista saw Dunnere the Heathobard cut down. Somewhere, a dog howled in pain.

'Back! Form on me!' Ballista retrieved his weapon, took quick steps back to the young Angle holding the white *draco*. Maximus was on one shoulder, Tarchon the other.

Often in battle there came a pause. Having cleared the barricade, the Brondings held off as they lapped around the defenders.

A tight knot of men, completely surrounded. Perhaps twenty left; half the hearth-troop gone. Young Mord howling defiance over Ballista's shoulder. An Olbian muttering 'Let us be men' in Greek. No point in trying to run, begging would do nothing. Die

like a man among men. The heartbreaking sorrow of never seeing his sons again.

A tremor, like wind through a cornfield, among the Brondings.
Heads turning, anxious words.

Battle-Sun shook in Ballista's hands. The Rugian pilot was dead
at his feet, near cut in half. Ballista's right shoulder stung. The
mail was broken, blood hot on his arm. He was panting with
pain, or shock, or effort.

The ring of Brondings backed away. Then, at a command,
turned and ran, clambering over the ruined barricade.

Ballista and the survivors stared at each other, not yet daring to
hope.

'Look, out to sea.' It was Maximus, keen-eyed as ever.

Ballista looked, struggling to comprehend the turn of events.
The seaworthy Geat longships were retreating, the Wylfings following. On the far shore, Dauciones were running back to their
boats.

'Fuck me,' Maximus said. 'You never would have thought it.'

A great forest of masts out at the entrance to Norvasund.
Any number of longships, under oars, coming down the Little
Belt from the north. Banners flew above them: the White
Horse of Hedinsey, the Deer and Fawn of Varinsey and the
Three-headed Man of the Wrosns. Four of the Bronding
reserve were swinging out line abreast to delay them. But the
largest enemy ship, the one with the huge black flag showing
Fenris the wolf in silver, was pulling out of Norvasund and
away south into the Little Belt. Unferth was fleeing from the
fleet of the Himlings.

Morcar stood at the edge, where solid ground gave way to
mud. The other leaders of the fleet stood a little apart; his
brother Oslac, *eorl* Eadwine, Hathkin son of Heoroweard, and
Hrothgar of the Wrosns. The marsh was no distance inland

from Norvasund. As they and the crowd waited for the cowards, he listened to the wind hissing through the alder scrub, and turned things over in his mind.

Mercy, in the two days since the battle, had been on everyone's lips, along with forgiveness and reconciliation. Morcar had used the words as assiduously as any. It had been necessary. Half the Geats had got away, and three ships of the Wylfings, but not a single vessel of the Dauciones had escaped south down the Little Belt, and the only Bronding longship to win clear had been that carrying Unferth himself. Conspicuous mercy and many assurances had been required to bring some three thousand defeated and trapped warriors and their *eorls* back into allegiance to the Himlings. But mercy was a virtue which all too easily could be interpreted as weakness. It had to be balanced by severity. Politics had precluded severity to the losers, but it had to be exhibited. The cowards among the victors would provide that display.

Morcar felt strangely alone. It was not so much that the other leaders were standing at a slight distance, the crowd further away still, more that neither his two particular confidants nor his son were at his side. It had been essential that Glaum, son of Wulf-maer, stay on Hedinsey. Someone reliable had to be with Isangrim, otherwise the old *cyning* was all too susceptible to malign influences. Swerting Snake-Tongue had been a long time in the west. He should have returned by now. Perhaps it had proved necessary for Swerting to travel into Gaul to the court of Postumus. If so, that might not be good. And Mord had vanished with Dernhelm.

In the distance a guard of warriors could be seen through the oaks bringing the convicted to the marsh.

Where had Dernhelm gone? Why had Mord gone with him? The very day of the battle, Dernhelm had retaken command of his longship *Warig*, quietly gathered his hearth-troop, Mord among them, and slipped away. The last time Dernhelm had vanished he had returned in triumph with the head of Widsith. Now most likely he had slunk back to Hedinsey, to their father. Glaum could deal with that.

Morcar smiled. Norvasund had been a triumph to rank with any of those won by the Himlings of the past, with those of Hjar over the Franks or Starkad over the Heruli and Goths. The *scops* would sing of it for generations. And it was not Dernhelm's but Morcar's own. Morcar had ordered the beacon fires not be lit when Unferth's fleet was spotted in the Sound. Instead he had trailed the enemy. Fast ships had summoned Oslac and Hrothgar. They had met with him off the north coast of Varinsey. Under his command, they had pursued Unferth down the Little Belt, caught him at the entrance to Norvasund, and there crushed his pretensions to the title of Amber Lord.

Doubtless the *scops* would make much of Morcar being first to board a Bronding longship, of how he had cleared its prow, struck down five warriors with his own hand. It had been a creditable feat of arms, but it was nothing compared with the leadership he had shown.

It had always been about leadership, everything, all the hard things he had done. All of it had been for the good of the Angles. A people could have only one leader, and the *theoden* must be the best man. It was a fact of nature. Froda had been vainglorious and thoughtless. Froda had been their father's favourite. A man of no substance, as *cyning* he would have brought disaster to the Himlings and the Angles. Eadwulf had been fickle, drunken, intemperate in all things. It would have been better if he had been executed, as Morcar had intended, but his exile for the murder of Froda had dealt with Eadwulf Evil-Child. Morcar claimed no credit for Dernhelm being sent away into the *imperium*. It had been luck, or the will of the *Norns*. But the betrayal of Arkil in Gaul had been a second masterstroke. It had been a difficult decision, not reached without consideration. That so many valuable Angle warriors had had to be sacrificed with Arkil had been unfortunate. Yet leadership was indivisible. It demanded hard choices. When Isangrim stepped down, as the old man soon must, Oslac would stand aside. The Angles would be united under one Himling ruler. Morcar knew he would give them the leadership they needed.

All had been in place, and then Dernhelm had returned. Isangrim doted on his youngest son, doted on Dernhelm in a way their father had never doted on Morcar himself. Dernhelm had to be removed again. Unsurprisingly, Oslac had shown himself weak. Morcar had arranged for his brother to find his whore of a wife alone with her old lover outside the feast, and Oslac had done nothing but whine and quote gloomy lines about betrayal from the verse of the Romans. Still, the *Norns* had given Morcar a new thread. Back on Hedinsey, the imperial envoy Zeno had made a clandestine approach. The repulsive little Greek claimed Dernhelm was carrying secret orders from Gallienus, orders to overthrow their father and take the throne himself. When confronted with documentary evidence of such treachery, of attempted parricide, the senile affections of Isangrim must give way. There could be no punishment for the hateful crime except death.

The condemned were herded down through the poles which marked the sacred site. Morcar felt no more sympathy for them than did the bleached skulls, the visible symbols of ancient piety, which were set on top of every one of the ash stakes. Each of the six men had hung back from the fight, had thrown down their swords like *nithings*. The cowardice of each had endangered their companions.

At the edge of the marsh, Morcar spoke the ritual words. 'Deeds of shame should be buried out of the sight of men, stamped down, trodden deep. Take them.'

One by one, the bound men were thrown into the marsh. Some struggled and sobbed, others lay still; all alike again unmanned by the weakness that had brought them to this. The wattled hurdles were brought down, and they were drowned.

341

The crowd – the loyal Angles and Wrosns, and the Brondings, Wylfings and the rest returned to allegiance – watched in solemn silence.

Morcar turned away, satisfied. No one would mistake the Himlings' mercy of the last two days as weakness.

THE ISLAND OF ABALOS

The new moon had risen. It was a clear night. From the copse, Ballista watched the isolated farm about half a mile away. Behind the dark line of the fence and the outbuildings, the high ridge of the hall was silhouetted against the azure sky. Grey smoke puffed up, smudged the stars and was pulled away to the east. Chinks of light came from the shutters. Now and then one of the doors was opened, and the sudden spill of golden torchlight threw everything else into blackness. When his night vision returned, Ballista could see the dark standard flying from the gable. He could not make out its insignia, but he knew it bore Fenris the wolf in silver.

They had sailed direct from Norvasund. The wind on the starboard beam, the current had helped them south down the Little Belt. The westerly had remained constant as they steered southeast around Varinsey and the islands of Latris, then north-east past Cape Arcona and across the open sea to Abalos. It had been a fast passage, just three days.

Behind Ballista, someone smothered a sneeze. It should not

343

matter. They had come up from the south. The wind was across their faces. Ballista raised himself on his elbow, and looked back. The men were blackened and muffled, their outlines broken and indistinct in the banded moonlight under the trees. A Black-Harii such as Wada the Short could have found little at which to complain. After Olbia and Ouiadoua Bank, even the Romans and Olbians must be becoming accustomed to night fighting. At least those who survived.

The hearth-troop had been hit hard at Norvasund. Twenty-three had fallen there: Dunnere Tethered-Hound and another three Heathobards, the Rugian pilot, four Romans, seven Olbians and seven of the young Angle nobles. All had been cut down around Ballista on the hill, except two Angles who had met their end fighting under Wada at the palisade, and another lost from one of the boats commanded by Ivar Horse-Prick. When all those left had been gathered, just thirty-six men had filed on to the *Warig*, several of them carrying wounds.

The previous afternoon, they had put in at a deserted stretch of coast near the main port of Abalos, hidden the *Warig* in a creek. Mord had volunteered to go on foot into the settlement. His grandmother was a Bronding. He had relatives there who would not betray him. Eadric, son of Eadwine, had gone with him. To look peaceful, they had taken off their helmets and coats of mail, left behind their shields and bows. It had taken much courage from both of them.

The young men had returned in the gloaming. The news they brought could not have been better. Unferth had withdrawn from the port. He was with his sworn companions in his hall on Gnita-heath.

Mord had led them to this concealed vantage point. Ballista looked up through the branches at the moon. They must have lain here for four hours or more. At first, messengers had come and gone up the road to the hall, riding hard. Unferth must be trying to gather what support remained to him, plan his next move. After Norvasund, Ballista could not imagine what that might be. But a cornered animal was always dangerous.

Now the doors of the hall had not opened and there had been no movement for some time. The light seeping around the shutters had dimmed to almost nothing.

Ballista whispered for Castricius, Ivar Horse-Prick and Wada to come close. He outlined his plan. Like those at Gudme, the hall had two main doors. They were situated opposite each other in the long walls. Ballista would take the one facing west with ten men. Castricius with the same number would take the other. There might be smaller doors. Ivar and five warriors were to ring the north of the building, Wada and the remaining five the south. They should stay at a distance and be vigilant. Some halls had underground passages designed for those inside to escape. When they were all in position, Ballista would call on Unferth to surrender, or those around him to give him up. Most probably, these would be refused. If the defenders were so minded, Ballista's men would let any women and children leave. Then they would break open the doors. They had brought axes, but it would be better if they could find timbers among the farm buildings with which to batter down the doors. If all else failed, they had tinderboxes.

With not much noise, they separated into the four groups. Huddled around Ballista were Maximus, Tarchon, Rikiar the Vandal, the Romans Diocles and Heliodorus, and Mord, with four other young Angles. There was no telling how many fighting men were in the hall with Unferth. The thirty-four of Ballista's party might be outnumbered, possibly by some margin. Surprise would be lost by the summons, but it could not be helped.

Ballista smiled at Mord in the gloom. The youth grinned back. Ballista thought of what lay ahead of the *atheling*. Vermund the Heathobard and Hieroson the Olbian were back at the boat with the prisoner. When they returned to Gudme and the court of the *cyning*, when finally the captive was unmasked, the words he would be forced to repeat would strike at the heart of Mord's young life. If, of course, Mord or any of them lived to return to Varinsey. Ballista put it all out of his mind.

There was nothing to be gained by delay. *Do not think, just act.* Ballista got to his feet. The others got up, too. He led them out of the wood.

In the blue moonlight, they jogged along a hedge which divided two meadows. They could hear nothing over the thump of their boots, the creak of leather, their grunted breathing. Ballista's bow and quiver banged against his back, his shield dragged at his arm.

Silent on great white wings, an owl glided overhead.

From nowhere, Ballista half remembered a line from Plato: 'The greatest hunting is the hunting of men.'

The ridge of the hall loomed closer.

No alarm rang out.

Ballista reached the fence. With his dagger, he cut the rope securing the wicket gate. He slipped into the farmyard, the others at his back.

The homely smells of woodsmoke and animal dung, the reek of a midden. Hard-trodden earth underfoot. The sounds of a horse shifting in its stable. Still no outcry. No dogs or geese loose to give a warning. Ballista angled to the left, close under the over-hanging eaves. He stopped before the western door. Dark shapes around him. Ivar and his men passed behind.

Ballista whispered for Rikiar and Heliodorus to look for a tim-ber which could serve as a ram. They disappeared into the outbuildings. Ballista waited. So far, so good. They had outrun the news of their coming, outrun all expectation. Unferth had no sentries posted. He had arrived on Abalos but hours before them. No one would have considered such close pursuit.

Heliodorus spoke in Ballista's ear. Beams could be pulled from a cowshed, but it would make a noise. Ballista said they would do it later.

Ballista drew Battle-Sun. The serpentine pattern in the blade shimmered in the moonlight. Alone, he walked to the door. It was tall and wide. There was a pile of dry chickweed to one side. He put his ear against the boards; why, he was not sure. The sound of a man snoring, of more than one, reverberating in the big space.

Ballista straightened up and struck the pommel of Battle-Sun against the door. The boards jumped and rattled. The sound boomed into the hall, out over the yard. He struck again.

'Unferth! You are surrounded. It is over. Surrender.'

Shouts from inside. The crash of a table or bench overturning. Feet drumming on the floorboards. The scrape of steel; weapons being tugged free.

Ballista stepped back, locked his shield with the others. They crouched in the night, linden boards well out and angled upwards. If the door opened, the first response might well be a flight of steel-tipped shafts.

Above, a shutter squealed and swung open from a previously unseen window in the thatch. So, the hall had a loft. The head and shoulders of a man in the opening. The face glittered with cold, immobile metal.

'Who is there?' The mask gave an inhuman quality to the voice.

'Dernhelm, son of Isangrim, the one the Romans call Ballista.'

The carved face looked down. 'The killer of my son.'

'You know me then. Unferth, do not make your followers share your death. Show yourself a man. Release them from their oaths. Give yourself up.'

There was something uncanny about the silent, unmoving regard of the silvered mask.

Ballista raised his voice. 'You Brondings and any others in there, your leader has no more luck. Hand him over, and you will go free.'

'No!' A shout came from the floor of the hall, behind the door. 'We gave our sword-oath. We would be dishonoured.'

347

Keeping his eye on the upper window, Ballista addressed the unseen warrior. 'There is no dishonour in renouncing an oath extracted under compulsion, an oath to an evil man.'

The voice answered from behind the door. 'Save your cunning arguments for yourself, Oath-breaker. We stay. Every man must give up the days that are lent to him.'

Ballista called up to where Unferth still stood in the window. 'If there are women and children in there, we will let them depart unharmed.'

The mask nodded. 'It is not possible to bend fate, nor stand against nature. It will be as you say.'

'Have them come out of this door, no other.'

The mask withdrew, pulling the shutters to behind it.

They heard the bar lifted, then the door opened. Only the low remains of the hearth fire illuminated the cavernous interior. A dozen figures emerged: three children, nine women, one with a swaddled babe in arms. Before the door closed, Ballista saw the dull gleam of serried ranks of helms and mailcoats. Many men would die before the hall could be cleared; perhaps too many.

'Wada, have two of your men lead them away,' Ballista called.

Grim and another Heathobard went up to the women.

'Wait!' It was Maximus. 'That one in the middle – the big one with the broad shoulders – grab her!'

The woman threw her cloak in Grim's face. Steel flashed from a concealed blade. It cut deep into Grim's leg. He howled as he fell. The other Heathobard hacked down the warrior disguised as a woman.

Screaming, the women and children scattered into the night. Their cries and the ways they ran vouched for the genuine nature of their gender and age.

Grim was dragged away. As his compatriot tied a tourniquet around the Heathobard's thigh, Ballista gave new orders to Diocles.

When the Roman had vanished around the hall towards

Castricius, Ballista and his men moved back into the obscurity between two farm buildings. They unslung their bows, notched arrows and trained them on the door.

From the far side of the hall came the noise of heavy things being manhandled, of loud hammering.

Ballista knew it was a terrible thing that he had decided to do, but he could see no other way.

The noise from the east side stopped. All was quiet in the farmyard, as if it were a normal night, as if awful things were not unfolding. When a cow lowed in its byre, it sounded unnaturally loud.

'What are they doing in there?' Mord whispered.

'Waiting,' Ballista said. The women would have loved ones in the hall. They would spread the news. It was only four or five miles to the port. Time was not an ally to the attackers. At any moment Fate could turn them into quarry, hunted down across a dark, alien landscape. You could never rely on *Wyrd*.

Diocles rounded the hall, Castricius and eight of his men in his wake. 'All done,' he said.

'Nailed up tight as a vestal's cunt,' Castricius said. 'I left two to keep watch.'

'The chickweed,' Ballista said.

Diocles darted forward. As he crossed the twenty or so paces of open ground before the doors, an arrow whipped out from the tiny window high above. It missed the soldier by a hand's breadth. He dived under the overhanging thatch.

Sparks dropping in the darkness. A glow from under Diocles' hunched body.

When the chickweed was well alight, Diocles leaned out and swung it high on to the thatch. It hung there. The fire in it seemed to diminish. Then little tendrils of flame snaked out across the roof.

Diocles moved away north under the protection of the drooping eaves, took a roundabout route back.

Maximus touched Ballista's arm, pointed. Three men with torches were moving towards the southern end of the building. They threw them cartwheeling over the gable wall, then faded back into the shadows.

The weather had been dry. The west wind breathed life into the flames.

Ballista sent runners to call Wada and Ivar and their followers to him. As in the east, just two warriors were to remain at the northern and southern ends. The wounded Heathobard Grim was to remain with the latter.

'Watch the door,' Ballista said. There should be twenty-six men spread out around him in the darkness. Each should have his bow trained on the door. He wondered if it would be enough.

'The *daemons* of death are close.' Castricius spoke softly in Latin. In the baleful firelight, smeared with soot, he looked like one himself.

The middle of the roof was blazing fiercely, the southern end flaring up. If the women had not already done so, this ghastly beacon would raise the countryside. Would relief arrive before the fire drove the defenders out or buried them under falling timbers?

'Watch the door,' Ballista said.

The outlines of black figures emerged up on the roof. Balanced precariously on the beams, they hacked at the burning and smouldering thatch. The great lumps they threw down fell like molten waterfalls.

There was no need for orders. Out of the darkness, arrows flew. The defenders on the roof were illuminated by the fires. They could not see the missiles coming. One after another, shafts found their mark and figures pitched into oblivion.

Above the door, a man's tunic caught fire. In an awful dumbshow, he beat at it with his hands, until he missed his narrow footing and crashed to earth like a northern Icarus.

After that, the defenders withdrew, and no more ventured on to the roof.

The fire roared. The heat of it was hot on Ballista's face even at a distance. Deep in the thatch, it seemed to breathe like a great beast. There was a horrible smell, all too like roast pork. Ballista thought of the Goths before Novae, the Persians at Arete, his own at Aquileia; all the men he had seen burnt.

A deep groan from within the hall, a sharp crack, and the southern end of the roof sagged. The first of the beams had burnt through. They must come soon. No one could abide in that inferno.

'Watch the doors.'

The words were still on Ballista's lips when the door flew open. On an instant arrows thrummed into the opening. The two warriors pushing the doors fell transfixed by many shafts.

Looking into the hall was like looking into a scene of divine punishment yet to be tenanted. The orange glow played on the empty high seat, the first pairs of great columns. No man could be seen in the swirling smoke.

They came with a yell, out from both sides where they had been huddled against the walls. They rushed together to form a shield-burg in the doorway. They were too slow, too clumsy in their desperation. Arrows plucked men off their feet, hurled them backwards. They collided with those behind. Those on the floor tripped those still on their feet. Ballista released, notched, released again. All around him others did the same. The doorway was filled with shafts flitting like bats.

Standing on their companions, treading them down, a dozen or more defenders linked shields in the opening. Arrows sprouted in the bright-painted boards. The men launched forwards. Arrows sliced all around them. They ran off to Ballista's right, towards the southern gate in the fence. Wada the Short rose in front of them, other shapes at his side.

A terrible clatter as the fight was joined. Warriors cutting, hacking in the infernal light.

Ballista sensed men near him moving to join the melee. He searched but could not see the flash of the silver mask.

'Maximus, Tarchon, Rikiar, Mord, stay with me.'

Heliodorus was reeling. The Egyptian's helmet had been knocked off. His bald pate shone. A swordsman cleaved Heliodorus's shoulder open. Wada cut Heliodorus's killer near in half.

Still no silver mask. Ballista's eyes flicked between the fight and the empty door.

Wada was in the middle of the foe. His blade flickered too fast to follow. The Harii was shouting, the words unintelligible in the uproar. His enemy fell around him. His brother was being avenged.

A flash of something moving in the hall. Gone before Ballista could focus.

Wada staggered. The man behind him swung another blow at his legs. Wada went down, swallowed in the chaos.

Distracted, Ballista did not see the men come from the hall. Six men, their leader's face a mask of metal. They were on Ballista before he could shoot. He dropped the bow, snatched up his shield. Unferth's blow split through the lindens, buckled the boss. Agonizing pain; Ballista dropped his shield. He got Battle-Sun in the way of the next downward cut. Unferth swung left and right. Ballista blocked. Sparks bright as lightning as steel met steel. Ballista was driven back. Everywhere the din of fighting, stunning the senses.

Ballista's back bumped into the wall of an outbuilding. Cattle stamping and shifting, bellowing with fear on the other side. Unferth thrust. Ballista twisted. The tip of the blade scraped off his mail, jabbed into the wood. For a moment Ballista's face was against the cold surface of the mask. The face of a young man, inhuman in its calm beauty.

Unferth grunted, stepped back, turning. Behind him, Rikiar

hacked at his other leg. Unferth's shield splintered under the blade. Pivoting, all his weight in the blow, Ballista swung. Battle-Sun took Unferth's right arm, near the elbow. A scream, obscured by the metal. Unferth's sword fell from his hand. Rikiar chopped into the back of Unferth's thighs. Ballista thrust. Rings of mail cracking, steel rasping through flesh and bone.

Ballista withdrew Battle-Sun, pushed with his damaged left hand. Unferth took two faltering steps and fell on his back. Ballista, his boot on the bloodied chest of his enemy, the tip of his blade at his throat, reached down and ripped off the mask.

'You have my luck in the palm of your hand.' Unferth's voice was steady.

'Yes,' Ballista said, and thrust down.

Ballista held the silver mask high. 'Unferth is dead.'

The clamour of battle died as men took up the shout. '*Unferth is dead! Unferth is dead!*'

There were six or seven defenders left. They pulled away into a huddle. Backs to the burning hall, they tossed their weapons to the ground. Castricius and the others faced them in a semicircle.

In death, Unferth's face was unremarkable. Perhaps fifty years old, swarthy skin, long black hair shot with grey.

'A southerner,' Maximus said.

'Where his name tell he from?' Tarchon asked.

'It tells nothing,' Ballista said. 'It means unrest. His son called himself Widsith.'

'*Stranger*,' Rikiar said.

Maximus looked sharply at Ballista. 'Do you know it is him?'

'No.'

They all studied the dead man. The firelight moved over his face.

'Then you know what you must do,' Maximus said.

'Yes,' Ballista said. He raised his voice. 'Kill all the others.'

XXXI

THE ISLAND OF VARINSEY

The procession fanned out when it reached Gudme Lake. With the other dignitaries, Oslac followed the *cyning* through the sacrificial grove of oaks to the field of the trophies. There were many memorials to past victories of the Himling dynasty. They were simple constructions: a stake about the height of a man driven into the ground, a helmet placed on top, a crossbeam to which was nailed a shield and sword. Other weapons taken from the conquered were piled at the foot of each. Time and the elements had reduced the oldest, those set up back in the days of Starkad or even Hjar, to nothing but a weathered wooden pole and some corroded iron. The impermanence, like the modest scale, was intended to prevent any affront to the gods.

In front of the new trophy, much more war gear from the victory of Norvasund was heaped up down by the waterline. Isangrim picked up a rock the size of his fist from those laid out ready. The *cyning* himself cast the first stone. It bounced off a shield. Oslac and the others made their throw. The hail of stones rattling and pinging off the weaponry disturbed a raven perched on a nearby trophy. The large black bird took to the air and flapped out across the lake away from Gudme.

The ritual stoning complete, the *cyning* and his court watched as warriors went down to the lakeside to break up the offerings. Shields with fine metal fittings were hacked apart with axes. Yew longbows were snapped in half, arrows of ash and pine broken. Chapes and mouths of ivory and gold were wrenched from scabbards. Long days of skilled craftsmanship were negated as pattern-welded blades were snapped on an anvil.

Oslac watched Kadlin out of the corner of his eye. Had she looked over at Dernhelm? He had caught her gazing at him at Heoroweard's funeral. Oslac felt the familiar lurch of his jealousy as he remembered finding them together in the darkness outside the feast before Dernhelm left for Norvasund. She had given him no reason for doubt since then. As far as he knew, she had not been alone with his half-brother. Indeed, over the last days she had been particularly affectionate, and in their marital bed she had been unusually demonstrative. Was it just designed to reassure him, or was it all to allay his justified suspicions?

Dernhelm was not looking at her. He seemed distracted. As Oslac watched, he twice glanced back down the road they had taken from Gudme. Since his return from Abalos, apart from this morning, Dernhelm had only come to their father's hall the once to announce the death of Unferth. The rest of the time he had remained with the closest of his hearth-troop, almost all of them foreigners, in the household of *eorl* Eadwine at Gudmestrand.

The weaponry ruined beyond repair, the warriors began to toss the remains out into the lake. The whole was a strange ceremony. The procession and the trophy might well have been borrowed from a Roman triumph, but the rest – the stoning, breaking and deposit in the lake – had their roots deep in the north. Perhaps that was how it went, Oslac thought. The *imperium* could not be ignored. Peoples took things from the great power in the south, but adapted them to their own usages.

As the last broken weapons splashed into the water, there was an awkwardness. Everyone knew it was time for the sacrifices, when warriors from the defeated would be hung in the oak trees like the Allfather was hung from Yggdrasill. Unlike the Lord of the Gallows, the warriors would not survive. Given the circumstances, that could not happen. Hygelac of the Geats, Yrmenlaf of the Wylfings, Eudosius of the Dauciones, and Brecca, newly appointed ruler of the Brondings and brother of the king murdered by Unferth, had all returned to their allegiance and stood with the Himlings.

The bloodied silver mask of Unferth and his great battle-standard, Fenris in silver on black, were hauled high into the branches. Those assembled, the sometime rebels as much as any, *hoomed* their approval. Oslac searched his memory of the *Aeneid* for suitable sentiments on reconciliation. None came to mind.

No man expressed his pleasure more evidently than Morcar. Oslac regarded his brother with mistrust. Morcar had spoken many smooth words to those who had served Unferth. Their actions were enforced, and thus there should be no recriminations or reprisals. All was forgiven and forgotten. Oslac doubted the sincerity of those statements. The former rebels would be wise to do the same. Morcar had always been vengeful, ever since they were children; vengeful and cruel. His cruelty had been apparent yet again when insisting on the drowning of those Angles deemed cowards. The suspicion remained that Morcar had delayed the intervention of the fleet at Norvasund to ensure his own greater glory, so that like a deity he had turned imminent disaster into victory. Certainly, try though he had, Morcar had been unable to hide his fury when Dernhelm had returned with the evidence of the killing of Unferth.

There were more personal reasons for Oslac's misgivings. In Himling's tomb, Morcar had quoted the curse of the *wicce*. Somehow, Morcar had spied on his own brother, spied on the one member of the family who had always supported him, always defended him from the contempt of Froda, from the laughter of Eadwulf and Dernhelm, had always spoken out in the hall when men accused him of being overbearing. And there was the feast. It was Morcar who had told Oslac that Kadlin was outside with Dernhelm. In the face of his bitter accusations, Kadlin had said it was Glaum, son of Wulfmaer, who had suggested she leave the hall to see why the serving women had been slow bringing things from the kitchen. Glaum was ever by Morcar's side.

Tables had been spread further along the shore of the lake. Isangrim led the way. Oslac was seated between Kadlin and Yrmenlaf of the Wylfings of Hindafell, and opposite young Mord. Oslac and the Wylfing toasted each other, the beer drunk from Roman vessels designed for wine. The food was brought round, great platters of roast meat.

A sudden silence spread along the boards. Dernhelm was standing. He pointed to a group approaching on foot down the road. *Eorl* Eadwine and his son Eadric flanked a tall, hooded and bound man. Four of Dernhelm's men followed after: the *daemon*-haunted little Roman, the Hibernian with the end of his nose missing, the ill-favoured Vandal and the warrior from the distant Caucasus – a villainous crew.

'Take off the hood,' Dernhelm said.

The prisoner swayed as it was done. His face was swollen and mottled from old beatings, his long hair matted with dried blood. A murmur of recognition ran along the benches: Swerting Snake-Tongue.

'What is the meaning of this?' Morcar was on his feet, pale with anger.

'Retribution,' Dernhelm said. 'Snake-Tongue, tell the *cyning*.'

'No,' Swerting said.

Eorl Eadwine walked to face Isangrim, but raised his voice so all could hear. 'Snake-Tongue has spoken before witnesses, myself and my son among them.'

'I warn you to stop this. If you value your life, Eadwine, you will stop,' Morcar said.

'No, let Eadwine continue,' Isangrim said. The old man's face was set.

Glaum, son of Wulfmaer, went to stand behind Morcar. And, although he looked bewildered, so did Mord.

'Snake-Tongue has confessed to arranging the betrayal of the *atheling* Arkil and the Angles with him in Gaul. He acted on the orders of Morcar.'

'That is a lie!' Morcar said. 'A lie.'

'There is worse,' Eadwine continued. 'Snake-Tongue perjured himself when he gave evidence against Eadwulf. It was not the exile who murdered Froda. It was Morcar.'

'Lies!' Morcar shouted. 'Evil-Child killed Froda, no one else. Swerting has been tortured. A man will say anything under torture.' Morcar turned to his father, tried to rein in his fury. 'You cannot believe this.'

Everyone looked at Isangrim. The old *cyning* sat motionless.

Morcar spun around. 'You, Eadwine, how did Swerting come into your hands?'

The *eorl* gave back stare for stare. 'Dernhelm put him in my custody. Eadwulf captured Snake-Tongue off the Frisian coast. Snake-Tongue was on his way back to Gaul.'

Morcar swung back to his father. 'Dernhelm, Evil-Child: both exiles, worthless; both hate me. I am not the traitor. Dernhelm is the traitor. The little Greek Zeno told me Dernhelm carries secret instructions from Gallienus – there on his belt – instructions to overthrow the *cyning*, kill his father, take his place on the throne.'

From his wallet Dernhelm removed a small ivory-bound dip-
tych. He passed it to his father.

Isangrim opened the document and read. 'This orders him to
take all measures to look to the safety and success of the embassy,
if necessary to take command from Zeno; nothing more.'

Morcar spun around. The Greek was nowhere to be seen.

Morcar rounded on Dernhelm. 'Oath-breaker, blood follows
you. What you do now will turn against you.'

Dernhelm stood still. 'Some things just happen.'

Morcar spread one hand in supplication to his father; the other
jabbed at Dernhelm. 'I will clear my name. I demand a duel.'

The silence was complete. Not even a bird sang.

'No,' Isangrim said.

'A duel – it is my right. I demand a duel.'

Isangrim looked down. He seemed even older. Eventually, he
looked up. 'I would not see my sons fight. One of you can go into
exile.'

'Never!' Morcar was lost in his emotion. 'I am innocent.'

'Dernhelm, you are returning to the *imperium* anyway.' There
was pleading in Isangrim's voice. 'You could leave now.'

'No.'

'So be it.' Isangrim raised his chin. 'Let the hazel twigs mark
out the ground before the hall.'

'Not the homecoming I had hoped for,' Ballista said.

Maximus continued to check the shoulder pieces of Ballista's
mailcoat.

'Fratricide is a terrible thing.'

Maximus was pulling at the straps as he would a horse's girths.
'Sure, Morcar is an evil bastard.'

'I was thinking about myself.'

Maximus stopped what he was doing, gripped Ballista's shoulders, forced his friend to look into his eyes. 'You can think about

that when you have killed him. Empty your mind of everything except the fight.'

Ballista nodded.

'And if you are dying, I will challenge, kill fucker very dead.' Tarchon beamed at the latter prospect. 'I keep his skull as another cup. Every time I drink, I think of revenge for you.'

Ballista grinned. 'You are not an Angle. He would not have to accept.'

'But he could not refuse my challenge,' young Eadric said. 'If you fall, I will take revenge.'

Ballista saw Maximus put his thumb between his fore and middle fingers to avert evil.

'Morcar is a duel-fighter of much experience.' Ivar Horse-Prick was very solemn. 'He defeated the Bronding, killed the champion of the Hilleviones before both armies. He has won four judicial duels among our people. If he wins today, I will fight him. He is of our generation. It is for us to wipe away the dishonour.'

'Enough about losing,' Maximus said. 'Give the man some space.'

When the others had drawn back, Maximus leaned close. 'He is not your brother. He is your brother's killer. Empty your mind. Nothing but the fight.'

Ballista unsheathed his dagger an inch or so, snapped it back, did the same with Battle-Sun, touched the healing stone tied to its scabbard.

'Watch the blade. Get your feet moving straight away. Treat each blow on its merit.' Maximus hugged him, kissed him on both cheeks. 'Time to go. Watch the blade.'

It was very bright outside the hall, the sky very high.

The dense crowd parted to let them get to the duelling place. Morcar was waiting. Mord was with him, holding his two other shields.

Ballista and Maximus stepped over the sprigs of hazel. Six paces by six, the cloth seemed tiny.

360

A high seat had been set up to one side for the *cyning*. Isangrim sat hunched on it. Ballista tried not to imagine his father's thoughts.

Ballista took a shield in his bandaged left hand. He stepped up to Morcar.

'You and me,' Morcar said, 'like snow blowing from one tree to another.'

Ballista said nothing.

Morcar stepped back. As the challenger, he had to wait for the first blow. He settled into the ox guard; half turned, shield out, blade held palm down, jutting down like a horn.

Ballista hefted his sword high, shifted to the left then the right, getting himself moving, his muscles warm.

Quick steps, feet close together, Ballista closed in, swinging down from the right at Morcar's head. In a fluid motion, he dropped to one knee, switched the strike towards the ankle. Morcar brought his shield down. The impact ran up Ballista's arm. He took the counter-blow on the boss. Pain flared in his injured left hand. Ballista surged up, shoving Morcar away. He stepped back.

They watched each other. Morcar moved into a charge guard, his sword low and hidden behind his body.

Ballista remembered how Morcar had fought the Bronding. A long defence, then a sudden attack. Ballista could wait. Time was no issue. Not taking his eyes off his brother's sword, he moved around the cloth, feeling its footing, exploring its edges, memorizing its dimensions.

With no warning, Morcar attacked. He feinted a cut from the left, rolled his wrist, chopped from the right. The steel sliced through the leather rim of Ballista's shield, cracked the boards.

'Shield!' Ballista shouted.

Morcar pulled back, the tip of his blade pointing to the cloth.

Ballista took his second shield from Maximus. Blood was seeping through the bandages around his left knuckles.

361

No sooner was the shield in Ballista's hand than Morcar tore in again. A surprisingly wild overhand vertical chop. Ballista brought his shield up. Morcar pulled the blow, hooked the pommel of his sword over the rim of Ballista's shield, dragged it forward, the blade arcing down. Ballista twisted down and away. The edge of the steel slid off his shoulder piece. He stepped forward and to the right. They were wedged together, Morcar's shield jammed between them.

'Snow – one tree to another,' Morcar hissed. 'We are the same, nothing to choose between us.'

Ballista staggered as Morcar heaved him backwards. Morcar stepped forward. A low, rising cut. Ballista lowered his shield. Morcar kicked it across Ballista's front, jabbing to the neck with the inside edge of his weapon. Ballista ducked. A metallic clang as the top of his helmet crest was sheered off. Ballista pivoted on his left foot, kicked his right boot hard into his brother's right shin.

Morcar grunted in pain. 'Rest!'

Ballista backed away. His ears were ringing from the blow to his helmet. His left hand hurt.

As Morcar took a drink offered by his son, he flexed his right leg.

The sacred truce over, Morcar hung back. Ballista feinted high and low from one side and the other, working him around. Morcar was favouring one leg, reluctant to put weight on his right. Ballista knew he had to finish it now, before his brother could work off the pain.

With three quick blows, Ballista drove Morcar into a corner. Morcar crumpled as his leg gave. The killing blow was open. Ballista shaped to strike. He remembered the Bronding. He side-stepped to the right. Morcar, suddenly recovered, thrust. His blade whistling where Ballista's stomach would have been, Morcar overshot. As he passed, Ballista hacked to the back of the thighs.

Two, three steps, Morcar crashed to the ground. His shield rolled out of reach. He rolled on to his back, brought his sword up. Ballista beat it aside, got his boot on his brother's sword arm, the point of his blade to his chest.

'The same,' Morcar said, 'one tree to another.'

As Ballista hesitated, a movement. Morcar's left hand wrenching his dagger out.

Ballista thrust down, all his weight behind it. The steel tip of Battle-Sun broke the closely wrought rings of mail, broke open the ribcage they guarded.

XXXII

THE ISLAND OF HEDINSEY

Vengeful furies, punishers of sinners, black torches in your hands, hear my curse. Ballista sat on the high table in his father's hall in Hlymdale, but in his mind he saw a village in the Caucasus, a dark village under a lowering sky. A woman standing in the rain, her hair unbound, her words cursing him.

There were many bad things he had done. Twice, he had broken the *sacramentum*. Rather than put the safety of the emperor above everything, as the Roman military oath demanded, he had stabbed Maximinus Thrax in the throat. With the emperor Quietus he had used his bare hands; thrown him to his death from a high place. He had sworn a terrible oath to return to captivity before the throne of Shapur, King of Kings. He had not returned. And now . . . now he had killed Morcar. As they said, the hand's joy in the blow is brief. The Oath-breaker had become the Brother-killer.

Dernhelm, son of Isangrim, the one the Romans called Ballista, knew himself cursed. Let him live – in poverty, in impotence, loneliness and fear. Let him wander the face of the earth, through strange towns, among strange peoples, always in exile, homeless and hated. He had failed to save old Calgacus, and now he had killed his own brother. There was a special place reserved in Hades for men like him. Brother-killer.

Isangrim rose to his feet. 'My people, it is time for the dispensation.'

Ballista looked past Oslac to their father, and beyond him to Eadwulf. Twenty-eight winters had taken their toll on Eadwulf. His long, blond hair was turning grey. His nose had been broken, spread across his face. He was much heavier set. Yet Eadwulf shone with the joy of his return. And Ballista was leaving again.

The hall waited for Isangrim in silence.

'The Suebian Sea is once more at peace. Abalos, Hindafell, Solfell, the Scadinavian coast – all have returned to their rightful allegiance. This peace will be protected. My son the *atheling* Oslac will build a new hall on Gnitaheath. My grandson Mord will travel with him to Abalos. The eastern Lords – Brecca of the Brondings, Yrmenlaf of the Wylfings, Hygelac of the Geats and Eudosius of the Dauciones – will swear their sword-oath to Oslac. In the south, the islands of Latris will be held by Hrothgar of the Wrosns. To Hrothgar we betroth our granddaughter Aelfwynn, daughter of Oslac. Hrothgar will oversee the Langobardi, Farodini and Rugii of the mainland. In accordance with the oath sworn in the hall of their king by our son the *atheling* Dernhelm, we welcome the Heathobards into an equal alliance. My son the *atheling* Eadwulf will go to the west. He will be accompanied by my grandson Aethelgar, son of Oslac. All the peoples of the peninsula, from the Cimbri in the north to the Reudigni in the south, will give Eadwulf their sword-oath. After his many years among them, Eadwulf brings the friendship of the Frisii. He will lead longships of the Frisii with those of the Angles against the coasts of Gaul held by the false-Roman Postumus, as desired by our son

Dernhelm. Our regent on Varinsey will be *eorl* Eadwine, and here on Hedinsey it will be Hathkin, son of Heoroweard. Given the youth of the latter, *eorl* Godwine will act as his advisor. Now let those appointed give me their oaths.'

The gift-stool was brought out, and Isangrim took his seat. Oslac was the first to kneel before the *cyning*.

It was an impressive ceremony, and it promised unity for the time being. But it did not do the same for the future. Who would inherit the throne? Oslac and Eadwulf had been given wide domains, but neither held the heartlands of Hedinsey and Varinsey. When Isangrim died, would either stand aside? And what of the younger Himlings? Would Aethelgar be content to see his uncle, not his father, as *cyning*? And there was Mord. He had been brought up with his father, Morcar, as the unacknowledged heir. In time he would have thought to sit on the high throne himself. And there were the other great *eorls*. Two generations before, Eadwine's Waymundings had ruled Varinsey as independent kings. A roll of the dice on Hedinsey, and the *cynings* would have come from Hathkin's Wuffingas, and not the Himlings.

Eorl Godwine swore his oath to support Hathkin in all things, to be true in word and deed. Just one thing remained for Isangrim to say. Ballista's thoughts shied away from it. They turned to Rome. He had done what Gallienus had ordered. He had turned the Himlings against Postumus. But what would happen when the northern longships appeared off the coasts of Gaul? What would Postumus do to Arkil and the other Angles in his power? Ballista had killed one brother with his own hand. Would he now be responsible for the death of another? Brother-killer.

Isangrim got to his feet, the years heavy in his movements. 'Tragedy has come to the halls of the Himlings. Morcar challenged Dernhelm to the duel. There is no compensation to be paid. But I would have Mord reconciled to Dernhelm.'

Both Ballista and Mord stood. They did not look at each other.

Ballista spoke first. 'Although, by our customs, compensation is not due, I will offer it. Let the *cyning* set the blood price.'

'No,' Mord said.

Ballista looked along the high table.

Mord stood very still, his anger holding him rigid. 'I will never carry my father in my money pouch. Either I will go the same way as he did, or I will take vengeance for him.'

Mord looked at Ballista now, his eyes full of hatred.

'I am sorry for it,' Isangrim said. 'Dernhelm leaves tomorrow for the south, Mord for Abalos. By my order, no revenge will be sought within my lands.'

Ballista sat down, the words of the curse in his mind. *Vengeful furies, punishers of sinners, kill his wife, kill his sons, all those he loves, let him wander the face of the earth, in loneliness and fear, always in exile, homeless and hated.*

Perhaps the words would prove true; perhaps they would not. There was no doubt that Mord hated him. And there could be no question that he had to leave his childhood home. Ballista had killed his half-brother; he could not kill Morcar's son as well. Yet he was reluctant to leave the north. It was still so much the same. It looked and smelt the same. The new buildings were much like the old. There were those here he loved: his father, his mother and Eadwulf. Most likely, he would never see them again. And there was Kadlin. But it could not become his home once more. Perhaps his sons might be young enough to make the transition, but his wife, never. And even if Julia did, there was Kadlin.

At least he was not leaving alone. He would lead the expedition back to the *imperium*, back by a more westerly branch of the Amber Road that would bring them via friendly tribes to Pannonia, and down into Italy at Aquileia. He would bring them all back safe: those he loved – Maximus and Castricius; those he cared for – Tarchon and Rikiar: and the others – like Diocles and

367

Amantius. Who would have imagined the portly eunuch would survive when so many others had died?

And he was not going into exile. When he reached the *comitatus*, he would petition the emperor. It might be Gallienus would give him permission to retire to Sicily. Of course, the villa was Julia's. But it was where his sons were. It was where his wife was. He missed his books, the baths, the garden with the view of the Bay of Naxos. Perhaps he and Julia could make things better, make them more what they had once been between them. Perhaps in a sense he was returning home, returning to protect his wife and his sons.

It had not been that difficult to arrange, but Kadlin knew the risk she ran. The leaving feast continued in the hall. The drink was flowing. Most were drunk. When she saw him go, she had told her serving women what she wanted them to do. They had not been unwilling. They had taken his closest companions away; most likely taken the Suanian and the Hibernian to their beds. Was that what she wanted for herself? She was bathed, perfumed. She had dressed her hair and chosen her clothes with care. It was for him, not for her husband. Did she want him to take her to bed? Throughout her life she had overheard the whispers that she was no better than a whore. The whispers that had started all those winters ago were his fault, and perhaps they were true. If she was caught, that was what Oslac would assume, what everyone would assume. If that was what Dernhelm wanted, she would not be in a position to resist. Was that what she was doing, giving herself no choice, putting the choice, and all its ramifications and guilt, on him? No, she told herself, that was not the reason. He was leaving, and before he left he must be told. Most likely there would never be another chance.

Muffled in the big, hooded cloak, she slipped into the outlying hall. It was empty. His hearth-troop were still drinking in the great hall. She climbed the stairs. Light showed around the door. She lifted the latch and went into the bedchamber.

The shutters were open. Dernhelm had been sitting, staring out at the dark trees. He twisted to his feet, hand reaching for the hilt of the sword propped against his chair.

She pushed back her hood.

'Kadlin.'

She walked right up to him. His hands fell to his sides. She touched his forearm. *It was wanting you that made me sick.* The line of poetry came into her mind.

'Were you going to leave without seeing me?' she asked.

'No.' He spoke quickly, but she heard the uncertainty.

'I thought you –' He stopped, obviously unsure what to say. '– With your daughter being betrothed tonight, I thought you might not want to see me.'

She took her hand from his arm, stepped back, suddenly furious. He was a fool; all men were fools. 'Aelfwynn will marry for duty, as I did.'

He stood irresolute, thrown by her sudden change. 'Does Oslac treat you well?'

'Yes.' Was that all he could say? She could not imagine how, coming here, she had desired him.

'I was sorry to hear your son Starkad was one of those taken in Gaul.'

She wanted very much to hit him. If she had been a man, she would have knocked him down. Her sister would have knocked him down. Starkad was in Gaul. His son was in Gaul, and very likely this man, his father, had ensured he would die there.

'May the gods hold their hands over you, see you safely back to your wife and sons.' She turned to go.

'Kadlin . . .'

She stopped.

He held his hand out. She did not take it.

'Kadlin, you know I never wanted to go, never wanted to leave you.'

'I know.' She managed to smile. 'I never wanted you gone.'

He moved to put his arms around her.

'No.' She stepped back.

He looked hurt.

'Life has not been kind to us,' she said. 'Now, I must return.'

She did not look back. Outside, in the dark night, she began to cry.

> Our lips had smiled to swear hourly
> That nothing should split us – save dying –
> Nothing else . . .
> Some lovers in this world
> Live dear to each other, lie warm together
> At day's beginning; I go by myself.

Epilogue I
Gallia Lugdunensis, AD264

As he had not had sex with his wife, at dawn the emperor Postumus went out into the atrium to his household gods. The pleasures of the flesh had not been on his mind, not since the news last night. A fleet of Angle and Frisian longboats were off the coast of Gaul, their leader a barbarian called Evil-Child. The towns of Caracoticum and Iuliobona had been sacked and burnt.

Postumus pulled a fold of his toga over his head. He picked up the incense box and with his right hand scattered a pinch into the fire on the little altar. The painted *genius* of the house mirrored the emperor: togate, veiled, incense box in hand. Two *lares* flanked the *genius*. A drinking horn in one hand, a wine bucket in the other, they danced, their short tunics flaring out. Their happiness did not reflect his mood. The statuettes of the gods – the deified emperors Augustus, Trajan, Marcus, and Pius, Alexander, Neptune and Hercules Deusoniensis – had a more sombre demeanour.

It was the sort of legalistic question which entranced his son. Treachery makes a group of men your hostages. They prove their loyalty, but further treachery turns their countrymen into your enemies. Do you reward them for their own behaviour, or do you punish them for their compatriots' betrayal? Such questions were all very well in the fictive world of Postumus Iunior's *Controversiae*, but very different in the hard, indeed lethal, arena of imperial politics.

The Angles of Arkil had done well at the battle of Curia. They had resisted the blandishments of Gallienus. One of their leaders, called Wiglaf, and his men had stayed and died fighting a rearguard action. Arkil and the others had got to their horses and cut their way out of the disaster. Arkil had taken a bad wound. Like Xenophon taking command of the ten thousand, a young Angle warrior called Starkad had led the survivors over the Alps back to Postumus in Lugdunum. The Angles had remained true to the oath they had sworn.

The Angles had been the only good thing about the disaster at Curia; an army lost, the province of Raetia lost. The governor Simplicinius Genialis had only just managed to get clear. And it was all caused by the treachery of Bonosus. The Spanish drunkard had suborned Legio III Italica Concors, and with its desertion all had been lost.

It was late in the season, probably too late for Gallienus to mount another campaign. But there was no doubt he would come next year. He had more options now he held Raetia. From that province he could strike north-west into Germania Superior, or he could move west from northern Italy into Gallia Narbonensis. Gallienus had a large Mediterranean fleet; Postumus did not. Superiority at sea meant Gallienus could strike direct at the south coast of Gaul, or even as far afield as Spain.

Bonosus had turned traitor, and he was not the first. The betrayal by Lollianus still hurt. Lollianus had been there from the start. He had been a friend, and he had been well rewarded. If Lollianus had not proved trustworthy, who would? *Who guards the guardians?* Wearing the purple had shown Postumus that trust and mercy were both finite qualities.

Postumus placed his right hand on his chest and prayed to his patron Hercules Deusoniensis for guidance. What should he do with the Angles? Late the previous night, he had put the same question to his hastily summoned *consilium*. His councillors had produced various arguments and advice, most of it severe. The Angles of Arkil could no longer be trusted. They would not fight against their own. Of the latter, Postumus was convinced. They should be disarmed and sold into slavery, sent to work in the mines, thrown to the beasts. Simplicinius Genialis had led a minority of voices which dissented. The Angles had fought well at Curia. Outnumbered two to one, they had nearly broken the Pannonian legionaries in front of them. In the face of disaster, they had held true to their *sacramentum*.

Postumus looked to the sky. There was not a bird in sight. He looked at the fire. It did not waver. Neither Hercules nor any other deity whispered in his mind. He would have to make his decision without divine aid. In the midst of his field army, Arkil and his men were impotent in his power. Postumus had faced a similar decision once before. When the citizens of Colonia Agrippinensis had surrendered the Caesar Saloninus along with Silvanus, the *Dux* of the German frontier, all options had been open. Postumus had ordered them beheaded; his *consilium* had urged it. The decision had troubled him ever since. Saloninus had been no more than a child, an innocent child. Saloninus had not desired to be Caesar any more than Postumus wanted to be emperor. All too often, Postumus had imagined the boy's fear as he was led out, knowing he would be killed, knowing he would be denied burial, and that his soul would be condemned to wander the world for ever without hope. Severity too easily declines into savagery.

Postumus made his decision. The Angles would live. They would not be sold into slavery. Fighting men such as they were not to be thrown aside. But they would have to be far away from their kinsmen. They would be sent to garrison southern Spain, the province of Baetica. From that distant latitude, they could not ever hope to return home.

Epilogue II
The Island of Abalos in the Suebian Sea, AD265

Zeno came out of his hut and walked up through the wood, taking the longer path through the birch and aspen and avoiding the grove of oaks and the marsh. He stopped and knelt to tie a loose lace on his rough leather boots. The wind moved through the trees. The leaves were turning already. It would soon be his second winter in Hyperborea.

Standing, Zeno brushed down his trousers. He was a Hellene, born in Arcadia under the sheer peak of Cyllene. A *eupatrid*, his ancestors had fought at Plataea. He was a Roman equestrian, a *Vir Perfectissimus*. He had governed a province, and advised the emperor. Now he lived in a thatched hut and dressed as a barbarian.

It was all the fault of Ballista. Piece by piece on the journey up, the northerner had chipped away his authority. When they were among the Heathobards, Zeno had vowed to bring down the northerner, but accepted that he had to bide his time. Eventually, he had revealed to Morcar the existence of the secret imperial *mandata* carried by Ballista. His half-brother evidently hated Ballista. It should have gone well, but it had not. With typical barbaric lack of foresight and self-control, Morcar had blurted out the information at the most inappropriate moment. In his profound ignorance, the ruler of the Angles had failed to see the meaning implied in the imperial orders: *to take all measures to look to the safety and success of the embassy.* In the uproar, Zeno had slipped away from the feast. He had remained out of the way during the duel. Almost insultingly, no one had searched for him. In fact, the Angles had almost completely ignored him, until the embassy was preparing to leave for home.

Zeno entered the settlement by the southern wicket gate. Most of the outbuildings still bore evidence of smoke damage, but the hall at Gnitaheath was clean and raw in its newness. As ever, the session would be in there. There had been nothing he could have done when given the orders. Ballista had the imperial *mandata* allowing him to take command. Ballista had armed men around him. Zeno was to remain in the north as *a Studiis* to Ballista's half-brother Oslac.

Zeno remembered how, on the journey, he had compared himself to Ixion and Odysseus. But the wheel bore Ixion up as well as down, and Odysseus returned home. All the gods, Zeno hated Latin literature, especially Virgil.

Life flutters off on a groan, down among shadows.

Appendices

Historical Afterword

The Gallic Empire

The essential modern study of the breakaway regime founded by Postumus is J. F. Drinkwater, *The Gallic Empire: Separatism and Continuity in the North-western Provinces of the Roman Empire AD260–74* (Stuttgart, 1987). Also useful is R. J. Bourne, *Aspects of the Relationship between the Central and Gallic Empires in the Mid- to Late Third Centuries AD with Special Reference to Coinage Studies* (Oxford, 2001).

Raetia

An altar discovered in 1992 at Augsburg records a victory over the Semnones and Iuthungi, two Germanic tribes returning from a raid into Italy, by an army composed of troops from the provinces of Raetia and Germany and the local militia. It was led by Marcus Simplicinius Genialis, equestrian acting governor of Raetia. The inscription (*AE* 1993, 1231) was dedicated on 11 September in the year when Postumus Augustus and Honoratianus were consuls (most probably AD260). The battle had taken place months earlier, on 24 and 25 April. In these novels, the following interpretations are made. The Semnones and Iuthungi were a part of the Alamannic invasion whose main contingent was defeated by Gallienus near Milan (most probably in AD260). Simplicinius won his victory in the spring while still loyal to Gallienus, and erected the altar in the autumn to mark his later change of allegiance to Postumus.

Olbia

Although about a third of the site has been lost to the waters of the Bug (Hypanis) river, Olbia is a rich and much studied archaeological site. Overviews are provided by E. Belin de Ballu, *Olbia: Cité antique du littoral nord de la Mer Noire* (Leiden, 1972); S. D. Kryzhytskyy et al., 'Olbia-Berezan', in D. V. Grammenos and E. K. Petropoulos (eds.), *Ancient Greek Colonies in the Black Sea*, vol. I (Thessaloniki, 2003), 389–505 (a stilted English translation); and S. D. Kryjitski and N. A. Leïpounskaïa, *Olbia: Fouilles, Histoire, Culture: Un État antique sur le littoral septentrional de la Mer Noire* (Nancy, 2011).

On Olbia in the time of the Roman empire, see V. V. Krapivina, 'Olbia Pontica in the Third to Fourth Centuries AD,' in D. V. Grammenos and E. K. Petropoulos (eds.), *Ancient Greek Colonies in the Black Sea 2*, vol. I (Oxford, 2007), 591–626; and the chapters by V. V. Krapivina (pp. 161–72) and V. M. Zubar (pp. 173–8), in D. Braund and S. D. Kryzhitskiy (eds.), *Classical Olbia and the Scythian World from the Sixth Century BC to the Second Century AD* (Oxford, 2007).

The most useful classical text is Dio Chrysostom, *Oration 36, The Borysthenitic, Delivered in His Native Land*.

(NB No attempt has been made here to standardize the variant transliteration of proper names of these authors.)

Leuce/ The Island of Achilles

Much of Chapter 3 is drawn from the *Heroicus* of Philostratus in the excellent translation of E. Bradshaw and J. K. Berenson (Atlanta, 2001). S. B. Okhotnikov and A. S. Ostroverkhov, 'Achilles on the Island of Leuce', in D. V. Grammenos and E. K. Petropoulos (eds.), *Ancient Greek Colonies in the Black Sea* 2, vol. I (Oxford, 2007), 537–62, offer a guide to the archaeology and history of the island, often rendered nearly incomprehensible by the English translation.

The North

One of the pleasures of researching the *Warrior of Rome* novels is learning about new areas of the classical world. The superb articles, maps, plans and illustrations in *The Spoils of Victory: The North in the Shadow of the Roman Empire* (Copenhagen, 2003), a catalogue of two exhibitions held at the National Museum in Copenhagen in 2003–4, edited by L. Jørgensen, B. Storgaard and L. G. Thomsen, opened my eyes to ancient Scandinavia.

Other extremely useful articles are to be found in O. Crumlin-Pedersen (ed.), *Aspects of Maritime Scandinavia* AD200–1200 (Roskilde, 1991); A. N. Jørgensen and B. L. Clausen (eds.), *Military Aspects of Scandinavian Society in a European Perspective*, AD1–1300 (Copenhagen, 1997); B. Storgaard (ed.), *Aspects of the Aristocracy in Barbaricum in the Roman and Early Migration Periods* (Copenhagen, 2001); and T. Grane (ed.), *Beyond the Roman Frontier: Roman Influences on the Northern Barbaricum* (Rome, 2007).

Map of the North

We have no literary source which describes the north in the third century AD. To people this world I have drawn on earlier classical works, especially the *Germania* of Tacitus and the *Geography* of Ptolemy, and later Anglo-Saxon poetry, mainly *Beowulf* and *Widsith*, as well as various much later Norse sagas. It should be stressed that the map makes no claims to historicity. The tribes on it may not have been contemporary with each other, may not all have been in those areas at that time, or ever, and in some cases may not have existed at all. The map just sets out to create a plausible world.

Himlingøje (Hlymdale in the novel)

The archaeology is well published in U. Lund Hansen et al. (eds.), *Himlingøje – Seeland – Europa* (Copenhagen, 1995). This very important site is a large burial ground. I have given it a port, and a settlement further inland by a forest. For what it is worth, although they have not been identified, the former must have existed, and most likely the latter did, too. Pollen analysis shows there were woodlands at a distance. The two graves described in Chapters 24 and 25 are composites, rather than based on specific examples. The construction technique is borrowed from Mound 2 at Sutton Hoo: M. Carver, *Sutton Hoo: Burial Ground of Kings?* (London, 1998). Somehow, although a northern setting seems to demand them, I managed to stop myself including both an anachronistic ship burial, and the Viking sex and death stuff from Ibn Fadlan.

The name Hlymdale is borrowed from *The Saga of the Volsungs*.

The 'treasure-fires' kept alight on top of the funeral mounds are invented from the idea in the Norse sagas that the location of buried hoards was revealed by supernatural fires, e.g. *Grettir's Saga*, ch. 18.

Gudme and Lundeborg (Gudmestrand in the novel)

A brief and thought-provoking introduction to these linked sites is provided by L. Hedeager, *Iron Age Myth and Materiality: An Archaeology of Scandinavia* AD400–1000 (Abingdon and New York, 2011), 150–63, 184–6. Neither site has been fully published, but substantial articles can be found in P. O. Nielsen, K. Randsborg and H. Thrane (eds.), *The Archaeology of Gudme and Lundeborg* (Copenhagen 1994).

The name Gudme may well be ancient. Lundeborg is not, so in this novel it is given the fictional name Gudmestrand.

Gudsø Vig (Norvasund in the novel)

Illustrations and discussion of the sea barrage at Gudsø Vig are provided by A. N. Jørgensen, 'Fortifications and the Control of Land and Sea Traffic in the Pre-Roman and Roman Iron Age', in Jørgensen et al., *The Spoils of Victory* (2003), 194–209. The village demolished to create palisades is borrowed from Priorsløkke; ibid., 206–8. The name Norvasund usually referred to the Straits of Gibraltar, but here is taken from an unidentified place in *The Saga of the Volsungs*, 9.

The Himling Dynasty

From the start, back in 2006 when I began planning the *Warrior of Rome* series, the hero had to be an outsider. In a classicist's terms, he had to be Polybius rather than Tacitus of the *Annals*. An outsider may lack the depth of understanding, but he always comments more openly and naturally on what an insider may take for granted. Ballista became Germanic because we know more about that culture than that of any other people beyond the frontiers, thanks to the *Germania* of Tacitus (obviously, here the Roman senator was writing as an outsider). Having gone that far, I made Ballista an Angle because his descendants, if they survive, will one day become English. At that stage, I imagined his father as a petty northern chieftain. Archaeology was to prove me wrong.

From the mid-second century AD the archaeology of southern

Scandinavia shows a great increase in riches and Roman imports. These are found both in deposits of war booty and in aristocratic burials, the latter particularly at the site of Himlingøje on the Danish island of Sealand. Danish archaeologists have argued convincingly that from the Marcomannic wars (AD162–80) onwards, the Roman empire backed the rise of a Baltic hegemony ruled by the native dynasty which interred its dead at Himlingøje. Both sides benefited. The new client kingdom received rich diplomatic gifts, possibly weapons, and could send some of its potentially troublesome young men overseas. Rome got the service of additional northern warriors, and a friendly power to the rear of the ones on the frontier, who were often hostile. For an accessible introduction to the 'Himlingøje empire', see B. Storgaard, 'Cosmopolitan Aristocrats', in Jørgensen et al., *The Spoils of Victory* (2003), 106–25.

As a newcomer to this field of study, it struck me that the modern literature conspicuously avoids addressing two issues. First is the relationship of the burial site of Himlingøje on Sealand with the rise of the settlement of Gudme on Funen. Second, and far more understandable, scholars are reluctant to link any of the peoples named in literary sources to the dynasty of Himlinøje (see above, 'Map of the North'). A novelist need not be so constrained. In *The Amber Road* I create a fictional narrative that joins Himlingøje and Gudme. The Angles were recorded in Denmark both before and after the third century. So were lots of other peoples, but none had the same resonance for me. The name of the fictional dynasty was created by abbreviating the modern place name for the burial site.

Ballista's father, Isangrim, stands revealed as a ruler of the highest consequence.

Northern Battle Standards

The tribes of the north used standards in battle. When discovered at Vimose in 1849 the gilded bronze head of a gryphon originally from a Roman parade helmet had been mounted on a pole with a red and blue flag (X. Pauli Jensen, 'The Vimose Find', in Jørgensen et al., *The Spoils of the North* (2003), 237). I gave this standard to the Heathobards. For the others, I used images from contemporary art (the page references are to illustrations in Jørgensen, ibid.): the bull with silver horns of the Brondings of Abalos (p. 13), the golden dormouse of Varinsey (p. 244), the gold and black rampant lion of the Wylfings of Hindafell (p. 268), the double-headed beast of the Geats of Solfell (p. 273), the silver (changed from gold) on black wolf of Unferth (p. 286), the three-headed man of the Wrosns, the deer and fawn of Varinsey, and the killer and slain man of the Dauciones (p. 293). The white horse of the Himlings of Hedinsey and Ballista's own white *draco* have been described already in previous novels.

Ships

The majority of scholars consider that northern ships lacked masts and sails in the third century AD (e.g. O. Crumlin-Pedersen, 'Large and Small Warships of the North', in A. N. Jørgensen and B. L. Clausen (eds.), *Military Aspects of Scandinavian Society in a European Perspective*, AD1–1300 (Copenhagen, 1997), 184–94). For a robust attack on this view, see J. Haywood, *Dark Age Naval Power: A Reassessment of Frankish and Anglo-Saxon Seafaring Activity* (revised edn, Hockwold-cum-Wilton, 1999).

Amber

The most important discussion of amber in classical literature is in Pliny the Elder, *Natural History* XXXVII.xi.30–xiii.53. It contains the fascinating story of a Roman equestrian who was sent to the Baltic to procure amber to adorn a display of gladiators in the reign of Nero. This anecdote was the original inspiration for *The Amber Road*.

Zeno

Aulus Voconius Zeno is known via one inscription (*AE* 1915, 51). He was appointed *a Studiis* while governor of Cilicia under Gallienus (*PLRE* Zeno 9). L. de Blois, *The Policy of the Emperor Gallienus* (Leiden, 1976), 49, n.21, reverses these posts. The Zeno of *The Amber Road* owes a lot to various of the *Characters* of Theophrastus: Obsequiousness (no. 5); Petty Ambition (no. 21); and Cowardice (no. 25). He is given an origin in Arcadia in the novel and used to explore some of the ambiguities of being a Greek under Roman rule. A good introduction to this fascinating topic is Greg Woolf, 'Becoming Roman, Staying Greek: Culture, Identity and the Civilizing Process in the Roman East', *PCPhS* 40 (1994), 116–43. A more comprehensive study is provided by Simon Swain, *Hellenism and Empire* (Oxford, 1996). In the novel, the irony that Zeno affects to despise Virgil while often thinking in images from the *Aeneid* is quite intentional.

Quotes

The battle song of the Angles in Prologue One is adapted from the translation by J. L. Byock of the anonymous *Saga of King Hrolf Kraki* (London, 1998, p. 41).

When the *Iliad* of Homer is recited – by Gallienus in Chapter 2, Zeno in Chapter 14 – it is, as ever in these novels, in the translation of Richard Lattimore (Chicago and London, 1951).

The passage of the *Odyssey* wheeled out by Zeno in Chapter 14 is in the translation of Robert Faggles (London, 1997).

In Chapter 5, Simplicinius Genialis's quotations from the *Letters* and the *Panegyric* of Pliny are in the translation by Betty Radice (Cambridge, Mass. and London, 1969).

The *Historia Augusta, Gallieni Duo* 11.7–9, claims that the epithalamium in Chapter 12 was composed by Gallienus. The translation here is by D. Magie (Cambridge, Mass., 1932). The lines that slip the emperor's mind in this novel can be found in the *Latin Anthology*, i.2, p. 176, no. 711.

The defence speech of the father with the Cynic son in Chapter 16 is from *The Lesser Declamations* attributed to Quintillian abridged and slightly altered from the translation of D. R. Shackleton Bailey (Cambridge, Mass. and London, 2006) – which would be particularly fitting if they were really written by Postumus Iunior, as in the unlikely claim of the *Historia Augusta* (*Tyranni Triginta* 4).

The prophesies of the witch in Chapter 20 are taken from the *Völuspá* in *The Elder Edda: A Book of Viking Lore*, translated by A. Orchard (London, 2011). The scene also takes sentences verbatim from *Eirik's Saga*, translated by M. Magnusson and H. Palsson in *The Vinland Sagas* (Harmondsworth, 1965), and the curse at the end draws on *Grettir's Saga* in the translation by J. Byock (Oxford, 2009).

All lines from *The Aeneid* of Virgil are translated by F. Ahl (Oxford, 2007): Oslac in Chapter 20; Zeno in Chapter 32 and Epilogue Two.

In Chapter 21, the line of *Beowulf* which comes to Ballista is in the translation by Kevin Crossley-Holland in *The Anglo-Saxon World* (Woodbridge, 1982), with *wyrd* reinstated for the modern English 'fate'.

Kadlin's thoughts of *Wulf and Eadwacer* in Chapters 22 and 32, and *The Wife's Complaint* in Chapter 32 are from M. Alexander, *The Earliest English Poetry* (London, 1991).

The invocation on the Scorn-Pole in Chapter 24 is altered from *Egil's Saga*, translated by B. Scudder (London, 1997).

Rikiar the Vandal's poems in Chapters 26, 27 and 29 are taken, and in places adapted, from *Egil's Saga*, as translated by B. Scudder (London, 1997).

Other Novels

In all my novels I include homages to a couple of writers who have given me pleasure and inspiration.

As *The Amber Road* involves much travelling up a river in small boats, I reread *Black Robe* by Brian Moore (1985). As I remembered, its authenticity and action, combined with its character development and profundity of theme, brings the historical novel close to perfection. Probably it says something that all I took from it were some images of paddling.

Consciously, I borrowed just the subtitle from *Blood Meridian: Or the Evening Redness in the West* (1985), but the influences of Cormac McCarthy's magnificent prose and unflinching vision are both challenging and inescapable.

Something at a very different level occurred to me as I was typing up the contents page. Hyperboria was the world of Conan the Barbarian. When I was twelve or thirteen, I loved the pulp fiction of Robert E. Howard. Not having reread any, I cannot tell if it has left its mark.

Thanks

Once again I thank almost all the same people, but my pleasure in doing so does not diminish.

Family at home in Woodstock and Newmarket: my wife, Lisa, and sons, Tom and Jack, my mother, Frances, and aunt, Terry.

Colleagues at Oxford: Maria Stamatopoulou of Lincoln College, John Eidinow of St Benet's Hall and Richard Marshall of Wadham College. The latter exhibited even wider scholarship than before in helping compile the List of Characters and Glossary.

Students at Oxford, especially Tim Bano and Dan Draper, who both had far more talk of Ballista than tutorials.

Friends at various locations: Kate and Jeremy Habberley, especially in Cromer and Chipping Norton, and Peter Cosgrove and Jeremy Tinton all over the place.

Finally, the professionals: Alex Clarke, the editor of my first six novels, Sarah Day, the copy-editor of the same, and James Gill, my agent, for those and beyond.

Harry Sidebottom
Newmarket
February 2013

Glossary

The definitions given here are geared to *The Amber Road*. If a word or phrase has several meanings, only that or those relevant to this novel tend to be given.

A Memoria: The emperor's keeper of records.

A Rationibus: Official in control of the emperor's finances.

A Studiis: Official who aided the literary and intellectual studies of the emperor.

Ab Epistulis: Secretary in charge of the emperor's correspondence.

Abalos: Island famed in antiquity for its amber, visited by the Greek explorer Pythias in the fourth century BC, but whose exact location is now unknown. In *The Amber Road*, this island is identified with Bornholm and populated by the Brondings.

Abasgia: Kingdom on the north-east shore of the Black Sea, divided into an eastern and a western half, each with its own king.

Abritus: Battle fought in AD251 against the Goths in what is now eastern Bulgaria. A disaster for the Romans, the emperor Decius and his son were killed in combat.

Achilles Pontarches: Achilles, Ruler of the Sea, a demi-god widely worshipped in the region surrounding the Black Sea.

Acropolis: Sacred citadel of a Greek city.

Actio Gratiarum: Speech of thanks delivered to the emperor by a newly appointed consul.

Adlected: Someone personally promoted by the emperor to a higher social or civic status.

Aegir: Norse god of the sea.

Aeneid: Epic poem by Virgil recounting the ancestral myths of the Romans.

Aenus: Modern river Inn, running from the Alps to the Danube.

Aestii: German tribe living at the eastern end of the southern coast of the Baltic Sea.

Agora: Greek term for a marketplace and civic centre.

Agoranomos: Official in Greek cities, responsible for the *agora* and the food supplies of the population.

Ala (plural, *alae*): Unit of Roman cavalry, usually numbering around five hundred cavalrymen.

Alamann (plural, *Alamanni*): Federation of German tribes along the border of the Roman province of Germania Superior.

Alani: Nomadic tribe north of the Caucasus.

Albania: Kingdom to the south of the Caucasus, bordering the Caspian Sea (not to be confused with modern Albania).

Albingauni: Gallic tribe living around modern Albenga on the Italian Riviera.

Alexandria: Capital of the Roman province of Egypt, second-largest city in the empire.

Alfheim: In Norse myth, the home of the light elves.

Allfather: Epithet of Woden, the supreme god in Norse mythology.

Alpes Maritimae: Roman province including the mountain ranges of the southern Alps and the Mediterranean coast roughly between Marseilles and Genoa.

Amazons: In Greek mythology, a legendary tribe of female warriors.

Amber Road: Collective name for a number of trade routes leading south from the Baltic to the Roman empire.

Amicitia: Friendship. Important Roman concept that included notions of social obligation.

Amicus (plural, *amici*): Latin, friend.

Amphitrite: In Greek mythology, a sea goddess and wife of Poseidon.

Amphora (plural, *amphorae*): Large Roman earthenware storage vessel.

Anabasis: Greek term for an expedition upcountry.

Andreia: Greek, manliness, courage.

Angeln: Land of the Angles.

Angles: North German tribe, living on the Jutland peninsula in the area now occupied by southern Denmark and the German state of Schleswig-Holstein, and in this novel on the Danish islands of Funen and Zealand.

Aphrodite: Greek goddess of love.

Apollo: Greek god adopted by the Romans, with many spheres of responsibility. Worshipped in Olbia as Apollo Prostates, Stands-in-Front, he seems to have been a protector of the city.

Aquileia: Town in north-eastern Italy, where the emperor Maximinus Thrax was killed in AD238.

Aquitania: Roman province covering south-west France.

Arabia: Roman province including the Sinai peninsula and modern Jordan.

Arcadia: Geographical region of Ancient Greece lying in the centre of the Peloponnese.

Archon: Greek title for a leading civic official; literally, ruler, lord.

Arelate: Modern Arles, city in the Roman province of Gallia Narbonensis.

Arete: Fictional town on the Euphrates, based on Dura-Europos, scene of the action in *Fire in the East*.

Argestes: Greek name for the north-west wind.

Armatura: Roman military drill performed in full armour.

Armenia: Kingdom bordered by the Roman empire and Parthia, over which both struggled for influence.

Arsacid: Dynasty that ruled Parthia from 247BC–AD224.

Asclepius: Greek god of healing and medicine.

Asgard: In Norse mythology, the realm of the gods and site of Valhalla.

Assessor: Advisor to a Roman judge.

Atheling: Anglo-Saxon, lord.

Athena: Greek goddess of wisdom and courage.

Atrebatic cloaks: Produced by the Atrebates tribe in north-western France.

Atrium: Central court of a Roman house.

Augusta Ambianorum: The modern town of Eu, just inland from the coast of northern France.

Augusta Raurica: The modern town of Augst in Switzerland, situated on the southern bank of the river Rhine.

Augustodunum: Roman town, now Autun in eastern France.

Augustus: Name of the first Roman emperor, subsequently adopted as one of the titles of the office.

Autochthonous: From the Greek, literally, people sprung out of the earth.

Autocrator: Greek, one who rules alone. Title applied to the Roman emperor.

Auxiliary: Roman regular soldier serving in a unit other than a legion.

Avarini: German tribe living along the Vistula river.

Aviones: German tribe inhabiting a part of the Jutland peninsula.

Baetica: Roman province occupying south-western Spain.

Balder: In some Norse myths, the son of Woden, killed by a trick of Loki.

Banausic: From the Greek term for a manual labourer, hence common or vulgar.

Barbaricum: Lands of the barbarians. Anywhere beyond the frontiers of the Roman empire, which were thought to mark the limits of the civilized world.

Barritus: German war cry.

Basilica: Roman public hall, used as an audience chamber and law court.

Batavians: German tribe living around the Rhine delta in the modern Netherlands.

Bifrost: In Norse mythology, the bridge connecting the world of men and Asgard.

Boeotia: Region of Greece north-west of Athens.

Borani: German tribe living near the Sea of Azov.

Borysthenes: Greek name for the Dnieper river.

Borysthenetica: Literally, pertaining to or regarding the Borysthenes river.

Bosporus: Roman client kingdom in the Crimea.

Boule: Council of a Greek city; in the Roman period made up of local men of wealth and influence.

Bouleuterion: Greek, council house, where the *Boule* met.

Bravoll: Legendary battle mentioned in Norse sagas.

Brisings: In Norse mythology, four dwarf smiths, makers of the goddess Freyja's necklace.

Britannia Superior: Roman province of southern England and Wales.

Brondings: Unidentified tribe named in Beowulf; in this novel inhabiting the island of Abalos (Bornholm).

Bucinator: Latin, trumpeter.

Bucolic: From the Greek *boukolikos*; literally, pertaining to shepherds; rustic.

Byzantium: Greek name for the modern city of Istanbul.

Caelian Hill: One of the Seven Hills of Rome, a fashionable residential district in antiquity.

Caesar: Name of the adopted family of the first Roman emperor, subsequently adopted as one of the titles of the office.

Caldarium: Hot room in Roman baths.

Caledonian: Roman name for people from the modern Highlands of Scotland.

Calumnia: Roman legal term for a false or malicious accusation.

Camarae: Flat-bottomed ships with arched covers used on the Black Sea.

Cambodunum: Modern Kempten, a town in southern Germany at the foot of the Bavarian Alps.

Campania: Region of west-central Italy, renowned in antiquity for its gentle climate and fertility.

Cantabrians: Celtic peoples of northern Spain, long under Roman rule.

Cape Arcona: Headland on the island of Rügen, lying off the eastern Baltic coast of Germany.

Cape Hippolaus: Name given by Herodotus to a promontory lying between the Hypanis and Borysthenes rivers.

Capua: Town in Campania, notorious for the luxurious lifestyle of its inhabitants.

Caracoticum: Modern town of Harfleur, lying on the north-western coast of France.

Carpi: Tribe living north-west of the Black Sea.

Carthage: Ancient Punic city in North Africa, destroyed by the Romans in 146BC, and later rebuilt as a Roman colony.

Castle of Achilles: In this novel, the most northerly Greek settlement along the Hypanis.

Castle of Alector: According to Dio of Prusa, a fort near the mouths of the Hypanis and Borysthenes.

Centurion: Officer of the Roman army with the seniority to command a company of around eighty to a hundred men.

Chalcedon: Town sited opposite Byzantium on the shores of the Bosporus, now a suburb of the modern city of Istanbul.

Chali: German tribe living on the Jutland peninsula.

Charon: In Greek mythology, the ferryman who rowed the souls of the dead to the underworld.

Choosers of the Slain: Literal meaning of 'Valkyrie'. In Norse mythology, maidens who picked out men to be slain in battle and transported them to Valhalla.

Cilicia: Roman province in the south of Asia Minor.

Cimbric peninsula: Ancient name for the Jutland peninsula, from the Cimbri, an early tribe who migrated from there into Gaul in the first century BC.

Circus Maximus: Great chariot-racing stadium in Rome.

Civilis Princeps: Courteous or civil ruler, one who treats his subjects with respect.

Clavenna: Modern Ciavenna, a town on the Italian side of the Alps near the border with Switzerland.

Clementia: Latin, the virtue of mercy.

Cognomen: Third name of a Roman citizen, often a family

name or a nickname, but could also be earned in notable military victories.

Cohort (plural, *cohortes*): From the Latin *cohors*. Unit of Roman soldiers, usually about five hundred men strong.

Cold Crendon: In this novel, a village of the Angles on Varinsey; literally, Cold Creoda's Hill.

Collegium: Latin, an association or society.

Colonia Agrippinensis: Important Roman city on the Rhine, capital of Postumus's breakaway empire; modern Cologne.

Colonia Vienna: Major Roman city on the banks of the Rhodanus river in western France; modern Vienne.

Comes (plural, *comites*): Latin, companion; term applied to an emperor's attendants.

Comitatus: Latin, a following or retinue; term originally used of barbarian war bands, but came to denote a mobile field army under the direct command of the Roman emperor.

Commilito (plural, *commilitones*): Latin, comrade, fellow-soldier.

Comum: Town in the Italian Alps, giving its name to the modern Lake Como.

Concordia Augusta: Deified abstraction of Imperial Accord, worshipped as a goddess; also a guardian of matrimonial harmony.

Consilium: Council, body of advisors, of a Roman emperor, official, or elite private person.

Consul: Originally the highest office of the Roman Republic; two consuls were elected annually. Under the emperors, it became a largely honorific position, with many favourites installed by appointment each year.

Consul Ordinarius: One of the consuls in office at the beginning of the year, the most prestigious position as the year would thereafter be known by the name of the office-holders: 'the year in which X and Y were consuls'.

Controversiae: Form of showpiece legal speech dealing with model cases taken from history and mythology, the more melodramatic the better.

Contubernium: Group of ten (or perhaps eight) soldiers who shared a tent.

Cornucopias: Large horns filled with food, emblems of the *lares*.

Cornutus (plural, *cornuti*): Latin; literally, horned ones. Roman military units raised from the German tribes.

Corrector Totius Orientis: Overseer of all the Orient; a title applied to Odenathus of Palmyra.

Corycus: Town on the southern coast of modern Turkey, scene of one of Ballista's victories over the Persians.

Croesus: King of Lydia, proverbial in antiquity for his wealth.

Ctesiphon: Capital city of the Parthian and Sassanid empires, south of modern Baghdad.

Cubicula: Latin; literally, a little room; bedchamber.

Cularo: Roman town in the Alps, modern Grenoble.

Curia (1): Roman public building in which a town council met, modelled on the senate house or *curia* of Rome.

Curia (2): Small Alpine village controlling the Julier pass; modern Chur.

Cursus Publicus: Imperial Roman posting service, whereby those with official passes, *diplomata*, could send messengers and get remounts.

Cybele: Eastern mother goddess adopted by the Greeks and Romans.

Cyclops: In Greek mythology, mythical one-eyed giant who imprisoned the hero Odysseus.

Cyllene: Mountain in the Peloponnese associated with various deities in Greek mythology.

Cynics: Followers of the counter-cultural philosophy founded by Diogenes of Sinope in the fourth century BC.

Cyning: Old English, king.

Cyreneans: Philosophical sect advocating pure hedonism, founded by Aristippus in the fourth century BC.

Cyzicus: Greek city on the southern shore of the Sea of Marmara.

Dacia: Roman province on the northern bank of the Danube, occupying much of the Carpathian mountains and modern Romania.

Dactylic hexameter: The rhythmic meter of ancient epic poetry.

Daedalus: Skilled craftsman in Greek mythology, credited, among other things, with building the labyrinth.

Daemon: Supernatural being; could be applied to many different types: good/bad, individual/collective, internal/external, and ghosts.

Damocles: Courtier of Dionysius II of Syracuse; after praising the good fortune of the king, he was made to sit on the throne under a sword suspended by a single thread to appreciate the constant fear in which he lived.

Danubian: Inhabitant of one of the Roman frontier provinces abutting the Danube river.

Dauciones: Germanic tribe living in eastern Scadinavia.

Decorum: Latin, seemly, proper, well-mannered.

Delphi: Sanctuary in central Greece, sacred to the god Apollo.

Demeter: Greek goddess of the harvest.

Deuso: Settlement of the Lower Rhine, probably located in the modern Netherlands.

Diana of the Lake: Roman goddess of the moon, hunting and the underworld, worshipped at Lake Nemi.

Didyma: Greek sanctuary on the western shore of modern Turkey, now known as Didim.

Dignitas: Important Roman concept which covers our idea of dignity but goes much further; famously, Julius Caesar claimed that his *dignitas* meant more to him than life itself.

Dioscuri: Roman name for the divine twins Castor and Pollux, said to appear at times of crisis to help those who worshipped them.

Disciplina: Latin, discipline. Romans considered that they had this quality and non-Romans did not.

Dominus: Latin, Lord, Master, Sir; a title of respect.

Draco (plural, *dracones*): Latin, snake or dragon; name given to a windsock-style military standard shaped like a dragon.

Dramatis personae: Latin, characters of the drama, play.

Duguo: Old English, a warrior with experience of combat.

Duguth: Old English, the veteran warriors of a warlord's retinue.

Dux: Roman commander, or duke, of a frontier or field army.

Egnatii: Roman family name attested from the second century BC onwards.

Eorl: Danish, an earl, nobleman.

Ephesus: Major Greek city on the western coast of Turkey where Ballista was forced to rescue his family from an earthquake.

Epicureans: Greek philosophers who either denied the gods existed or held they were far away and did not intervene in the affairs of mankind.

Epigrammatic: From short, pithy poems called *Epigrammata* in Greek, originally carved on to funerary monuments; grew into a major ancient literary genre.

Epiphany: From the Greek, a miraculous, sudden appearance.

Epithalamium: Roman word borrowed from Greek; literally, before the bedroom; a wedding poem sung in praise of the bride and groom.

Equestrian: Second rank down in the Roman social pyramid, the elite order just below the senators.

Equites Singulares Augusti: Permanent cavalry bodyguard of the emperor.

Equites Singulares Consularis: Temporary unit recruited from auxiliary cavalry to be the bodyguard of a provincial governor.

Eros: Greek god of love.

Ethiopia: Ancient term for the whole of sub-Saharan Africa.

Eupatrid: From the Greek, well-born, an aristocrat.

Eutes: Tribe that migrated to the Steppe from the area of modern Denmark and adopted nomadism.

Euxine: From the Greek word *euxenos*; literally, kindly to strangers. Ancient name for the Black Sea.

Exegesis: From the Greek; literally, to lead out; a critical discussion or investigation.

Fairguneis: Thunder god. One of the most important deities of the Goths.

Falernian: Very expensive white wine particularly prized by the Romans.

Familia: Latin, family, and by extension the entire household, including slaves.

Farodini: North German tribe; in this novel placed south of the Jutland peninsula.

Feliciter: Good luck, hurrah; according to the Roman poet Juvenal, the cry of guests at weddings.

Felix: Latin, lucky; an attribute of emperors and some legions.

Fenris: In Norse mythology, a monstrous wolf that will break its chains at the end of days, Ragnarok, and devour Woden, father of the gods.

Ferryman: In Greek and Roman mythology, rows the souls of the dead across the river Styx to the underworld. Required a toll, thus the practice of leaving coins in the mouths of the dead.

Fides (1): Latin, faith, as in 'good faith', keeping one's word to men and the gods.

Fides (2): Name of a patrol boat on the Ister river.

Fiend: Old English for an adversary or enemy.

Fifeldor: Legendary battle mentioned in Norse sagas.

Fimbulvetr: In Norse mythology, a series of severe winters that foretell the end of the world, Ragnarok.

Finni: Nomadic tribe of hunter gatherers living in the far north of Scadinavia.

Fiscus: Originally the private assets of the emperor, the *fiscus* eventually played the role of state treasury.

Flyting: In Norse and Germanic cultures, the ritualized exchange of insults and abuse, a competition of invention, quick thinking and hardiness.

Forum: Public square of a Roman town, the centre of administration, commerce and legal business.

Forum Romanum: Ancient political and legal centre of Rome.

Forum of Trajan: Complex of public buildings erected by the emperor Trajan in central Rome, held to be the most magnificent in the whole of the empire.

Framadar: Persian military officer.

Franks: Confederation of German tribes.

Freyja: Norse goddess of fertility.

Frisia: Coastal region along the shores of the modern
  Netherlands and western Germany.
Frisii: North German tribe inhabiting Frisia.
Frugundiones: Also called *Burgundiones* in ancient sources, a
  German tribe living along the Vistula river.
Frumentarius (plural, *frumentarii*): Military unit based on the
  Caelian Hill in Rome; the emperor's secret police;
  messengers, spies and assassins.
Gallia Belgica: Roman province occupying northern France
  and southern Belgium.
Gallia Lugdunensis: Roman province of north-western and
  central France.
Gallia Narbonensis: Roman province roughly corresponding
  to the French regions of Provence and Languedoc.
Gallic Channel: Literal translation of the Roman name for
  the English Channel.
Gaois: Old Norse, the growing or whirling one. A sword
  inscribed with this name has been excavated in Norway.
Geats: North Germanic tribe; in this novel inhabiting
  Solfell, the island of Gotland.
Genius: Divine part of man, some ambiguity, whether exter-
  nal (like a guardian angel) or internal (divine spark); that of
  the head of a household was worshipped as one of the
  household gods, that of the emperor publicly worshipped.
Gepidae: East German tribe.
Germania: Lands where the German tribes lived; free (as
  opposed to Roman) Germany.
Germania Inferior: Roman province along the south bank of
  the lower Rhine river, occupying much of modern
  Belgium and parts of the Netherlands.
Germania Superior: Roman province astride the upper
  Rhine, in the French region of Alsace and the German
  Rhineland.

Germanicus Maximus: Title adopted by the Roman emperors symbolizing victories over the German tribes.

Gesoriacum: Modern Boulogne, a major military and naval base used by the Romans' Channel fleet.

Getae: Thracian tribe living along the banks of the lower Danube in modern Romania and Bulgaria.

Gift-stool: Literal translation of the Old English term for a throne or seat for formal occasions.

Gladius: Roman military short sword; generally superseded by the *spatha* by the mid-third century AD; also slang for penis.

Gladsheim: Old Norse, bright home, the meeting house of the gods in Asgard.

Gnitaheath: Old Norse; literally, Glittering Heath; in this novel, a heath on the island of Abalos where Unferth has his hall.

Goths: Loose confederation of Germanic tribes.

Graeculus (plural, *Graeculi*): Latin, Little Greek; Greeks called themselves Hellenes; Romans tended not extend that courtesy but called them *Graeci*; with casual contempt, Romans often went further, to *Graeculi*.

Grethungi: Gothic tribe living on the Steppe north of the Black Sea.

Gudme: Major early settlement and trading post on the island of Varinsey (modern Funen).

Gudmestrand: Fictional name for the port of the settlement at Gudme, known today as Lundeborg.

Gymnasium: Exercise ground. Formed from the Greek word *gymnos*, naked, as all such activities were performed in the nude.

Hades: Greek underworld.

Hansa: Gothic, army, band or force.

Harii: Germanic tribe living around the headwaters of the Vistula.

Hearth-companions: Translation from the Old English, retainers, companions.

Hearth-troop: From the Old English, a war band bound to a particular leader through ties of personal loyalty.

Heathobards: German tribe; in this novel, living south-east of the Jutland peninsula.

Hecate: Sinister, three-headed underworld goddess of magic, the night, crossroads and doorways.

Hedinsey: Island in the Baltic known from the Norse sagas, here identified as Zealand.

Heimdall: Norse god who watches for signs of the beginning of Ragnarok.

Hel: Underworld in Norse mythology, reserved for those who do not die a warrior's death.

Helisii: German tribe living along the banks of a tributary of the Borysthenes.

Hellas: Greek name for Greece.

Hellene: Greeks' name for themselves. Often used with connotations of cultural superiority.

Hellenism: Civilization of Ancient Greece.

Hellespont: From the Greek, Sea of Helle (a figure in Greek mythology); narrow channel separating Europe and Asia and linking the Black Sea to the Mediterranean, also known as the Dardanelles.

Hercules: Hero who became a god, popular among Greeks and Romans. Known to the former as Heracles.

Hercules Deusoniensis: Hercules of Deuso, a localized version of the god Hercules.

Herul (plural, *Heruli*): East Germanic tribe living to the north of the Black Sea, having migrated from Scandinavia in the early third century AD.

Hibernia: Modern Ireland.

Hilleviones: German tribe living on Scadinavia.

Himlings: Fictional dynasty ruling over the Angles from the island of Hedinsey.

Hindafell: Literally, Deer Mountain, a place mentioned in the Norse sagas; here identified as the island of Öland, and home of the Wylfings.

Hispania: Roman name for Spain.

Hispania Tarraconensis: Roman province covering much of the Iberian peninsula except the south-western corner, which was shared between two much smaller provinces.

Hlymdale: Literally, Valley of Uproar, a place name mentioned in the Norse sagas and here given to the ancient site excavated at modern Himlingøje on the island of Zealand; home of the Himlings on Hedinsey.

Hoi polloi: Greek written as English, the many: thus the common herd.

Homonoia: Greek political concept of concord, unity, the absence of factionalism.

Homunculi: Latin, little men, dwarfs.

Hronesness: Headland of the Whales, a place mentioned in the Norse sagas.

Hubris: From the Greek *hybris*, pride, which expresses itself in the demeaning of others, and taken to excess results in divine punishment.

Humanitas: Latin, an important ethical concept incorporating notions of humane, civilized, cultivated conduct; the opposite of *barbaritas*. The Romans thought themselves and Greeks (at least upper-class ones), and occasionally other peoples (usually very remote) possessed it, while the majority of mankind did not.

Hygeia: In Greek mythology, the daughter of the god Asclepius, the goddess of health and cleanliness.

Hylaea: Area of forests and marshes bordering the Borysthenes river.

Hymen: Greek god of marriage and weddings.

Hymenaee Hymen, O Hymen Hymenaee: Traditional song
chanted at Roman weddings, invoking the god Hymen.

Hypanis river: Flowing north-west to south-east in western
Ukraine, now known as the Southern Bug river.

Hyperborea: Land of fantastical peoples of the extreme
north, beyond the north wind and far from civilization.

Iberia (1): Ancient name for the lands of modern Spain and
Portugal, taking its name from the Ebro river.

Iberia (2): Kingdom to the south of the Caucasus (the name
led some ancient writers to state that its inhabitants had
migrated from Spain).

Icarus: In Greek mythology, boy whose artificial wings
melted as he flew too close to the sun, with tragic
results.

Iliad: Great epic poem of the Greeks, telling the story of
the Trojan War; written by Homer.

Ilion: Alternative name for the legendary city of Troy.

Imperator: Originally an epithet bestowed by troops on
victorious generals, became a standard title of the
princeps, and thus origin of the English word 'emperor'.

Imperium: Power to issue orders and exact obedience;
official military command.

Imperium Romanum: Power of the Romans, i.e. the Roman
empire, often referred to simply as the *imperium*.

Interamna: Literally, Between Rivers; modern Terni in the
Italian region of Umbria.

Invictus: Unconquered, a title of the Roman emperors.

Invidia: Latin for malicious envy; *phthonos* in Greek.

Io Cantab!: Hurrah, Cantabrians!

Ionic columns: Style of column originating in Ionia, the

eastern coast of modern Turkey settled by Greeks in antiquity.

Isis: Egyptian goddess of reincarnation, adopted by the Romans.

Islands of the Blessed: In Greek myth, a place in the west where the souls of the fortunate dead dwell.

Ister: Ancient name for the lower reaches of the Danube river.

Iuliobona: Modern Lillebonne, a town on the north-western coast of France.

Iuthungi: German tribe belonging to the Alamanni confederation, living to the north of the headwaters of the Rhine and Danube.

Ixion: In Greek mythology, the first man to kill a member of his own family (his father-in-law). Punished by being broken on a wheel.

Julier pass: Important mountain pass though the Alps in south-eastern Switzerland.

Juno: *Genius* of a woman.

Jupiter Optimus Maximus: Jupiter Greatest and Best, the chief god of Roman religion.

Kalends: First day of the month.

Kurgan: Name for a burial mound in the Slavic or Turkic languages spoken to the north of the Black Sea.

Lacedaemon: Alternative name for the Greek state of Sparta, renowned for its warlike inhabitants and militaristic society.

Laestrygonians: Tribe of mythical giants in the *Odyssey* of Homer which practised cannibalism.

Lake Benacus: Roman name for Lake Garda in northern Italy.

Langobard (plural, *Langobardi*): Latin, Tribe living on the banks of the river Elbe in central Germany.

Lares: Gods worshipped domestically by the Romans, protectors of the home and its inhabitants.

Latris: Baltic island mentioned by Pliny, here identified as the group of islands to the south of Zealand and home of the Wrosns.

Legio I Minerva: First Minervan Legion. Originally raised by the emperor Domitian in AD83; stationed in Germania Inferior, its fortress was the modern city of Bonn. Although troops on detachment fought for Gallienus, the legion itself supported Postumus. Commanded by Marcus Aurelius Dialis.

Legio II Adiutrix: The Helpful Second. Formed by Nero in AD66/67, later stationed in Pannonia to defend the Danube frontier.

Legio II Parthica: Second Parthian Legion. Raised by Septimius Severus in AD195/196 for his campaigns in the east. Detachments formed the core of Gallienus's *comitatus*.

Legio III Italica Concors: Third Harmonious Italians. Recruited by Marcus Aurelius in AD165, stationed in Raetia and falling within Postumus's empire. At one time commanded by Simplicinius Genialis, now by Bonosus.

Legio IV Scythica: Fourth Scythian Legion; from the second half of the first century AD, based at Zeugma in Syria Coele; commanded by Ballista against the Persians.

Legio V Macedonica: Fifth Macedonian Legion. Raised in the civil wars of the Roman Republic, stationed in Dacia from AD167. Loyal to Gallienus, detachments saw service in his *comitatus*.

Legio VII Augusta: Seventh Augustan Legion. First raised by Julius Caesar for the conquest of Gaul, stationed at modern Strasbourg in Germania Superior from AD70.

Detachments saw active service in the field army of
Simplicinius Genialis.

Legio XI Claudia: Eleventh Claudian Legion. Stationed in
Moesia Inferior from the beginning of the second
century AD; detached *vexillationes* for service around the
Black Sea region.

Legio XXII Primigenia: Twenty-second First-born. Founded in
the mid-first century AD and quartered for much of the
time thereafter in the modern city of Mainz in Germania
Superior, a province controlled by Postumus.

Legio XXX Ulpia Victrix: Thirtieth Ulpian Victorious Legion.
Recruited by Trajan and taking one of his names, was
posted in AD122 to the modern city of Xanten in Germania Superior. Commanded by Lollianus, an adherent of
Postumus.

Legion: Unit of heavy infantry, usually about five thousand
men strong; from mythical times, the backbone of the
Roman army; the numbers in a legion and the legion's
dominance in the army declined during the third century AD as more and more detachments, *vexillationes*,
served away from the parent unit and became more or
less independent units.

Legionary: Roman regular soldier serving in a legion.

Lesbian: From the Greek island of Lesbos. Wine from this
island was highly praised in antiquity. To accuse a man
of 'playing the Lesbian' was to accuse him of perform-
ing fellatio.

Leuce: Greek, White Island, lying in the Black Sea off the
coast of the Ukraine. Sacred to Achilles in antiquity, now
known in English as Snake Island.

Lex de Imperio: Resolution of the senate conferring power
on an emperor, a constitutional fiction not always
observed.

Libation: Offering of drink to the gods.

Licinii: One of the most important families in early Rome, providing many of the consuls.

Liguria: Ancient name for the north-western area of Italy, modern Piedmont and Genoa.

Little Belt: Sea channel between the Cimbric (modern Jutland) peninsula and the island of Varinsey (modern Funen).

Loki: In Norse mythology, the trickster, bad god.

Lucullan: From the Roman Lucullus, a notorious gourmand.

Lugdunum: Important Roman city in central France, modern Lyon.

Lugii: Confederation of German tribes living roughly in the region of modern Poland.

Macedonia: Roman province covering much of the southern Balkan peninsula, not to be confused with the modern state.

Macriani: Collective name for the family of Macrianus the Lame, a general who proclaimed his sons emperors in AD260.

Maeotis: Sea of Azov.

Maiestas: Latin, majesty. The majesty of the Roman *imperium* was a core component of imperial ideology. Offences against Roman *maiestas*, personified by the emperor, were considered treasonous and punishable by death; in time, the term began to be used for the crime as well as the positive quality.

Mandata: Instructions issued by the emperors to their governors and officials.

Manimi: Tribe belonging to the Lugii.

Manubiae: Latin, spoils of war. A Roman general was

expected to be open-handed with the plunder won on campaign, sharing it among his soldiers. Yet at the same time, under the principate, according to the law, it was all to go to the emperor.

Marcomanni: German confederation of tribes that invaded the Roman Danubian provinces in the late second century AD, and were expelled only with great bloodshed.

Maremma: Breed of Roman hunting dog from northern Italy.

Massilia: Roman port on the southern shores of Gaul; modern Marseilles.

Mauretania: Area of western North Africa divided into two Roman provinces, Tingitana and Caesariensis, covering much of modern Morocco.

Mediolanum: Roman city in north Italy; modern Milan.

Megareans: Followers of the philosopher Stilpo of Megara, who taught the essential unity of all things.

Middle Earth: In Norse culture, the world of men, as opposed to Asgard, the realm of the gods.

Miletus: Major Greek city on the western coast of modern Turkey, saved by Ballista from the Goths.

Mirkwood: Name of several great forests in the legends of the Norse sagas.

Moesia: Ancient geographical region following the south bank of the Danube river in the Balkans.

Moesia Inferior: Roman province south of the lower reaches of the Danube river, bordering the Black Sea.

Mos (plural, *mores*): Latin, customs, modes of conduct.

Mos maiorum: Important Roman concept: traditional customs, the ways of the ancestors.

Murmillo: Type of heavily armed gladiator who could be

recognized by the shape of his helmet, which had a crest
in the shape of a fish.

Museum: Temple of the Muses in Alexandria, an institution
that attracted leading intellectuals from all over the
Greek world, who came to study in its vast library and
would lecture in its precincts. Origin of the modern
word 'museum'.

Myrgings: Saxon clan living to the south of the Angles
along the Eider river.

Naharvali: German tribe of the Lugii. According to Tacitus,
they worshipped at a sacred grove led by a transvestite
priest.

Narbo: Roman city on the southern coast of France; modern Narbonne.

Nasu: Persian, Demon of Death. Name by which the
Persians know Ballista.

Necropolis: Greek; literally, city of the dead; a cemetery.

Nemean lion: Mythical beast killed by Hercules whose pelt,
impervious to mortal weapons, was subsequently worn
by the hero as a cloak.

Nemi: Roman sanctuary sacred to Diana, whose priest was
an escaped slave. His position was precarious, as he
could be replaced by a challenger through a fight to the
death.

Neophytes: From the Greek, recent converts to a religion or
cult; those who must undergo an initiation ritual.

Neo-Pythagoreans: Philosophers who revived the teachings
of Pythagoras in the first century BC, reintroducing an
element of spirituality and mysticism into the then
dominant philosophy of Plato.

Nereids: In Greek mythology, the fifty daughters of the son
of Pontus (the sea); water spirits.

Nerthus: Germanic earth goddess.

Niflheim: In Norse mythology, the underworld for those who do not die in battle.

Nithing: Germanic word for a coward, a wretch. Highly derogatory.

Nocturnal council: In the ideal state sketched by the philosopher Plato, a body meeting before sunrise which seems to have been entrusted with the preservation of the constitution and education of future leading citizens.

Noricum: Roman province lying to the south of the Danube river, occupying most of modern Austria.

Norns: In Norse mythology, the three goddesses responsible for weaving the destinies of gods and men.

Norvasund: The Narrow Sound, an unidentified place mentioned in the Norse sagas and here identified as the modern Gudsø Vig, an inlet on the Jutland peninsula.

Novae: Town on the south bank of the Danube; successfully defended from Gothic attack by the future emperor Gallus in AD250.

Numidia: Ancient geographical region and Roman province on the coast of North Africa; now modern Algeria and western Tunisia.

Odyssey: Greek epic poem telling the long, difficult and dangerous journey home of Odysseus from the Trojan War; written by Homer.

Oikoumene: Greek, the inhabited world; term became synonymous with the Roman empire.

Olbia: City originally founded as a Greek colony near the mouth of the Hypanis river; in modern southern Ukraine.

Olympus: Mountain in northern Greece, its peak thought to be the home of the gods.

Ombrones: German tribe living north of the source of the Vistula river.

Oneiromancy: Interpretation of dreams to divine the future. Elaborated into a complex system and widely practised in antiquity.

Optio: Junior officer in the Roman army, ranked below a centurion.

Ordo: Latin, social or professional class.

Orpheus: Entered the underworld in a doomed attempt to bring back his wife, became a popular figure in ancient literature and religion.

Ouiadoua bank: A river of this name is mentioned by the geographer Ptolemy; probably the modern Oder; the shallow waters and lagoons at its mouth are now known as Stettin Bay.

Oxygala: Greek sour milk or yoghurt.

Paideia: Culture; Greeks considered it marked them off from the rest of the world, and the Greek elite considered it marked them off from the rest of the Greeks.

Palatine: One of the Seven Hills of Rome, overlooking the *forum*; eventually engulfed by the imperial palace.

Palmyra: Now-abandoned city in central Syria. In the chaos of the third century AD, its ruler was put in charge of the Roman province of Syria by the emperor Valerian.

Palmyrene: Inhabitant of Palmyra.

Panegyric: Highly formalized speech of praise delivered to an emperor in gratitude for some favour.

Pannonia: Ancient geographical region lying south of the upper reaches of the Danube river and north of the Dalmatian mountains, in the region of modern Austria and Slovenia, divided into two Roman provinces.

Pans: Greek gods of the mountains, shepherds and rustic music; half man, half goat.

Panticapaeum: Greek: literally, All-cradling. Trading city at the eastern end of the Crimean peninsula, capital of the kingdom of the Bosporus, now modern Kerch.

Parthian: From the empire centred around north-eastern Iran, conquered in AD224 by Ardashir I, founder of the Sassanid empire.

Patrician: Men of the highest birth in Rome, whose families could trace their aristocratic origins back to the legendary foundation of Rome and the first senate.

Pax: Roman personification of Peace, worshipped as a goddess.

Peace-weaver: In Germanic culture, a woman who acts to establish peace between feuding families or individuals.

Pegasus: Winged horse of Greek mythology, famed as a battle charger.

Pelion heaped upon Ossa: In Greek mythology, the sons of Poseidon attempted to climb to heaven by stacking Pelion and Ossa (mountains in north-eastern Greece) on top of Mount Olympus; an image used in the *Aeneid* of Virgil.

Peloponnese: Large peninsula formed by southern Greece.

Peripatetics: Literally, the wanderers; philosophers who followed the scientific and physical teachings of Aristotle.

Peristyle: From the Greek, surrounded by colonnades.

Phalanx: Greek, a military formation; heavy infantry standing in line, many ranks deep.

Phoenician: To act the Phoenician was to perform cunnilingus, considered by the Romans to be a disgusting and degrading act. Slang term originating in the ethnic stereotyping of the Phoenicians, a people of the eastern Mediterranean, early enemies of Rome; *see Lesbian*.

Phthonos: Greek, malicious envy; *invidia* in Latin.

Pius: Latin, god-fearing, properly religious; a quality of all good Romans.

Plataea: Battle in which a small alliance of Greek states fought successfully for their freedom against the invading Persians.

Platonist: Follower of the philosophy of Plato.

Platonopolis: According to Porphyry, a project conceived by the philosopher Plotinus and patronized by the emperor Gallienus to refound a ruined city in Campania that would be run along the lines of the ideal state theorized by Plato.

Plebs: Lowest social class in Rome, more or less despised by the elite; often referred to as the dregs of the population.

Polis: Greek, a city state; living in one was a key marker in being considered Greek and/or civilized.

Pontifex Maximus: Chief priest of the Roman religion, an office assumed by the emperor and included among his titles.

Poseidon: Greek god of the sea.

Praefectus Castrorum: Roman officer in charge of the baggage train and camp; normally an ex-centurion.

Praefectus Legionis: Equestrian commander of a legion.

Praefectus Vigilum: Important administrator in the city of Rome; in charge of the *vigiles*.

Praetorian Prefect: Commander of the *Praetorians*, an equestrian.

Praetorians: Members of the Praetorian Guard, the emperor's bodyguard and the most prestigious and highly paid unit in the empire.

Praetorium: Tent of a Roman general; a military headquarters.

Prefect: From the Latin *praefectus*, a flexible term for many officials and officers; on its own, typically the commander of an auxiliary unit.

Prefect of Cavalry: Senior military post introduced in the
mid-third century AD.

Prefect of the City: Official controlling the judiciary of
Rome; also commanded a military unit for the mainten-
ance of order in the city.

Priene: Greek town on the eastern coast of modern Turkey.

Primus Pilus: Senior centurion of a legion; on retirement,
could expect to be made an equestrian.

Princeps (plural, *principes*): Latin, leading man; thus a polite
way to refer to the emperor. In the plural, often denoted
senators or great men of the empire, but might also be
used of any important persons.

Princeps Peregrinorum: Commander of the *frumentarii*.

Protector (plural, *protectores*): Group of high-ranking military officers singled out by the emperor Gallienus to act
as his staff.

Puer (plural, *pueri*): Latin, boy; used by owners of their
male slaves, and by soldiers of each other.

Pulchritude: From the Latin, beauty.

Pythagoreans: First followers of the philosopher Pythagoras,
who taught a form of mysticism based on mathematics.

Quadi: Bellicose tribe of Germans living on the Roman
frontier beside the Danube river.

Quaestors: Most junior office in the public career system of
the Roman elite, granting the holder the rank of senator.

Raetia: Roman Alpine province including the modern
Tyrol and parts of Switzerland and Bavaria.

Ragnarok: In Norse paganism, the death of gods and men;
the end of time.

Ran: Norse goddess of the sea.

Reiks: Gothic chief or warlord.

Res Publica: Latin, the Roman Republic; under the emperors, continued to mean the Roman empire.

Reudigni: German tribe living on the Jutland peninsula.

Rhodanus: Roman name for the Rhone river.

Rotomagus: Important Roman city in northern France; modern Rouen.

Rugii: German tribe living on the southern coasts of the Baltic.

Rugium: Town of the Rugii named by Ptolemy; here placed on the lower Vistula.

Runes: Germanic writing system, thought to have magical powers.

Sacramentum: Roman military oath, taken extremely seriously.

Sacred Way: Road leading from the *forum* in Rome, used as a processional route for state occasions.

Salus: Roman personification of safety and prosperity, worshipped as a goddess.

Samarobriva: Roman city in north-western France; modern Amiens.

Sarcophagus (plural, *sarcophagi*): Greek; literally, flesh-eater; a stone coffin, often highly carved and displayed above ground.

Sarmatians: Nomadic peoples living north of the Danube.

Sassanid: Persian, from the dynasty that overthrew the Parthians in the 220s AD and was Rome's great eastern rival until the seventh century AD.

Saxons: North Germanic tribe.

Scadinavia: Ancient name for the southern part of the Scandinavian peninsula, thought to be an island in antiquity.

Scop: In Norse and Angle culture, an itinerant poet, reciting epic verse on heroic themes of battle.

Scrithiphini: Scandinavian tribe.

Scylla and Charybdis: Two monsters from the *Odyssey*, guarding either side of a narrow strait.

Scythians: Nomadic peoples living north and east of the Black Sea, roughly bordered by the Danube in the west, the Volga in the east and the Caucasus to the south. A source of fantastical tales for ancient geographers.

Sebaste: Elaiussa Sebaste, a Roman town on the southern coast of Turkey where Ballista successfully routed the Persians.

Semnones: German tribe belonging to the Alamanni confederation, living to the north of the headwaters of the Rhine and Danube.

Senator: Member of the senate, the council of Rome. The senatorial order was the richest and most prestigious group in the empire, often entrusted with military commands and imperial offices.

Serapis: God of the harvest, worshipped by the Greek inhabitants of Egypt and later adopted by the Romans.

Sesterces: Standard denomination in the Roman coinage system.

Seven Hills: The city of Rome encompassed seven hills, the tops of which were popular residential districts among the rich and powerful, the poor crowding into the valleys in between.

Shield-burg: From the Old English, a shield fort or castle.

Shield-maiden: In Germanic society, a woman who chose to fight as a warrior, though more common in legend and folklore. Also a name for the Choosers of the Slain.

Silentarii: Body of servants whose sole job was to maintain the awed hush in the imperial audience chamber.

Skalks: Gothic, slave.

Skoll: In Norse mythology, the wolf who chases the chariot of the sun's horses across the sky and, at the end of time, catches them.

Solfell: Sun Mountain, place mentioned in the Norse sagas; here identified as the island of Gotland, the home of the Geats.

Soli: Greek city in southern Turkey, scene of Ballista's victory over the Persians and sacking of Shapur's harem.

Sophist: Famous public speakers who specialized in display oratory.

Sorn-pole: Also known as a *nithing* pole. Wooden stake covered with curses carved in runes and capped by a horse skull, activating the malevolence of the Norse goddess of death. Thought to be a highly potent form of magic.

Sound, The: Sea channel between Hedinsey (modern Zealand) and Scadinavia (modern Sweden).

Sparta: Region in the centre of the Peloponnese and Ancient Greek state, notoriously militaristic.

Spatha: Long Roman sword, the usual type carried by all troops by the mid-third century AD.

Stephanephor: Greek; literally, Crown-wearer; title of magistrate in some Greek cities.

Stipendium: Latin military term for a soldier or sailor's pay.

Stoics: Philosophers who practised self-control and suppression of the emotions in the search for moral perfection. Very popular among the Romans; the second-century emperor Marcus Aurelius even wrote Stoic treatises.

Strategos: Greek, general, commander.

Suania: Kingdom in the High Caucasus; included the modern district of Georgia called Svaneti.

Suebian Sea: Ancient name for the Baltic.

Susurration: From the Latin *sussuratio*, a whispering.

Swinehead: Germanic/Norse attacking formation in the shape of an arrow.

Syria Coele: Hollow Syria, Roman province covering the northern half of the coast of modern Syria.

Syria Phonice: Phoenician Syria, Roman province occupying the southern half of the coast of modern Syria.

Taifali: Gothic tribe settled to the north-east of the lower Danube river; accused of very strange customs by Ammianus.

Talasio: Very ancient cry raised at weddings; its origins and meaning were unknown to the Romans themselves.

Tanais: City at the mouth of the river Tanais (the modern Don), located on the extreme north-eastern shore of the Sea of Azov.

Tara: Sacred hill on which the high kings of Hibernia were crowned.

Tauromenium: Town in Sicily (modern Taormina), where Ballista and Julia own a villa.

Teiws: God of war worshipped by the Goths.

Telones: Greek, a customs or tax official.

Tervingi: Gothic tribe living in the region between the Danube and Dnieper rivers.

Testudo: Latin; literally, tortoise; by analogy, a Roman infantry formation with overlapping shields, similar to a northern shield-burg.

Thebes: Greek city north-west of Athens. Site of a legendary siege captained by seven mythical heroes.

Theoden: Old English, king, ruler.

Thermae: Public baths.

Thessaly: Region of north-central Greece.

Thetis: In Greek mythology, one of the Nereids, mother of Achilles.

Thiazi: In Norse mythology, a giant whose eyes were placed as stars in the heavens by Odin.

Thrace: Ancient geographical region corresponding to the

European portion of modern Turkey and southern Bulgaria.

Tiber: River flowing through Rome.

Toga: Voluminous garment, reserved for Roman citizens, worn on formal occasions.

Tribune (Latin, *Tribunus*): Junior rank in the Roman civic or military hierarchy, generally filled by the sons of the elite.

Tridentum: Roman town lying in the foothills of the Italian Alps; modern Trento.

Trierarch: The commander of a *trireme*; in the Roman forces, equivalent to a centurion.

Trireme: Ancient warship, a galley rowed by about two hundred men on three levels.

Troy: City on the southern shore of the Hellespont, scene of the legendary siege recounted in the *Iliad*.

Ubi tu Gaius, ego Gaia: Where you (are) Gaius, I (am) Gaia. The traditional vow made by a woman during the Roman marriage ceremony, which Romans themselves found hard to explain. The names may have been chosen because they were typical (Mr and Mrs Smith), or might be garbled versions of an archaic word meaning happy.

Ultio: Roman concept of revenge as a form of justice, once a powerful motivating factor in the politics that created the empire.

Urugundi: Gothic tribe settled along the Don river.

Uxorious: From the Latin, to be fond of one's wife.

Valhalla: In Norse mythology, the hall in which selected heroes killed in battle would feast until Ragnarok.

Vandals: German tribe living in the area of southern Poland.

Varini: German tribe living on the Jutland peninsula.

Varinsey: Island in the Baltic known from the Norse sagas, here identified as Funen.

Venedi: Tribe living along the upper reaches of the Dnieper.

Vesontio: Roman town lying by the foothills of the French Alps; modern Besançon.

Vestal: Virgin priestesses of the Roman goddess Vesta; if they broke their vow of chastity, they were punished by being buried alive.

Vexillationes: Troops detached from their parent units for special service.

Via Claudia Augusta: Roman military road driven through the Alps, linking northern Italy to the provinces of the Rhine frontier.

Via Flaminia: Major road leading north out of Rome.

Vigiles: Large paramilitary organization stationed in Rome, fulfilling the duties of fire brigade and police force.

Vir Egregius: Knight of Rome, a man of the equestrian order.

Vir Ementissimus: Highest rank an equestrian could attain; e.g. Praetorian Prefect.

Vir Perfectissimus: Equestrian rank above *Vir Egregius* but below *Vir Ementissimus*.

Virtus: Latin, courage, manliness and / or virtue; far stronger and more active than the English word 'virtue'.

Vocontii: Gallic tribe living on the east bank of the Rhone river in the foothills of the French Alps.

Wade: Sea giant of Norse mythology; a great warrior.

Warhedge: Old English poetical term for a shieldwall; a hedge of spears.

Warig: Old English; literally, Filthy, Muck-tub, Brine-stained; here the name of a native longship given by the king of the Harii to Ballista.

Waymunding: Leading family on Varinsey; later a royal
    dynasty mentioned in the epic poetry of the Angles.
Whale Road: Old English poetical term for the sea.
Wicce: Old English, a sorceress, witch.
Woden: High Norse god.
Woden-born: Descended from Woden.
Woden's Hall: Alternative name for Valhalla.
Wrosns: Royal dynasty mentioned in the Norse sagas; here
    the ruling dynasty of Latris.
Wuffingas: Noble dynasty of the Angles on Hedinsey,
    became the first rulers of the Anglo-Saxon kingdom of
    East Anglia in England with a burial ground at Sutton
    Hoo.
Wylfings: German tribe; in this novel inhabiting Hindafell,
    the island of Öland.
Wyrd: One of the *Norns*, often translated as 'fate'.
Yggdrasill: In Norse mythology, the immense tree that
    supports the worlds of the gods and men.
Zephyr: From the Greek name for a gentle west wind.
Zeus: King of the gods in Greek mythology, worshipped in
    many guises; as Zeus the Saviour, he brought protection
    and was commonly toasted at dinner parties.

List of Roman Emperors of the
Time of The Amber Road

AD193–211	Septimius Severus
AD198–217	Caracalla
AD210–11	Geta
AD217–18	Macrinus
AD218–22	Elagabalus
AD222–35	Alexander Severus
AD235–8	Maximinus Thrax
AD238	Gordian I
AD238	Gordian II
AD238	Pupienus
AD238	Balbinus
AD238–44	Gordian III
AD244–9	Philip the Arab
AD249–51	Decius
AD251–3	Trebonianus Gallus
AD253	Aemilianus
AD253–60	Valerian
AD253–	Gallienus

List of Characters

To avoid giving away any of the plot, characters usually are only described as first encountered in *The Amber Road.*

Achilles (1): Greek hero of the *Iliad*, Homer's epic poem of the Trojan War. Worshipped as a demi-god, his cult was especially popular around the coast of the Euxine.

Achilles (2): Iulius Achilles, *a Memoria* to Gallienus.

Acilius Glabrio: Gaius Acilius Glabrio, a young patrician, one of Gallienus's *comites* at Mediolanum in AD260.

Aelfwynn: Daughter of Kadlin and Oslac, a young Angle.

Aelius Restutus: Governor of Noricum in the service of Gallienus.

Aemilianus: Postumus's governor of Hispania Tarraconensis.

Aeneas: Trojan hero of the *Aeneid*, Virgil's epic poem telling of the legendary origins of Rome.

Aeneas Tacticus: Greek author of a handbook on how to survive sieges, written *c.* 350BC.

Aeschylus: Athenian tragic dramatist of the sixth to fifth centuries BC.

Aethelgar: Son of Kadlin and Oslac, a young Angle.

Aeva: Sweetheart of Eomer.

Albinus: *See* Nummius Ceionius Albinus.

Alexander (the Great): 356–23BC, son of Philip, King of Macedon, conqueror of Achaemenid Persia.

Amantius: Publius Egnatius Amantius, an imperial eunuch from Abasgia.

Amelius: Gentilianus Amelius, leading disciple of the philosopher Plotinus.

Anacharsis: Scythian philosopher who settled in Athens in the sixth century BC, sometimes numbered among the Seven Sages of Greece.

Antony: Marcus Antonius, Roman statesman and general, committed suicide in Egypt when it became clear he had lost the civil war with Augustus, 30BC.

Ariadne: Mythical heroine who fell in love with Theseus, only to be abandoned by him shortly after saving his life.

Arkil: An *atheling* of the Angles; son of Isangrim (1) and a woman of the Frisii, full brother of Eadwulf Evil-Child, older half-brother of Ballista. He fights under the banner of the Himlings of Hedinsey, a white horse on a green field.

Ashhere: Angle warlord.

Attalus: King of the Marcomanni, father of Pippa.

Augustus: First Roman emperor, 31BC–AD14.

Aulus Voconius Zeno: Roman equestrian, once governor of Cilicia and *a Studiis* to Gallienus, but afterwards acting as a Roman emissary. Having visited the tribes near the mouth of the Danube, is now heading for the Angles in the far north of Germania.

Aurelian: Lucius Domitius Aurelian, known as Hand-to-Steel, a Roman officer from the Danube. A friend of Ballista at the court of Gallienus.

Aureolus: Once a Getan shepherd near the Danube, now Gallienus's Prefect of Cavalry, one of the *protectores*.

Ballista: Marcus Clodius Ballista, originally named Dernhelm, son of Isangrim the *Dux*, war leader, of the Angles; a diplomatic hostage in the Roman empire, he has been granted Roman citizenship and equestrian status, having served in the Roman army in Africa, the far west, and on the Danube and Euphrates; having defeated the Sassanid Persians at the battles of Circesium, Soli and Sebaste, and killed the pretender Quietus, he was briefly acclaimed Roman emperor three years before this novel starts.

Bion: Deputy *strategos* of Olbia.

Bonitus: Roman siege engineer, one of Gallienus's *protectores*.

Bonosus: Commander of Legio III Italica Concors, a drunkard in the service of Postumus.

Brecca: Ruler of the Brondings.

Brutus: One of Julius Caesar's assassins.

Caesar: Gaius Julius Caesar, Roman statesman and general, assassinated for tyranny on the *ides* (15th) of March 44BC.

Calgacus: Marcus Clodius Calgacus; a Caledonian ex-slave, originally owned by Isangrim and sent by him to serve as a body servant to his son Ballista in the Roman empire, and manumitted by the latter. He was murdered by Hippothous the year before this novel starts.

Caligula: Gaius Julius, Roman emperor AD37–41; as a child, nicknamed Little Boots, *Caligula*, because his father had him dressed in miniature soldier's uniform.

Callistratus: Foremost *archon* of Olbia.

Camsisoleus: Egyptian officer of Gallienus, brother of Theodotus; one of the *protectores*.

Carus: Marcus Aurelius Carus, a young officer from Narbo, one of Gallienus's *protectores*.

Cassius: One of Julius Caesar's assassins.

Castricius: Gaius Aurelius Castricius, Roman army officer risen from the ranks, Prefect of Cavalry under both Quietus and Ballista.

Cato the Censor: Marcus Porcius Cato, also known as Cato the Elder (234–149BC), stern moralist of the Republican age.

Catullus: Roman poet (*c.* 80–*c.* 51BC).

Celer (1): Roman general from Italy, one of Gallienus's *protectores*.

Celer (2): *Frumentarius* in the service of Postumus.

Censor: Governor of Gallia Narbonensis under Postumus.

Censorinus: Lucius Calpurnius Piso Censorinus, *Princeps Peregrinorum* under Valerian and the pretenders Macrianus and Quietus; now serving as Praetorian Prefect under Gallienus.

Ceola: Son of Godwine, a young Angle warrior in charge of coastal defence.

Chosroes: Exiled client king of Armenia, now resident at the court of Gallienus.

Cicero: Roman statesman and prolific author (106–43BC).

Circe: Mythical witch, also involved in the homecoming of Odysseus from the Trojan war.

Claudius: Marcus Aurelius Claudius, a Danubian officer of Gallienus, one of the *protectores*.

Claudius Natalianus: Gallienus's governor of Moesia Inferior.

Clementius Silvius: Titus Clementius Silvius, governor of both the provinces of Pannonia, Superior and Inferior, under Gallienus.

Cominius Priscianus: Gallienus's *a Studiis*.

Cormac: Cousin of Maximus.

Dadag: *Agoranomos* of Olbia.

Dardanos: Legendary founder of Troy.

Demetrius: Marcus Clodius Demetrius, a slave purchased by Julia to serve as her husband Ballista's secretary; manumitted by the latter, now a freedman with Roman citizenship living in the household of the emperor Gallienus.

Dernhelm (1): Original name of Ballista.

Dernhelm (2): Lucius Clodius Dernhelm, second son of Ballista and Julia.

Dido: Legendary founder and Queen of Carthage, spurned lover of Aeneas in the *Aeneid*.

Dio of Prusa: Also known as Dio Chrysostom, the Golden-Mouthed; a Greek philosopher of the first to second centuries AD.

Diocles: *Optio* of a military unit sent to Olbia.

Diogenes: Cynic philosopher, *c.* 412/403–*c.* 324/321BC.

Diophanes: Student of the philosopher Plotinus.

Domitianus: Italian officer of Gallienus, one of the *protectores*; claims descent from the emperor Domitian.

Dunnere Tethered-Hound: Heathobard warrior.

Eadric: Angle, son of *eorl* Eadwine of Gudmestrand.

Eadwine: Angle *eorl* of Gudmestrand, of the Waymunding family.

Eadwulf Evil-Child: Son of Isangrim (1) and a woman of the Frisii, full brother of Arkil, half-brother of Ballista.

Eomer: Angle *duguo*.

Eudosius: Ruler of the Dauciones.

Fabius Cunctator: Quintus Fabius Maximus Verrucosus Cunctator, appointed Dictator (for the second time) to defend Rome from Hannibal in 217BC. Avoiding pitched battle, and thus defeat, he earned the name Cunctator, the Delayer.

Fabius Labeo: Ex-consul, governor of Syria Coele for Gallienus.

433

Faraxen: Charismatic leader of a native revolt against Rome in North Africa; uncertain if he is dead.

Faustinus: Roman senator with wide estates in Narbonensis and Lugdunum.

Firmus: Castricius Firmus, Roman senator; identified as a follower of the philosopher Plotinus by Porphyry.

Flaccinus: Valerius Flaccinus, a young relative of Gallienus's father, Valerian. Fell into the hands of the Quadi and was rescued by Probus.

Freki: Alamann, commander of the German bodyguard of Gallienus.

Froda: Son of Isangrim (1) and a Langobardi woman, older half-brother of Ballista.

Gallienus: Publius Licinius Egnatius Gallienus, declared joint Roman emperor by his father, the emperor Valerian, in AD253, sole emperor after the capture of his father by the Persians in AD260.

Gallus: Gaius Vibius Trebonianus Gallus, a successful general on the Danube, he defended Novae from the Goths in AD250; emperor AD251–3.

Gifeca: Counsellor of Heoden, king of the Harii.

Giton: Slave boy belonging to Marcus Aurelius Julianus, named after a character in an ancient novel who was also used sexually by his master.

Glaum: Son of Wolfmaer, an Angle confidant of Morcar.

Godwine: Angle *eorl*, father of Ceola.

Grim: Heathobard warrior.

Gunteric: Ruler of the Tervingi Goths.

Guthlaf: Duguth of the Angles.

Hama: Legendary hero in the poems of the *scops*, a warrior and dragon-slayer.

Hannibal: General of Carthage in the Second Punic War against Rome (247–183BC).

Hathkin: Angle, son of Heoroweard and Wealtheow, cousin of Starkad.

Hector: Legendary hero in Homer's *Iliad*, the greatest warrior of Troy and sworn enemy of Achilles.

Helen: Greek princess abducted by Hector's brother and brought to Troy; the war waged for her return is the subject of the *Iliad*.

Heliodorus: Sailor serving on the *Fides* patrol boat, originally from Egypt.

Heliogabalus: Derogatory nickname for the emperor Marcus Aurelius Antoninus, AD218–22. Said to be remarkably perverse.

Helm: Ancestor of Heoden, founder of the royal line of the Harii.

Heoden: King of the Harii, maternal uncle and sometime foster-parent of Ballista.

Heoroweard Paunch-Shaker: Brother of Kadlin, husband of Wealtheow; a childhood friend of Ballista.

Heraclian: Marcus Aurelius Heraclianus, a *protector* of Gallienus.

Herodotus: The Father of History; fifth-century BC Greek historian of the Persian wars.

Hieroson: Olbian guide attached to Ballista's embassy.

Hippolytus: Legendary Greek figure. As punishment for spurning Aphrodite's advances, the goddess made his stepmother fall madly in love with him. Similarly rejected, her jealousy ultimately resulted in Hippolytus's death.

Hippothous: Claimed to be from Perinthus originally; joined Ballista as *accensus* (secretary) in Rough Cilicia, murdered Calgacus.

Hjar: *Cyning* of the Angles, great-grandfather of Ballista.

Holen: Wrosn of the islands of Latris, first husband of Kadlin.

Homer: Epic poet and father of Greek literature, author of the *Iliad* and *Odyssey*; probably lived in the seventh or eighth century BC.

Honoratianus: Governor of Gallia Lugdunensis; *Consul Ordinarius* with Postumus AD260.

Hrothgar: Brother of Holen, brother-in-law of Kadlin and ruler of the Wrosns.

Hygelac: Ruler of the Geats.

Ingenuus: One-time governor of Pannonia Superior and one of Gallienus's *protectores*, rebelled and was killed in AD260.

Ion: Slave boy belonging to Amantius.

Isangrim (1): *Dux*, war leader, of the Angles, father of Dernhelm/Ballista.

Isangrim (2): Marcus Clodius Isangrim, first son of Ballista and Julia.

Ivar Horse-Prick: Angle warrior and older contemporaryof Ballista.

Julia: Daughter of the late senator Gaius Julius Volcatius Gallicanus; wife of Ballista.

Julius Marcellinus: Roman officer in the service of Gallienus, assistant to Bonitus.

Kadlin: Wife of Oslac and mother of Starkad, an Angle *eorl*.

Laelianus: Ulpius Cornelius Laelianus, legionary commander in then governor of Germania Superior, a supporter of Postumus.

Leoba: Sibling of Kadlin and Heoroweard, an Angle shield-maiden.

Lepidus: Governor of Gallia Belgica for Postumus.

Liberalinius Probinus: Officer serving under Lollianus.

Licinius: Licinius Valerianus, son of Valerian and half-brother of Gallienus, *Consul Ordinarius* in AD265.

Lollianus: Commander of Legio XXX Ulpia Victrix, advised Postumus to rebel, promoted to Prefect of Cavalry.

Lucillus: Egnatius Lucillus, designated *Consul Ordinarius* for AD265, possibly a relation of Gallienus.

Macarius: Marcus Aurelius Macarius, *stephanephor* of Miletus.

Macrianus: Titus Fulvius Junius Macrianus, son of Macrianus the Lame and known as Macrianus the Younger. With his brother, Quietus, usurped the throne in AD260 and died in AD261.

Macrianus the Lame: Fulvius Macrianus, father of the usurpers Macrianus and Quietus. Was unable to assume the throne himself as he was physically deformed in one leg, so arranged to have his sons acclaimed joint emperors in AD260. Died in AD261.

Maecianus: Prefect of Postumus's Equites Singulares Augusti.

Marcellus Orontius: Roman senator identified as a follower of the philosopher Plotinus by Porphyry.

Marcianus: Aurelius Marcianus, one of Gallienus's *protectores*.

Marcus Aurelius: Marcus Aurelius Antoninus, emperor AD161–80.

Marcus Aurelius Dialis: Postumus's governor of Germania Inferior.

Marcus Aurelius Julianus: Roman knight, ambassador of Gallienus.

Marinianus: Publius Licinius Egnatius Marinianus, youngest and sole surviving son of Gallienus.

Marius: Postumus's *Praefectus Castrorum*.

Maximinus Thrax: Gaius Julius Verus Maximinus, Roman emperor AD235–8, known as *Thrax* (the Thracian) because of his lowly origins.

Maximus: Marcus Clodius Maximus, bodyguard to Ballista; originally a Hibernian warrior known as Muirtagh of the Long Road, sold to slave traders and trained as a boxer then gladiator before being purchased by Ballista. Now a freedman.

Menoetius: Legendary Greek hero and father of Patroklos, accompanied Jason and the Argonauts in their search for the Golden Fleece.

Montanus: Marcus Galerius Montanus Proculus, *strategos* of Olbia. The tomb of his great-grandmother, who lived to the remarkable age of ninety, still survives.

Morcar: Son of Isangrim (1) and a woman of the Brondings; full brother of Oslac, elder half-brother of Ballista.

Mord: Young Angle, son of Morcar.

Mussius Aemilianus: Lucius Mussius Aemilianus, rebelled as Prefect of Egypt *c.* AD261–2 but was captured and replaced by Theodotus.

Naulobates: King of the Heruli.

Niger: Gaius Pescennius Niger, short-lived usurper in the east, AD193–4.

Nummius Ceionius Albinus: Prefect of the City in AD256 and AD261–3, and *Consul Ordinarius* for the second time in AD263.

Nummius Faustinianus: *Consul Ordinarius* with Gallienus in AD262.

Odenathus: Septimius Odenathus, Lord of Palmyra/Tadmor, appointed by Gallienus as *corrector* (overseer) over the eastern provinces of the Roman empire.

Odysseus: Legendary Greek hero of the *Odyssey*, encountered many trials and monsters on his ten-year return home from the siege of Troy.

Oslac: Stepfather of Starkad (2) and second husband of

Kadlin, son of Isangrim (1) and a Bronding woman, full brother of Morcar, elder half-brother of Ballista.

Palfurius Sura: Gallienus's *ab Epistulis*.

Patroklos: Greek hero killed at Troy and avenged by Achilles, thought by some in antiquity to be his lover.

Petronius: First-century AD author of the Latin novel *The Satyricon*; usually identified with Petronius Arbiter, sometime friend of Nero.

Philip the Arab: Marcus Julius Philippus, Praetorian Prefect under the emperor Gordian III (AD238–44), became Roman emperor himself AD244–9.

Pindar: Greek lyric poet.

Pippa (or Pipa): Daughter of Attalus, king of the Marcomanni, known as Pippara to Gallienus.

Pius: Titus Fulvius Aelius Hadrianus Antoninus Augustus Pius, sometimes shortened to Antoninus Pius, Roman emperor AD138–61.

Placidianus: Julius Placidianus, Gallienus's *Prefectus Vigilum*. An inscription in his honour survives from Grenoble.

Plato: Athenian philosopher, *c.* 429–347BC.

Pliny: Pliny the Younger, a prolific letter writer and author of a surviving speech in praise of the emperor Trajan (AD61/62–c. 113).

Plotinus: Neoplatonist philosopher, AD205–69/70.

Postumus: Marcus Cassianus Latinius Postumus, once governor of Lower Germany, from AD260 Roman emperor of the breakaway Gallic empire; murderer of Gallienus's son Saloninus.

Postumus Iunior: Son of the Gallic emperor Postumus, serving as a tribune of the Vocontii.

Potamis: Slave trader on the Dnieper river, whose unpleasant character was referred to in *The Wolves of the North*.

Priam: Legendary king of Troy during the siege recounted in Homer's *Iliad*.

Probus: Marcus Aurelius Probus, a young tribune from Pannonia, rescuer of Flaccinus.

Proculus: Gallic prefect in the service of Gallienus.

Pyrrhus of Epirus: King of Epirus, stunned by a roof tile while assaulting Sparta and subsequently beheaded (319/318–272BC).

Pythonissa: Daughter of King Polemo of Suania; a priestess of Hecate.

Quietus: Titus Fulvius Iunius Quietus, son of Macrianus the Elder, proclaimed Roman emperor with his brother Macrianus the Younger in AD260, and killed by Ballista in AD261.

Quirinius: Aurelius Quirinius, Gallienus's *a Rationibus*.

Ragonius Clarus: Gaius Ragonius Clarus, a Roman senator, originally from Macedonia, a supporter of Postumus, had previously served as Ballista's legate in Cilicia.

Rebecca: Jewish slave woman bought by Ballista.

Regalianus: One-time governor of Pannonia Inferior, who claimed descent from the kings of Dacia before the Roman conquest; rebelled against Gallienus and was killed in AD260.

Regulus: *Trierarch* in charge of transporting Ballista's embassy.

Respa: Son of Gunteric, brother of Tharuaro; Gothic warrior of the Tervingi killed by Ballista at Didyma.

Rikiar: Ugly Vandal warrior, member of Heoden's hearth-troop, composer of poetry.

Rufinus: Gallienus's *Princeps Peregrinorum*, spymaster, commander of the *frumentarii*.

Rullus: Publius Servilius Rullus, tribune of the Roman

people in 63BC, proposed a set of radical measures to resettle the urban poor as farmers. Three of Cicero's speeches against the proposals survive.

Sabinillus: Roman senator; identified as a follower of the philosopher Plotinus by Porphyry.

Saitaphernes: Member of the *Boule* of Olbia.

Salonina: Egnatia Salonina, wife of Gallienus.

Saloninus: Publius Cornelius Licinius Saloninus Valerianus, second son of Gallienus, made Caesar in AD258 on the death of his elder brother, Valerian II; executed by Postumus in AD260.

Saturninus: L. Albinus Saturninus, consul in AD264.

Scipio: Publius Cornelius Scipio Aemilianus Africanus Numantinus, usually shortened to Scipio Aemilianus; raised the city of Carthage to the ground in 146BC.

Scyles: Half-Greek king of the Scythians, *c.* 500BC.

Septimius Severus: Lucius Septimius Severus, Roman emperor AD193–211.

Servilius Rufinus: Commander of Legio XXII Primigenia in Germania Superior, a supporter of Postumus.

Shapur I (or Sapor): Second Sassanid King of Kings, son of Ardashir I.

Silvanus: Governor of Germania Superior and *Dux* of the Rhine; his unreasonable requests forced Postumus to rebel in AD260.

Simon: Young Jewish boy owned by Ballista.

Simplicinius Genialis: Marcus Simplicinius Genialis, acting governor of Raetia and supporter of Postumus, later confirmed in his post and made *Consul Ordinarius* in reward.

Solon: Law-giver of the Athenians, *c.* 600BC.

Starkad (1): Chief of the Angles, son of the *cyning* Hjar, Ballista's grandfather.

Starkad (2): Son of Kadlin, an Angle *eorl*. His banner is a white *draco*.

Swerting: Angle, once friend of Eadwulf.

Tacitus (1): Marcus Claudius Tacitus, Roman senator of third century AD (most likely) of Danubian origins; one of the *protectores*; may have claimed kinship with or even descent from the famous historian, but this is unlikely to be true.

Tacitus (2): Cornelius Tacitus, *c.* AD56–*c.* 118, the greatest Latin historian.

Tarchon: Warrior from Suania rescued by Ballista and Calgacus.

Tatius: Ex-centurion attached to the embassy of Marcus Aurelius Julianus.

Tetricius: Gaius Pius Esuvius Tetricius, Postumus's governor of Aquitania.

Tharuaro: Son of Gunteric, brother of Respa; Gothic warrior of the Tervingi killed by Ballista at Miletus.

Theodotus: Aurelius Theodotus, Prefect of Egypt after putting down the revolt of Mussius Aemilianus; brother of Camsisoleus; one of the *protectores*.

Thersites: Troublemaking and ugly Greek soldier mentioned by Homer in the *Iliad*, probably of low birth.

Theseus: Legendary Greek hero, accepted help from the besotted Ariadne but later abandoned her on the island of Naxos.

Tiridates: Son of King Chosroes of Armenia, serving in the army of Gallienus.

Trajan: Marcus Ulpius Trajan, Roman emperor AD98–117.

Trebellius Pollio: *Amicus* of Postumus; a highly uncomplimentary biography of Gallienus circulates under his name.

Trimalchio: Fictional character in Petronius's novel *The*

Satyricon; vulgar and immensely rich host of a bizarre dinner party.

Tulga: King of the Grethungi Goths, father of Tuluin.

Tuluin: Gothic warrior, son of Tulga.

Unferth: Ruler of the Brondings; as leader of an uprising against the authority of the Angles, assumes the title Amber Lord. In Old English, his name means something like Unrest or Harm Peace.

Valerian (1): Publius Licinius Valerianus, an elderly Italian senator elevated to Roman emperor in AD253; captured by Shapur I in AD260.

Valerian (2) the Younger: Publius Cornelius Licinius Valerianus, eldest son of Gallienus, grandson of Valerian, made Caesar in AD256; died in AD258.

Vandrad: Childhood alias of Ballista taken from the Norse sagas; literally, Won't-be-Told.

Venutus: Valerius Venutus, a *frumentarius* in the service of Gallienus.

Vermund: Heathobard in Ballista's hearth-troop.

Victorinus: Marcus Piavonius Victorinus, *tribunus* of Postumus's Equites Singularis Consularis in Germania Inferior, encourages Postumus to rebel, rewarded with post of Praetorian Prefect in the new regime.

Virgil: Roman national poet (70–19BC).

Virius Lupus: Governor of Arabia.

Vocontius Secundus: Gaius Vocontius Secundus, Postumus's *Princeps Peregrinorum*.

Volcatius Gallicanus: Gaius Julius Volcatius Gallicanus, *amicus* of Postumus and cousin of Ballista's wife, Julia.

Volusianus: Lucius Petronius Taurus Volusianus, Gallienus's Praetorian Prefect, an Italian risen from the ranks; one of the *protectores*.

Wada the Short: Childhood friend of Ballista with his

brother, Wada the Tall; warriors of the Harii, they attach themselves to Ballista's retinue.

Wada the Tall: Brother of Wada the Short.

Wealtheow: Wife of Heoroweard Paunch-Shaker, mother of Hathkin.

Widsith Travel-Quick: Warlord among the Brondings, the son of Unferth; known by the title The Young Lord. In Old English his name means something like Stranger.

Wiglaf: Angle *eorl*. His banner is a red *draco*.

Wulfmaer: Angle, father of Glaum.

Xenophon: Athenian soldier and writer (*c*. 430–*c*. 350BC); author of the *Anabasis* (March Upcountry), an account of the escape from Persia of ten thousand Greek mercenaries who fell under his command after their original general was murdered.

Yrmenlaf: Ruler of the Wylfings.

Zenobia: Wife of Odenathus of Palmyra.

Zik Zabrigan: Persian commander, *framadar*, defeated by Ballista at Corycus, now in Roman service.